D0113857

E. C. MYERS

QUANTUM COIN

an imprint of **Prometheus Books**
Amherst, NY

Published 2012 by Pyr®, an imprint of Prometheus Books

Cover illustration © Sam Weber
Jacket design by Jacqueline Nasso Cooke

Inquiries should be addressed to
Pyr
59 John Glenn Drive
Amherst, New York 14228–2119
VOICE: 716–691–0133
FAX: 716–691–0137
WWW.PYRSF.COM

16 15 14 13 12   5 4 3 2 1

Library of Congress Cataloging-in-Publication Data

Myers, E. C. (Eugene C.), 1978–
    Quantum coin / by E.C. Myers.
        p. cm.
    Sequel to: Fair coin.
    Summary: Ephraim thought his universe-hopping days were over, but when his girlfriend's twin sister from a parallel universe crashes their senior prom, the three must work together to save the multiverse.
    ISBN 978–1–61614–682–5 (hardcover)
    ISBN 978–1–61614–683–2 (ebook)
    [1. Science fiction.] I. Title.

PZ7.M98253Qu 2012
    [Fic]—dc23

                                                          2012019305

Printed in the United States of America

For Carrie, my only love

ACKNOWLEDGMENTS

The more I learn about publishing, the more I realize that it takes teamwork to bring books to life.

I would like to thank the many friends who sponsored me in the Clarion West Write-a-thon and provided extra motivation to finish that messy first draft. As always, my writing group, Altered Fluid, helped me shape this into the book I wanted it to be. Eddie Schneider, Joshua Bilmes, and Jessie Cammack at JABberwocky frequently go above and beyond the call of duty on my behalf and have probably saved the day in ways I'll never realize.

I have tremendous gratitude and admiration for everyone at Prometheus Books and Pyr, who consistently turn their authors' words into beautiful books. I would especially like to thank Lou Anders, Jill Maxick, Meghan Quinn, Gabrielle Harbowy, Julia DeGraf, Jackie Nasso Cooke, Liz Scinta, Jennifer Tordy, and Catherine Roberts-Abel; if you knew all they do to produce great fiction and get it in the hands of readers, you would thank them too.

Finally, my sincerest appreciation goes to my fellow Apocalypsics and everyone who read *Fair Coin*, blogged about it, wrote reviews, mentioned it to friends, hosted interviews or readings, or was generally awesome in countless other ways. I hope you feel your valued contributions to my debut novel's successes are fairly rewarded by this sequel.

CHAPTER 1

Ephraim Scott sat at the bar and swirled the ice cubes in his glass. He wondered why he always ended up alone at parties, even when he had a date. This was a big night for him and Jena, but so far she had spent most of their senior prom hanging out with friends.

"Quarter for your thoughts."

Ephraim jumped at the voice behind him. Grapefruit juice splashed on his hand, and an ice cube clattered on the bar top. He twisted around on the stool and faced the large eye of a camera lens, with Nathan Mackenzie behind it. Its screen cast an eerie glow on his best friend's pale face and reflected off his glasses, obscuring his eyes.

"Nervous?" Nathan asked.

Ephraim put the glass down and wiped his hand dry with a napkin.

"You just surprised me," Ephraim said.

"That's a great shot for the video," Nathan said. He perched on an adjacent stool and fiddled with the camera controls. He tilted the screen toward Ephraim.

"*Quarter for your thoughts?*" Nathan repeated onscreen. Ephraim watched himself leap a foot off his seat, accompanied by a small geyser of ice and juice. He smiled despite himself. Nathan had the uncanny ability to capture Ephraim at his worst moments.

"Thanks for that," Ephraim said.

"Wait. Here." Nathan played the footage back in slow motion, which looked even more comical. "This one's gonna go viral. I can feel it."

"That's what you said about the last twenty videos." Ephraim cleared his throat. "What did you mean by that comment, anyway?" he asked.

"Which?" Nathan was panning his camera over the dance floor, getting one of those directorial wide shots he liked so much.

"'Quarter for your thoughts?'" He swallowed the last of the grape-fruit juice and winced at the bitterness. He'd never told Nathan about the strange quarter he'd found last year that had whisked him off to a series of parallel universes each time he'd flipped it. He watched his friend carefully to make sure he was really the Nathan he'd grown up with.

"It's just something people say," Nathan said. He held the camera at arm's length and tested the limits of the zoom function to get a better shot of Leah Donner's shimmying butt on the dance floor. That footage was more likely to go viral than anything else he'd shot.

"No, they don't. Nobody says that." Ephraim tugged at his bowtie to loosen it. He sighed when it unraveled completely. It had taken him half an hour to get it right. He'd wanted to wear the clip-on, but his mother insisted that if she was paying for the tuxedo rental, he was at least going to learn to tie the real thing. "People say '*penny* for your thoughts.'"

"I adjusted for inflation. You can't get anything for a penny these days. A quarter doesn't buy much either, for that matter. Remember those little juices we'd buy in junior high? My favorite was the blue one. It actually tasted like *blue*, you know?"

"So you didn't mean anything in particular by it?" Ephraim asked.

"What's the big deal, Eph?"

The big deal was that Ephraim had been thinking about a partic-ular quarter a lot lately, and Nathan's choice of words had triggered paranoia that he had never quite rid himself of. The coin he had was now inert, and it was the only one of its kind as far as he knew. But if there were others out there, any of his friends could be replaced at any moment, or he could be swapped into another universe and another life, powerless to do anything about it.

"Nothing. Never mind," Ephraim said.

"Everything okay?"

"I'm fine."

"Is everything okay with you and Jena, I mean?" Nathan asked. "The plan's still in effect?"

"Yeah. Of course." Ephraim gave Nathan a sidelong look. "Why? Have you heard anything?"

"No one tells me anything, dude. But I have five eyes, and I haven't seen you two together much tonight."

"Five?"

Nathan pointed his camera at Ephraim and grinned.

"Jena went to the bathroom," Ephraim said. He glanced at the clock above the bar. "Thirteen minutes and forty-five seconds ago. Not that I've been keeping track, because that would be weird."

"Right," Nathan said. "Was Shelley with her?"

"Naturally," Ephraim said. "And Mary. I've barely had five minutes alone with my girlfriend all evening."

"You and Jena danced that once," Nathan said.

Ephraim groaned. "Those were the five minutes. Please tell me you didn't get that on video." He hadn't danced with Jena so much as moved erratically in her vicinity in an approximation of rhythm.

"It's my job to get embarrassing footage of you. I'm building a catalog of your failures, to keep you ever humble. And to blackmail you with them when you become rich and powerful. Besides, I didn't think you were that bad."

"*You* wouldn't. I stepped on her toes. Twice."

Even after surviving a trip to a dangerous and twisted version of his own universe last summer, dating Jena was still the most amazing thing that had ever happened to him. Part of him had been waiting for their relationship to end, like some marvelous dream. Even Dorothy eventually returned to Kansas.

"Could you put that camera down for just a minute?" Ephraim asked. "I feel like I'm talking to a teenage cyborg in a bad suit," he said.

"I. Do. Not. Want. To. Miss. Anything," Nathan said in a robotic monotone. "What's wrong with my suit?"

"Purple hasn't been in since . . . ever. And I hate to disappoint you, but a giant monster is not going to attack Summerside during prom."

"But you can't know that for sure." Nathan reluctantly put the camera down on the bar, pointed toward the mirror behind it. He studied his reflection, smoothed back his gelled blond hair, and adjusted his glasses, then gave Ephraim his full attention. The camera had left a vertical red crease down his cheek that looked like a scar.

"Odds aren't good, in any case. The only things rampaging tonight are teenage hormones," Ephraim said.

"I already have plenty of footage of that. The MPAA might up the rating on this production to R," Nathan said. "Anyway, you don't have anything to worry about with Jena. She loved that necklace you gave her, whatever it's supposed to be. I'm sure that if she's in the bathroom, she hasn't dumped you, she's just taking a—"

"*Thank you*," Ephraim said. "No, really. It's such a relief that you—"

Nathan giggled.

Ephraim sighed. "'Relief'?"

Nathan nodded, still laughing. He wiped tears from the corners of his eyes.

"When are you going to grow up?" Ephraim asked.

"Toilet humor never gets old," Nathan said.

"But it always stinks."

"Nice," Nathan said.

Ephraim's stomach flip-flopped, and he pressed his hand to his cummerbund. Just when he thought he was going to be sick, the queasiness disappeared just as quickly as it had come.

What was that? The pang had felt almost like the first time he had crossed over to a parallel universe. But the quarter that had taken him there and back again didn't work anymore, and he didn't even have it with him.

"Uh. You okay?" Nathan asked.

Ephraim stood and looked around the room wildly, trying to spot any changes. Had that banner been blue before, or had it been lavender?

"What were we just talking about?" Ephraim asked.

"We were engaging in some scatological repartee," Nathan said. "Seriously. What's wrong?"

Ephraim was worried that he'd shifted into another universe again—or been bumped by someone else—but Nathan remembered the conversation they'd been having. He hadn't seemed to change, and everything else looked the same as it had a moment ago.

"You don't look so hot. Or actually, you look a little too hot," Nathan said. "In the literal, not colloquial, sense, though objectively speaking, as a guy, I recognize that your appearance is not entirely unappealing. No doubt thanks to exceptional genes from your mother, who also looks exceptional in jeans."

"I'm okay now," Ephraim said.

"No, you aren't. You didn't even react to my remark about Maddy."

"I've given up on discouraging your bizarre crush on my mother."

"Oh, there she is," Nathan said.

"My mom?" Ephraim asked.

"Your date." Nathan grabbed his camera from the bar and pointed it over Ephraim's shoulder. "And . . . action!"

Ephraim swiveled around on his stool. Jena was at the entrance to the ballroom, looking around the room. She had changed into a tank top and denim shorts. She looked frantic.

"Where's her dress?" Nathan asked.

Jena's prom dress had been a very pleasant surprise, considering her wardrobe favored unrevealing T-shirts and jeans. The crimson sleeveless gown pushed up her breasts, though she'd kept tugging at it self-consciously to keep too much from showing. She had crossed her arms for the whole limo ride, annoyed at Nathan's insistence on documenting it. Now that Ephraim thought about it, maybe her avoidance of him all night had more to do with Nathan's constant surveillance.

"Something's wrong." Ephraim headed for Jena, with Nathan trailing close behind, whispering stage cues.

"You haven't seen her in a long time. You've been pining for her," Nathan prompted him.

"It's been fifteen minutes," Ephraim said.

"*Pining*. I want a tearful reunion. How good are you at crying on demand?"

"Nathan. Quit it. This isn't the time."

A smile spread across Jena's face as Ephraim approached. In fact, she looked happier than she had all night. She ran toward him, dodging couples on the dance floor. What had gotten into her?

They met in the middle of the dance floor. She hesitantly placed a hand on his arm, as though not quite sure he was real. Then she held on more tightly. Her face was flushed, and she was breathing heavily. Sweat plastered her short dark hair to her forehead. A strand clung to the back of her neck.

"Ephraim?" Jena said. There was something odd about her eyes. They were bright, shining. She looked at him so intensely, he was abruptly at a loss for words. She'd had that effect on him since the second grade, until they finally got to know each other last summer.

"You missed her," Nathan murmured softly, so only Ephraim could hear him.

"I missed you," Ephraim said. "Are you—"

She cut him off with a kiss. He stopped thinking about anything except how soft her lips were.

Jena was not into PDA. She was barely comfortable with him in private, which always made him worry whether he was doing something wrong. But this kiss was different. All of her was in it.

It wasn't a new feeling though, it was an *old* one.

Panic seized Ephraim. He had the sudden impression that this was wrong. It shouldn't be happening. *Couldn't* be happening.

He pulled away and stared at her.

She sighed dreamily and opened her eyes. Her clear *blue* eyes. They widened as she saw his expression change.

"What's wrong?" she asked.

Jena's eyes were brown.

She hadn't changed her dress. *She* had changed.

"Zoe," he whispered.

Now he noticed the tiny indentation above Zoe's right nostril, from the nose ring she'd been wearing the last time he saw her. And he should have noticed immediately that she wasn't wearing the necklace he'd just given Jena, which was suddenly a very important detail.

"You thought I was someone else," Zoe said. She backed away.

"Zoe, how did you get here?" he asked.

"Oh, crap," she said. "Ephraim?" Her voice was raw.

"How—no, why are you here?" Ephraim asked. His voice rose. He ran a hand through his hair, coating his fingers in sweat and sticky hair gel.

She looked around, as if seeing where she was for the first time. "I don't belong here."

"No, you don't," he said. His voice came out harsher than he'd meant it to.

That snapped her out of her daze. She grabbed his hand. "I know you have questions, but you have to come back with me. Right away."

"What? I can't." He looked around. "It's *prom*."

"Do you still have the coin?" Her voice was urgent.

At mention of the coin, Ephraim's hand went cold, and he jerked it out of her grasp. He looked her over. There it was: a clamshell-style cell phone tucked into her right front pocket. But he knew that it wasn't a phone, just like the coin wasn't actually a coin. The device Zoe carried was a controller, which worked in tandem with the coin to shift from one reality to another. Now he knew how she'd gotten back to his universe.

"What the hell?" Nathan asked. Ephraim and Zoe turned to see Nathan pointing his camera at them. Ephraim had forgotten he'd been standing there the whole time. "Is this some kind of kinky roleplaying you guys do? I have to say, I didn't expect it from you, Jena, but I fully approve."

"Dammit, Nathan. Turn that thing off," Ephraim said.

Zoe swiped at her eyes with the back of one hand. "How can you associate with that creep after what he did?"

"This is *Nathan*. He had nothing to do with all that," Ephraim said.

"But he's capable of it," Zoe said.

The same thought had occurred to Ephraim, which was why he'd decided not to involve Nathan in anything having to do with the coin or tell him about what had really happened with *his* double Nate last year. Things seemed simpler that way. Easier. But that whole experience was coming back to haunt him now. It would be hard to explain who Zoe was. He had to get her out of here before more people saw her.

"Zoe, I thought I'd never see you again," he said.

"Obviously," she said. Her eyes were focused on something behind him. She clenched her jaw.

"That's weird," Nathan said, aiming his camera in the same direction.

With a sick sense of dread, Ephraim turned around. He felt like he was moving in slow motion, caught in another bad moment in one of Nathan's videos.

Jena stood in front of the bathroom entrance, staring at him and Zoe. She had put her glasses back on, vivid red secretary frames that matched her prom dress. Aside from her outfit, Jena was as identical to Zoe as the twin Morales sisters were to each other; Mary and Shelley stood on either side of Jena, openly shocked by the sight of their best friend's double.

"Crap," Ephraim said. "Um. How long has she been watching us?"

Judging from Jena's stormy expression, she'd been there long enough.

"I'll distract her. You run for it," Nathan said.

Ephraim shook his head. "She's faster than me, even in a dress."

"In that case, any last wishes?" Nathan asked, shoving the camera in his face.

Ephraim sighed. "Wishes got me into this mess in the first place."

CHAPTER 2

Ephraim considered Jena, Zoe, Mary, and Shelley. The two pairs of identical girls sat across from him and Nathan in the parked limousine, watching Ephraim expectantly. The perceived double vision was messing with his head.

Jena took a deep breath. "Okay, we're somewhere we can talk. So talk." She snuck a sidelong glance at Zoe, then quickly looked away.

He'd convinced Jena to leave the dance floor with him and Zoe before they attracted any more attention. The limo was the most private place he could think of on short notice. But he hadn't planned on having an audience; after what they'd seen, there was no way to ditch the Morales sisters and Nathan. With Nathan's camera recording the proceedings, the whole thing felt like *Ephraim on Trial*.

Shelley nodded. "Who the hell is this and why was Ephraim kissing her?" she asked.

"And why does she look like Jena?" Mary asked.

Ephraim took a deep breath. He didn't know where to start explaining. He turned around first to make sure the divider was up and that the driver couldn't hear them.

"Her name's Zoe," Jena said. "Zoe Kim. She's me. In a parallel universe."

Mary snorted. "Yeah, right. Who is she really, Jena?"

Shelley frowned, staring at Zoe.

Zoe looked at Jena in surprise. "He told you?" Zoe asked.

Jena fingered the silver chain of her necklace thoughtfully. "He told me the day I saw him pop from thin air into my backyard. But on some level, I didn't completely believe him. I guess I do now."

"I told her everything," Ephraim said.

"Not quite everything," Jena said. "I *would* like to know why you were kissing Zoe."

"I'm sorry you saw that," he said.

Jena narrowed her eyes. "You're sorry it happened, or you're sorry I saw it?"

"Both?" Ephraim glanced at Zoe apologetically. "Look, I didn't have any reason not to assume she was you. I thought all that was over."

He wiped his sweaty hands on the knees of his pants. They slid across the smooth synthetic fabric. He couldn't get a grip. "I'm sorry I made a mistake," he said.

"A mistake," Zoe said softly. She turned to Jena. "It was a mistake. *I* kissed Ephraim. But I wish I hadn't."

Ephraim bunched his eyebrows together.

"I didn't know you two were together, Jena," Zoe said. "I should have expected it, I guess. It's been a year. It's my fault for not stopping to think about it. So if you're angry, be angry at me."

"Oh, I'm plenty pissed at both of you," Jena said. "He should have realized sooner."

"He isn't the most observant guy sometimes," Zoe said.

"Most of the time," Jena said.

"True," Zoe said.

"But still," Jena said. "That's not really an excuse."

"No, it isn't," Zoe said.

"This is so screwed up," Ephraim said. While dating twins might be one of Nathan's dreams, this was more of a nightmare. "Give me a tiny break. Your hair was much longer last summer, Zoe, but now it's as short as Jena's. Exactly like Jena's. I mean, how many people can tell Mary and Shelley apart?"

"I can," Jena said.

"Me too," Nathan said. He ducked back behind his camcorder.

"Yup," Zoe said. "And I just met them."

Thanks for the help, Zoe.

But Ephraim had to admit he could tell the Morales twins apart too, even when they weren't color-coded like tonight in their matching lavender and rose mini dresses. It had taken a while, but once you got to know them, it was easy to distinguish between them.

Mary's knees were touching, her legs tucked back at an angle, but Shelley's long legs were extended and crossed at the ankles. It was the little details.

That was the problem. He should have known it was Zoe, but somehow he'd missed the clues. Or ignored them.

"At least I can tell the difference in a blind taste test," he muttered.

Nathan chuckled. Zoe smiled for a second before regaining her stern composure.

Despite the circumstances, it was good to see her again. It had taken months for him to stop being reminded of Zoe every time he looked at Jena.

"Will someone please tell us what's going on? This . . ." Mary waved her hand at Jena and Zoe. "This is just—"

"Freaky," Shelley said.

Ephraim sighed. "Jena was telling the truth. Zoe is kind of a doppelganger, what we call an analog of her: a double from another reality. They're twins like you, sort of like quantum sisters."

"So they're the same person?" Shelley asked.

"You actually buy this?" Mary asked.

Shelley shushed her. Mary looked surprised.

"Biologically, yes, they're the same person," Ephraim said. "They might even have the same fingerprints. But they're as much unique individuals as you and Mary are."

Shelley smiled.

"I know you and Jena read a lot of fantasy, but I prefer fact over fiction, Ephraim," Mary said.

"It isn't fantasy. It's science," Shelley said.

Mary rolled her eyes. "You're so gullible, sis."

"Am not," Shelley said. "He's talking about the multiverse."

"The multiverse," Mary said. "What?"

"Nathan's been loaning me his comic books." Shelley blushed. "The alternate reality stories are my favorites. The multiverse is what they call a collection of multiple universes."

Ephraim and Jena exchanged incredulous glances.

"It's kind of cool," Shelley said. "I like the idea of all you poor singletons having twins somewhere out there. Or right here, as it turns out." She smiled.

"You've been spending time with Geekazoid?" Mary asked. She shot a scornful look at Nathan.

"We started talking about comics at Ephraim's birthday party last August. I mentioned the only ones I read were the little strips in Mama's Sunday *Journal News*. Then a comic book he'd recommended appeared in my locker with Post-It notes on the pages, explaining the backstory with cute little drawings." She smiled. "After I finished reading it, I slipped it into his locker."

"And I left another one for her," Nathan said. Apparently Ephraim wasn't the only one keeping secrets.

"We've been exchanging them every day for a few months." Shelley's face was bright pink now.

"You whore," Mary said.

Zoe stretched her legs out. "Listen, long story short: there are many parallel universes where lots of things are pretty much the same, but some little things are really different. And vice versa. Most of them have alternate versions of all of us, doubles that we call 'analogs.' For instance, in one universe, analogs of Shelley and Nathan are swapping more than just comic books."

"Awesome," Nathan said.

"Ew," Mary said.

"And in another universe, Nathan is dead," Zoe said, looking at her nails casually.

"Not awesome," Nathan said. He glanced at Ephraim. "You never mentioned any of this to me." His expression showed how hurt he was.

"Can you blame me? It's hard to explain," Ephraim said.

"But you told Jena."

"That's different. She saw me arrive in this universe. She saw Zoe leave. I had to tell her what was going on. Would you have believed me?"

"Probably not," Nathan said. "But I would have tried, if you had trusted me."

"It's not that I didn't trust you," Ephraim lied. He glanced at Zoe. No help there. "It's complicated."

"The multiverse is just theoretical though," Shelley said softly, almost defensively.

"Do I look theoretical to you?" Zoe said.

Shelley studied her and Jena. "It shouldn't be possible to move between parallel universes."

"And yet here I am," Zoe said.

"About that," Ephraim said. "You were supposed to destroy the controller."

"I did." Zoe pulled the controller from her pocket. "Mostly. I dismantled it after you left, but I kept the parts. I thought that would be enough." She shrugged. "Nathaniel said we might need it again someday. And today's that day."

"Nathaniel?" Nathan asked. "Is he one of my, uh, 'analogs'?"

"He's you from a universe twenty-five years ahead of ours," Ephraim said. It felt good to be sharing all of this with his friend finally. It would have been better if the situation hadn't forced him into it, though if Zoe hadn't returned, he probably never would have initiated this conversation.

"He's a time traveler, too?" Nathan asked.

"Sort of. His universe's timeline is different from ours." In that universe, scientists had figured out how to travel to parallel dimensions. Nathaniel and another Ephraim had visited and cataloged other universes, until Nathaniel had gotten stuck in Zoe's universe without his partner.

Ephraim reached over and took the controller from Zoe. The small device had caused a lot of trouble for them. People had died because of it. It should have been destroyed.

"That's a cell phone," Mary said.

"Looks can be deceiving," Zoe said.

"This is a controller," Ephraim said. "It records coordinates of different universes and lets you program in the one you want to go to."

The controller resembled a standard flip phone, with a hinged case, numeric keypad, and a digital display. But it was far more sophisticated than that, perhaps more sophisticated than anything else in the world. *This* world.

The controller's blue metal case was scuffed and cracked, and secured in places with duct tape and superglue. He shook it, and something loose rattled inside.

"I'm pretty sure you've voided the warranty," he said.

"I misplaced one of the screws," Zoe said. "And I couldn't figure out where every little piece fit."

Ephraim unfolded it, and the hinge clicked and wobbled. The screen on the top half stayed dark. He rotated his finger around the round depression in the lower half, just above the keypad, where a quarter-sized disc could just fit.

"Is it broken?" Nathan asked, pointing the camera at it.

Ephraim handed the controller to Nathan, and the screen blinked on. Nathan nearly dropped it.

"Whoa," he said. "How'd I do that?"

"It only responds to certain people. You and Zoe. And all your analogs from other universes, of course."

Ephraim glanced at Jena, realizing that her biometrics could activate it too.

"Is it radioactive?" Nathan asked.

"Maybe. Probably," Ephraim said. "I don't really know what's inside it."

Nathan handed it back to him carefully and rubbed his hand on the plush seat. The screen flickered and went out as soon as Nathan's skin lost contact with it. Ephraim passed the controller to Zoe. Their fingers brushed against each other. The hairs on the back of his hand tingled.

"That's how you got here?" Mary asked. "That thing can travel between dimensions?"

"There's another piece," Jena said. She lifted the chain around her neck and drew a silver disc from her cleavage. It dangled in front of her chest, spinning slowly with light glinting dully from its smooth sides.

Zoe shot Ephraim a look that was both questioning and accusatory.

The coin had brought Ephraim and Jena together, in a way, and he'd wanted to show her he was firmly committed to her and their universe. He'd thought it little more than a souvenir, with its power drained and the controller gone, and it had felt right to let it go—especially tonight.

"Your pendant?" Mary asked.

Jena pulled the necklace over her head and lowered it into Ephraim's palm.

The metal was warm in his hand, not from weird quantum energy but from prolonged contact with Jena's skin. He got distracted for a moment, thinking about where the coin had just been.

"Ephraim," Zoe said.

He popped the coin out of its bezel, glad he hadn't drilled a hole in it like he'd originally considered doing. He handed the chain back to Jena and held the coin up between forefinger and thumb.

"This is the coin," he said.

"It doesn't look like a coin," Mary said.

Zoe flipped open the controller and held it out. Ephraim slotted the blank disc into the round groove in the controller. She pressed a button, and George Washington's head slowly shimmered onto the face of the coin. Ephraim knew the reverse side would now show the island of Puerto Rico.

"Nice magic trick," Mary said.

"It isn't magic or a trick," Ephraim said. "This coin serves as the guidance system for the controller, a kind of gyro. Combined, they form a portable coheron drive. Or 'Charon' for short."

"'Charon'?" Shelley asked.

"It's a corruption of 'coherence,' the quantum effect that forms new universes," Zoe said.

"And, of course, a reference to the Greek ferryman who takes dead souls across the river Styx for the price of a coin," Jena said.

"And people make fun of our names," Mary and Shelley said simultaneously.

"Just like only analogs of me and Nathan can use the controller, only Ephraim and his analogs can handle the coin," Zoe said.

Mary and Shelley considered Ephraim. Their matching expressions said, *Why him?* He'd wondered that himself often enough.

"Uh. Anyway, the coin draws its power from the controller," Ephraim said. "It's blank when it's drained, but it's recharging now."

"But why does it look like a quarter?" Mary asked. "Why does the controller look like a cell phone?"

"Nathaniel said my analog carried around the quarter his whole life. I don't know why," Ephraim said.

"It's camouflage. Another security feature," Shelley said. "Just like the restricted users and the complementary components. So if anyone finds one of the pieces, they won't know what they have."

Zoe nodded. "That's what my Ephraim thought too."

"The controller is used to program dimensional coordinates for a specific universe, but it needs the coin to get there," Ephraim said. "Either piece of the device can be used independently, in a limited way. I can use the coin alone if I flip it, but it takes me to a universe pretty much randomly. The controller can home in on the coin though and shift to the same universe."

"Whoever invented the Charon device was paranoid," Shelley said.

"Wouldn't you be if you developed something this powerful?" Zoe asked.

"It just seems too dangerous to use at all," Shelley said.

"I agree," Ephraim said. "In any case, you wouldn't want to use the coin by itself if you could help it. Without contact with the controller, I switch places with my analog when I shift to his universe," Ephraim said.

Shelley shuddered. "Creepy . . ."

"I don't switch *bodies*," Ephraim said. "We just exchange quantum positions. Clothes and everything go with you."

"So you could use the coin to displace your analog on purpose?" Nathan asked. "Like, to take over his life?"

Ephraim exchanged a worried look with Zoe. "Who would want to do something like that, Nathan?"

"You got me. I'm just saying, that's messed up," Nathan said.

Ephraim relaxed. Nathan's analog Nate hadn't had any reservations about doing whatever he wanted, and he had done a lot worse than switch lives with his analogs.

"Can I come?" Shelley asked. Mary pinched her hard on the forearm. "Ow! I mean, can you take anyone with you?"

"As long as we're physically touching, sure," Ephraim said.

"Don't humor them, sis." Mary pulled her long brown hair behind her neck. "*No*," she said. As if rejecting the notion would reassert her idea of how the world was supposed to work. "There's some other explanation for all of this."

"Like what, Mary? You're always so stubborn." Shelley said. "Ephraim, how did you get mixed up in this?"

Ephraim quickly explained how he'd discovered the coin a year ago: how a duplicate Ephraim from a parallel universe had brought the coin to their universe and died. Zoe closed her eyes while he related the accident. That duplicate had been her universe's Ephraim. Her boyfriend.

Ephraim told them about Nathaniel's analog Nate, who had been abusing the technology to steal money, to hoard stuff from parallel universes—and to hurt people. Ephraim and Zoe had eventually gotten the controller away from Nate and stranded him in a universe where he couldn't cause any more trouble.

Ephraim and Zoe had decided that they each belonged in their own universe and that the technology was too dangerous to keep. So they parted ways. Zoe had destroyed the controller, and Ephraim's coin had run out of power.

"Or at least I *thought* she'd destroyed the controller," Ephraim said.

"Yes. Why did you reassemble it, Zoe?" Jena asked.

Zoe pursed her lips. "Nathaniel said I had to."

"That's my analog from the future?" Nathan asked. "I thought you were from different universes."

"We are," Zoe said.

"So how did he get in touch with you?" Ephraim asked.

"Ham radio," she said.

Ephraim and Nathan laughed.

"Really," Zoe said.

"Come on," Jena said.

"*That's* the part of this you don't believe?" Mary asked.

Ephraim stared at Zoe. "You have a radio that can contact other universes? How does that even work?"

"I made some modifications to boost the sensitivity."

"With what?"

"Pieces from the controller. But it's all modular," she said. "Nathaniel and I agreed on a schedule. Once a week I scan all the radio bands, listening for him. Most of the time I can't get through, but every couple of months I find the right frequency, and we can talk for a little while."

"Why did you two set this up?" Ephraim really meant, *Why did you exclude me?*

"It was supposed to be an emergency channel. Just in case."

"In case of what?" Ephraim asked.

"In case he needs us." Zoe shrugged.

"'Us' as in you and Ephraim?" Jena asked. "For what?"

"I don't know. But it might have something to do with how I got here."

"You didn't track the coin's coordinates with the controller?" Ephraim asked.

Zoe shook her head. "I tried. But I couldn't lock onto it."

"The coin was dead," Jena said. "So how *did* you get here?"

"I don't know. As soon as I got Nathaniel's message, I put the controller back together and turned it on. When I couldn't find a signal from the coin, I got worried. I hoped that even if the coin were drained, it still might retain a latent charge. Most electronics do. If I was close enough to its spatial location in your universe, I might be able to track it.

"So I went to the Memorial Fountain in Greystone Park and the library. I went by your old apartment, thinking you might keep the coin at home, but nothing. I biked all over town, all afternoon. Then I remembered what day it was."

"You were planning to skip prom?" Jena asked.

"The whole school was skipping prom. Summerside hasn't had one in three years."

"You don't have prom in your universe?" Shelley asked.

"We don't have a lot of things," Zoe said. "Not since the Soviet Union shot down that commercial jet. But some of the other kids were talking about it in school today, how we would have had a prom tonight if we weren't in the middle of a war. It always used to be on the first Saturday after May Day—"

"You were in school today?" Mary asked.

Zoe stared at her. "Yeah. So?"

"It's Saturday!" Mary was triumphant, as if Zoe's entire story were invalidated by that one small detail.

"They have classes on Saturday," Ephraim said. "And all summer long."

"No!" Shelley said.

"Yes, I know, it's a horrible place," Ephraim said. "But, Zoe, how did you know where we were?"

"The Hudson Club is closed in our universe, but it's the only place where you can have an event like this."

"And that's how you found the signal from the coin?" Jena asked.

Zoe shook her head. "I still didn't pick it up. I decided to try inside. I climbed through a broken window around back, and as soon as I entered the ballroom, I shifted—before I even took the controller out of my pocket." She put a hand on her stomach. "It felt different from before."

"Maybe you accidentally triggered the controller," Ephraim said.

"I didn't butt-dial your universe, Ephraim. Remember, it's touch-sensitive." Zoe tapped the face of the controller with her index finger thoughtfully. "It was like I was drawn to you," she said.

"Oh, please," Jena said.

Zoe held up the controller. "I mean, I think this was drawn back to the coin as soon as they were near each other, almost overlapping spatially, in adjacent universes. It pulled me here. And if that happened spontaneously, something really strange must be going on."

"Nathaniel didn't tell you why he needs us?" Ephraim asked.

"I didn't actually talk to him this time. He was broadcasting a message on repeat. He probably wanted to be sure he wouldn't miss me," Zoe said.

"What did it say?" Nathan asked.

"'We have trouble, Z. We need you and your better half. Bring Charon home,'" Zoe said.

"That's it?" Ephraim asked.

"'Your better half'?" Jena frowned.

"He means the coin," Ephraim said.

Zoe brushed her hair behind her ear. "I know it isn't much, but the message was pretty clear. Something is happening, and he needs us to bring the coin and the controller back to him as soon as possible."

Ephraim leaned forward with his elbows on his knees. "Even if there were some problem Nathaniel needs help with, why not just send another team with another device?" Ephraim asked. "Why does he need us?"

"It's *Nathaniel* asking, Ephraim," Zoe said. "Isn't that enough?"

"I know that look, Ephraim. You don't have to do this," Jena said.

Ephraim glanced between Jena and Zoe. He didn't want to disappoint either of them. But he didn't even know for certain that anything was wrong, or that he could trust Zoe anymore. Or Nathaniel for that matter. A lot could happen in a year.

He spread his hands helplessly. "I never agreed to be on call, Zoe. I'm done with universe-hopping."

"If it's nothing, we can get you back home right away," Zoe said.

"It's not like he's popping off to the grocery store for milk," Jena said. "It's another *universe*. And you just said the controller or the multiverse or whatever isn't behaving the way it should. What if he can't get back?"

"That's why we have to check in," Zoe said. "We owe Nathaniel that much. He saved my life and got you home, Eph. He wouldn't ask if it wasn't important."

"He shouldn't have asked at all," Ephraim said.

Nathan's camera beeped loudly. Everyone turned to stare at him. He fiddled with it. "Oops. Out of storage space," he said.

"Thank God," Jena said. She uncrossed her arms.

"Don't worry, I brought plenty of memory cards with me. I just hope I got all that." He pressed "Play" on the camera and watched the footage on its tiny screen. A hyper pop song played through the speaker.

"Zoe, can't this at least keep until tomorrow morning?" Ephraim asked.

Zoe glared at Ephraim. "This from the guy who made us backtrack through like a dozen multiple universes just to put his analogs where they came from? The guy who insisted on protecting Nate, because killing him would make us as bad as he is?"

"Good on you, bro," Nathan said. He held his palm out for Ephraim to slap in solidarity. Ephraim ignored him.

"This is your responsibility, Ephraim," Zoe said. "I shouldn't have to remind you of that."

"I have responsibilities here, too," he said. "This is where I belong."

"Eph?" Nathan said. "You should see this. It's kind of . . . I don't know. Wrong." He shook the camera for a second and went back to watching the video, chewing on his upper lip.

"The bottom line is: If anything's wrong, we have to help fix it," Zoe said.

"Guys, you have to look at this," Nathan said. "Seriously."

Nathan pulled the memory card out of the camera and inserted it into a slot on the monitor above his seat. He turned the screen on, hands shaking.

"Why us, Zoe?" Ephraim asked. *Why me?*

"Because we can. Because we have these." Zoe held out the controller with the coin mounted in it.

He placed his first two fingers on the coin and rested his hand on hers for a moment. He felt a warm buzzing sensation at her touch, as though she were closing a circuit between them. He told himself it was from the contact with the device.

"Guys! Everyone, look at this!" Nathan pointed at the screen. All Ephraim saw was static.

"*What,* Nathan?" Ephraim asked.

"Shhh," Zoe said. "We're in the middle of something."

"Oh, we're in the middle of something, all right," Nathan said. "Something bizarro. And I have it on video."

CHAPTER 3

Ephraim moved to the other side of the limo to get a better view of the screen. After a moment of hesitation, he wedged into the seat on Jena's right, keeping her between him and Zoe.

Onscreen, the camera zoomed in and focused on Ephraim and Zoe kissing. The image was shaky, but Ephraim saw the surprised look on his face then watched his earlier self close his eyes and lean into it blissfully. He still felt her warm lips against his mouth. Jena tensed beside him.

"Could we skip past this part?" Ephraim asked, his voice strained.

Nathan pressed a button on the remote, and the video played in double-time. It focused on Jena and Mary and Shelley, then jumped to show couples dancing. Nathan slowed the picture down to normal speed.

"Wait for it," Nathan said.

Something flickered in the corner of the screen. Static burst over the image, and when the picture stabilized, a blurry ghost trail followed everyone's movements on the floor.

"Did you break the camera?" Jena asked.

Nathan shook his head. "Watch."

The image zoomed in on a couple, Michael Gupal and Katrina Allen slow dancing in the corner, their transparent doubles superimposed over them. As the camera focused, it caught them clearly for a moment. The hazy ghost Michael grabbed the ghost Katrina's ass. She jerked upright, smacked him, and stalked off. The ghost Michael stared after her, then stumbled away in the other direction, while the real Michael and Katrina continued dancing, completely unaware of the paths their other selves had taken.

"What the holy hell?" Jena said.

"What was that?" Mary squeaked. "Their *souls*?" She made the sign of the cross.

"Couldn't be. Michael doesn't have a soul," Nathan said.

"Quantum branching," Ephraim said. "The moment a parallel universe—"

"Splits off from its original one," Shelley chimed in. "In theory, it happens every time we make a choice."

Mary gaped at her.

"But it's not supposed to happen in a universe when the coin and controller are in it," Zoe said. "Otherwise there'd be tons of other Ephraims and Zoes and Nathaniels running around with their own Charon devices."

"Can you be sure there aren't?" Jena asked.

"Play that back, Nathan," Zoe said.

"Can you slow it down?" Ephraim asked.

Nathan rewound it and played it again at half speed.

Ephraim pointed at the screen. "See? That transparent Michael and Kat didn't peel off from our universe," Ephraim said. "They were already in a different universe. Michael just made a different decision in that one."

"And faced the consequences," Jena said.

Zoe moved next to Nathan and grabbed the remote from him. She advanced the footage, her brow knit with worry. "So the camera's picking up other parallel universes bleeding into this one, overlapping like a double-exposed photograph. And we're seeing people's other selves, like . . ."

"Ghosts of a chance?" Nathan suggested.

Shelley groaned.

"How can a camera pick up quantum . . . phantoms?" Ephraim asked. "Where'd you get that thing, Nathan?" He looked at it skeptically.

"I bought it used online," Nathan said.

"Maybe the Charon device is causing interference? It looks like it started recording other realities just after I appeared with the controller," Zoe said.

She rewound the recording once more, taking it back before she had kissed Ephraim. She pressed "Play."

The screen showed the mirror behind the bar, reflecting the camera on the counter and Ephraim and Nathan. They were out of focus, but their conversation was loud and clear.

"*When are you going to grow up?*" said the Ephraim of thirty minutes before.

Hard to believe that only half an hour ago, his life had been so normal. Relatively speaking.

"*Toilet humor never gets old,*" Nathan said.

"*But it always stinks.*"

Mary sighed.

"*Nice.*"

The image flickered and broke apart into colorful pixels, like an old video game that was malfunctioning. The picture snapped back, and for a moment, the distorted image showed a long line of Ephraims and Nathans reflected in the mirror. The recursion effect was accompanied by the loud whine of audio feedback. The Ephraim at the front doubled over and pressed his hand to his stomach. When he straightened, all the other reflections collapsed into him, and the picture cleared up.

Jena drew in a sharp breath. She, Mary, and Shelley were literally on the edge of their seats, pressing closer to the small video monitor. Ephraim realized he was clenching his right hand into a tight fist. He relaxed his fingers.

"*What were we just talking about?*"

"*We were engaging in some scatological repartee. Seriously. What's wrong? You don't look so hot. Or actually, you look a little too hot. In the literal, not colloquial, sense, though objectively speaking, as a guy, I recognize that your appearance is not entirely unappealing. No doubt thanks to exceptional genes from your mother, who also looks exceptional in jeans.*"

Shelley crossed her arms, her lower lip protruding.

"*I'm okay now.*"

"*Oh, there she is.*"

The camera picture tilted and swung around to face the bathrooms. Half of Ephraim's face stayed in frame in the foreground. It blurred as Zoe came into focus in the background. In the picture, Ephraim turned slowly.

"We don't need to see *that* again," Jena said.

Zoe paused the video.

"The recording went screwy at the precise moment that I popped into this universe," Zoe said.

"So, the camera isn't broken?" Nathan asked.

"No, but I'm afraid something else is," Zoe said. "Or maybe I *am* causing interference."

She picked up Nathan's camera. "Give me another memory card."

Nathan pulled a small blue memory card from his coat pocket and handed it to her. Zoe slid the chip into the camera, popped the lens cap off, and rolled the window down. She angled it out at the parking lot and tapped the round red icon on the touchscreen with a red fingernail to start recording. Her nails were longer than Jena's, another small difference Ephraim had failed to pick up on.

"Hold up," Nathan said. He pulled a thin cable from another pocket and plugged one end into the camera and the other into the side of the monitor. He pressed a button on the remote, and the screen displayed everything the camera saw.

"Look at that," Zoe said.

Ghostly images of people moved in the empty parking lot. The image zoomed in, and Ephraim saw two transparent people making out in the back seat of a Hyundai.

"Looks cramped," Mary said.

Jena squinted. "I think that's Leah Donner and . . . Serena Renfield? What are they . . . *oh*." Her cheeks flushed.

"That's hot," Nathan said.

"Down, boy," Shelley said.

"You're getting all this, right?" Nathan asked.

Zoe closed the camera, and the screen turned black. "I think we've seen enough."

Nathan grabbed for the camera, but she held it just out of his reach.

"This is bad news, isn't it?" Jena said.

"This is news," Zoe said. "Considering Nathaniel's call for help, it probably isn't good news."

"I bet the Old Ones are busting into our universe!" Nathan said.

"What is it with you wanting giant creatures to attack Summerside?" Ephraim asked. "If it has anything to do with virgins, I don't want to hear it."

Nathan pursed his lips and remained silent.

"I thought so." Ephraim sighed.

"Like I've been saying. We need to get to Nathaniel as soon as possible." Zoe looked at Ephraim.

"Okay," Ephraim said. He tried to keep his voice steady. "I'm in."

"At last." Zoe held up Nathan's camera. "Can we borrow this? It could come in handy."

Nathan looked stricken.

"Let me rephrase that. I'm going to take this." She wrapped the strap around her wrist definitively.

"It took me six months to save up for that," Nathan said.

"We'll get it back to you, buddy," Ephraim said. He hoped he'd be able to keep that promise.

"We should send these clips to a scientist. Or Eyewitness News," Shelley said.

"That could cause a panic," Jena said.

"If this is real, we have to tell someone," Mary said.

"We will. The only person qualified to explain what's happening and do something about it," Zoe said. "Nathaniel."

"We'd better get going then," Jena said.

"You are *not* coming with us," Zoe said.

"That isn't your decision," Jena said.

"Jena, maybe it's better for you to stay here," Ephraim said.

Jena crossed her arms. "You gave the coin to me, darling. If you want to use it, I'm coming along. I don't like losing things that belong to me." She smiled sweetly at Zoe.

"I can be so damn stubborn sometimes," Zoe said.

"Most of the time," Ephraim said. Jena and Zoe glared at him.

Zoe knocked on the partition.

"We're *driving* to this other universe?" Mary asked.

Ephraim smiled. "The Charon device can move us across dimensions, but not over distances. Unless you're swapping quantum positions with your analog, you appear in the same geographic location you started from. The limo will just get us to a better place to shift."

The partition slid down with a mechanical whir. Hip hop music blared into the passenger cabin.

The driver twisted around to face them. "Where to?" he asked. He had a gentle voice with a Russian accent. Zoe started when she heard it. Ephraim remembered that back in her reality, the country was at war with the USSR, along with almost everyone else.

"Take us to Greystone Park," Ephraim said. He looked at Zoe questioningly, and she nodded her approval. In Nathaniel's universe, it was the site of an institute devoted to studying parallel universes.

"Park's closed," the driver said.

"We aren't going inside."

"Suit yourself."

"Hang on," Ephraim said. "Do you two want to get out here?" he asked Mary and Shelley.

The twins exchanged a look.

"We're coming with you," Shelley said.

"At least as far as the park," Mary said.

"What about your dates?" Ephraim asked. "I forget their names."

"Exactly," Mary said. "I never thought I'd say this, but I'd rather hang out with you."

"This is much more interesting." Shelley smiled at Nathan.

"Someone has to document this," Nathan said. He pulled a pocket-sized video camera from his back pocket and grinned.

"You're kidding," Ephraim said.

"I always carry a backup," Nathan said.

"You can ride with us to the park too and drop us off." Ephraim leaned toward the front of the cabin and raised his voice over the music. "Hey, what's your name?"

"Maurice," the driver said.

"Okay, Maurice. Step on it."

"You bet." Maurice tipped his hat.

The partition rose, and the cabin was silent again. The car engine rumbled under them, and they were moving.

CHAPTER 4

The car slowed, then stopped. The partition lowered, and Russian rap with a pounding bass invaded the passenger compartment.

"We're here," Maurice said.

Ephraim and the others climbed out of the limo and gathered on the sidewalk in front of Greystone Park by the bus shelter, directly across from the Summerside Public Library where Jena and Ephraim worked. Ephraim ducked back into the car to grab the ice bucket. He unloaded the bottles of soda and water onto a seat, then dumped the ice out into the gutter. He handed the bucket to Jena.

"Hold onto that," he said.

Jena raised an eyebrow but tucked the bucket under her arm. "We're just going to do this here?" she asked. "In the street?"

"We can't stay in the car. If we're sitting, we'll fall when we shift. Plus Maurice will notice if we vanish from the back seat. Which reminds me . . ." Ephraim walked over to the driver's side, and Maurice lowered the window.

"Nothing here," the driver said.

"No, not yet," Ephraim said. "Listen, can you drive around for about ten minutes, then come back here to pick us up? Some of us are arranging other transportation from here."

Maurice shrugged. "No problem," he said. He started the engine.

Ephraim smiled. "Thanks."

He rejoined the others. They were so engaged in conversation they didn't notice the limo pull away.

"—going to the *future*?" Mary asked.

"Not exactly. It's another universe where it's already 2037," Zoe said.

"How is that different?" she asked.

"It's *a* future, but not necessarily *our* future," Nathan said.

"'Other times are just special cases of other universes,'" Shelley said.

"Is that from a TV show?" Mary asked.

"I was quoting David Deutsch. He's a physicist," Shelley said.

"When were you reading all these books and comics? Under the covers with a flashlight?"

"You don't give me enough credit," Shelley said. "I do a lot of things you wouldn't approve of."

"Hey, what happens if this machine moves you to a universe where there's something already occupying the space you're standing in?" Nathan asked. "Like a building or an obelisk?"

"An *obelisk*?" Ephraim asked. "Why would there be an obelisk here?"

"Because it's the future! The future has obelisks. And zeppelins. There are always zeppelins in alternate universes."

"I suppose if we shift into an obelisk, it would hurt," Ephraim said. "I don't think the Charon device would let that happen."

Zoe flipped open the controller. "We'll take our chances," she said.

"You have the coordinates for Nathaniel's universe?" Ephraim asked.

"Yup. And the coin's fully charged." She held the controller out to show him the coin still nestled in its place.

Ephraim grinned at Nathan, Jena, and the twins, and waggled his fingers over it. "Behold," he said.

"Goofball." Zoe pressed a button on the controller, and the coin slowly floated up until it hovered a couple of inches above the controller. "Woooo," she said in a spooky voice.

Ephraim smiled. Zoe was getting into the spirit of it.

Mary and Shelley moved to opposite sides of the controller and leaned over to stare at the weightless coin.

"Impressive," Nathan said. "Gravity-defying." He was looking down their dresses instead of at the coin. Ephraim smacked him in the back of the head.

"You ain't seen nothing yet," Zoe said.

"I know," Nathan said.

She pressed another button. The coin began spinning, faster and faster. Mary's and Shelley's hair stirred in the breeze caused by its rapid rotation. They backed away slowly.

Ephraim placed his right hand over the coin and felt the heat emanating from it. His palm itched with anticipation.

The coin slowed, then froze in midair, tilted at an oblique angle. It still radiated intense heat.

Zoe slipped her right hand into his left and nodded almost imperceptibly in Jena's direction.

She wanted to leave Jena behind.

He was surprised, and immediately shamed, that he was actually considering it. Jena would never forgive him if he abandoned her, especially if he left with Zoe. But this was his last chance to keep her out of this mess, to keep her safe. He could even try to make it look like an accident—not that she'd believe that for even a second.

His hand crept toward the controller. He pulled his hand away just as Zoe nudged the coin closer. He glared at her.

"You'd better hold on to us, Jena," he said.

Jena approached his other side and gripped his right forearm tightly. He grimaced as her fingers dug into his skin, grateful that she kept her nails trimmed short so she could use the touchscreen of her smartphone. She tucked the empty ice bucket under her other arm.

Nathan pulled out his pocket camera and pointed it at them.

"Do you have to?" Ephraim said.

"This is for Maddy," Nathan said. "She might want proof that I haven't murdered you and buried your body in the park."

Ephraim's eyes widened. "Oh, crap! I have to call my mother."

"Really? Now?" Zoe said. "Do you want her to sign a permission slip for our field trip to another universe?"

"She'll worry. You know how she is," he said.

"I knew a different Mrs. Scott," she said. "She didn't pay much attention to my Eph."

Zoe had also known Ephraim's dad. In her universe, David Scott had stayed with his family, but that still didn't get them a happily ever after. He'd ended up killing his wife, then himself, and that act had inadvertently caused his son's death in Ephraim's universe.

Ephraim's dad was irresponsible, unpredictable, and violent, but his analog had been much worse. Sometimes Ephraim still missed him, even though he knew deep down that he and his mother were better off without him.

"It'll just take a second," Jena said.

Mary and Shelley nodded in tandem. Their mother was a nurse at Summerside General, and she had helped Madeline Scott after her attempted suicide last year. The twins knew about it but had the decency not to share the gossip with their classmates. Ephraim had always appreciated that.

Ephraim's mother was still convinced that whenever he walked out the door, it would be the last time she'd see him alive.

"Think about how Mom and Dad would feel if you suddenly disappeared, Zoe," Jena said.

"*My* dad wouldn't notice," Zoe said. She switched off the controller and turned away. "Mom died when I was born. Just make it quick, Ephraim. I want to get out of here."

"Use my phone." Jena handed Ephraim her smartphone and gave his hand an encouraging squeeze.

Ephraim had never owned a cell phone of his own, but his mother had implied he might receive one for a graduation present.

He pressed the little picture of his face on the touchscreen to dial his apartment. He walked a few feet away from the group as the phone rang.

"You never told your Mom about all this quantum thinginess either?" Nathan asked, trailing behind him.

Ephraim shook his head. "She wouldn't get it."

He started to get anxious when she hadn't picked up after six rings. Was it her AA night? No, that was on Tuesdays. If he had to face the truth, Ephraim was probably more worried about his mother than the reverse. And this call wasn't so much about easing her concern as it was to assuage his guilt that he was leaving her again.

She finally answered after the eighth ring.

"Yes?" She sounded oddly out of breath—and a little annoyed.

"Mom?" Ephraim asked. "Uh. Is this a bad time?"

"Oh, Ephraim. It's *Ephraim*," she repeated to someone. "Hi, honey. Jim and I were just . . . watching TV."

"Gross, Mom," Ephraim said. Nathan shot him a questioning look. "They're fooling around," Ephraim explained.

"Who's in jail? Is Nathaniel in trouble?" she asked.

For a moment he thought she was referring to the older Nathaniel, which was right on the mark. But she always called Nathan by his full name for some reason and let him address her by her first name.

"I heard my name," Nathan whispered. "Is she talking about me?"

"Why do you assume something's wrong?" he asked into the phone.

"Because you're the only boy at any prom anywhere tonight who's on the phone with his mother." He heard her murmur to Jim. "I don't know. I'm trying to find out." Her voice became louder and clearer. "Is everything all right with Jena?"

Ephraim glanced over at Jena and Zoe.

"They're fine," he said.

"They?"

"I mean, *she's* fine. Everyone's fine." *So far.* "Look, I want to tell you what's going on, but I don't think you'll believe me."

"I don't like where this is going," she said. She had that two-smoke edge to her voice, which meant she was seriously stressed out, and it would take two cigarettes to calm her down again. "Have you ever lied to me before?" she asked.

"Never."

"Then I'll believe you."

"Okay. Here goes." He took a deep breath. "What would you say if I told you that multiple universes exist, and that I've been to other worlds just like ours and met lots of different versions of you?"

His mother was quiet for a long moment.

"I don't believe you," she said.

"Nice." He rolled his eyes.

"But since just about anything else you came up with would

sound more plausible, I have to assume you're telling the truth. Or you think you are. Maybe you should go to a hospital."

"I've had enough of hospitals," he said. "That's it! Mom. Remember how I acted last June, just after you got out of the hospital?"

"You were upset because of . . . what I did. Going through one of your phases," she said. She'd picked that up in a parenting magazine and used it to excuse anything weird and unexpected he did. But no magazine could advise her on what he was about to spring on her, except maybe *Scientific American*.

"No. That wasn't me," he said.

"I know. You weren't yourself." She'd told him that in their AA meetings, they emphasized how saying "I wasn't myself" wasn't an apology and it wasn't an excuse. It was a way of avoiding responsibility and continuing bad behavior.

"No, I mean it literally," he said. "That Ephraim was one of my doubles from a parallel universe. I came back in August. Remember? You said it was like I'd reverted back to normal overnight. I kind of did."

"That was a figure of speech." She lowered her voice. "Ephraim. You haven't been drinking, have you?"

"After all the times I've lectured *you*?" Ephraim asked.

"Drugs?"

"Drugs, Mom? I don't even take aspirin."

"Fine. Why are you telling me all this now?"

"Because I have to go away. To another universe." He knew how that must sound. "But I'll be back."

"Absolutely not," his mother said.

"I'm sorry, but you don't get a vote on this."

"I'm your mother, which gives me veto privileges over whatever stupid thing you're planning."

"You've always trusted me. I'm asking you to trust me now. This is really important."

"You're going to a 'parallel universe,'" she said. "That's your official story."

"Nathan will explain when I'm gone."

Nathan's eyes widened.

"Nathaniel won't be with you?" she asked.

Ephraim smiled. "No." Not the one she was thinking of, anyway.

"I feel better already. What about Jena? Is she involved?" his mother asked.

"Yes."

"But you're not eloping."

"Definitely not."

"And she isn't pregnant."

"Holy crap. Mom! Do you have to be such a *mom* right at this moment?"

"Ephraim, I don't know . . ."

"This is something I have to do."

"I see," she said, her voice tight. "Well, then, it doesn't really matter why you're doing whatever it is or where you're going. You're almost eighteen so I guess I can't stop you. I just want to know: Will you be safe?"

He could have lied. It would have made her feel better. "I hope so. I don't even know what we're dealing with yet."

"Can you contact me when you get there?"

"Doubtful. Unless Jena's phone has a really good service plan." He remembered that Nathaniel had contacted Zoe through a radio. "But if there's a way, I'll let you know that I'm all right."

"You're not giving me much here."

"I know."

"Well, thanks for calling instead of just . . . disappearing. And I do trust you," she said.

"Thanks." Ephraim swallowed. "Listen, Jim's a super nice guy in every universe. He'll take good care of you, if you let him."

"Do I need taking care of?" She laughed. "What am I saying? You're right. Is there anything I can do?"

He swallowed. "Just be here when I get back."

"I'm not going anywhere. I love you, hon."

"I love you too, Mom." His voice wavered, and he half-turned away from Nathan, who was pointedly looking in the other direction, hands stuffed in his pockets.

Ephraim tapped the phone's screen to end the call and stared at it for a while, blinking back tears. "So, that went well," he said.

"She'll be okay," Nathan said. "I'll make sure of it."

"Thanks."

"Unless . . . do you want me to come along too?" Nathan asked hopefully.

"I'll feel much better knowing you're here watching out for her. She's really important to me."

"Okay. But if you want company, all you have to do is ask." Nathan pointed his camera at Ephraim's face. "There are those tears I was looking for!" he said.

Ephraim scowled and wiped his eyes. "Let's go."

When he returned to Zoe's side, she silently opened the controller and held it out to him. She pressed a button, and the coin rose so he could take it. There was no need to reprogram the coin; the air around it was hot, indicating it was primed to go as soon as he touched it.

"Ready?" Zoe said. She grabbed his arm, and Jena took his left hand.

Ephraim reached for the coin. Just before he touched it, the disc wobbled and the controller's screen flickered. He pulled back his hand.

"You're sure that thing's working?" he asked.

Zoe frowned and tapped the screen. The coordinates for Nathaniel's universe flickered back on, and the coin repositioned itself by ten degrees. "Yes?"

"Great . . ." Jena said.

"Maybe you should stay behind," Zoe retorted.

Ephraim shrugged. "In for a quarter, in for a pound."

"It's 'in for a penny,'" Jena said.

"Inflation." He dipped his hand and closed it around the coin, pulling it out of the air.

The air rippled, expanding spherically from the coin in his fist. The parking lot became a hazy mirage around them, and Ephraim glimpsed a tall, dark building from another universe: the Institute where Nathaniel worked. He'd seen it once before, from the inside, when they'd dropped the older man off.

Then the shimmery sphere around them abruptly contracted, like a taut rubber band being let go, and the coin pulsed with sudden heat.

But they were still in his universe.

"Is this it?" Jena asked. She burped and covered her mouth. "Sorry. I suddenly don't feel well."

"Something's wrong," Zoe said. "We didn't shift."

Ephraim shook his head. He'd felt *something*. As if his stomach were being stretched like taffy and then pounded back into shape with a sledgehammer.

"What are we doing here?" Shelley asked.

"Wait. What?" Ephraim asked. He looked at Shelley. "Are you all right?" He looked around. "Where's Mary?"

"Right here," Shelley said. She waved her hand. "*Hello*. But why aren't we at the prom? Where's the limo?"

"Mary was standing right next to me," Nathan said. "They both were."

"What are you talking about?" Shelley asked.

"Your sister," Jena said. "Where's your sister?"

She stared at Jena. "Where did you come from?" She looked at Zoe. "I didn't know you had a twin, J."

"*You're* supposed to have a twin, Shelley," Jena said.

"I think I'd remember that," Shelley said. "And why are you using my middle name?"

They stood in stunned silence.

"Ephraim," Jena said. "What's going on?"

"I don't know," Ephraim said. "I've never seen this before. In some universes there's only one Mary Shelley Morales. Twinning is a random event, so it's just a matter of probability—"

"How can you be so calm? Something happened to our friend!"

He didn't remind Jena that he'd once watched Nate shoot one of her analogs dead right in front of him. It was hard to say which was the worse way to go.

"She's gone," Zoe said. "I thought I imagined it. I only saw it out of the corner of my eye while we were shifting. It was like one of them merged into the other one."

"Guys, what are you talking about?" Shelley asked.

"Just a second, Shell . . . er, M.S." He looked at the others. "We need to talk." Ephraim and the others walked over to the closed gates of the park. He looked back at the single, confused Morales girl. He'd never seen anyone look so lonely before.

Jena was crying. "Is she dead?"

Ephraim shook his head. "She might be . . . nonexistent."

"Then we shifted to another universe, after all," Jena said. "We just left her behind, and this is a different version of her."

Ephraim looked at her empty bucket and at Nathan. "No, we didn't. Zoe, is it possible that an analog switched places with her at the moment we shifted?"

"Anything's possible at this point. But I don't think so. I saw them . . . combine. That's the only way I can describe it. I'm sorry. This is effed up." She tapped her upper lip nervously. "It must be related to what just happened with the coin and controller."

"Why doesn't she remember everything that happened tonight?" Nathan asked. He looked pale and completely freaked out. "She acts like Shelley, but it isn't her. It's like she's both of them."

"Did you see what happened when we tried to leave?" Zoe asked.

"You sort of went wispy," Nathan said. "Like the ghosts. Then you were back. I recorded it."

"I thought I saw Nathaniel's universe for a moment," Zoe said.

"Me too. We almost made it, but something . . . blocked us," Ephraim said. He'd felt some sort of resistance. He wanted to sit down. He wanted to go home.

"What do we do about Mary and Shelley?" Jena asked.

"Whatever's happening is bigger than them, or any of us." Zoe sighed. "I know it isn't much consolation, but they're fine in another universe. There's a reality right next door to ours where they're both still at prom with you and Ephraim and Nathan. Where I never appeared to . . ." She looked around. "To cause all this."

"You don't know your presence had anything to do with this," Ephraim said.

"But the controller . . . if I'd destroyed it?"

"You can't blame yourself," he said.

"I think that's usually my line." She smiled.

"What do we do about Mary and Shelley?" Ephraim repeated. "We stick to the plan. We find out what's wrong with the multiverse. We try to use the Charon device again."

"What good will that do if we were blocked the first time?" Jena asked. "Something else might happen to one of us."

"That's also true if we do nothing," Zoe snapped.

"Try another set of coordinates?" Ephraim said. "Just to make sure the controller's working. We'll go to your universe, Zoe."

"Mine?" Zoe said.

"Why there?" Jena asked.

"Because if we make it, I can try to contact Nathaniel." Zoe grinned. "Smart, Ephraim."

He glanced at Jena. She nodded. Zoe dialed up her universe's coordinates.

The limo pulled up alongside Mary Shelley. She climbed into the back. The tinted window lowered, and Maurice stuck his head out.

"Hey, you guys ready to go somewhere else?" he called.

"We're working on it," Ephraim said. "Give us a couple more minutes."

The driver pulled his head back into the car and drove off.

Ephraim slotted the coin into the controller. Once again, it spun to get a fix—this time on Zoe's universe. When it settled, the three of them linked arms, and Ephraim reached for the coin.

He made eye contact with Nathan. His friend was devastated and afraid, so shaken he didn't even switch on his camera.

"Bye, Eph," Nathan said.

"Stay frosty," Ephraim said.

He grabbed the coin. The parking lot rippled around them, then warped back into focus. His stomach seemed to contract into a dense ball and rapidly expand to normal size. He tasted his dinner and swallowed hard to keep the bitterness down.

Ephraim blinked. Nathan was gone. So was the limo.

No, it was Zoe, Jena, and he who had disappeared. They'd made it to Zoe's universe.

"I'm going to—" Jena pivoted and buried her face in the bucket Ephraim had given her. She bent over and retched.

Shifting between universes invariably made people sick their first time, but the effect was brief, and subsequent trips between universes got easier. After all the trips he'd taken, Ephraim shouldn't have felt anything at all. It had been a while since he'd shifted, but the fact that he'd also felt a twinge earlier when Zoe burst into his universe, and that his stomach felt rather unsettled now, might be another sign that something was wonky.

"Welcome back, Eph." Zoe didn't let go of Ephraim's hand until he pulled away. She preoccupied herself with the controller as he turned to make sure Jena was okay.

He was supposed to hold her hair or something, he thought. But his girlfriend shoved him away.

Jena looked up and got her first look at the shuttered library. Her expression turned even bleaker.

"Now that really makes me sick," she said.

The dim moonlight revealed that its facade was drab and in disrepair, like most things were here. The glass doors were broken and covered in spray-painted plywood. The lion sculptures on either side of the steps, which Ephraim thought of as Bert and Ernie, were no longer identical—Bert was missing his head. Ephraim looked around, but the broken granite wasn't in sight. Who would steal a stone lion's head?

Jena had volunteered at the library since junior high, and worked there part-time ever since she was legal. She would have spent all of her time there anyway, so it was just gravy to get paid to be around all those books. It was practically a second home for her.

Zoe put a hand on her shoulder. "It's been a rough night, but we should get back to my house."

Jena shrugged Zoe off. She rubbed her eyes with the back of her arm and took a deep breath.

Ephraim fingered the coin in his hand. He tucked it safely into the front right pocket of his slacks at the same time that Zoe stowed the controller in her own pocket. Just like old times.

Not quite. As awful as the evening had turned out, it could get even worse if he didn't watch himself with Jena and Zoe. He suddenly felt very alone.

I wish I were anywhere but here.

CHAPTER 5

Zoe's bedroom hadn't changed much in the last year, aside from the addition of the massive black radio sitting on her desk and tangles of wire and microchips scattered among the familiar landscape of books.

Ephraim sat next to Zoe and examined the radio while she pulled a pair of old metal headphones around her neck and placed a microphone carefully in front of her. The polished tin plate screwed into the front of the machine read "RCA AR-88 Radio Receiver."

"This is how you've been communicating with Nathaniel?" Ephraim asked. He glanced at Zoe's reflection in one of the three glass panes covering the large dials on the radio's face.

"Beautiful, isn't it?" she asked, patting the radio's chassis with her right hand. He noticed a tattoo on the inside of her wrist: a barcode with a string of numbers printed beneath it. His gaze traveled along her bare arm, up to her shoulder, then her face.

"Yeah," he said, finally meeting her eyes.

She tilted her head and smiled. "What is it?"

"Um. I was just wondering, what happened to your nose ring?" he asked.

"The piercing got infected," she said. "And I guess I never bothered to put the stud back in. I only got it to piss off my father anyway."

"Too bad. I liked it," he said. "But the new tattoo's nice. Have they started tagging citizens here?"

She jerked her arm down to her lap and held it against her stomach to hide the tattoo.

"Did you get that to piss off your dad, too?" he asked.

"No. This was for me."

"Let me guess: A library thing? The barcode from your favorite book?" he asked.

"Something like that. It's private, Ephraim."

Then it shouldn't be on your wrist. "Okay. I'm sorry," he said.

He turned back to the radio, the only safe thing to look at when she was sitting this close to him.

"Let me show you how this works," she said. She sounded relieved.

She twisted the knob in the lower left corner from "Off" to "Rec. C.W." It clicked into place, and an amber glow lit each of the dials.

"It takes a little time to warm up," she said.

The large dials on the left and right of the radio panel were labeled "Tuning" and "Tuning Meter." Their purpose seemed clear enough, but the smaller dial in the center above the round red and white RCA logo was marked for something called "Vernier."

He counted ten small knobs labeled things like "Tone," "Noise Limiter," "Range," and "Audio Gain." The big knob in the center was also labeled "Tuning."

"I can't believe this old radio can contact another universe," he said.

"It's not old, it's *vintage*. Respect my ham shack," Zoe said.

"So how can a *vintage* radio receive signals from another dimension?" Ephraim said.

"I made some custom modifications to the radio and mounted a thirty-foot homebrew antenna on the roof that boosts the range. Turns out, I'm kind of a genius with this stuff."

"I know you like old TV shows and books, but how did you get interested in antiques?" he asked.

"This is the closest thing the Kims have to a family heirloom. It belonged to my grandfather. I'd forgotten all about it until Nathaniel suggested setting up an emergency channel. I had fun learning all this stuff. I guess it's in my blood."

A wooden crate next to her bed was stuffed with coiled cable, stacked soldering boards, computer chips, glass tubes, and printed schematics. Ephraim pulled out a worn instruction manual for the

"General Purpose Communications Receiver Model AR-88." He carefully thumbed through its brittle, yellowed pages. He skimmed a diagram filled with technical terms that he couldn't make any sense of.

"What's a, uh, 'vibrator power supply'?" he asked, reading from a list of parts.

Zoe eyed him suspiciously.

"Hey, Zoe?" Jena said.

Ephraim spun his seat around and saw his girlfriend's head poking from the open bathroom door. He felt guilty for forgetting she was cleaning up and changing clothes while he was talking to Zoe.

"Do you have anything a little less, um . . . skanky?" Jena asked.

Zoe raised her eyebrows. "Sorry, I just packed my non-skanky clothes away with my winter wardrobe."

The bathroom door opened the rest of the way, and Jena slunk out with a glum expression. She tossed her prom dress onto Zoe's bed and hugged her arms over her chest.

She was wearing a clingy black tank top, denim shorts, and navy Chucks. Except for the colors, the outfit was identical to Zoe's ensemble of a blue tank and red Chucks. She looked just as stunning as her analog, but showing that much skin clearly made her uncomfortable.

"Here," Zoe said. She pulled a baby-blue hoodie from the back of Ephraim's chair and tossed it to Jena.

"Thanks for letting me borrow your clothes. Everything fits perfectly." Jena zipped up the hoodie.

"Good. I was worried they'd be a little snug on you," Zoe said.

Jena gritted her teeth.

Ephraim coughed. "You guys are so cute in your matching outfits. Just like—" He stopped himself when he saw Jena's expression change as she remembered what had happened to Mary and Shelley.

"Uh, you should check this out, Jena," Ephraim said. He stood and gestured to his seat in front of the radio.

Her face brightened. "Is that Grumps' radio?" Jena asked. She hurried over and sat next to Zoe.

"'Grumps'?" Ephraim asked. He perched on the edge of the desk, scooting some books back with his butt to make room.

"That's what I called my grandfather when I was three," Jena and Zoe said simultaneously. "Stop that," they said.

Ephraim laughed. They both glared at him in perfect sync.

"Not funny," they said.

"You're right. It's getting spooky," he said. "So was he grumpy or something?"

"He was the sweetest, smartest man I've ever known," Jena said.

"I just called him that because I couldn't say 'grandpa' yet. And it stuck," Zoe said.

"Where did you find this?" Jena asked.

"It's been in the attic since he passed away," Zoe said.

"Here too?" Jena said. She ran a hand across the radio's chassis. "It looks terrific."

"Thanks. I refinished it. Everything but this." Zoe pointed out some letters and numbers scratched into the top corner of the case.

Ephraim stood to get a better look at it. "WB2IXW," he read. "I don't get it."

"That was his call sign," Jena said. She brushed her fingers over the engraved letters. "It actually works?"

"Like new," Zoe said. "Actually, better than new. I had to replace some parts, and I upgraded a few components with modern technology. There's a bunch of Internet forums that gave me some tips on repairing it, and you can order everything really cheaply." She fiddled with some wires behind the radio. "The hacker nerds at school were all too happy to help. We even started a ham radio club. There used to be one at Summerside High in the sixties. We figure when we get drafted, we can get into radio operations and engineering. The kind of thing that makes it less likely you'll be shot at."

"I always meant to try this out," Jena said. "Grumps loved it so much."

"It's not that hard. I can teach you the basics. You'll probably pick it up even more quickly than I did."

"Thanks."

Jena and Zoe looked at each other awkwardly for a moment, as if unsure how to proceed without sniping at each other.

"I'd still like to know how you can reach Nathaniel's universe with this," Ephraim said.

"I'll show you." Zoe tugged the plug of the headphones out of its jack, and static hissed over the small speaker beside the radio. She nudged a knob, and the volume increased.

"During the summer, sporadic E propagation in the ionosphere sometimes allows the six-meter wavelength band to pick up transmissions from all over the world, depending on certain conditions," Zoe said. "With a tall enough antenna and the right amounts of sunspot activity, cloud ionization, and luck, you can experience some amazing and unique radio phenomena and make contact with other countries. It's called DXing. That's why hams—ham radio operators—call the six-meter band the 'magic band.'"

"Magic, huh?" Ephraim said. "I've heard that before."

Jena picked up a stack of rumpled schematics. "This receiver isn't rated for the frequency range you'd need."

Zoe smiled. "It is now. I found a 50 mHz converter online. Imagine: People might be talking to parallel universes all the time through the magic band. But no one ever realizes it. Even if you found someone else who spoke the same language as you, you'd hardly think to confirm you were both in the same dimension."

"How'd you figure this out?" Jena asked.

"Nathaniel told me what to look for. I found everything online. Ham forums are great resources for beginners."

"Is that when he told you not to destroy the controller?" Ephraim asked. His question sounded harsher than he'd intended, but she didn't react.

"He instructed me to DX the magic band every Saturday before school for half an hour. As soon as I got back here, I rescued the receiver from the attic and started setting up my shack." She spun the dial slowly, and snatches of words crackled from the radio. "It's not like I had anything better to do."

"Are we hearing people in parallel universes right now?" Jena asked.

"Not yet. I need parts from the controller to really boost the signal." Zoe pulled the controller from her pocket.

"You aren't going to take it apart again," Ephraim said.

"No need," she said. She rummaged around behind the radio and grabbed the end of a bare copper wire. She slid a small antenna from the top of the controller and coiled the wire tightly around it.

"I didn't notice that antenna before," Ephraim said.

"I added it. It's just a conductor. It connects to the controller's motherboard so I can plug it into the radio without cracking the controller open," Zoe said. "There."

The speaker went nuts. Dozens of overlapping voices spilled out at once.

"Wow," Zoe said. "There's a lot of activity tonight. Most of the time I can't pick up anything at all."

Zoe worked through the dial incrementally. Static hissed, then they heard a series of strange beeps.

"Morse code?" Jena asked.

"Just interference," Zoe said. She clicked a knob over three settings, and the noise cleared a bit. "None of it ever makes any sense." She pointed at the dial. "I think this is the frequency where I heard Nathaniel's SOS this morning. It's hard to say. These old radio dials are very imprecise. I should really install a more accurate digital tuner, but I hate to spoil the elegance of the original design."

All Ephraim heard from the speaker was something like Darth Vader breathing.

"This is CHARON2 to CHARON1. Do you read?" The microphone had a squeeze bar that Zoe pressed to transmit while she spoke. She relaxed her grip. "No answer."

Ephraim crouched beside her chair. "We can't wait until next Saturday."

"We couldn't get through with the Charon device for a reason, and I'm hoping he'll realize that and will be listening for us," Zoe said. "Unfortunately the magic band is kind of fickle."

Ephraim rested his hand on the radio. The casing was warm and hummed gently under his fingers. This machine was older than the three of them combined. It was antiquated tech, but he knew as much about how it worked as he did the coheron drive. It might as well have been magic to him.

A sharp tone blasted from the speaker. He lifted his hand and backed away while Zoe turned down the volume on the speaker.

"What did you do?" she asked.

"I don't know. I barely touched it!" he said.

He moved his hand closer to it, but nothing happened until he touched the case. The same loud tone shrilled out of the speaker.

"Ephraim, what's in your pocket?" Jena asked.

"Huh?" He realized his other hand was in his pocket holding the coin: an old habit that had come back way too easily. He pulled the coin out and tapped it against the radio's metal chassis. The sound got sharper when it made contact.

"Interesting," Zoe said.

"I have an idea," he said. "Zoe, pick up the controller?"

As soon as she touched it, more static hissed. They heard fragments of words, random syllables. She touched the radio with her other hand, and the machine began to thrum.

"Huh," Zoe said.

"Open it," Ephraim said.

She flipped the controller open, and he placed the coin into its slot. The static dropped away to a gentle, steady hiss in the background.

"You did it!" Jena said. "You did something, anyway."

The coin lifted off an inch and hovered over the controller. Static sizzled and popped on the radio, and the coin trembled in midair.

Ephraim nudged the tuning dial on the radio to the right, and the horizontal coin tilted gently in the opposite direction, torquing slightly along its y-axis. He kept turning the dial through the frequencies, through silence, then white noise, and then people speaking in different languages. As he tuned different frequencies, Washington's face slowly rotated clockwise, and the coin turned around and over.

"'We are controlling transmission,'" Jena intoned in a deep voice. "'We will control the horizontal. We will control the vertical. . . . You are about to participate in a great adventure. You are about to experience the awe and mystery which reaches from the inner mind to *The Outer Limits*.'"

Zoe slapped Ephraim on the shoulder. "Eph, you're stupid brilliant!" She leaned over the controller, the neck of her tank top dipping.

"Eyes on the coin, Ephraim," Jena warned in a low voice.

"Nothing I haven't seen before," he muttered.

Jena punched him hard on his other shoulder.

"Mmph," he said.

Zoe grinned. "You've boosted the signal by like five hundred percent. We could probably talk to *aliens* right now. The radio's getting every frequency out there, and I think it's getting multiple signals from each. The neat trick is going to be parsing out the one we need out of all the possibilities. Keep tuning that big dial. I'll take these other two," she said, gesturing to the smaller dials flanking it on the radio.

Ephraim spun the dial back in the other direction, and the coin repeated its aerobatics in reverse. He kept it moving slowly, and the coin gradually turned belly-up until it was showing tails, with an image of the island of Puerto Rico and a tiny frog.

"Look," Zoe said. She poked the screen of the controller to life in her free hand as he turned a dial. Numbers blinked in and out, alternating with the sounds of static and active channels. It seemed that it was picking up a signal from a parallel universe on every fifth frequency.

Zoe smiled. "I guess we're still a great team, Eph."

Jena cleared her throat. "How long is this going to take?"

"You have somewhere else to be?" Zoe asked.

Jena glanced wistfully at the time on Zoe's VCR, almost hidden by a tower of old videotapes labeled "The Many Loves of Dobie Gillis" in Mr. Kim's neat print. It was just after 1 a.m.

"Not anymore," Jena said. She'd been planning the details of their prom night for months, but this hadn't figured into any of them.

"We have time, Jena. Your folks aren't expecting you until tomorrow," Ephraim said.

"Oh?" Zoe said.

"They think I'm staying with . . ." She swallowed. "Friends."

"Miss Perfect lied to her parents?" Zoe asked. "What debauchery did you have planned this weekend?"

Jena and Ephraim exchanged glances.

"Oh!" Zoe said. She looked away.

"It's not just that. I mean, we have classes on Monday. Exams coming up," Jena said. "I have to write my speech for graduation." Her voice rose, and she was talking more quickly, on the verge of a panic attack.

"Jena, remember what happened to your friends," Zoe said. "This is important."

"I know, but . . ." She looked at Ephraim helplessly. "This isn't part of the plan," Jena said. "My life's important too. I have a future to think about."

"I'm so sorry this happened at such an inconvenient time for you." Zoe plucked the coin away from the controller. The radio hissed its displeasure. "He can drop you off right now in your universe, if you're that worried about your *future*."

"Hey," Ephraim protested. "Hold on."

"Honestly, you're kind of redundant here, Jena," Zoe said.

"Speak for yourself," Jena said.

"I just did."

"Guys. Let's just get on with this," Ephraim said. "The sooner we get in touch with Nathaniel, the sooner we can all get back to our lives. Agreed?"

Zoe nodded.

"Are we good, Jena?" he asked.

"I'm staying with you," she said.

"Okay." He smiled.

Ephraim took the coin from Zoe. It was still warm from its time in the machine. He slid it back into the controller, and it wobbled into the air a couple of inches above its groove.

"Can't we just set the coordinates for Nathaniel's universe with the controller to program the radio?" Ephraim asked.

Zoe pulled them up on the screen, and the coin reoriented, but nothing changed on the radio.

"It looks like the Charon device can't control the radio," Zoe said. "It was a good idea, though."

"That makes sense," Jena said. "We can use the coin and controller to monitor the frequencies, and it's obviously boosting the range significantly, but the information exchange only goes one way."

"So we'll know when we have the correct coordinates, but we can't take any shortcuts," Zoe said. "If I had enough time, I could probably set up a two-way interface. The easiest thing would be to solder the motherboard from the controller to the radio . . ."

"And if you break the controller, the nearest service facility is in the universe we're trying to find," Ephraim said.

He spun the knob as far to the left as it would go. The coin spun rapidly and shuddered to a stop. The arrow on the dial shot to the left, and gears rumbled within the radio.

Ephraim yawned as he nudged the knob forward the tiniest bit.

"We'll just have to do this the slightly-easier-but-still-annoyingly-hard way," he said. "It's gonna be a long night."

CHAPTER 6

Ephraim advanced the dial a tiny bit and heard only the hiss of open air on a dead frequency. Zoe sat in a chair beside him, clutching the controller in her left hand. She shook her head. The coin remained still over the controller and the screen was blank.

"Next," Zoe croaked.

They had painstakingly crept through all the stations one frequency at a time. Then they'd done it again in the opposite direction. They had picked up dozens of transmissions from other universes, but not once had they heard Nathaniel's voice. Nor had the unique ten-digit sequence that identified his universe appeared on the controller's display. Even so, Zoe repeated her call sign over and over again.

Forward, back, forward. Over and over, they sent her voice out into the ether. But were they even getting through to anyone?

Ephraim twisted the knob.

"Too far!" Zoe said.

"Sorry, my fingers are cramping," he said.

"Mine too." She swapped the controller to her right hand, then flexed the fingers of her left hand. She had to maintain contact with the controller to keep it active while they scanned the frequencies.

"You need a break," Ephraim said.

She shook her hand out. "We have to keep going." She cleared her throat.

It was already nearly three in the morning, and Ephraim was starting to worry they weren't going to get through tonight. Zoe had said the magic band was unreliable. Or it could be that Nathaniel wasn't listening for them after all—or maybe he couldn't anymore.

"Jena can take over," he said.

"No, I can do this," Zoe said. Her voice rasped and she coughed.

She put down the controller in disgust. The coin dropped into its slot, and the radio went dead. "Fine. I'll get us some coffee."

When Zoe stood and stretched her back, Jena looked up from the book she was reading, tucking a finger between the pages to hold her place. She'd gathered several selections from Zoe's extensive library. At the moment she was working her way through *Sanditon* by Jane Austen.

"Any luck?" Jena asked. Her cheeks were flushed, and she looked flustered.

Zoe left the room without answering her.

"Not yet. We could use some assistance over here," Ephraim said. "Tag, you're it."

Jena walked over slowly, still reading her book. If Ephraim could hit a bookstore before going home, he could find the perfect graduation present for Jena. And perfect presents for her next twenty-five birthdays, holidays, and their anniversaries. Except the money here was different, and the multicolored bills with different presidents' faces that he'd brought back to his own universe were all hidden at the back of his desk drawer at home.

Jena sat down in front of the radio and slowly turned a page.

"Is that any good?" Ephraim asked.

"It's wonderful," Jena said, missing his sarcasm. "I've never read the whole thing before."

"I find that hard to believe. You're an Austen fanatic."

"She didn't finish writing it in our universe." Jena glanced at the bookcases around them wistfully. "A lot of these have never been published. So, how can I help?"

"You just have to hold something for me."

She raised an eyebrow.

"The *controller*," he said. "Jeez. You've been hanging around Nathan way too much."

"And whose fault is that?" She picked up the controller. Her hand jumped when the screen lit and the coin floated above it.

"Careful," he said.

"It caught me by surprise," she said. "Why can only Nathan, Zoe, and I use this thing?"

Ephraim nudged the tuner knob back to the previous frequency, just to be sure they wouldn't miss anything.

"Nathaniel and his universe's Jena Kim operated the controller on the survey teams that recorded the different realities in the multiverse. Even though it's coded to specific biometric readings for security, you're all indistinguishable as far as the device is concerned."

"And the coin only works for you and your analogs," she said.

"So far," he said.

Nathaniel had once mentioned that the Charon device had four authorized users, and that it could be programmed for any new pair of users if necessary. But Ephraim didn't know if that meant the controller would operate for a third person, or if the coin also worked for someone else. Was there anyone who could use both the coin and the controller? That would be a lot of responsibility and a lot of risk.

Ephraim leaned over to look at the controller's screen. "Do you know what you're looking for?"

"Nathaniel's coordinates. 909.877.111 . . . 9?"

"Good memory," Ephraim said.

"It's like a phone number. Or a library call number. So—" Jena said.

Ephraim hushed her and leaned closer to the speaker. A low, gravelly voice was murmuring, but he didn't recognize it. It certainly wasn't Nathaniel.

He shook his head and reached for the tuner.

Jena grabbed his wrist to stop him. "Wait," she said. "I recognize that voice."

"Who is it?"

"It's . . . Grumps." Jena turned up the volume.

". . . is all I'm saying. I simply don't think he's man enough for the job." The response was garbled. Ephraim reached for the dial again, but Jena slapped his hand away.

"Don't touch it," she snapped.

"I'm just trying to get a better signal," he said.

"You might lose it, and we'll never get it back again." He and Zoe hadn't heard the same quantum frequency twice that night, which didn't bode well for getting in contact with Nathaniel again.

"Oh, my God," Jena whispered. "It can't be, but it's really him."

"Nathaniel?" Zoe asked. She came back into the room bearing a tray with a platter of sandwiches and three steaming mugs of coffee.

"It's our grandfather," Jena said, holding up the microphone.

Zoe put the tray down on her bed and rushed over.

Grumps' voice cut back in. "That's right! I'm so pleased you said that. You know what this country needs, and it isn't—"

"Grandpa Dug!" Zoe said. "Wow."

"How long has it been since you talked to him?" Ephraim asked.

"Eight years," Jena said. "We lost him to colon cancer."

Zoe put a hand on Jena's shoulder.

"That's awful. I'm sorry," Ephraim said.

He remembered when Jena had missed a week of school in fifth grade. His week had been bad enough with her absent, but that was nothing compared to what she'd been going through. She'd been even more withdrawn for a few months, until Mary and Shelley managed to draw her out again. He knew someone in her family had died, but at the time, he hadn't really known what that felt like; now he was all too acquainted with death. That was also when his mom had kicked his abusive dad out and started divorce proceedings, so he'd had other things on his mind.

Jena turned to Zoe. "He sounds so young."

"Don't forget, alternate universes can be at different points in our timeline," Zoe said.

"Right. So he *is* younger. Can we talk to him?"

"He won't even know us. We haven't been born yet, from his perspective." But Zoe tapped Ephraim on the shoulder and gestured for him to get up.

She took his chair and studied the number on the controller in

Jena's hand. Ephraim looked over Jena's shoulder. The last digit of the frequency flickered between two numbers, corresponding to interference on the station.

"Hmmm. The signal isn't very strong," Zoe said.

"If we save these coordinates, can the coin take us there?" Jena asked.

"That probably isn't a good idea. But you ought to learn this anyway in case you have to use the controller," Zoe said.

She showed Jena how the menu worked and walked her through saving both sets of coordinates.

"No telling when this is," Zoe said. "He bought this radio in 1953, I think, when he emigrated from Korea after the war. If that's still the same, and he's a young man, it's probably not long after that. He would be twenty-something."

"It's tempting to try to visit, isn't it?" Jena asked. "I love the 1950s."

"Me too," Zoe said. She gestured at the piles of videotapes and DVDs of old TV shows from her father's collection, identical to the state of Jena's room back in her and Ephraim's universe. "Obviously."

Ephraim wandered over to the tray Zoe had made for them and grabbed a peanut butter sandwich and a mug of coffee. He was surprised he wasn't sleepier, but he often stayed up this late on weekends playing computer games with Nathan.

He watched Zoe show Jena how to transmit by squeezing the activator bar on the microphone, and then hand it over.

Jena leaned closer to the radio, her lips almost brushing against the metal grille on the old microphone. She squeezed the bar.

"Grumps?" she asked. "I mean, Dug Kim? Is that you?" Jena's knuckles were white as she clutched the microphone. Zoe touched the back of her hand and murmured something. Jena loosened her grip.

"Try his call letters," Zoe said.

"Oh, yeah." Jena read off the numbers scratched into the top of the radio. "Calling WB2IXW. Come in. This is, uh, CHARON2?" She glanced at Zoe. Zoe shrugged.

The radio crackled. "Who is . . ." Static popped and a piercing tone sounded, then his voice faded to silence.

"What happened?" Jena said. "Get him back!"

"I don't think I can," Zoe said.

"But we got the coordinates?"

Zoe nodded. The coin spun around once, twice, trying to lock onto something.

Jena grabbed the microphone again. "Hello? Hello?"

"Hello?" Her voice came back out of the radio.

"Just an echo," Jena said. She threw the microphone down in frustration.

"Hey, careful with that," Zoe said.

"Is anyone there? Over." The staticky voice spoke again—Jena's voice.

Jena and Zoe froze, staring at each other. They looked at the microphone. Neither of them had touched it.

Ephraim swallowed a mouthful of peanut butter painfully. "*That* wasn't an echo," he said. He gulped the coffee to clear his throat and winced as the hot beverage scalded its way down his throat.

"That sounded like us," Jena said.

"That's it! We've made contact!" Zoe snatched the microphone and tilted it toward her while Jena continued to hold on to the controller. "Hello! This is CHARON2. Is someone there? Come in. Over."

"CHARON2, this is CHARON1. Am I ever glad to hear from you. Over." This was becoming downright surreal—Jena and Zoe were speaking to another of their analogs.

"Finally! We've been trying you all night," Zoe said. "CHARON1, is Nathaniel there? Over."

"His hands are full," the voice went on. ". . . multiverse . . . flux. I could lose your frequency again at any mo . . . can't keep this channel open for long. We need you here ASAP. Over."

"We tried to shift to your universe, but something blocked us. Over," Zoe said.

"Say again?"

"We couldn't shift to your universe," Zoe repeated slowly.

"Excellent," the voice said.

Ephraim, Jena, and Zoe exchanged a look. Why was that a good thing?

"Who's with you?" the voice asked.

"I'm Zoe Kim. I'm here with my analog Jena. And Ephraim Scott."

There was a prolonged silence. Zoe released the microphone.

"Did we lose her?" Ephraim asked. He reached down to adjust the frequency, but Jena shook her head. The coin was steady, the signal was as strong as it was going to get.

Finally the voice from the radio spoke. "Ephraim's there?" She sounded hopeful. Relieved. "He has the coin?" A moment later: "Of course he has it if he's in your universe."

Ephraim put his hand on Zoe's shoulder and leaned over the microphone. He nodded, and she squeezed the activator bar.

"Yes, I have the coin," he said. "Hi. Uh, who's this?"

"Dr. Jena Kim," she said.

Zoe dropped her hand from the microphone. "Doctor?" she asked.

"It's the future," Ephraim said. "She wouldn't still be in high school. Even Michael Gupal couldn't get left back twenty-five times, and you're considerably smarter than him."

"A doctor," Jena said. "Dad would be so proud."

"Hmph," Zoe said.

"Are you still there? Hello?" Dr. Kim asked. "It's, um . . . 3:06 a.m. here."

Zoe glanced at the time on her VCR and squeezed the microphone. "The same here," she said.

"Then our next window will be at 3:33," Dr. Kim said. "We have . . . time it for periods with less quantum . . . ference. You live near Greystone Park . . . there by then?"

Zoe released the microphone. "What do we do?"

"This is what we've been waiting for," Ephraim said.

"I'd feel better if I heard it from Nathaniel," Zoe said. "I don't know this woman."

"But she's us," Jena said. "I say we go. It's better than sitting around here."

"I guess we won't get any answers otherwise," Ephraim said.

"Hello?" Dr. Kim called. "Are . . . there?"

Zoe leaned into the microphone and transmitted. "We'll be there," she said.

"Splendid. Use the Charon . . . 3:33 a.m. *precisely*." Noise drowned her out. "see you. Ov—"

Zoe adjusted the tuner a couple of times, but the coin was flat and motionless, and the empty radio channel sizzled and sputtered back at them.

"She's gone," she said. She switched off the radio and carefully stowed the microphone next to the headphones.

"Where are we supposed to go? I couldn't make it out," Jena said.

"The fountain," Ephraim and Zoe said.

"The one in the park?"

"It's a hunch," Ephraim said. "The Memorial Fountain is located smack in the center of the Institute. It's where we dropped off Nathaniel last year."

He reached for the coin in the controller, but he stopped an inch away from it when he felt the heat radiating from it. Instead, he used the pocket square from his tux to pick it up and let it cool. Even through the cloth, his hand tingled with energy. It felt like the coin could jump from his hand and flip itself.

"But we made contact, and we have a plan. Not bad for a night's work," he said.

"I get the impression our work has just begun," Zoe said.

Jena shuddered. "I hate hearing my own voice."

"Thanks," Zoe said. "But I know what you mean." They both smiled.

"So we're headed back to the park. We can get there in ten minutes if we walk fast." He yawned. "So much for sleep."

"You weren't really planning to get any tonight, were you?" Zoe asked. He shot her a look. Zoe smiled slyly. "Sleep, I mean."

Jena blushed. "I, for one, am too wired to sleep. I can't believe we actually talked to Grumps! Sort of."

Zoe pulled a red hoodie out from under her bed, brushed off some dustballs, and tied it around her waist. She opened the top drawer of her dresser and pulled something out of it. Something dark and heavy, which she tucked into the back of her shorts. It looked like—

"Holy crap! Is that a gun?" Jena asked. "Where did you get a gun?" She whirled to face Ephraim. Her face had become a shade paler than Zoe's. "Why does she have a gun?"

"We confiscated it from Nate," Ephraim said. "I can't believe you kept it, Zoe."

"I live in a tough world," she said. "Guns aren't dangerous if they're in the right hands."

"No one should carry a gun around," Jena said. "Least of all an eighteen-year-old woman."

"You know that isn't true even in your universe," Zoe said. "I don't expect you to understand. I know how to use it. I spend a lot of time at the shooting range at school."

"There are so many things wrong with that statement," Jena said.

"Whatever," Ephraim said. "Just be careful with that, Zoe."

She'd kept the controller. She'd kept the gun. He wondered what else she was keeping from him.

"Don't worry about me," Zoe said. "I can handle myself."

"I'm not worried about *you*," Ephraim said. "Let's just go."

Zoe snapped her fingers. "I need one more thing. Be right back," she said and went into the bathroom.

"What did she forget? Nunchaku?" Jena asked.

Ephraim pulled on his tuxedo jacket and slid the coin in the handkerchief into the breast pocket. When Zoe returned a couple of minutes later, he caught the familiar glint of silver over her right nostril.

"You have a nose stud!" Jena said. "Dad must have freaked."

"That was the idea. But it's kind of who I am now." She smiled at Ephraim.

"It looks so badass on you. Maybe I'll get one in college," Jena said. "Or a tattoo. If I can think of something I would want on my body for the rest of my life."

Zoe frowned and pulled on a fingerless glove that covered the bar-code on her wrist.

Ephraim looked at the two of them.

"We make an interesting trio," he said. He tightened his bowtie.

"One guy in a tux and a pair of twins . . . this is the perfect setup for a sitcom," Jena said.

"All we need are some wacky hijinks and an easily avoided mis-understanding," Zoe said. She scratched at her nose.

Ephraim smiled. Now that Jena and Zoe were getting along, mostly, this situation might not be so bad after all. He was with two beautiful women who liked him, and he . . .

His smile faded. This situation could be more dangerous than he'd bargained for; he'd just realized that he might be caught between two women, and that never ended well, even in sitcoms.

CHAPTER 7

Ephraim, Jena, and Zoe stared up at the chained and padlocked gates to Greystone Park.

"I think it's closed," Ephraim said. The padlock was coated in reddish-brown rust. "Forever."

"Let me guess: high crime rates in your universe?" Jena asked.

"An underground community of draft dodgers was squatting on the old estate," Zoe said. "This is supposed to prevent that."

She pointed out a crumbling section of the wall next to the gates. "Just do what I do," she said.

Zoe scaled the wall, finding cracks and crevices to take hold of so easily it was clear she'd done this before, and often. Ephraim concentrated on watching where she placed her hands and feet instead of how good she looked doing it. He'd forgotten how much more athletic she was than Jena.

Zoe crouched on the wall on the balls of her feet, fingers pressed against the old stone in a classic Spider-Man pose, only with cleavage visible from her tank top.

"Who's next?" She stage-whispered, even though they probably were the only people around.

"Me," Jena said. She cracked her knuckles and jogged in place for a moment. She pulled two paperbacks out of her sweatshirt pockets and handed them to Ephraim. "Carry my books, boyfriend?"

"My pleasure, madam." He squinted at the covers in the soft yellow glow from the old-fashioned wrought-iron lampposts flanking the gates: *The Dark Tower* by C. S. Lewis and *The Sense of the Past* by Henry James. "Does Zoe know you stole these?" he asked.

"They're library books," Jena said. "Consider them checked out."

Jena climbed, more slowly and clumsily than Zoe at first, but she picked up speed as she went. Her calf muscles strained with the effort, and she had more trouble pulling herself up.

A foot away from the top, she hesitated, testing out a couple of toeholds. As she tentatively applied weight on her right foot, a section of the wall disintegrated, and she slipped with a short shriek.

Ephraim leapt forward to help. He reached up and pushed against her butt. Her right hand swung loose from the wall. Zoe was holding onto her left hand, her feet hooked over the far edge of the wall for leverage.

"I've got her," he said. "You can let her go. Slowly."

Zoe shook her head. "Push on three. One. Two . . ."

On three, he heaved Jena up, and Zoe hauled her up with both hands. Jena grabbed onto the wall with her right hand, pulled herself over, and sprawled on her stomach on the top of the wall.

"Thanks," Jena gasped. She remained flat on her stomach and pivoted around until she was lying lengthwise along the one-foot-wide wall, looking like a contented cat. She rested her head on her hands and gave Ephraim a Cheshire grin. "And *you*. Watch where you put your hands, mister."

Ephraim stared at the wall. Jena's struggle had collapsed more of it, knocking out several bricks he had planned to use as footholds.

"Now how do I join you two?" he asked.

"Maybe there's another section that's easier to climb," Jena said.

He scanned the wall, squinting at the long shadows cast by the moonlight and the flickering fluorescent glow of the light inside the dilapidated bus shelter.

He prodded the wall, watching for more crumbling gray bricks. "I can do this," he said. He tossed Jena her books one at a time, and she caught them easily.

He backed up about ten feet and looked up at Jena and Zoe, their silhouettes dark against the sky so he wasn't sure which was which, aside from their positions. "Catch me?" he asked.

"*Catch you?*" Jena said. "Hold on—"

But Ephraim was already racing toward the wall as if he intended to smash headlong into it. He nearly broke off his approach, but instead he leaped as high as he could, his right sneaker catching the first toehold Zoe had found. He used his momentum to push him up and to the left, boosting himself on a lateral crack in the wall and up the rest of the way. Broken brick and mortar tumbled under him.

His hands scrabbled painfully against the rough stone, and he took one last step on a section that cascaded down immediately. But he had enough speed now to launch him almost to the top of the wall.

He reached out, and Zoe and Jena each grabbed one arm, tugging him up and forward, like they were breaking a giant wishbone. His right shin banged against the corner of the wall, and his left scraped along the top. Soon he was kneeling shakily between the two women.

In his head, he'd imagined it like a ninja scaling a cliff face, but in practice he'd probably never looked more awkward. It was a good thing Nathan hadn't been there to witness it with his camera.

Zoe stretched her arms and winced. "That was—"

"Impressive?" Ephraim said. He stood to take a bow and nearly lost his balance.

"Stupid," Jena said. "Next time a little more warning, huh? Or hire a stunt double."

"Ha ha," he said.

"Even you have to respect the laws of physics, Ephraim," Zoe said.

"Not if they don't respect me."

They lowered themselves down the other side of the wall before dropping the rest of the way. Ephraim felt the shock of impact in his feet and legs but shook it off, and they headed toward the fountain.

Like the library, the old Memorial Fountain was untended and overgrown with weeds. It was in worse shape than when he'd last seen it; the cement basin was cracked down the length of its middle, bisecting it in two halves. It was full of mounds of trash: discarded cans, broken bottles, Styrofoam cartons, condoms, and plastic wrappers. The bronze statue of Atlas in the middle was tarnished, black in the darkness. Withered vines twined around his legs and obscured his chest, dry remnants dangling from his arms.

"Depressing," Jena said.

"It's 3:31," Zoe said. She retrieved the controller and held it out to Ephraim. He slid the coin into its slot, and she set the coordinates. "Ready," she said.

Ephraim thought the hovering coin was tilted at the same angle it had been when they'd been communicating with Dr. Kim through the radio. Jena linked arms with Ephraim, then took Zoe's hand. Jena looked at their clasped hands with barely suppressed revulsion.

"This feels weird," Jena said.

Zoe positioned herself at the other point of their little triangle, where Ephraim could easily reach the coin with his right hand.

"3:32 and fifty seconds," Zoe said.

"Ready," he said. "Steady . . . go!"

He scooped the coin from the controller and squeezed Jena's hand.

The earth dropped away and quickly lurched back up to meet his feet. His stomach heaved, and he shut his eyes against a sudden, intense brightness. He sneezed.

He slowly cracked his eyes open. As they adjusted to the change in lighting, he saw Zoe and Jena blinking at him, hands shading their eyes. They were indoors, with bright spotlights shining down at them.

Jena groaned. Despite the pained expression on her ashen face, she didn't seem to be in imminent danger of throwing up again.

Zoe looked woozy too. "Was that a rougher trip than usual?"

Jena wiped sweat from her forehead. She glanced around them in awe.

"Holy crap," Jena said. "Where are we?"

"The Everett Institute for Many-Worlds, uh, Research Something Something," Ephraim said.

"Relativity Waves and, uh, Mechanical Probability?" Zoe said.

"Usually 'Crossroads' for short." Ephraim grinned.

Jena gaped at the gleaming silver statue of Atlas in the center of the enclosed courtyard. Nearly a story tall, it stood exactly where its smaller, bronze version existed in other universes at the center of the Memorial Fountain.

Atlas's muscular shoulders supported a fixed, vertical brass ring about five feet in diameter, which framed three inner concentric circles: two more brass rings and a round, flat gyrocompass in the center. The golden surface of the giant disc reflected the yellow spotlights and shone down on them like a small sun.

"What is *that*?" Jena asked.

"The Coheron Drive," Ephraim said. "The big brother to the Charon device."

"You mean it's like the coin and controller?" She looked from him to Zoe.

"So I'm told," Ephraim said. He shielded his eyes against the light and studied the large-scale version of the portable device he and Zoe used. A logo was stamped in its center: a figure eight with the letters E in the left loop and I in the right.

He'd never seen the machine in action. The last time he and Zoe had been here, they'd only stayed for a few minutes—just long enough to drop off Nathaniel and say their good-byes.

Ephraim peered at the skylight ten stories above their heads. At noon, the sunlight must fall directly on the disc, but right now the square window was pitch-black.

Jena followed his gaze. "No windows," she murmured.

The interior walls of the courtyard were covered in large steel plates. He saw four surveillance cameras trained on the plaza below. He wouldn't have been surprised if there were also laser cannons. Maybe they were hidden inside the walls. One of the cameras rotated to stare directly at him.

"Very welcoming," he said.

Machinery clicked and whirred behind him. Ephraim turned just as a thick metal door in the wall whooshed up, revealing a long, lit corridor. Zoe stood beside the door with her hand on a shiny black panel with the outline of a hand on it.

"How'd you do that?" Jena asked. She walked to the door and peered inside curiously without crossing the threshold. Ephraim joined her. A difference in air pressure drew air from the enclosed courtyard into the building. Jena's hair wafted in the gentle breeze at their backs.

"I just put my hand there," Zoe said. "Nathaniel did it last time."

She stepped aside, and Jena placed her hand on the panel. The door slammed shut, inches in front of Ephraim. He felt it whiz by his face as he stumbled backward.

"Jeez," he said. His heart pounded.

Jena looked at her hand and wiggled her fingers. "Nifty."

"It must be programmed for us," Zoe said. "Just like the Charon device. If it were reading our handprints, it would know we aren't Dr. Kim."

"You try it, Eph," Jena said.

Ephraim placed his hand against the panel. The door didn't respond. He looked around the courtyard. There were three other doors like the one in front of them. He assumed at least one of them must lead outside into Greystone Park, or whatever was on that property in this time.

A high-pitched alarm suddenly went off, reverberating in the enclosed space.

"Not again," Zoe shouted, hands clamped over her ears.

"Turn it off!" Jena said.

"I didn't turn it on," Ephraim said. The panel was flashing white and red under his hand. He slapped his palm against it again, but nothing happened. He pressed harder. Was it a general intruder alert, or had it been set specifically to respond to his touch?

A door on their right slid open, and a man hurried out. He turned to the panel beside the door he'd emerged from and drew his forefinger clockwise in a circle on it. A digital keypad lit up on the screen. He tapped in a sequence, and the alarm stopped. After the echo died down, Ephraim still heard a faint ringing in his ears.

The man drew a counterclockwise circle, and the panel darkened, then he placed his hand on the screen, and the door closed. He turned around and walked slowly out of the shadows toward them with a familiar gait.

He was a forty-two-year-old man with short dirty-blond hair, in

a white button-down shirt and dark jeans—an older version of
Ephraim's best friend, Nathan Mackenzie. And he had a wide grin on
his face.

"Hey, old man," Ephraim said.

"Hey, kid," Nathaniel said. "Causing trouble already, I see."

"Isn't that why we're here?"

Ephraim reached out to shake Nathaniel's hand. Instead, the man
gathered him into a bear hug. Ephraim patted him on the back.

Nathaniel let him go and scrutinized him.

"Looking snazzy." Nathaniel straightened Ephraim's bow tie.
"Didn't the RSVP say casual attire?"

"You caught us at prom," Ephraim said.

Nathaniel glanced at Jena. "Sorry about that."

"Yeah," Ephraim said.

"I'm glad to see you again, though I really hoped this day
wouldn't come." He turned to Jena. "And I finally get to meet your
lady friend."

Jena blinked up at him. The spotlights made a gentle halo of
Nathaniel's light hair. "Hi. I'm Jena Kim."

"Of course you are," he said.

"I've heard a lot about you," Jena said.

He shook her hand. "If you're anything like your analogs, you'll
be a big help."

She smiled at that. Finally, Nathaniel turned to Zoe.

"Hey, Z," he said.

She embraced him in a fierce hug.

"I missed you," she murmured.

"Me too," Nathaniel said. He folded her in his arms.

Ephraim looked away. When had those two gotten so close? She
couldn't have feelings for him, could she? He couldn't imagine her
and Nathan Mackenzie getting together in any universe, especially a
version of him more than twice her age.

Nathaniel pulled away and stared at Zoe. "You're packing?" he
asked.

She rolled her eyes. "Not you, too. I know how to handle a gun."

"That isn't the point. You don't need a weapon here." Nathaniel held his hand out, palm up.

"Really?" Zoe asked.

"Come on, Z," Nathaniel said. "If you're armed, you can't come in."

Zoe sighed, but she reached under her hoodie and pulled out the compact pistol. She handed it to Nathaniel.

He examined the gun carefully. It looked much smaller in his hands. Ephraim felt a shiver run down his spine.

"Safety's on," Zoe said.

Nathaniel pressed a button, and the magazine dropped out of the short handle. He pocketed it and squinted at the gun.

"Smith and Wesson Bodyguard 380," Nathaniel murmured. "The gun that shot me. I'm surprised at you, Zoe. I'll hold this in my office until after school."

He put the gun in his pocket and shook his head. "But that reminds me. How's M.S. doing?"

"She's finishing her senior year in Spain. But she won't be back any time soon. Her parents didn't want her getting drafted," Zoe said. "Their family has a house in the country. I considered going with her, but . . . I didn't want to leave Summerside, in case you needed me." She glanced at Ephraim.

Ephraim cut in. "Speaking of Mary Shelley, we've seen some really screwed up things tonight. It's great to catch up and all, but we were hoping you and Dr. Kim could explain what the hell is going on."

"It felt strange shifting here this time," Zoe said. "And we couldn't get through at all before, like there was some kind of resistance."

"Doc set up a quantum barrier around our universe. Like a firewall on a computer network." Nathaniel slapped his forehead. "And I almost forgot to turn it back on. I'll be right back. You guys stand far away from the LCD."

"LCD?" Jena asked.

"The Large Coheron Drive." He pointed at the mechanism in the center of the courtyard and hurried back to the room he'd appeared from. He pressed his hand to the security panel and ducked inside, leaving the door open. The squeal of machinery filled the atrium, and the Large Coheron Drive shuddered into motion.

The central disc, like a giant version of Ephraim's coin, slowly tilted to a horizontal position and remained level, while the two rings around it began spinning—one of them horizontally, the other vertically. They picked up speed until it looked like the disc was surrounded by a shimmering transparent orb, generating a strong air current that pulled at their hair and clothes.

The air around it rippled like heat waves, and in fact, the air was definitely warmer.

Nathaniel emerged from the room and slapped the panel on his way back to them, closing the door behind him. "Now nothing gets in or out of this universe," he shouted over the roar of the machinery.

Ephraim placed a hand over his breast pocket, feeling the coin inside. It was useless until they switched off its larger counterpart. He was basically trapped in this universe, and he didn't like it.

"Come on," Nathaniel said. "The Doc will meet us up in the lab."

Nathaniel opened the door and ushered them inside. Zoe hurried along beside him, telling him about everything that had happened that day. Ephraim noticed she omitted any mention of their kiss.

Ephraim glanced behind him. He glimpsed Atlas straining under the weight of the spinning gyroscope before the door slammed shut, cutting off the light from the courtyard.

Jena slipped her hand in his and squeezed lightly as they followed Nathaniel and Zoe down the long, dark corridor.

CHAPTER 8

So far, the interior of the Everett Institute resembled Summerside High School, with speckled gray floor tiles, pale-yellow walls, and a long corridor with unmarked doors that could have led to classrooms, for all Ephraim knew. This was supposed to be the future, but it was fairly indistinguishable from his time, let alone the previous century.

"This place is huge," Zoe said.

"Ten years ago, we had more than a hundred physicists and nearly a thousand engineers, data analysts, mathematicians, materials scientists, machinists, chefs—you name it. You never had to leave the place because it had everything you needed." Nathaniel sighed. "Today we have barely, maybe, five percent of the staff." He glanced at her. "But we're actively recruiting."

"What happened to everyone?" Jena asked.

"We couldn't afford to keep them on after we lost our government grants," Nathaniel said. "Fortunately for them, most of them were already being offered jobs elsewhere."

The hall ended at a pair of large elevator doors, and Nathaniel pressed the button. The doors dinged open, and the group piled into the expansive elevator. It easily could have fit twenty people. Nathaniel jabbed the top button.

The doors slid shut. If the green numbers above the door hadn't been increasing, Ephraim wouldn't have known they were rising at all.

"Was it because you disappeared?" Zoe asked.

"I'm flattered you think I'm that important." Nathaniel scratched the back of his neck. "But that *was* related. The big issue was that we promised results that we could no longer deliver without the coin and controller. And the government was only interested in funding us when they thought we were building a weapon. A small private

investor is keeping us operational, but they could back out any day if
we don't show them we're making progress. And this is the worst possible time for us to be shut down."

"Is it really bad?" Zoe said.

"Let me put it this way. If we'd had the coin and someone to use
it, I would have seriously considered robbing banks in other universes.
And it may still come to that." He glanced at Ephraim.

"Why didn't the Institute just make another Charon device?"
Ephraim asked. "Or at least try to retrieve you?"

Nathaniel looked down at his feet. "Dr. Kim worked on it. But
the situation is complicated. You'll understand soon. But that isn't
our main concern right now."

Ephraim felt a gentle bump under his feet, and the doors opened.

"Sorry, I've been meaning to fix that." Nathaniel pulled a tablet
from his back pocket and made a note on it with a plastic stylus.

"Welcome to the main research and development lab," Nathaniel
said. "Uh, the only research and development lab anymore." He
strode out.

"Hello?" he called. "Dr. Kim? Anyone?" His voice echoed back at
them. "I guess she's still on her way over from the manor. While we
wait, I'll give you the fifty-cent tour. Follow me."

Ephraim, Jena, and Zoe stepped out of the elevator and stopped
to stare.

The floor wrapped around four enclosed walls in the center. The
wall opposite the elevator was dominated by a hundred-inch video
screen.

Nathaniel turned to face them and walked backward toward the
wall, leading them like a tour guide.

"The building was constructed around the LCD," Nathaniel said.
He knelt and rapped his knuckles against the wall under the video
monitor. There was no sound. "These interior walls are reinforced with
five feet of solid steel."

"What for?" Jena asked.

"To shield us if the machine blows up," Nathaniel said. "The atrium is designed to channel the force of the explosion up and out of the skylight, so this building doesn't come apart with it."

"I'm both impressed and concerned that you factored the potential for that kind of damage into this building's design," Jena said.

"Don't worry, we're safe up here. Probably. If you believe the math." Nathaniel tapped the screen behind him. "Since windows would compromise the integrity of the blast shielding, we've mounted a viewscreen on each of these internal walls, with video from cameras on the other side. This is cool . . ." He gestured for them to join him.

As Ephraim drew closer to the screen, he realized it was displaying a three-dimensional image of the courtyard they'd shifted to. The effect was like looking *through* the wall—a virtual window. Slowly the LCD below came into view, still spinning at high speed. He told himself he was just imagining that the frame around the central disc was trembling.

"I need to get a TV like this," Jena said.

"The price has dropped a lot since we installed them. You could probably get one on sale for around six hundred and twenty-five thousand dollars," Nathaniel said.

Zoe whistled.

Nathaniel moved slowly to their right, still walking backward.

"We're a LEED gold–certified green building, which is pretty good considering how much energy you need to punch holes through the universe," he said. "The building is almost entirely self-sustaining. There are solar panels and wind generators just above our heads, and a roof garden to grow our own food. We couldn't afford to keep the gardener though, so it isn't producing much anymore. I hope you like beets."

"So this is the place to be during a zombie apocalypse," Ephraim said.

"Yeah." Nathaniel laughed.

He spread his arms out. "This is the south end of the floor, what we call 'downtown.' It's mostly cubicles with computer workstations and swing space for nontechnical work. You wouldn't believe the amount of paperwork there is for a business that doesn't make any money. We used to have an entire floor dedicated to administrative personnel, but after cutbacks, we were forced to consolidate almost everyone up here. We closed the other floors except for the dormitories, gym, and mess hall one level down, and the forge and machine shops on the first floor."

"You have your own forge?" Ephraim asked.

"We design, mold, and cast every one of the LCD's components in-house. It's all custom. It's also more secure to manufacture the parts on our own."

Nathaniel pointed to a window—a real window—to the left of the elevator, which had gone down to the basement. "If you look out there, you'll see something you ought to recognize," Nathaniel said.

Ephraim, Jena, and Zoe bunched around the glass and saw the park sprawling below, wilder and more overgrown than in Ephraim's universe.

"The Institute bought this land from the city in the 1970s, and assembled its first laboratory in Greystone Manor. It now holds a private library and small apartments for senior staff. Your rooms are already set up," Nathaniel said.

Ephraim was more interested in the skyline rising above the park. The lighted windows of the towering buildings in the distance looked like stars in the night. This world's Summerside had grown into a mini-Manhattan in the last quarter century.

"This is incredible," Ephraim said.

Nathaniel led them around the corner to the east side of the floor, which featured clusters of lab tables and offices with sliding glass doors. The office in the center was the only one with frosted glass that afforded some privacy. A black nameplate outside read "N. Mackenzie, Chief Engineer." Below it was one of the Institute's ubiquitous hand panels. Ephraim looked at every office door they passed, but he didn't see his own name on any of them.

They reached the north end of the building. The wall was entirely made of glass, affording a view of the streets. Jena and Zoe looked at the library across from the Institute. The two-story building was identical to the one Ephraim had grown up visiting, but it was dwarfed by larger buildings on either side of it.

"It looks the same," Jena and Zoe said.

"They do that a lot?" Nathaniel asked Ephraim.

Ephraim nodded.

Nathaniel smiled. "Dr. Kim renovated the Library when the Institute opened. It's still a lending library for the public, but now it also has one of the best scientific research collections in the world. Of course, it's all online too."

Judging from the storefronts Ephraim saw, the boulevard around the library had grown into a main street. There were even elevated train tracks on the far end of the block, stretching off into the distance. There'd often been discussions of extending the New York City subway system to downtown Summerside; it looked like they'd finally done it here.

The group passed through equipment racks loaded with servers, their lights blinking like Christmas trees, and long lab benches covered with mechanical parts. The air hummed with overworked air-conditioning and a cacophony of beeping and whirring machinery. Ephraim glimpsed what looked like a half-assembled controller on one table, wires spilling out of it, but he couldn't stop to examine it more closely.

They followed Nathaniel around the last corner. The west end of the floor held more offices; a kitchenette with a cooking range, microwave, refrigerator, coffeemaker; and cafeteria-style seating for about fifty people. The door next to a glass-walled conference room was labeled "J. Kim."

Nathaniel stopped on the far end of the corridor, near the corner of the south and west walls. They had completed a counterclockwise circuit and were back where they'd started, in front of the elevator.

Nathaniel pointed out a glowing exit sign to the left of the elevator. "There are stairs here and on the opposite corner of the building. But you would need security clearance to access this floor from the other side, even if the power were out. The doors are on the same emergency generators as the servers."

"Of course," Jena said.

He grinned. "So that's pretty much it. Home sweet home."

The elevator dinged.

"Excellent timing," Nathaniel said.

The elevator doors opened, and a woman emerged. She stopped short when she saw them all staring at her.

"Oh," Dr. Kim said.

Even though Ephraim had known who she was, had been expecting it, he was still unprepared to see her.

She was twenty-five years older, but it was undeniably Jena Kim. Ephraim got a chill looking at her. Jena and Zoe simultaneously took a small step forward, as if pulled toward her against their will.

Dr. Kim's black hair was streaked with gray and bound up in a loose bun, with strands drifting free and floating around her head. Under a disheveled white lab coat she wore a plain blouse and gray slacks. Though she was slightly heavier than her young counterparts, her face was gaunt and lined with worry.

She looked Jena and Zoe over critically, and her mouth stretched into a thin smile.

"I forgot how damned pretty I was," she said. "I wish I'd flaunted it like that while I could have."

Her voice was huskier than Jena's. It was kind of . . . sexy.

"You're still pretty," Ephraim blurted out.

All three Kim analogs looked at him. Nathaniel covered his smile with a hand.

Dr. Kim's expression softened.

"Doc, this is Ephraim Scott," Nathaniel said.

"I know who he is," she snapped. "How could I forget?"

She stepped close enough to Ephraim for him to see the delicate creases in her forehead, around her eyes, in the corners of her mouth. Jena's overwhelming cuteness had matured into something else. He hadn't just been trying to be polite—the doctor *was* pretty. Maybe not conventionally hot like her eighteen-year-old self, but still attractive.

God, she was the same age as his mother. He couldn't berate Nathan anymore for his comments about Madeline Scott.

"Ephraim, it's good to see you—" She bit off her sentence. Was she about to say "again"?

"It's nice to meet you," Ephraim said.

She blinked. "I feel like I know you already." She laughed, but there wasn't any joy in it. "You didn't have to dress up, but a woman always appreciates when a man puts in some effort. A real tie, too," she said.

"Their prom was tonight," Nathaniel said.

"I wish we hadn't had to interrupt it," she said. "It was a very special night for us."

Ephraim wondered if she and her Ephraim had slept together for the first time after their prom, like he and Jena had planned. Why did the thought of that squick him so much?

Dr. Kim regarded her analogs.

"And what are *your* names?" she asked slowly, like she was speaking to five-year-olds.

"Jena Kim," Jena said.

Her older self nodded.

"And I'm Zoe," Zoe said.

The doctor's eyes lit up.

"Nathaniel's friend," she said. "Thank you for coming so promptly. Thank you, all."

"We would've been here sooner, but we had some trouble—" Zoe started.

"We should have warned you, but we weren't at all sure it was working until you confirmed it for us."

"So what do we call you?" Jena asked.

The woman gave her a cool look. "Dr. Kim."

"Right," Jena said.

Ephraim cleared his throat. "Well, we've traveled a long way . . ." he began.

"What's going on and what can we do about it?" Zoe asked.

"Direct and to the point. I suppose you get away with a lot looking like that." Dr. Kim patted her hair bun. "Before I explain, I need you to return the Charon device."

Ephraim and Zoe exchanged worried looks.

"It's okay," Nathaniel said. "We just need to run some diagnostics and sync the equipment to our database. Routine maintenance every three hundred thousand universes. You'll get them back. Right, Doc?"

"They are the property of the Everett Institute, Nathaniel," Dr. Kim said. "You know we need them."

Ephraim felt uneasy letting it go, but she was right. It didn't belong to him. It was a part of this universe. She had a claim to it, especially if it had belonged to the Ephraim she knew.

He dipped his hand into his breast pocket and pulled the coin out between his index and middle fingers.

He knew it wasn't magic, but it still represented freedom to him. Possibilities. Without it, he, Jena, and Zoe were all stuck here. Then again, even with it, they wouldn't be able to leave unless the LCD downstairs was switched off, which made him even more apprehensive.

Dr. Kim smiled encouragingly. Something about her expression sent a shiver down his spine. He carefully placed the coin in her open left hand, feeling her cool skin brush against his as she closed her fingers.

"Thank you," she said softly, like a sigh. The coin disappeared into the right-hand pocket of her lab coat. "And the controller?" Dr. Kim said. She looked at Zoe and Jena expectantly.

Zoe stepped up and sullenly passed the controller to her older self. Dr. Kim took it delicately, avoiding contact with Zoe.

The doctor examined the device, her lips tight together and her face growing a shade redder.

"What have you done to it?" Dr. Kim asked.

"I took it apart," Zoe said. "But I put it back together again."

"With . . . duct tape?" Dr. Kim seethed.

Zoe waved a hand at the controller. "Those scratches and dents were there when I got it. Most of them."

"The Charon device is not a toy. It's a precision instrument." She glared at Nathaniel. "This is what happens when you leave things in the hands of children."

"Don't you need the help of these 'children'?" Zoe asked. "Nathaniel certainly did, to get back here last year."

"I'm not comfortable with the fate of the multiverse resting on a device held together with tape and glue. Nor should you be." Dr. Kim shook the device. She closed her eyes in exasperation when she heard the rattling on the inside.

"It got us here all right," Zoe said.

"Wait, wait, wait," Ephraim said. "What do you mean, 'the fate of the multiverse'? That's just an exaggeration, right?"

Dr. Kim thrust the controller at Nathaniel. "Check it thoroughly. Make sure there isn't any damage and see if you can recover additional coordinates. Feed them directly into the catalog and lock down the database."

"You got it, Doc," Nathaniel said.

"I can help you," Zoe said. "I know how it's put together."

He smiled. "Thanks. But I know its parts better than my own anatomy." He scratched his bristly chin. "Just a figure of speech."

"I know you're a hands-on kind of guy," Zoe said.

Everyone looked at her.

Dr. Kim pulled a silver case from her lab coat. She opened it and selected a cigarette. She lit it with a Zippo lighter and squinted at them through a haze of smoke. Zoe coughed pointedly, waving her hand in front of her face.

"I'm afraid I was not speaking with hyperbole, Ephraim," Dr. Kim said. "We believe that there is an unprecedented interaction between the quantum wave states of individual universes in the multiverse."

"Which means what?" Ephraim asked.

"Universes are merging," Nathaniel said.

"We already knew that," Zoe said.

Dr. Kim's eyebrows shot up. "How?"

"We've seen it." Zoe produced Nathan's video camera from one of the pockets of her hoodie. "We recorded it."

"You *recorded* it?" Dr. Kim shot a questioning look at Nathaniel.

"This is the first I've heard of it," he said. "*What* did you see, Zoe?"

"We saw—" Zoe began.

"We saw our friends . . ." Jena swallowed. "Our friends sort of combined into one person."

"Mary and Shelley Morales," Ephraim said. "They're . . . they were twins. But just before we shifted, they merged into one person. M.S. She didn't even know anything had happened."

Nathaniel grimaced. "I'm sorry."

"This is marvelous," Dr. Kim said. "I must examine that footage immediately."

Zoe clutched the camera against her chest. "This belongs to us," she said.

"Zoe," Ephraim said. "Let her have it."

Zoe glanced at him. She handed the camera to Dr. Kim and folded her arms.

"You still haven't told us why the universes are merging. Or how," Jena said.

"We're still figuring that out. We may know more once we've reviewed your recording," Dr. Kim said. She dropped the camera into a pocket of her coat and kept her hand inside. She puffed on her cigarette thoughtfully.

"You're *welcome*," Zoe said.

Dr. Kim continued speaking as if she hadn't heard Zoe. She looked directly at Ephraim.

"What we do know is that readings from the LCD suggest the number of universes has just started to decrease at an alarming rate. And the process is accelerating."

"That's . . . bad?" Ephraim asked.

"It isn't good, especially if you're in one of the universes that disappears or merges," Nathaniel said. "The rate of branching and quantum decoherence are usually balanced."

"One thing's clear," Dr. Kim said. "If this goes unchecked, we don't know if the process will ever stop. It could end up affecting *every* universe."

"You mean, what happened to Mary and Shelley. It could happen to any of us?" Jena asked.

"We think so. But we aren't experts on this," Nathaniel said.

"Shouldn't you be? Isn't that your *job*?" Zoe said. "What are you a doctor of, anyway?" she asked Dr. Kim.

"Psychology," Dr. Kim said.

Zoe threw up her hands. "*That's* useful."

"I need a new major," Jena said in a small voice.

Nathaniel glanced at Dr. Kim. "Look, I don't know about you, but I'm so tired I can't think straight," he said.

"You're right," Dr. Kim said. "It's very late and you have all had an eventful night. Get some rest. Nathaniel will show you to the manor."

"You're sending us to our rooms?" Zoe said. "If the multiverse is screwed up, we can't afford to wait. We should do something about it now."

"What?" Ephraim asked quietly. "We don't even know what's causing this. Anything we do could just make it worse."

"There must be someone who can figure this out," Zoe said.

"There is, but we'll go over that tomorrow morning," Dr. Kim said. "Don't worry, we have a plan."

"When people tell me not to worry, that's when I start worrying," Zoe said.

Nathaniel pressed the elevator call button, and the doors slid open. Jena hesitated, then walked inside.

Ephraim put a hand on Zoe's arm. "I'm pretty tired, Zoe. We all are," he said. "We'll figure this out in the morning."

She shrugged his hand off. "Fine." She flounced into the elevator. Ephraim and Nathaniel joined her.

"Good night," Ephraim said to Dr. Kim before the doors closed, but she had already turned around and started walking to her office.

Nathaniel pressed the 1 and the 3 buttons at the same time, and they heard a gentle tone. The elevator descended.

"This is how you get to the basement entrance to Greystone Manor," Nathaniel said. "We found an old network of tunnels that were used in the Civil War to move slaves to the Hudson River and then north to Albany."

Jena clapped. "A secret tunnel! I love it."

"1 and 3," Zoe said. "Clever."

At Ephraim's questioning look, Jena explained. "One plus three equals B."

"Ohhh," he said, a moment later.

"I can't believe that woman," Zoe muttered.

"I know!" Jena said.

"She was nice," Ephraim said. "To me, anyway."

"The Doc's very focused on her work and worried about, frankly, the end of life as we know it, and possibly the entire fabric of space and time," Nathaniel said. "That hasn't done wonders for her mood, I'll tell you."

"You'd think she'd treat us of all people better, though," Jena said.

"Doc has always been hardest on herself," Nathaniel said. "She blames herself for . . ." He looked at Ephraim. "Well, everything. She's taking all of this very personally. All I'm saying is cut her a little slack. She's a good person when you get to know her, and she's the one who will get us through this. Whatever it is."

The elevator jolted to a stop.

"Sorry, sorry," Nathaniel said.

The doors opened onto plush maroon carpeting. They followed Nathaniel through the air-conditioned corridor, and he led them up a short flight of wooden stairs to the first floor. All the polished brass and dark wood paneling reminded Ephraim of a hotel.

"Only the west wing is open right now. The rest was under renovation when the money ran out. Ephraim, you're here." Nathaniel stopped in front of a door and opened it.

"Jena will be next door, and Zoe is just across the hall. I'm the last door on the left if you need me. Every room has its own bathroom and a stocked mini-fridge if you're hungry. I'll collect the three of you for breakfast around ten."

Jena stifled a yawn.

"Thanks, Nathaniel. Good night, everyone," Ephraim said.

He walked into a comfy room with a wide four-poster bed, a writing desk in the corner, and some green velvet armchairs. The windows on the far wall looked out on the park, with the dark tower of the Everett Institute looming beyond the trees a hundred feet away. The outside of the Institute was just as utilitarian as the inside. With its gunmetal gray walls and solar paneling, it looked like a modern fortress.

Ephraim closed the door and headed straight for the bed, shedding his jacket and tie on the way. He quickly stripped down to his boxers and collapsed face-first into the pillows. He was asleep almost as soon as he closed his eyes.

CHAPTER 9

Ephraim picked at his plate. The microwaved pizza was singed to a crisp on one edge, soft and soggy on the other, and slightly frozen in the center. And the soda was flat. This was far from the breakfast of champions he'd expected.

He bit into it anyway, too hungry to quibble over quality. It wasn't the worst thing he'd had to eat. He had subsisted largely on a diet of Pop-Tarts and Chef Boyardee before his mother had discovered that not only could she cook—albeit with child supervision—but that she enjoyed it.

They were seated around a long table in the conference room next to Dr. Kim's office. Her head was bent to read a translucent computer screen at one end of the conference table, hands typing on the bare table. Ash dropped from a cigarette dangling from her lips, but she didn't notice. A series of numbers scrolled in front of her face in green text, backward, from Ephraim's perspective. The controller was positioned next to the screen with the coin rotating slowly above it.

Oddly, the other end of the conference table held a dusty contraption that Nathaniel told him was an overhead projector. It was designed to display information from clear plastic sheets onto a white screen suspended from the ceiling, but the lightbulb inside had burned out.

Ephraim took another bite. The scorched crust of the pizza jarred a tooth and cut into the roof of his mouth. He dropped the hard pizza onto his plate with a solid thump and pushed it away.

Dr. Kim looked at him through her computer screen, startled. She stared at him as though seeing him for the first time.

"Ephraim," she said.

"Yes?" He ran his tongue inside his bloody mouth, surveying the damage.

"Where did you get those clothes?" she asked.

"I found them in the closet. They were a pretty close fit. A little baggy." He met Nathaniel's eyes. "Was that okay?"

Nathaniel swallowed. "I put him in *his* old room," he said.

"Oh." Dr. Kim stared at Ephraim without actually seeing him. "Yes, that's fine. I always liked that shirt on you."

Ephraim had been so thrilled to change from formal wear into a gray button-down shirt and jeans, it hadn't occurred to him that he was wearing his analog's clothes. A dead man's clothes.

"Well." Dr. Kim cleared her throat. "If everyone's done eating, then I suppose we're ready to begin," she said. She puffed on the cigarette once more before grinding it out on her uneaten, congealed slice of pizza.

Jena and Zoe shoved their paper plates forward simultaneously, pizza slices only half-eaten.

"Good morning," Dr. Kim began. "Did I say that already?"

"*Good morning, Dr. Kim,*" Ephraim, Jena, and Zoe chorused.

Dr. Kim leveled a stern gaze at them over her screen. Jena had given him that annoyed look before, but this was the first time she'd been on the receiving end of it. Jena leaned back and pushed her glasses higher on the bridge of her nose with a finger, unnerved. Ephraim smiled.

Dr. Kim tapped a couple of invisible keys, and a 3-D image of the coin and controller appeared on the monitor behind her. "The Charon device," she said. "Also known as a portable coheron drive. How much do you know about the science behind it?"

Ephraim leaned forward, feeling like he was taking a pop quiz he was in no way prepared for. He glanced at Nathaniel.

"We know which buttons to press," Ephraim said. Nathaniel smiled.

Dr. Kim tsked.

Zoe folded her hands in front of her. "I only have a vague idea of how microwave radiation works, but I don't need a physics degree to nuke a pizza. Though it might have helped in this case." She flicked the edge of her plate.

Dr. Kim stood and leaned on the back of her chair. She reminded Ephraim of his English teacher, Ms. Nolan. Had she had the same teacher in her senior year of high school in this timeline? How similar were their histories? He thought that might give him an idea of how closely their futures might track.

"Let's start with the footage you recorded," Dr. Kim said.

"Nathan recorded it," Ephraim corrected. "My universe's Nathan."

Dr. Kim swept a finger across her screen. The overhead lights dimmed, and the glass wall tinted black. Ephraim relaxed slightly. He'd felt like a goldfish in a bowl, exposed to the forty Institute staff members working in the R&D lab. When the fate of the multiverse was in the balance, you didn't get Sundays off.

Nathan's video footage played across the screen at nearly life-size scale, with a clarity and depth that made Ephraim feel like he was back at the prom.

"I enhanced the video quality as best I could," Nathaniel said. He leaned toward Ephraim and lowered his voice. "I also edited out some of the personal drama to make you look better."

"Thanks for using your creative skills for good instead of evil," Ephraim said. He wondered what Dr. Kim had thought of all that when she saw it.

Ghostly images popped onto the dance floor.

"We're very lucky Nathaniel's analog discovered this," Dr. Kim said. "Perhaps we should sell all our expensive monitoring equipment in exchange for a twenty-five-year-old camcorder and a high school kid."

"Can't we just share in our combined accomplishments?" Nathaniel asked. "What's his is mine, and all that."

Dr. Kim smiled, the first sign that she'd retained any kind of sense of humor.

"All parallel universes are superimposed over each other, occupying the same space but in different dimensions," she said. "They're there all the time, but under ordinary circumstances, we can't see them—let alone jump from one to another. But as this video shows, something is weakening the forces that separate the universes. And it's now weak enough that people are beginning to shift involuntarily without a coheron drive. That's what happened to your friends."

Jena closed her eyes for a moment. When she'd come out of her room that morning, they'd been red. She'd claimed they were irritated from the contact lenses she'd worn the night before.

"What's the bottom line, Doc?" Nathaniel asked. "What's the worst-case scenario?"

Dr. Kim sat down and passed her hand over her screen. The computer and monitor went dark, and the lights brightened. The glass wall faded to transparency again. A man in a white lab coat pulled his ear from the window in surprise and hurried away. Nathaniel glared at him and tapped something on his tablet.

"We lose . . . everything. It all disappears." She fell silent and her shoulders slumped. "As if all those universes never existed."

"But we're going to stop it, right?" Ephraim asked. He looked at Nathaniel and Dr. Kim. "You said you had a plan?"

"Before we can stop it, we have to understand it," Dr. Kim said, "or we're just stumbling around in the dark. It's even possible that this process is natural, cyclical, and if we interrupt it there could be terrible consequences."

"Your arrival here caused a noticeable spike in instability," Nathaniel said softly. "I don't need a camera to tell me it's all breaking down."

"But we're safe here?" Jena said. "The thing in the courtyard is protecting us?"

Nathaniel glanced at Dr. Kim. "The cancellation wave generated by the LCD is stabilizing this universe," he said. "But we don't know for how long. And *it* might be contributing to the damage, too."

Ephraim squeezed his hand. He could almost feel the coin in his fist. His mother, Nathan, Jim . . . everyone he cared about at home was in danger, along with their countless analogs in all the realities he'd visited and even more that he hadn't.

"Can we extend the LCD's protection to other universes?" he asked.

"You're just like him," Dr. Kim murmured. "Always worrying about other people."

"Isn't that why we're here?"

She frowned. "Of course. Perhaps we could protect other universes, at least the ones we have coordinates for," Dr. Kim said. "Once we know more."

"Could we bring more people here?" Jena asked.

Dr. Kim rubbed her upper lip with a knuckle thoughtfully. "That's also a possibility I've been considering."

"But only as a last resort," Nathaniel said.

"How would you choose?" Zoe asked. "How can you pick one analog to survive over another?"

"You can't keep the LCD running forever. Eventually it'll break down," Ephraim said. "Then what?"

"You said there was someone who could help," Zoe said.

"The only person who could figure this out passed away a couple of years ago," Dr. Kim said. "Hugh Everett."

"*Everett?*" Jena said. "That can't be. He'd have been over a hundred, easy."

"Who's Hugh Everett?" Ephraim asked.

"I'm surprised you don't know," Jena said. "This place is named after him. After you told me about the Institute, I looked him up. He existed in our world too. Dr. Hugh Everett III was the physicist who developed the many-worlds theory."

"He invented multiple universes?" Ephraim asked. "I wish he were still alive so I could punch him."

"It's more like he discovered them. In our universe, it was just a theory, and not a well-regarded one at that."

"Here, his ideas were wholly embraced in the 1950s and '60s, eventually leading to his development of coheron technology," Dr. Kim said.

"But the fifties . . . like I said, he would have been too old," Jena said.

Nathaniel cleared his throat. "Dr. Kim was talking about Hugh Everett III . . . the Second."

"A clone?" Ephraim asked. "You can do that?"

"No," Zoe said. "An *analog*."

Nathaniel smiled. "Head of the class, Z."

Oh. Now Ephraim knew why he and Zoe were here.

"The original Everett of this universe derived his theory of multiple worlds in 1954," Nathaniel said. "It was a game changer. The study of parallel universes took off, much in the way NASA did in your universe until the space program was shut down. Dr. Everett founded this Institute to discover proof that his theory was correct."

Dr. Kim leaned forward. "In 1999, Everett had a minor stroke while delivering a presentation on quantum coherence at a physics symposium. He recovered physically, but people close to him said his mind had been subtly changed. Everett started talking about opening a gateway to parallel universes. He disappeared from public view to work on what he called a 'coherence generator.'" She glanced at Nathaniel. "This is all before my time here."

"Everett's colleagues called it 'Everett's Folly,'" Nathaniel said. "But sixteen years later, he announced that he was close to success. That's where my Ephraim and I came in. We were hired right out of college, along with tens of dozens of other technicians, engineers, and scientists, to complete his prototype of the coheron drive.

"And it worked, sort of. The machine recorded wave patterns that Everett insisted were evidence of other universes. But as for traveling to other worlds . . ." Nathaniel shook his head. "It was one way only, and the destination was completely random. Everett considered it a failure."

"He obviously improved on it," Zoe said. She pointed to the Charon device beside Dr. Kim.

"He revealed the portable coheron drive a year later. It was a huge leap forward in design and functionality," Nathaniel said. "I still don't know how Everett did it, especially in secret. He was getting so old, I'm not sure he knew either. He was like some kind of savant at that point.

"Ephraim and I were the lucky ones assigned to use the portable coheron drive to study as many other universes as possible, so researchers could analyze their wave patterns and look for connections between quantum coordinates and the amount of variation from our own universe."

"I didn't join the team until 2024," Dr. Kim said. "Everett hired me because he wanted a trained psychologist to help him recruit his replacement. He was in pretty good shape for a nintey-three-year-old man who drank and smoke like an undergrad, but he knew his number was coming up. He insisted on operating the Charon device personally, even though it made him terribly ill, and I accompanied him in search of one of his younger analogs in parallel timelines."

"What happened to the original Everett?" Jena asked.

"He died shortly after we brought his analog back. He's buried in the courtyard."

"Ew," Jena said.

"With the help of makeup, and limited public exposure, no one noticed that he'd been replaced with a man nearly fifty years younger," Dr. Kim said.

"The second Everett was still alive when Nathaniel and Ephraim disappeared. Why didn't *he* build another Charon device?" Ephraim asked. "And go look for them?"

"He tried," Dr. Kim said. "But he was determined to develop the technology on his own, without relying on his predecessor's work. Ultimately his failure killed him."

"Ass," Zoe said.

"He was a proud man," Dr. Kim said. "A great man."

"He's buried downstairs too?" Jena asked.

"It seemed appropriate," Dr. Kim said.

"That's one word for it," Zoe said.

"No one knows he's dead," Nathaniel said.

"The public must assume he's long gone by now," Jena said. "He'd be, what? Like, one hundred and seven?"

"Every now and then some reporter comes sniffing around for a story, or a physicist with a flashy new idea wants to consult him like he's the Dalai Lama, but the breakthroughs in quantum mechanics aren't happening in this lab anymore. Which means they aren't happening anywhere. Visiting parallel universes doesn't have the same romance it once did. Space is the new hot thing."

"A little behind the times," Zoe said.

"So you want us to locate another analog of Hugh Everett and ask him what's going on?" Ephraim asked. "And coincidentally save this Institute from ruin?"

"That's the general idea," Nathaniel said.

"No way," Jena said. "We're going to meet Hugh Everett?"

"What do we do?" Zoe asked.

Dr. Kim picked up the controller. "You have to bring him back here. He may not have the same detailed knowledge that his counterparts did, but knowing Hugh, he kept copious notes in his private lab."

"You haven't read them?" Ephraim asked. "Maybe we should try there first. We might find some answers, something that can help us."

"His lab is keyed to his genetic imprint," Nathaniel said.

"Well, let's dig one of him up then," Zoe said.

Dr. Kim blanched and Nathaniel winced.

"Too soon?" Zoe asked.

"Locks also can be broken or picked," Jena said.

"But not all locks are rigged to destroy everything inside the room if the wrong person attempts access," Nathaniel said.

"Who *does* that?" Zoe said.

"Hugh Everett. He was very protective of his work."

"There's no other choice. I need Hugh," Dr. Kim said. She straightened. "We all do. He alone is uniquely qualified to figure out what's going on with the multiverse."

"There have to be other quantum physicists to consult," Jena said.

"We've been reaching out to other scientists with what we've observed, but they're either unconcerned or think we're trying to revive interest in our research. The press is buzzing with rumors that Dr. Everett is going to return with some new technology that's going to revolutionize multidimensional travel or quantum computing."

"We could show them the video," Jena said.

Dr. Kim shook her head. "I sent a clip to some of our former colleagues. They wouldn't even look at it."

"Not even Brian?" Nathaniel asked.

"Professor Greene won't return my calls. Unfortunately, video like this is too easily forged these days."

"Right." Ephraim shrugged. "Okay. How are we going to find another Everett?"

Nathaniel rested his right arm on the table and leaned forward. The cuff of his shirt dipped into a spot of tomato sauce, but he didn't notice. "We have the coordinates for the universe that Dr. Everett recruited his successor from. He's already gone from there, but if we specify an adjacent universe from the same branch, the reality might be close enough."

"Shouldn't we recruit an Everett from a universe where he founded an institute like this one?" Ephraim asked.

"The first Everett searched but never discovered another one this far along," Dr. Kim said. "For some reason, this universe and the LCD are as unique as it gets in the multiverse. You have to find a Hugh who's just old enough to have refined his theory, but young enough to be healthy. He'd be about my age, in his mid-forties."

"Let's say we find this ideal Everett. Then what?" Ephraim asked.

Dr. Kim walked over to Ephraim and pressed the coin into his hand. He shivered at her touch. "I'll talk to him, convince him to help us."

"I thought I was going with Ephraim," Nathaniel said.

"Not this time," Dr. Kim said.

"If this is because of—"

She held up a hand. "It has nothing to do with that. I know you're the best trained on the controller, but I'm the best person to talk to Hugh, to convince him to come back here. It's a matter of practicality."

Zoe stood up. "Wherever Ephraim goes, I go," she said.

"I'm not staying behind." Jena jumped up from her seat.

Here we go, Ephraim thought.

Dr. Kim shoved her hands into her lab coat pockets. "Three identical women will attract far too much attention."

"You mean two identical women, and someone who looks like their mother," Zoe said.

Dr. Kim's jaw flexed. "Ephraim doesn't need any distractions."

"Hey," Ephraim said.

Nathaniel looked bemused. "Maybe it's a good thing I'm getting benched on this one."

"Do I get a vote in this?" Ephraim asked.

"This is my decision, and it's final," Dr. Kim said.

Ephraim considered her for a moment. He put the coin down on the table in front of her.

"Then good luck," he said.

She stared down at it.

"Don't overestimate your importance, Ephraim," she said. "We can reprogram the coin for another user."

Ephraim stood and walked around the table. "So I've heard. But if you could do that, then you would have already. Regardless, you know I'm the best person for this job."

She picked up the coin thoughtfully. Ephraim couldn't shake the feeling that she wasn't telling him everything.

"The coin is useless while we're in lockdown," she said. She flipped it toward him and he caught it. "Without my authorization, none of you will ever see your home universes again."

"Jena," Nathaniel said. "Threats don't work with him."

"You have a funny way of convincing people to help you, Doc," Ephraim said.

He pocketed the coin. "I don't think a sane person would allow the multiverse to burn itself out just to get her way. And that isn't the kind of person I want watching my back. I'm not going anywhere with you."

Dr. Kim narrowed her eyes. "This isn't a game, Ephraim."

"We're deciding the fate of the multiverse with a flip of a coin. Heads or tails, Doc. If that isn't a game, I don't know what is."

She bowed her head. She started shaking. A moment later, he realized she was laughing.

"That's something Hugh would have said," she explained. "He treated everything like a game. Or a conquest." She sighed and smoothed her hair away from her face. She lit another cigarette and stared at the group, her face expressionless.

"All right," she said. "You can pick two people to go with you. But one of you stays here with me."

"A hostage?" Zoe asked.

The doctor blew smoke from the side of her mouth. "Not at all. But I can use some help on this end."

Ephraim watched the scientists working at the tables outside, the people walking past the conference room pretending they weren't curious why their boss was having a meeting with a bunch of teenagers, two of whom looked like her. She had plenty of backup here.

"So it's decided. Be ready to leave this afternoon, Ephraim. Time is of the essence," Dr. Kim said.

Zoe groaned. "Was that a time travel pun?"

"I've always wanted to say that," Dr. Kim said.

Jena, Zoe, and Nathaniel looked at Ephraim.

"Well?" Zoe asked.

"Who's going with you?" Jena asked.

Nathaniel raised his hand lazily. "Pick me. Pick me," he said in a bored voice.

Ephraim glanced at Dr. Kim nervously. She wore a self-satisfied smile. No matter whom he chose, someone would be disappointed or angry with him. He really hated making decisions, especially when every outcome was a bad one.

CHAPTER 10

"I thought the future would be shinier," Ephraim said from the passenger seat of Nathaniel's old Ford convertible.

The top was down, and the spring day was warm but not unpleasantly hot. They were driving down I-275 South in the year 2037 in order to get to Princeton, New Jersey, 1977. It was better to get there in this universe before shifting with the Charon device; if they did it the other way around, they'd have to get a car or find some other means of transportation from Summerside.

In at least one universe, Dr. Hugh Everett III had been a professor at Princeton University, where he had a lab dedicated to discovering proof of parallel universes. If all went well today, Ephraim and his friends would be the proof he'd been looking for.

"You expected flying cars or something?" Nathaniel snorted. "We still have paper books, you know. And television. Unfortunately, we also have reality TV."

"I was promised flying cars and jetpacks," Ephraim said.

"You got alternate universes. Don't be greedy," Nathaniel said.

Ephraim glanced in the passenger-side mirror. Jena's nose was buried in an eReader she'd borrowed from Dr. Everett's private library in Greystone Manor. She hadn't said a thing since she'd gotten in the car.

Jena had sworn that she'd never give up paper books, but she'd been won over by the eReader's light weight, its inexhaustible power supply (like the controller, it drew power through the air from electromagnetic sources all around them), and the 3-D holographic display that simulated real pages—for the reader. To Ephraim, she seemed to be turning invisible pages, which looked kind of ridiculous.

The real selling point was that Everett had a wide selection of books acquired from hundreds of alternate realities.

Hoping to get her attention, Ephraim twisted around in his seat, pulling against his seat belt.

"What are you reading?" he called over the roar of the car engine.

"Everything!" she shouted.

"I meant, what are you reading *now*?" Ephraim asked.

"What?" Jena leaned forward.

"Hold on," Nathaniel said. He pressed a button and the engine cut off.

Ephraim grabbed the dashboard and armrest in panic, but they continued at a steady eighty-eight miles an hour. Nathaniel had only cut off the sound of the engine. It was running on silent now. The only sound came from the wheels on the paved highway and the wind rushing by them.

"That's better," Nathaniel said.

"What did you do?" Ephraim asked.

"The sound of the engine is just a recording. When I converted the car from gas to electric power, I added it. The law says you need to have it on while you're driving in residential areas so people know a car is coming." He patted the dashboard affectionately. "Shiny enough for you?"

"This thing's electric?" Ephraim asked. "Sweet."

That explained why the skies were a clear blue and the air smelled fresher than any Ephraim had ever breathed. It reminded him of the camping trip to Bear Mountain that his dad had taken him on just before he left.

"I'm curious too," Nathaniel said. "What's so interesting on that screen, Jena?"

"The collected works of the collective Hugh Everetts." She paused. "Or is it Hughs Everett? At the moment, one of his biographies. You've probably read it already."

"I'm waiting for the movie," Nathaniel said.

"It seems like his favorite topic aside from parallel universes was himself," Jena said. "He has every book about him from multiple universes." She shoved her windswept hair out of her eyes. "Not that I blame him. He was a fascinating man."

"Let's hope he still is, somewhere," Nathaniel said. "And that we can find him and bring him home."

Nathaniel gunned the engine silently and swerved around a bullet-shaped BMW in front of them, which also drove quietly on the highway. Ephraim found it disturbing how all he heard now were tires on the pavement and the wind rushing past their heads.

Ephraim put his hand on the dashboard and felt the reassuring vibration of the motor. He wondered if that was faked too.

"Thanks for bringing me along for the ride," Nathaniel said softly.

"You're the one who's driving," Ephraim said.

"You know what I mean."

"Who else would I ask?" Ephraim said.

Nathaniel smiled. "You would have made things easier on yourself if you'd picked the girls."

"I don't think so."

"Maybe not." Nathaniel smiled.

"You have more experience at this kind of thing. And a car," Ephraim added.

Nathaniel glanced at Jena in the rearview mirror. "Zoe was pretty pissed, huh?"

Ephraim nodded. "I know Dr. Kim is your friend and all, but I don't trust her. She's up to something." He didn't see why Nathaniel was so loyal to her after she'd left him stranded in another universe for more than a decade.

"That's just the way she is," Nathaniel said. "She finds it difficult to trust people too, but she has good intentions. I'm sure of it. Is that why you asked Zoe to stay?"

"She trusts the Doc even less than I do. She'll keep an eye on her, and she'll watch our backs." They needed someone there who had their interests in mind if anything went wrong; if this universe's history was an indication, Dr. Kim wasn't that person.

Ephraim watched Jena in the mirror. "Besides, if I didn't bring my girlfriend with me, I'd really be in the doghouse," he said.

Nathaniel laughed. "You're smarter about women than my Ephraim ever was."

Jena suddenly leaned forward between the seats, her brow creased with concern.

"Jena, what are you doing?" Ephraim asked. "Put your seat belt back on!"

"Stop the car!" she said.

Nathaniel slowed the car. He half-turned toward Jena in his seat. "What? What's wrong?" he asked.

"I just realized: We have the wrong coordinates," she said.

"But we got them straight from the computer," Nathaniel said. He turned his head back to the road, the wind whipping his hair back. It was starting to thin.

Jena's own hair fanned behind her. "Think about it. We started from the same coordinates the original Hugh used in this universe. He retrieved his analog from a 1977 running on a parallel track, right? And that was when? About twenty years ago, in subjective time?"

Nathaniel nodded thoughtfully. "Oh, shit," he said.

"What am I missing?" Ephraim asked.

"It's been almost a year here since you and Zoe brought me back, right?" Nathaniel asked.

"Yeah. It'll be a year in August," Ephraim said.

"Same in this universe. Even though it's twenty-five years ahead of yours, time doesn't move any faster or slower in either. Twenty-four hours here is the same as twenty-four hours there. It's even the same time and day of the week.

"So we're just on separate tracks," Nathaniel continued. "Imagine: If shifting from one universe to another is like moving up or down to parallel layers, overlapping with one universe, then going to another timeline is like taking a jump to the left."

"Or a step to the right," Jena said wryly.

"It's all the same to the Charon device," Nathaniel said. "It's like a friend of mine used to say: 'Other times are just special cases of other universes.'"

"Shelley said the same thing," Ephraim said. "I get it. So?"

"If we use very similar coordinates to Everett's, like we planned, then we'll arrive in 1997," Jena said.

"Crap," Ephraim said.

"Damn!" Nathaniel said. "I'm really rusty at this. I know how the device works, I should have thought of it right away. Good catch, Jena."

"Yeah," Ephraim said.

She smiled.

"Hugh Everett might be alive in 1997," Ephraim said.

"Survey says . . . no," Jena said. "The Everetts I've read about died pretty young."

"How many have you read about?" Nathaniel asked.

She wiggled her eReader. "All of them. All the ones Everett had information on, anyway. He collated all their biographical information, as if he were trying to work out his own future from the data points. How's that for morbid?"

"That sounds like Dr. Everett," Nathaniel said.

"So what do we do?" Ephraim asked. "Abort the mission?"

"Not after we've driven all this way." Nathaniel looked at Ephraim. "I say we improvise. You think you can 'wish' us to a reality with a living Everett, Ephraim?"

"Didn't Everett and his team try that before? They went through dozens of realities before they found one of him."

"But no one's better at handling the coin than you. Not even your analog, and he was the first. You're like the coin whisperer," Nathaniel said.

"I don't know. Trying to influence the outcome with my thoughts is kind of imprecise. Almost random," Ephraim said.

"*Almost*," Nathaniel said.

Jena reached behind his seat and squeezed his arm. "You can do it, Eph."

"If you think so . . . why not? I'll give it a try."

"Good man. Our exit's coming up," Nathaniel said. He maneuvered the car toward the right lane. "Better start thinking about your wish, E."

"Yeah." Ephraim slouched back in his seat, the joy of the car ride lost. He had been ready for an adventure, assuming all he had to provide was their transportation between universes. But now he had to manage navigation too. The weight of their impossible scheme pressed down on him.

Nathaniel drove through the streets of Princeton, New Jersey, until he found parking in a garage on Hulfish Street. Jena excitedly directed them on foot to the main entrance to Princeton University, a large wrought-iron gate on Nassau Street. When they crossed through a side gate onto the campus, Ephraim felt like they'd already traveled back in time.

"This place hasn't changed much in twenty-five years," Jena said, panning Nathan's camcorder over the college walk.

"Old universities like this have a way of holding onto the past," Nathaniel said. He kicked a loose cobblestone on the walkway. "How do you know it so well?"

"Jena's going to Princeton next fall," Ephraim said. He had tried not to think about the difficulty of maintaining a long-distance relationship with her, since he was planning on going to the community college. But Summerside to Princeton wasn't as insurmountable as his universe to Zoe's.

And where had that thought come from?

"Congratulations," Nathaniel said.

"Whoa. I've never seen *that* before," Jena said. She aimed the camera at a building that didn't quite fit with the classic, red-brick architecture of the university. It was a tower of glass and steel, like the Everett Institute, only smaller, with more windows.

"That's the science center Hugh Everett donated to the university.

It has his name on it, naturally. He often talked about coming back to be president of the university one day and whip it into shape."

Nathaniel looked around and pointed out a nearby building. "Let's shift from over there to attract less attention," he said. "That building's been around for nearly a century."

Nathaniel pulled out the controller. It looked brand-new. He had replaced the casing with a sturdier black alloy, carefully cleaned all the circuit boards inside, and replaced the missing screws.

Ephraim palmed the coin. It was warm against his clammy skin.

Jena capped the camera and slung it on its strap over her shoulder. She pulled out a smartphone and spoke to it: "Dial Crossroads. Speaker on."

The line rang, and a moment later someone picked up. "Hello?" Zoe answered.

"It's us, Z," Nathaniel said. "We're just about ready here. Start the shutdown procedure, just like I showed you."

"Aye aye, captain. No problems on your end?" she asked.

"There's been a slight change in plans," Nathaniel said. "Jena pointed out that the coordinates we have are twenty-five years off."

Zoe cursed. "Because it's a parallel timeline that's been progressing respective to our universes. I should have thought of that."

"Me too," he said.

"Yes, you should have." Dr. Kim's voice broke in over the speaker.

"I'm an engineer, not a quantum mechanic," Nathaniel said.

"We'll discuss this later. How are you going to correct for the temporal drift?"

"Ephraim's going to guide us to the correct universe. The old-fashioned way."

Dr. Kim drew in a sharp breath. "Are you sure you can do this, Ephraim?" she asked. "There's very little room for error."

Nathaniel rolled his eyes.

"I guess," Ephraim said.

She sighed. "I suppose that's the best we can hope for. We're nearly ready here." Dr. Kim's voice muffled. "Zoe, watch the calibration. The gyro is listing. Correct it! No, the other lever. The *other* other lever. Better."

"What if the coin lands on tails?" Jena asked.

"What?" Dr. Kim asked.

Ephraim leaned toward the phone and raised his voice. "When I used the coin before, heads would take me to a 'good' reality, and tails would take me to a 'bad' one."

"Are you serious?" Dr. Kim asked.

"I know that isn't really what's happening, but she's right. It still might influence my thoughts," he said.

"I suggest you don't let that happen," Dr. Kim said.

Nathaniel clapped a hand on Ephraim's shoulder. "Eph, this is science. The coin functions based on its relative position in space and the parameters you set for it. That's it. Because you had a negative context for a coin that lands on tails, the coin adjusted according to your expectations. You have to not only understand that intellectually, but you have to believe it.

"Remember: There are countless realities where the year is 1977, where Dr. Hugh Everett III is studying multiple worlds at Princeton University," Nathaniel said. "We only need to find *one* of them."

Dr. Kim's voice blared from the speaker. "This is very important. You have to focus on filtering down to that specific subset of all the realities in the multiverse, and the coin will choose the best one at random based on its orientation when it makes contact with your skin."

"You can do it!" Zoe shouted from the phone.

Ephraim swallowed and nodded.

"We're ready here," Zoe said. "I'm reviewing footage from the surveillance cameras around the atrium now. I don't see any phantoms."

"No offense, but I'll double-check your settings," Dr. Kim said. "Nathaniel, as soon as your phone call drops, we're switching the LCD back on. We'll switch it off again for thirty seconds every hour, on the hour, local universal time. You each have watches synchronized with the home station."

"The hourly time will probably be the same," Nathaniel said. "It seems to be the default setting for the Charon device. But with you wishing, all bets are off, Ephraim, so we should be prepared for any variations in hour or day, aside from the year we want."

Ephraim nodded. He tried to clear his mind to concentrate on the wish.

"Okay," Nathaniel said. "Let's do it. Ephraim, whenever you're ready."

No pressure.

He opened his eyes. Nathaniel and Jena smiled encouragingly.

Ephraim extended his left hand to Jena. She took it in her right. Nathaniel took her left hand in his right hand, completing the human chain, and flipped open the controller in his left hand. The screen glowed dimly in the bright afternoon sunlight.

Ephraim coughed to clear his throat. "I wish—"

"Remember to specify 1977," Jena said.

"Okay," Ephraim said. "I wish—"

"And Hugh has to be a working physicist," Nathaniel said. "Studying parallel universes."

"I—"

"At Princeton!" Jena said. "That's important too."

"*Okay.*" Ephram waited for another interruption, but Nathaniel and Jena simply watched him expectantly.

"Get on with it," Jena said.

Ephraim scowled. "I wish . . ." He paused, looking at them. "I wish we were in a universe where it's still 1977 and Dr. Hugh Everett III is a physicist at Princeton University working on parallel universes." *1977. Dr. Hugh Everett III. Parallel universes.* He repeated it all to himself like a mantra, letting it shape the reality he wanted.

Jena wrinkled her nose. "My nose itches," she said.

"Nothing's happening," Ephraim said. He jiggled the coin in his hand, like a cupped die, but it wasn't even warm. He let her hand go.

"That's okay. It happens to everyone," Zoe said.

Jena scratched her nose, trying to hide a smile.

"You're still there?" Dr. Kim said.

"Unfortunately. Something's wrong," Nathaniel said. "Confirm: The LCD is off?"

"Confirmed," Zoe said. "It's frozen. And still no interference from adjacent universes on the monitors."

"All our state-of-the-art scientific equipment, and we're relying on cheap closed-circuit cameras to detect other universes," Nathaniel muttered.

He'd had to strip RF shielding from the Institute's video equipment to mimic the deficiencies of older technology like Nathan's camcorder, which was somehow more sensitive to the quantum wavelengths. They wouldn't be sure it was working until they saw a phantom from another reality, but they really didn't want to see a phantom.

"Try it again, Ephraim," Jena said.

"It's just performance anxiety," Nathaniel said. "You're out of practice."

"It's supposed to be an instinct, isn't it?" Ephraim said.

He dutifully repeated his wish again, word for word, concentrating hard on keeping it all in his head, shaping the reality he wanted—willing the coin to take them where they needed to be.

"Still nothing," Nathaniel reported after a moment.

"So what's the holdup?" Dr. Kim sounded impatient.

Ephraim examined the coin carefully: It was the right quarter and it was charged.

"It just won't respond. The coin's acted like this before, when I wished for something impossible, like a world where we have super-powers, or where the coin is programmed to respond to Nathan."

"I'm calling this," Dr. Kim said. "Head back to Crossroads."

"No," Ephraim said. "Nathaniel, hold out the controller for a second."

Ephraim placed the coin in its groove and wrapped his hand

around Nathaniel's over the controller. He closed his eyes and repeated the wish aloud slowly.

"The coin moved," Jena said. She had the camera trained on it. She was getting as bad as Nathan with that thing.

"I didn't touch anything," Nathaniel said.

"Good," Ephraim said, trying to hold his concentration. He opened his eyes. The coin wasn't moving anymore.

"When did it stop?" he asked.

"After you wished for it to be 1977," Nathaniel said.

"One out of three," he said. Ephraim repeated the wish and saw that Nathaniel was right. The coin rotated a few times for the first part of his wish but didn't budge when he mentioned Dr. Everett or Princeton.

Jena narrated what they were trying to do for Dr. Kim and Zoe's benefit.

"I was afraid of this," Dr. Kim said. "There may not be any universes left that match the criteria we need."

"But the multiverse is infinite," Ephraim said. "This should be a reasonable possibility."

"Perhaps once it was. Hugh was dabbling in something he called the preferred basis, in which the multiverse is dependent on the probability of certain outcomes. For whatever reason, the likelihood of Hugh's success with parallel universe research is very low. He began to suspect this when he initially had difficulty recruiting his replacement. That's why he went back to '77, after visiting dozens of contemporary universes," Dr. Kim said.

"I read about that theory," Jena said. "In universes where Everett went into computer science, he worked for the US government running nuclear war simulations during the Cold War. Some biographers speculated that if he hadn't designed the software that proved nuclear altercations result in mutual assured destruction, then we would have entered a nuclear conflict with the Soviet Union. No winners."

Nathaniel whistled. "In other words, odds are that most of the worlds where Everett studied parallel universes were destroyed by nuclear war."

"So we have to go a little farther back," Ephraim said. "Like when, the sixties?"

"We don't have the luxury of being able to try multiple universes hoping that you'll find a surviving Everett," Dr. Kim said.

"Do you want him or not?" Ephraim asked. "We're already here. We have to try. If we give up now then we've already failed."

"Guys!" Zoe called. "Monitors are picking up quantum phantoms in the atrium."

"Here too," Jena said. She showed Ephraim and Nathaniel the screen of the camcorder, and they noticed the ghostly images of students walking down the avenue around them, faint in the bright sunlight.

"I'm shutting this operation down," Dr. Kim said. "Sorry, team. Come home."

Ephraim covered the cell phone so Dr. Kim couldn't hear them. "Jena, when did Everett study at Princeton?"

"Graduate school?" She stared at him for a moment. "1953."

"Is that in most universes or just some of them?"

"All of them," she said. "A rare certainty in the multiverse. He always went to Princeton for graduate work. But it was only in about a quarter of them that he ended up coming up with the many-worlds interpretation. And it only went anywhere in a small fraction of those."

"Good enough for me," he said. "We're going to the 1950s. It's our best chance to make contact with a living Everett."

"He'll be too young. Practically a kid," Nathaniel said.

Ephraim and Jena glared at him.

"Not that there's anything wrong with that," Nathaniel said.

Ephraim related the plan to Dr. Kim and Zoe.

"Absolutely not," Dr. Kim said. "That's not what we agreed. I'm initiating the lockdown sequence now. It's too late. Come back home."

"Go, Ephraim!" Zoe said. "Make it quick."

"Release that lever, young lady. No, the other lever," Dr. Kim said.

"Jena! Remember Grumps!" Zoe said, just before the call cut off.

Nathaniel put his hand on Ephraim's shoulder. "Sorry, Eph. It was a ballsy idea."

"What did she mean by 'remember Grumps,' Jena?" Ephraim asked.

Jena was scrolling through the menus of the phone, muttering under her breath.

"Jena?" Nathaniel asked.

"Please shut up. I almost have it," she said. "How long do we have?"

"The LCD takes a few minutes to warm up," Nathaniel said. "The initialization sequence for the barrier may take even longer if Zoe's stalling the doctor."

"Got it!" Jena said. The coin started spinning.

She put her free arm around Ephraim's waist.

"Better grab on, Nathaniel," she said as the coin slowed, then stopped.

Tails up.

"Take it away, Eph," Jena said.

"But where are we—"

"No time. Let's go!" Jena said.

Ephraim grabbed the coin. Even though the tails orientation of the coin probably didn't mean anything, as the world shimmered around them, he tried extra hard to think positive thoughts.

CHAPTER 11

Everything looked the same. The campus even smelled the same, like freshly mowed grass and sunbaked stones. Then Ephraim peeked around the corner and saw that the Everett Science Center had been downgraded to a humbler brick structure. He sighed with relief.

"We made it," Ephraim said. "Somewhere."

"I'm more interested in *when*." Nathaniel examined their surroundings carefully.

"It's the mid-1950s," Jena said. "And I'm wearing entirely the wrong thing for this decade."

Expecting to be in the seventies, she'd worn a plain white blouse and black capri pants. Ephraim's white T-shirt, jeans, and tennis shoes were a bit casual for a university, but they fit in just about any decade. And Nathaniel had nailed the stuffy professor look: a tweed jacket with patches on the sleeves and a red bow tie.

"Where did you get these coordinates, Jena?" Nathaniel asked.

"Yesterday, when we were DXing on the radio, Zoe and I recognized our grandfather's voice. The frequency of the transmission wavered between two coordinates, which we recorded. His analog had to be in his twenties, so this is circa 1955." She smiled. "Which means Grumps is alive right now." She looked around, sweeping the area with the camera. "This is so excellent."

Jena loved the past, largely because of her father's job as a historian at the Paley Center for Media in New York. She'd grown up watching old television programs like *Leave It to Beaver*, *The Donna Reed Show*, *The Patty Duke Show*, and *The Twilight Zone*. And now she was practically in one of her favorite shows.

They explored the campus. Ephraim felt like he was on the set of a period film. Every man they saw walking around the campus wore a suit, many of them sporting stylish fedoras. They all looked at Ephraim, Nathaniel, and Jena curiously—especially Jena. Some of them looked annoyed.

"They act like they've never seen a girl," Jena said.

"It's more likely they've never seen a camcorder," Ephraim said.

"Oh." She checked the screen one last time, then switched it off, stowing it in her purse. "No phantoms, by the way."

They continued down the walkway.

"They're still staring at me," she said through tight lips. "I know women weren't admitted here until '61, but still."

Nathaniel cleared his throat. "Asian women were considered a bit . . . exotic in this time period."

She glared at him.

A man in a gray suit and a loosened, skinny tie was headed down the path toward them. As he brushed past Jena, he mumbled something under his breath that made her stop in her tracks. She looked as if she had just been slapped.

"What's wrong?" Ephraim asked. She didn't say anything. "Jena?" he asked softly.

Jena's face flushed. "That . . ." She swallowed. "He called me a . . ." She choked back a breath and her lower lip quivered.

"What?" Ephraim asked.

Jena lowered her head and balled her fists. Tears dripped from her eyes. "And he told me to go home to *China*." She spat the words out.

Ephraim took a step after the man, but Nathaniel grabbed the back of his shirt.

"Let go! Whatever he said to Jena he can say to me," Ephraim said.

"*No*," Jena said. She drew in a rattling breath and wiped her eyes dry with a sleeve, smearing mascara on the inside of her arm. She stared at the black streak on the thin white fabric. "I don't want to hear it again."

"But—" Ephraim said.

"It's a different era, Eph," Nathaniel said. Ephraim glowered at him.

"Of course that's no excuse," Nathaniel said quickly. "But we aren't here to open their eyes and alter society. We have a mission."

"Nathaniel's right," Jena said. "Let it go. Kids used to call me names like that. Worse. Usually I don't pay any attention; people like that are just ignorant. I was just shocked to hear it here." She looked up. "It isn't like it is on TV. Not that you saw Asians on TV back then."

"You okay?" Nathaniel asked.

"Let's just get on with this," Jena said. "All right?" She looked at Ephraim.

"If you say so," Ephraim said. He adjusted the stretched collar of his shirt.

If Ephraim hadn't taken after his mother's Scottish blood more than his father's Puerto Rican roots, he might have had to deal with that kind of behavior growing up, too. He didn't see how Jena could brush it off so easily. Maybe not *so* easily, looking at her now.

Nathaniel looked around. "We have to find out what year we're in. Perhaps we can find a campus newspaper."

There was another young man on the lawn, standing around and reading a book but sneaking curious glances at Jena.

"What?" Jena yelled at him, hands on her hips.

The man snapped out of it and dropped his thick book to the grass. Ephraim grinned. He sympathized completely—Jena had that effect on a lot of guys.

"What are you looking at?" Jena asked.

His eyes widened behind his wire-frame spectacles. "M-me?" he asked.

"Yeah, you," Jena said.

"I, ah." His shoulders hunched. "I'm sorry about that. I didn't mean to stare, but I've never seen a woman more beautiful than you. I've never seen a—"

"Stop there," Ephraim advised.

The young man had a soft voice and a British accent. He crouched to pick up his textbook. He fumbled it, and it spilled open facedown on the ground. *Mathematical Foundations of Quantum Mechanics*. He grabbed it by its spine and shook it out.

Jena opened her mouth, but words didn't come out.

"Come *on*," Ephraim muttered.

Jena smiled. "Can you tell us what day it is?" she asked.

The man stood with a perplexed expression. "Why, it's Sunday."

"No, today's date," Jena said.

He gave them all a peculiar look. "You must be pulling my leg. Today's the twenty-seventh of May."

Jena sighed. "For goodness' sake. What's the bloody *year*?"

"Fifty-four, of course." He took a step in their direction, but Jena turned away from him, and his stride faltered.

"1954," Ephraim said.

"Everett started in the fall of '53. He has to be here," Jena said.

The student finally moved away, discouraged, reading as he walked. His eyes found Jena one more time, and he tripped over his own feet.

"Jena, you can't just do that," Nathaniel said.

"Talk to strangers?" she asked. "Sorry, Dad."

"You're attracting way too much attention," Nathaniel said.

"That isn't my fault," she said. "Direct seemed like the best approach. The sooner we get back with Hugh Everett, the sooner we can all get back to our normal lives."

"It's better to keep a slightly lower profile when you're traveling in time," Nathaniel said.

"This isn't our past. We aren't going to change our own futures. We won't even change this universe's future, because it hasn't happened yet. Nothing we do here matters."

"We don't know what impact, if any, our presence will have on this timeline."

"I don't really care about this timeline," she said. "Not compared to every other timeline out there—yours and mine. Even Zoe's. Besides, kidnapping Hugh Everett is going to have a significant impact on this world, so I don't think asking a simple question about the day is going to ruin the rest of that young man's life."

A horn blared, tires screeched, and they heard a sickening thump just outside the Princeton gates. A woman screamed.

The blood drained from Jena's face.

Ephraim darted toward the street and saw a body crumpled by the curb near a stopped Ford Oldsmobile, its engine still running. A nervous little bald man in a pinstripe suit was standing by the driver's side door, staring down at the body in shock. A woman on the other side of the street hurried away without a second glance, hands pressed to her face to cover her sobs.

Ephraim crouched next to the injured man—it was the guy Jena had spoken to only moments before. His textbook was trapped under the car's rear tire, torn to shreds.

Ephraim looked up as Jena slowly approached and saw horror creep over her face as she realized what had happened.

"Is that . . . ?" she said. She lowered herself heavily to her knees on the other side of the body. "Is he . . . ?"

Ephraim fumbled around on the man's wrist, trying to recall the CPR lessons he'd taken at school. He repositioned his fingers and finally found a weak pulse.

"He's alive." He looked up at the motionless driver. "He needs an ambulance," he shouted. "Call 911!"

"911 doesn't exist yet," Jena said softly. She pulled out the cell phone Dr. Kim had given her and stared at it stupidly. "Neither do cell phones."

"Call for help!" Ephraim shouted. He pointed at the flustered driver and stood up. "You. Get help now."

The man's mouth opened and closed silently like a fish gasping for air. He jumped back into his car and tore off down the street.

"What the hell?" Ephraim said. "Did you get his plate number?"

"He has to find a payphone," Nathaniel said. He was breathing heavily from running down the avenue to the street. He leaned over and picked something up. A pair of wire-frame spectacles, bent out of shape, one lens with a Y-shaped crack. He squinted an eye and looked at Ephraim with the other through the broken glass.

"There should be a hospital nearby," Jena said.

She shuddered and flexed her fingers, eyes bright with welling tears. "*I* did this. If I hadn't yelled at him . . ."

Nathaniel knelt beside her. "You don't know that. It's just like you said: You haven't changed anything, because none of this has happened before."

She shook her head. "I talked to him. Distracted him. He would have been safe where he was, or if he'd left sooner he might have crossed the street in time."

"Or maybe he got in the path of a different car. The dumb kid was reading a book and walking. It was only a matter of time before something happened to him. And when it's your time, it's your time," Nathaniel said.

"I read while walking," Jena said.

"Not anymore," Ephraim said.

Nathaniel gently turned the man's body over, scrutinized his face, then reached into the victim's jacket pocket. He pulled out a brown leather wallet.

"What are you doing?" Ephraim hissed. "We probably aren't supposed to move him. And we definitely aren't supposed to rob him."

Nathaniel ignored him and thumbed through the cards in the wallet.

Ephraim studied the young man's face. He had a nasty gash on his forehead over the right temple, matted with a fringe of black hair. His skin was turning gray, and his eyelids fluttered rapidly. He was still breathing, though, and he didn't seem to have any broken bones that Ephraim could see. But you couldn't see internal damage.

"It isn't Everett," Jena said. A moment later, Nathaniel sighed with relief.

"Clifford Marlowe," he read from the young man's driver's license. He slipped the billfold back where he'd found it. "Good. Now let's get out of here."

Ephraim stared at him. "You want to leave him bleeding in the road?"

"Help's on the way. The hospital isn't far. We can't do anything for him, and we don't have much time. If the police start asking questions we'll be in trouble. The fake IDs we made are for '77."

"I don't know," Ephraim said.

Ephraim's analog had been hit by a bus. He'd likely died alone, thinking about Zoe. Maybe wishing he had a chance to tell her how much he loved her.

"Someone should be here if he wakes up," Ephraim said.

"I'll stay," Jena said. "You two go on. I'll catch up."

"No," Nathaniel said. "We're not splitting up. That's never a good idea."

"I'll just make sure he gets to a hospital," Jena said. "Besides, you'll have an easier time finding Everett without me attracting unwanted attention."

Ephraim put his hand over Jena's on the unconscious man's chest, which was rising ever so slightly with his breaths.

"We wouldn't have made it this far without you," Ephraim said.

Jena glanced down at the injured student. "I have to do this, Eph. You understand?"

He squeezed her hand.

"But since you're so helpless without me, here's something that might come in handy," she said.

Jena reached into the back pocket of her pants and pulled out the tiny eReader. "Here. I loaded it up with campus maps of Princeton from 1950 through 2030. If this is 1954, it'll be Everett's first year here, which should narrow things down a bit. I'd check the Graduate College first."

They heard a distinctive siren in the distance. The driver had come through after all.

"See? He'll be okay now," Ephraim said. "Come with us."

"We'll meet in front of FitzRandolph Gate in three hours, all right?" She pointed the gates out. "That should give you boys enough time to find Everett. We'll make the hourly window back to Nathaniel's universe."

Nathaniel offered her the controller. "Take this. Just in case."

"In case of what?" she asked.

"Take it. If we have to shift out of here quickly with the coin, you can use it to follow us," Ephraim said. He knew how difficult it was for Nathaniel to give up the controller.

"What could happen?" Jena asked. "The most dangerous thing in 1954 is—"

"The H-Bomb?" Nathaniel said.

"Right," Jena said. "I don't think anyone's going to bomb Princeton."

But she dropped the controller in her purse and offered him the camcorder. "Trade you?"

Nathaniel hung the camera strap around his neck and tucked it discreetly inside his sports coat.

"Be careful," he said.

"We'll meet at the gate in three hours," Jena reminded them.

Ephraim studied the surroundings. They were on Nassau Street, in front of a small side gate to the left of the larger, closed gates to the campus. It would be hard to miss the ornate wrought-iron entrance, crowned by the Princeton crest and flanked by stone eagles on massive columns.

He leaned over and kissed Jena on the cheek.

Nathaniel pulled Ephraim to his feet and propelled him quickly through the side gate back onto campus.

"Stupid, sentimental girl," Nathaniel said.

"I like that about her, actually."

Nathaniel gave him a sidelong look. "You would. I just meant it doesn't make sense to invest so much on one person when so many other lives are at stake."

"I don't agree with that," Ephraim said.

"You'll understand one day."

"When I'm older? I don't think I'll ever want to see anyone die needlessly."

Nathaniel grunted noncommittally. "So where are we headed?" he asked.

Ephraim consulted the 1954 map of Princeton Jena had pulled up and oriented himself. The 3-D display made the page float in front of his eyes. It also gave him a headache. He pointed west, toward a fancy Gothic bell tower that was unfortunately situated on the outskirts of campus. They had a bit of a hike ahead of them.

Nathaniel lowered himself wearily onto the base of a large bronze statue of a man in a chair. The man was named Andrew Fleming West, according to the plaque Nathaniel slumped against. He draped his jacket over one knee and rolled up the cuff on his left sleeve, then his right. The half-mile walk from the main campus had turned out to be too much for him.

"I wish we could have brought the car," Nathaniel panted. He wiped sweat from his forehead. "So where are we, navigator?"

"This is Thomson College," Ephraim said, checking the map. "Where the graduate students supposedly live."

They stood inside an enclosed courtyard with a large tree at their backs. Behind them to the right loomed Cleveland Tower, and the shorter Pyne Tower was behind them on the left.

Ephraim's stomach twisted, and he doubled over in pain. Cold sweat beaded on his forehead. He clenched his fists and waited for the wave of nausea to pass. He looked up and through a damp fringe of bangs he saw Nathaniel lean back against the statue, his face incredibly pale. He had one hand pressed to his left shoulder.

"You okay?" Ephraim asked. He straightened and took a hesitant step forward, unsure of his balance.

Nathaniel groaned. He opened his eyes.

"Did I just have a heart attack?" Nathaniel asked. "Am I dead?"

"It was just quantum reflux," Ephraim said.

"Nice," Nathaniel said. He checked his watch. "It's five o'clock. Right on schedule," he said.

"The LCD was just switched off?" Ephraim asked. "How could we feel it here?"

"Everything's entangled on the quantum level. Our presence must have linked the two universes," Nathaniel said.

He turned on the camera and panned it over the grounds. Despite himself, Ephraim smiled because he was suddenly reminded of his best friend doing the same thing only yesterday at prom.

"Picking anything up?" Ephraim asked.

"A couple of phantoms, but it doesn't look too—" Nathaniel suddenly jerked the camera to his left and up, pointed over Ephraim's shoulder.

"What?" Ephraim asked.

"I spoke too soon. Look at this."

Ephraim moved beside Nathaniel and watched the camera's screen. The picture crackled as he came near and then became even clearer. He saw the faint outline of a tower in the distance, back the way they'd come. It was translucent in the evening sunlight, but it looked just like Cleveland Tower, the building immediately to their right.

"That's back on the main campus, where we just came from," Ephraim said. "What's it doing there?"

"It must be bleeding through from a parallel universe," Nathaniel said. "Not good."

"Well, that would have saved us the walk."

As they watched, the tower faded away and Ephraim felt a tightness release in his body that he hadn't known was there. The time on his watch clicked over to 5:02.

"She's supposed to keep the window open for just thirty seconds," Nathaniel said. "I guess she kept it open longer to give us a chance to get back."

"Or Zoe did," Ephraim said.

"We really can't linger here any longer than necessary. Three hours, with that happening every hour, might be pushing our luck." Nathaniel closed the camera and slowly pulled himself to his feet. "Every time they switch off the LCD, this universe is vulnerable."

"The Charon device will protect us, won't it?"

Nathaniel shook his head. "The coin and controller are separated right now. Maybe that's affecting things too. This is all guesswork until we find Dr. Everett. Speaking of which . . ."

Ephraim looked around the courtyard. There were more than a dozen entryways to the buildings around them.

"Any idea where Everett's room is?" Nathaniel asked.

Ephraim paged through Jena's notes. "The records aren't that detailed," he said. "If rooms were randomly assigned, Everett could have occupied any of them in different universes."

"Is he behind door number one? Door number two? Or door number three?"

Ephraim located the first entryway on the map and pointed it out. "We may as well start at one," he said. "I'm hoping for fabulous prizes."

"I want a new washer and dryer," Nathaniel said. "But I'd settle for a trip to Disneyland."

They walked through the entryway and tried the door into the building. It was unlocked.

Nathaniel grinned. "Simpler times," he said.

They entered the building and walked up to the first-floor room. The building smelled musty, like an old library, with a hint of dried beer and stale cigarette smoke. Perversely, it reminded Ephraim of home.

"What do we do now?" Ephraim asked. The names of the residents weren't listed anywhere, and he didn't even see any mailboxes in the building.

"Maybe Jena had the right idea. We just ask." Nathaniel knocked boldly on the door.

After a moment, it opened. A man with a thin mustache blinked out at them. A cigarette stuck to his lower lip as he shrugged a black gown on over his gray suit.

"Yes?" the man asked. His eyes went from Nathaniel to Ephraim curiously.

"Hi, we're looking for a friend," Nathaniel said. "But we forgot his room number. Hugh Everett?"

"The name doesn't ring any bells," he said. "I think you're in the wrong entry."

"Entry?" Ephraim asked.

"First time on campus? Each of the dorms around this quad are an entryway," the man said. He zipped up his gown and took the cigarette out of his mouth.

"How many are there?" Ephraim asked.

"Twenty-one," the man said. "Including the North Courtyard."

"Phew," Nathaniel said.

"What school's your friend in?" the man asked.

"Physics," Nathaniel said.

"Then you might check Fine Hall over on main campus. He's probably studying for finals. I guess he isn't expecting you."

"Not even a little," Nathaniel said. "He should be very surprised to see us."

"You could also check at the Porter's Lodge," the man said. "If Daphne's there, tell her Gerald sent you. But the office will be closed now for dinner."

Ephraim's stomach grumbled at the mention of food.

"Excuse me, I should be getting to dinner myself," the man said.

Nathaniel stepped back as the man edged out of his room and closed the door. "Sorry I couldn't be more help."

"You've been very helpful," Nathaniel said.

Nathaniel and Ephraim followed in the wake of the man's ciga

rette smoke. He flicked his smoldering cigarette butt off into the grass
and headed for the dining hall.

Ephraim spotted several other students, all in black gowns bal-
looning in the wind, walking in the same direction.

"What's with the gowns?" he asked.

"I imagine they're pretty formal here. Old-world stuffy."
Nathaniel peered around. "Twenty-one dorms," he said. "Damn."

"He could be anywhere, if he's even on campus today." If they had
more time, they'd have a better chance of posting flyers and waiting
for Everett to contact *them*. "Lost Physicist. Answers to Hugh. Contact
Universe # 9098771119."

Nathaniel walked toward the second entryway. "Someone must
know him," he said. "Even if he isn't famous yet. He must have
friends. Everyone has friends."

"This could take hours," Ephraim said. "We'll cover more ground
separately."

Nathaniel frowned. "It's bad enough that Jena's off somewhere on
her own," he said. "I'm not going to risk losing track of you, too.
Damn, I wish we had working phones."

"Next time we'll bring walkie-talkies. Look, nothing's going to
happen to me on campus, and we already have a meeting place worked
out. We'll meet back here in two hours, in front of the bronze dude,
and go to FitzRandolph Gate together to collect Jena."

"No, Ephraim. I already lost one of you," Nathaniel said.

"And you have to stop being afraid that history will repeat itself."

"Funny," Nathaniel said. "Considering where we are."

Ephraim squinted at his older friend. "Or are you worried about
getting back home without me?"

"I'm worried about *you*."

Ephraim stared at him.

"I know that look," Nathaniel said. "You aren't going to change
your mind. Fine. Let me see that map."

Ephraim handed over the eReader and Nathaniel studied it. He

mimed tearing off a page and slapped it onto his watch. He tilted the
watch's small screen toward Ephraim, and he saw a copy of the page
of building plans floating above the time display.

"That's ridiculous," Ephraim said.

"I'll take the North Court and work my way from lucky thirteen
to entryway twenty-one. You take this courtyard. One's already down,
so you have twelve to go." He circled a block of entryways on the map.
"We'll meet back at that statue in two hours." He handed Ephraim the
reader and delivered a stern look. "And stay out of trouble," he said.

Ephraim spread his hands in a "Who me?" gesture. Nathaniel
grunted and trudged off on his own.

Each entryway in the quad had one to three apartments on each
floor, and some of them had as many as four floors. It was slow going,
but Ephraim settled on a methodical system. He knocked on every
apartment door and if no one answered, he snuck inside to try to iden-
tify the occupants. If someone did answer, he asked for Hugh Everett
and saved himself from checking the rest of the rooms in the entryway.

Finally, he hit the jackpot at entry 5—he found someone who
knew Everett.

"He's in entry 7," the birdlike man said. He was tall, with a long
hooked nose and a shock of gray hair, though he couldn't have been
older than twenty-five. He looked like he'd been sleeping off an epic
hangover. "I've been over there a few times for sherry."

"Do you know the room number?" Ephraim asked eagerly.

"7C, I think. Top floor."

"Thanks," Ephraim said.

"How do you know him?" the man asked, looking Ephraim over,
the first glimmer of suspicion he'd gotten from anyone so far.

"We share multiple connections," Ephraim said.

Naturally, Hugh Everett wasn't home. Ephraim checked all three
rooms in his small apartment and found a letter addressed to Everett
in one of the bedrooms, confirming that at last he had the right place.

He sat down on a threadbare couch, trying to decide what to do. It would be a waste of time to try to find Nathaniel early. Ephraim could wait here for Everett to return, but there was no telling when he'd be back.

Ephraim pulled up a picture of Everett on the eReader. It was black and white, taken around the time he'd been at Princeton, but he'd recognize the man if he saw him in person: broad forehead, thinning hairline, boyish face with a confident smile bordering on smugness.

Ephraim searched the bedrooms again. He found what he was looking for in one of the closets: a black dressing gown. It was a little too long for him, but it made Ephraim passable as a very young Princeton graduate student. He slicked his hair back with styling cream from the bathroom to match the fashion of most of the guys on campus. To complete his master disguise, he picked up a thick mathematics textbook and tucked it under his left arm.

Maybe he could also grab a bite to eat while he looked for Everett in the dining hall—just to avoid suspicion, of course.

CHAPTER 12

There were around a hundred students in the grand dining hall, but Everett wasn't among them. Ephraim kept an eye out for him in between bites of food. The meal was much better than the microwave pizza he'd had back at Crossroads: succulent roast chicken with buttery mashed potatoes, and chocolate cake for dessert.

A hand clamped down like a vise on Ephraim's shoulder. He stiffened and carefully put down his fork. The person behind him leaned close and whispered in his ear.

"Fancy meeting you here," Nathaniel said. He released Ephraim's shoulder and slid onto the bench across from him.

Ephraim rotated his shoulder painfully. "You have quite a grip, Spock." Nathaniel's furious expression shut him up.

"I thought you'd vanished on me," Nathaniel said. He picked up one of Ephraim's rolls and took a vicious bite from it. "As if it weren't hard enough to find Dr. Everett, I had to look for you too." His words were muffled as he chewed. He grabbed Ephraim's bottle of Coke and took a swig. He smacked his lips. "Mmm. This stuff was much better in the fifties," he said.

"I found Everett's room, but it was empty. I figured if I hurried, I could catch him here," Ephraim said. "Why are you here?"

"Looking for irresponsible teenagers and thinking up appropriate punishments makes me hungry."

"I was improvising. Hey, where'd you get those threads?"

Nathaniel had also changed into a black dinner gown. It was two sizes too small for him, so six inches of his sleeves showed and it was tight across his chest.

"I improvised too. I knocked out a student," Nathaniel said.

"Yeah, right." Ephraim stared at him. Nathaniel's face didn't betray even a hint that he was joking.

133

"I didn't hit him very hard, but eggheads go down easy. He might have been pretending."

"You've seen too many movies," Ephraim said.

"That isn't how you got your disguise?"

"I borrowed it from a closet in Everett's apartment."

Nathaniel's eyes scanned the room as surreptitiously as he could, which wasn't very. "I'm not sure I'd recognize Everett at this age."

"I found a picture," Ephraim said. He showed it to Nathaniel on the eReader screen. "I considered showing it around, but I don't think they're ready for 3-D displays yet."

Nathaniel started coughing.

"You okay?"

Nathaniel nodded and pointed through the 3-D image toward the entrance.

Hugh Everett had just walked in with two friends. They moved together toward the stack of food trays.

"It's really him," Ephraim said. "My plan worked."

"Your *plan?*" Nathaniel wheezed. He gulped down some more soda and cleared his throat. "We were lucky."

They stood up as one.

"I'll do the talking," Nathaniel said.

A wave of vertigo made Ephraim lose his balance. He pitched back onto the bench. Nathaniel braced himself against the table.

Ephraim tasted roast chicken and potatoes. His chest was restricted, and his stomach turned over like he was on a freefall ride at the amusement park.

"Not again," he said through clenched teeth.

"It's the next window opening," Nathaniel said. He turned to look at Ephraim. "Eph . . . you're disappearing."

Ephraim held his hand out. It looked as solid as usual to him. But he could see through *Nathaniel* to the dining room behind him. And through the dining hall to the grass and trees outside.

The students in the room were similarly fading, but they were oblivious to what was happening, except for the groups seated close to him and Nathaniel, who were glaring at Nathaniel. They didn't look at Ephraim at all.

"I'm not disappearing. You are!" Ephraim said.

Ephraim scrambled to his feet. He hastily gathered up the bottom of the gown so he could reach the pocket of his jeans. The coin jumped around in his hand, vibrating like crazy and burning hot, but holding it eased the sensation of his stomach being pulled every which way. He squeezed it tight and reached out to Nathaniel with his left hand.

"Grab my hand!" Ephraim said. "You're shifting without me."

Nathaniel reached for him, but their hands passed through each other. Meanwhile, he and the other people and the building around them continued to vanish.

"It's too late." Nathaniel squinted at Ephraim. "You still there, Ephraim?"

"I'm here," Ephraim said. He was the only one that was still there, as far as he knew.

"Good luck, kid. I don't know where I'll end up, but I'll find you," Nathaniel said.

His voice echoed hollowly, and Ephraim had to strain to hear him.

Then Nathaniel was gone.

A moment later, the coin settled in Ephraim's hand and abruptly cooled until it was practically freezing. The center of his palm throbbed in tandem with the quickened beating of his heart. He examined the coin: It was a plain disc again, its charge drained. Without power, he couldn't shift himself out of this world to what-ever universe Nathaniel had ended up in. If he hadn't been erased.

Ephraim tried to swallow, his mouth suddenly dry.

He was all alone on a grassy lawn with nothing much around him. A golf course was not far off, but the entire Graduate College had van-ished right along with his mentor. Ephraim crumpled to the grass and buried his head in his hands. He was all alone in a strange time, and the friends he'd come with could be . . . gone. As in, they'd never existed.

He pulled up a clump of grass. Then another one. A building was standing here a moment ago. It had stood for more than thirty years, but now that it was gone, grass grew undisturbed in its place. The building hadn't moved—it simply had never been.

Ephraim crawled around on his hands and knees, pulling up more and more wads of grass, turning up loose soil, leaving a scattered trail of broken stalks and sod behind him. He dug in the soft ground with his bare fingers, tossing dirt and rocks aside, not sure what he was looking for but desperate to find something, to *do* something.

Finally, he rolled over onto his back and stared at the clear blue sky, breathing heavily. His vision blurred. It wasn't fair that he could somehow lose everything on such a beautiful day.

Maybe not everything.

If Jena had been protected by the controller, the way the coin had anchored Ephraim in this universe, she would be waiting for him at the gates.

He spun around slowly, trying to imagine the campus the way it had been half an hour ago. College Road was missing, too. In this altered reality, there was no need for a street leading to nonexistent residence buildings. If there was no path, he would just have to make his own.

He ran across the field toward the main campus.

CHAPTER 13

Ephraim stood on Nassau Street, consulting his map anxiously. He was fairly certain that the car accident had happened right over there, but the gate Jena had pointed out wasn't in sight and neither was she.

"You look lost." An elderly man with a pointed gray beard stopped on the sidewalk. "What are you looking for?"

"Oh." Ephraim tucked the eReader behind his back. "Fitz-Randolph Gate?"

The man frowned. "If you mean FitzRandolph *Road*, you're on it."

"No, I'm looking for a giant metal gate." Ephraim described the gate as he remembered it, and the man's face lit up.

"Van Wickle Gateway! That's over on Prospect Avenue." He pointed across campus and rattled off some directions that Ephraim tried to follow. The campus had been rearranged more than Ephraim had thought. "You're sure you don't want to write this down?"

"Ephraim!" A familiar voice called from down the street.

"Never mind," Ephraim told the man. "Thank you."

He turned and saw Jena running toward him. She grabbed him and planted a kiss on his mouth.

When she let him go, Ephraim grinned. "What was that for?" he asked. That hadn't been like her at all, but he could get used to it.

"For Cliff," Jena said in a low, breathless voice. She nudged her eyebrows up and rolled her eyes to the side. Ephraim looked past her and spotted the car accident victim waiting about ten feet away, pretending he wasn't looking at them.

Cliff? Clifford Marlowe. That's what had been on his driver's license when Nathaniel went through the man's pockets.

Cliff looked absolutely fine, if somewhat glum. Even his glasses were intact, though one of the lenses had been cracked earlier.

"I told him I was going steady with someone, but he didn't believe me," Jena said.

"Oh. Then how about a kiss for *me*?" Ephraim asked.

She punched Ephraim on the shoulder.

"Ow! Was that for him, too?" He rubbed his arm.

"Where the hell have you been? I've been waiting for twenty minutes," she said.

"Where have *I* been? You told us to meet you here," he said.

"We were supposed to meet at the *gate*," Jena said. "Do you see a gate?"

"How was I supposed to know it was going to move? The campus is all turned around. It isn't even called FitzRandolph anymore," Ephraim said. "We really need to bring walkie-talkies next time."

"Where's Nathaniel?" she asked, craning her neck to peer around Ephraim. She looked down the street in the direction of the no-longer-existent Graduate College and frowned.

"I . . . I don't know," Ephraim said. "He vanished in that last quantum hiccup."

Jena covered her mouth with a hand. "That's awful."

Ephraim told her what he'd seen.

"The whole campus is gone?" Jena asked. "Hmmm. Do you have my book?"

Ephraim handed her the eReader and she started paging through it.

Cliff headed toward them. Ephraim put a hand over the eReader screen to hide it. Jena pulled it away from him.

"Don't worry," Jena said. "He knows." She continued thumbing through the virtual pages.

"He *knows*?" Ephraim asked.

The bespectacled man stood next to Jena and flashed Ephraim a friendly smile.

"Hello. I'm Cliff." He extended a hand.

Ephraim shook it. "Ephraim. Glad you're in better shape than the last time I saw you."

Cliff puffed his lips and blew air out through them. "That wasn't me." He glanced at Jena. "Apparently."

"Jena?" Ephraim asked.

"Cliff was unconscious during the whole ambulance ride to the hospital and in the emergency room," she said. "They were preparing to operate, but after everything in the world went all blurry, he sat up on the operating table."

"That was when the window opened. But how did it fix him?" Ephraim asked.

"It didn't. He insisted he wasn't hit by a car," Jena said. Half her attention was still on the eReader screen.

"I wasn't," Cliff said. "One minute I was walking down the street, reading a book, the next I was in hospital."

"He was displaced by his analog," Ephraim said. "Jeez."

Cliff took out a silver case and offered each of them a cigarette. They both refused, and he lit one for himself with a match.

With any luck, Cliff's counterpart had ended up near a hospital in whatever universe he'd been swapped into, or he might not have lasted long with those injuries. It was a good thing they hadn't already begun the surgery when he shifted out.

"I thought the Charon device was supposed to protect this universe," Jena said. She looked up from the eReader, spun around, and looked toward the center of campus. She checked the screen again and smiled to herself.

"Nathaniel's theory is that it's less effective when it's divided over long distances," Ephraim said. He didn't mention that Nathaniel was also worried that bringing the device to this universe in the first place had made it more vulnerable to whatever was happening to all the others.

"I get it. So the coin and controller protected us because we were carrying them, but no one else," Jena said. "If Nathaniel hadn't insisted I take the controller . . ."

"What are you doing?" Ephraim asked. "We need to figure out how to find him."

"That's what I'm doing. If I'm right, Nathaniel's still here," Jena said. "Somewhere. Originally there were two proposed locations for the Graduate College. Woodrow Wilson, who was president of Princeton at the time, wanted the College to be in the center of the university campus. But the dean, Andrew Fleming West—"

"There was a statue of him in the courtyard," Ephraim said.

"Yes. West wanted the College away from campus, in its own separate location."

"Is this really a good time for a history lesson?"

"History is everything right now," Jena said. "Eph, in our universe's history, Andrew Fleming West won that fight, and the College was built away from the undergraduate campus."

"But in other universes, he didn't?" Ephraim asked.

She pointed in the distance. "Doesn't that building look familiar?" she asked.

Rising amid the campus buildings in the distance was a tower he realized he had seen before.

"Cleveland Tower?"

"I don't know what it's called in this newly merged reality, but it's very distinctive, isn't it?" She showed him a holographic image of it on her eReader screen. It was the same building.

"But that was over at the Graduate College . . ." Ephraim said.

And Nathaniel's video camera had caught a glimpse of the tower's quantum phantom at the main campus. It had moved, just like FitzRandolph Gate had.

Jena tucked her eReader away with a smug expression.

"You think Nathaniel might have gone with the dining hall when the Graduate College shifted here?"

"I hope so," Jena said.

"Then let's go find him," Ephraim said.

"Ephraim. No, we can't." Jena looked stricken.

"What are you talking about? He's probably looking for us."

"Then let him find us. We still have a mission and we only have thirty minutes before the next window opens."

"We need him," Ephraim said.

She shook her head. "We have the coin and the controller. We should find Hugh first and bring him back to Crossroads."

Cliff had been listening intently to everything they said, but he perked up at that. Ephraim ignored him.

"I can't believe you're suggesting we abandon Nathaniel," Ephraim said. "He might have saved your life by giving you that controller."

"Not abandoning him. We'll come back for him when we can. I don't want to do this, but it's the most practical thing. It's what he would want."

"Zoe—" Ephraim stopped.

Jena narrowed her eyes.

"Zoe *what*?" she asked.

Zoe would never leave one of them behind.

"Zoe won't be happy if we come back without him," Ephraim said.

Jena made a dismissive sound.

"So we're off then?" Cliff asked. He stomped his cigarette out on the sidewalk and looked at the two of them eagerly.

"Excuse me?" Ephraim asked.

"Ms. Kim says that my roommate can explain what happened to me and help you sort the mess you're in."

"Really," Ephraim said. "Who's your roommate?"

"Hugh Everett," Cliff said. "Brilliant fellow. Always leaves his dishes in the sink, though."

Jena winked at Ephraim. "Small multiverse, huh?"

"I could kiss you, Jena," Ephraim said.

"Permission granted."

CHAPTER 14

Cliff opened the door to his apartment, in the same building Ephraim had visited earlier. It was in a different location now, where Jena's map said the School of Architecture had once stood. He wondered where all those students had gone after the last dimensional shift.

A man at the window slowly turned. Ephraim instantly recognized Hugh Everett from his photo. In real life, the man's hair was reddish-brown, almost fiery in the light from the window. He was about Ephraim's height; he'd looked taller in his picture, and more . . . black-and-white. It took Ephraim a moment to adjust his concept of Everett into the physical person who was standing right in front of him.

"Hugh?" Cliff said. "You'll never believe what just happened to me."

"Who's your friend?" Hugh asked. His piercing eyes were on Jena. She smoothed her wind-blown hair self-consciously. Ephraim stepped in front of her.

"Dr. Everett, I presume?" Ephraim said. "We have to talk."

"That's the second time I've been addressed that way today. I like the sound of the title, but I haven't earned my degree. Yet." He sipped a dark liquid from the glass in his hand.

"The second—?" Ephraim asked.

"Ephraim!" Nathaniel rose from the couch. "Jena. You found me. How?"

Ephraim swallowed his guilt and embraced Nathaniel. "You never shifted out of this universe. It rearranged itself and you moved across campus with the rest of the Graduate College."

"Fascinating," Nathaniel said.

"You're all right?" Ephraim asked.

"I am now." Nathaniel noticed Cliff. "Isn't that—? Aren't you . . . ?"

"Cliff Marlowe," Cliff said. They shook hands.

"I'm Nathaniel Mackenzie. You look pretty good for an almost-dead guy, Cliff," Nathaniel said.

"I'm aces," Cliff said. "But I understand that another me may not be so fortunate," he said with a thoughtful expression.

Ephraim took a deep breath. "Nathaniel, this isn't the Cliff from the car accident. He was swapped with his analog during the last quantum disruption."

Nathaniel paled. "Oh, that *sucks*."

"Yeah," Ephraim said.

"But I can't believe you're Everett's roommate," Nathaniel said to Cliff. "That's a hell of a coincidence."

"If you're right about these multiple worlds of yours, there are no coincidences," Hugh said. He stared at the bottom of his glass. He raised his eyes and looked at Jena. "I'm Hugh. And you are?"

"J-Jena Kim," she stammered. He took her hand and brushed his lips against the top of it. Ephraim wrinkled his nose.

"A pleasure to meet you," Hugh said.

"I'm Ephraim Scott," Ephraim said. Everett hesitated before shaking his hand. His palm was cold and wet from holding his drink.

"Your friend Nathaniel told me an incredible story at dinner," Hugh said. "He says you're all from other universes. Is he as insane as I think he is?"

Hugh sat on the edge of the couch, his eyes lingering on Jena in a way that made Ephraim want to punch him in the face. Jena leaned back against the door and flipped on her eReader, eyes focused on the screen self-consciously.

"He was telling the truth," Ephraim said. "We're from the future."

"The future," Hugh said. "Time travel is impossible, according to Einstein." He glanced at Ephraim. "That's Albert Einstein. He's a genius."

"I know who he is," Ephraim said. "He's famous where we come from." *Unlike you*, he almost added.

"It wasn't time travel, exactly," Nathaniel said. "We're from two possible futures, two different universes. Ephraim and Jena are from one where it's 2012. I'm from 2037."

Hugh's face didn't show even a glimmer of recognition. "How interesting." Hugh drained his glass. "I'll need more sherry," he said.

"You haven't heard of the many-worlds interpretation of quantum mechanics?" Ephraim asked.

"No, but I know what Mr. Mackenzie suggests is ludicrous. According to Niels Bohr and Werner Heisenberg's Copenhagen spirit of quantum theory."

"You haven't heard of it because you haven't come up with it yet," Jena said. She pushed off from the door and handed Hugh the eReader. "Here."

"Jena," Nathaniel said.

"We don't have time for this," she said.

Ephraim checked his watch. They had ten minutes before the next window opened.

"She's right," Ephraim said.

"What is this?" Hugh turned over the eReader and examined it from every angle.

"Just read it," Jena said. "You can turn the pages by waving a finger at the top of the screen."

He gazed at her for a long moment, then turned his attention to the device.

"You aren't showing him his autobiographies, are you?" Ephraim asked in a low voice while Hugh turned pages.

"That would be cruel," she said gently. "I pulled up a scan of his original paper on many worlds, which he won't start writing for around another year."

Hugh's hand was shaking. "These notes are in my handwriting," he said.

"Bingo," Jena said.

Hugh looked up at them, his face pale and his eyes very bright. "The man who wrote this is either mad or a genius."

"Modest, isn't he?" Ephraim muttered.

"Shh," Jena said.

"I should have figured this out myself," Hugh said.

"You would have," Jena said.

"May I see?" Cliff asked.

"You'd never be able to understand this." Hugh sneered.

"And he's kind, too," Ephraim said. "Can this guy help us if he hasn't even come up with this theory on his own?"

"He gets it though," Jena said. "Look. It usually takes people years just to wrap their brains around it, but not him. He got it right away. His mind came up with it, and that makes him most capable to understand what's going wrong."

"This isn't all, is it?" Hugh asked.

Jena smiled. She slipped the eReader from Hugh's hand. He snatched at it, but she tucked it close against her chest and folded her arms.

"There's more where that came from, back home. Think of it: the accumulated knowledge of the next eighty-three years."

Hugh frowned. "In the future, in some alternative universe?"

Jena nodded.

"It's hard to believe, even after reading the theory. I'd have to check the calculations—"

"That'll have to wait," Ephraim said. "We have to go. Now." He pointed at his watch, and Nathaniel moved toward them.

Jena leaned forward. "Come with us, *Dr.* Everett," she murmured. "You're needed."

"Anywhere you like, Miss Kim," Hugh said. He looked slightly dazed.

"It's Jena," she said. "Call me Jena."

"Jena," he said gently. "And I'm Hugh."

"I know exactly who you are," she said.

"It's time," Nathaniel said. "Coming, Everett?"

Jena pulled out the controller and flipped it open. Ephraim slipped the coin into it, and she set it spinning. Hugh stared at the floating coin.

"I'm with you," Hugh said.

"You're leaving with them?" Cliff asked. "You're going to . . . another world?"

"The paper this young woman showed me, *The Relative State Formulation of Quantum Mechanics*, is far more enticing than the military game theory I'd been planning to work on this summer. Do I win the Nobel?" he asked Jena.

"That would be telling," Jena said.

"Should I pack anything?" Hugh asked.

"I think you'll find we have everything you need," Nathaniel said.

Hugh smiled at Jena. "Indeed."

Ephraim clenched his teeth. He didn't like Hugh's fixation on Jena, but they had to do whatever it took to bring him back to their universe. And it was a good thing she knew how to play Hugh to get him to join them.

Ephraim wondered if she had ever used her wiles to manipulate *him*? Definitely.

He also hoped she was only acting with Hugh.

"Excuse me," Cliff said. He glanced at each of them. "But, if this is all real . . . if it isn't a dream, and I'm actually lying on some table in hospital somewhere, then this isn't my life, is it? Can you switch me back? Can you send me home?"

Ephraim stiffened. He looked down at the floor.

"We can't," Jena said softly.

"I'm sorry," Nathaniel said. "We don't know where you came from and unfortunately, we don't have the time to help you."

Ephraim looked up. "Cliff, what happened to you . . . it's happening to a lot of people. You probably wouldn't have known the difference if we hadn't told you."

"But I do know," Cliff said. "I don't belong here."

"Oh, it's all the same, Cliff," Hugh said sharply.

"No, it *isn't*," Ephraim said. "Cliff, if we succeed in fixing things, if I can, I'll come back here and get you home. I promise."

Cliff looked at him intently. He nodded.

"Now how does this gadget work?" Hugh asked. He drew closer to the Charon device. "Theory is one thing, but nothing in my research or our understanding of physics should allow for interdimensional travel."

There was a prolonged silence as Hugh looked at their awkward expressions.

Nathaniel cleared his throat. "Actually, we were hoping you could tell us."

"Me?" Hugh said. "I've only just seen this contraption for the first time."

"One of your counterparts invented it. We understand how to use the technology, but we need you to explain the deeper concepts," Nathaniel said, "Specifically, what side effects it might have on the multiverse."

"Multiverse?"

"The continuum of other worlds," Jena said. "Multiple universes. Multiverse."

"Catchy. But why don't you just ask the me of one your futures for assistance?"

"It's complicated," Nathaniel said.

"Naturally. If we can use this device to actually visit other dimensions . . . this changes *everything*," Hugh said.

"That's kind of the problem," Ephraim said. "The controller there, Jena uses that to set the dimensional coordinates. And then all I have to do is grab that little disc when it stops spinning and it transports all of us in the blink of an eye."

"So that disc is the key component of this device?" Hugh asked. "It must serve as some sort of gyrocompass."

"Exactly," Ephraim said. He had to hand it to Everett, he was a quick study. He might be able to solve this problem after all.

"And without the . . . controller, did you call it? The disc would work at random, I imagine. According to its orientation?"

"Yes," Ephraim said, surprised. How long had it taken Ephraim to grasp the concept, even after he'd been using the coin for a while?

Hugh nodded as though he was confirming some private thought.

"Cliff, don't rent my room out," Hugh said. "This shouldn't take more than a couple of days. Then I'm coming back here to claim my destiny."

Cliff stifled a laugh.

"You have the coordinates, Jena?" Nathaniel asked.

"Yup," she said.

The coin slowed and stopped. Hugh peered at it curiously.

"Why, that's a quarter," he said. "But it's odd. Why does it have the Commonwealth of Puerto Rico on it? It's not made out of silver, either."

Ephraim shrugged.

"Okay, everyone link hands," Nathaniel said, eyes on his watch. "The window's about to open."

Hugh grabbed Jena's free hand immediately.

"What makes the coin levitate in that fashion? A quantum field? The Meissner effect? That hasn't even been tested yet . . ." Hugh reached for the coin with his free hand. Ephraim felt a twinge of panic.

"Grab them!" Nathaniel rushed toward Jena and Hugh, reaching for the controller—just as they vanished with a soft pop of air. Something thudded to the hardwood floor.

Ephraim's stomach twisted, and he collapsed forward onto his knees. Nathaniel made it to the couch and slumped sideways with his head on the armrest. They waited out the now-familiar quantum reflux. It seemed to go on forever.

When it was over, Ephraim crawled to where Jena and Hugh had just been standing and picked up Jena's eReader. The screen was cracked down the middle.

Ephraim heard a strangled whimper and realized it was coming from him.

"What . . . where did they . . . ?" he asked.

"Back to my universe," Nathaniel said. "Without us."

"Are you blokes all right?" Cliff asked. "That was stunning. This is all really happening, isn't it?"

"I wish it weren't," Ephraim said.

"Damn it," Nathaniel said. "Why'd you let him touch the coin?"

"I didn't know he could use it," Ephraim said. It came out sounding whiny.

"He *invented* it," Nathaniel said.

"Yeah." Ephraim leaned back against the couch, his breath coming in gasps. "It's my fault. I should have stopped him when I saw him reaching for it, but I froze."

"No, I'm sorry. I should have warned you."

Ephraim stared at the broken eReader. Hugh Everett's bisected face peered up at him, smirking. Ephraim switched it off. Half of the screen blanked, but the other half still showed a faint image of Everett.

"It's broken," he said.

"Everything's broken." Nathaniel sighed.

"They'll come back for us, won't they?" Ephraim asked.

Nathaniel checked the time. "The window's closed."

"In an hour, then."

"Maybe. But if Jena's smart, and I know she is, she'll take Everett straight back to Crossroads. They can't waste any more time on retrieving us, especially if they can't be sure we're still here. Without the coin or the controller, we're completely vulnerable here."

"Maybe she'll call them and tell them what happened. Dr. Kim could shut down the LCD—"

"The Doc won't do that. Every time they turn it off, the multiverse breaks down a little more and risks further decoherence. Now that she has what she needs . . ." Nathaniel bit his lip and fell quiet.

"I thought we were important to the mission," Ephraim said.

"They have Everett now. He *was* the mission. And he can use the coin too, so . . ."

Ephraim's shoulders slumped. "They don't need me anymore."

CHAPTER 15

Cliff sat on the coffee table to face Ephraim and Nathaniel on the couch. He handed each of them half-full glasses of sherry. Nathaniel took Ephraim's glass from him and gave it back to Cliff.

"I've never seen anything like that," Cliff said. He lit a cigarette and puffed on it. "But you seem pretty calm for someone who was just abandoned in another universe."

"It's happened to me before," Nathaniel said.

"What are we going to do?" Ephraim asked.

He stood and paced around the living room. He felt like a caged animal. If they weren't retrieved, they could be wiped out the next time the multiverse threw one of its tantrums.

"We can't stay here," Ephraim said.

"It seems I have a room available," Cliff said.

"Thanks, but we won't be staying," Nathaniel said. He put down his empty glass and pulled a cell phone from his coat pocket.

"You can't call Crossroads with that," Ephraim said.

Nathaniel smiled cryptically.

"That isn't a cell phone," Ephraim said. He hurried over and took the small device from the older man. "It's another controller. You had a backup this whole time?"

"After spending ten years in your universe, did you think I would ever risk being stuck again?"

"You devil," Cliff said. "I'm impressed." He held his glass up to toast Nathaniel and took a sip.

"You've been holding out on us, old man. I thought you didn't have the resources to build another one of these." Ephraim returned it to Nathaniel.

"I didn't. This one was the prototype, I guess. Everett—the first one, I mean—gave it to me to reverse engineer and improve on the

LCD years ago. I got it out of the archive and finished reassembling it yesterday, using Zoe's controller as a guide."

"If you had this on you in the dining hall an hour ago, why didn't it anchor you with me?"

"It was switched off," Nathaniel said. "I was worried it would interfere with the other controller."

"So we can use this to get back? Can it lock onto the coin?"

"I hardwired a connection to the LCD so I could always get back there. There's just one small problem. If Jena called the Doc as soon as they arrived, the Doc knows that Hugh is there, and that's all she ever wanted. They aren't going to try to retrieve us. I don't think Dr. Kim is going to open another window for us."

"Zoe's still there," Ephraim said. He met Nathaniel's eyes. "She wouldn't leave us here."

"My thought exactly," Nathaniel said. "We just need a way to contact her so she knows we're okay and get her to switch the LCD back on."

"Right." Ephraim leaned his elbows on his knees and rested his chin on his hands. "It's not fair," he said.

"I know," Nathaniel said.

"When Nate had the controller, I would have done anything to stop him," Ephraim said. "Even if it meant I could never go home again. This is a worse situation, but right now, the only thing I want is to go home."

Nathaniel rubbed his chin. Cliff took his empty glass and went to the bar on the other end of the living room.

"Where's home for you?" Nathaniel asked.

"What do you mean?" Ephraim asked.

"In Zoe's universe, you still had Zoe. You said it wasn't the place, it was the people that made it home."

"Sure. My mom, my Nathan, Jim—I miss all of them too." He looked around the circa 1950s apartment. He'd loved the idea of visiting the past, but could he really be happy living there?

"Wherever or whatever home is, it isn't here," Ephraim said.

"Maybe it's selfish, but I'm glad for the company this time," Nathaniel said.

"How did you do it?" Ephraim asked. "You were trapped in the past just like we are, in a different universe. How did you survive that, without any friends, without going crazy?"

"I took it one day at a time," Nathaniel said. "And maybe I did go a little bit crazy there. But I knew I would see you again one day. I knew there was a way out, if I only waited for it. That counts for a lot." He tugged on his ear. "We won't always be stuck in 1954. In seven months, we'll be in 1955. Then 1956. We move forward because that's all we can do."

But there were countless dangers ahead for Americans living in the mid- to late-twentieth century. Ephraim should have paid more attention in history class.

Then again, he could be hit by a bus tomorrow. No history book could prevent that.

"*History*," Ephraim said. He sat up straight, struck by a sudden, hopeful thought. Maybe he'd learned something from history after all.

"Ephraim?" Nathaniel asked.

"We have a controller," Ephraim said. "All we need is a ham radio, and we should be able to contact Zoe. This decade is lousy with ham radios, yeah?"

Nathaniel frowned. "That's good thinking, but it isn't that easy. The reason we were able to make a solid connection on a quantum frequency was because of quantum entanglement."

"Huh?"

"We need a very specific radio. It has to be identical to the one we're trying to contact—its analog."

"Oh," Ephraim said.

They realized the answer at the same moment. "Grumps!" they said.

Nathaniel stood up. "Okay, all we need are wheels. I parked my car eighty-three years away."

"I can help with that," Cliff said. "Sorry, I eavesdropped."

"I don't care about that if you have a car," Nathaniel said.

"Hugh has one. And he never lets me drive it." Cliff picked up a key ring from a dish on the bar counter. "Where are we going?"

"Summerside, New York," Ephraim said.

CHAPTER 16

Ephraim guided Cliff through the lamplit streets of Summerside from the passenger side of Everett's Buick. When they drove past his block, Ephraim was shocked to see that instead of his apartment building, there was an old-fashioned movie theater. Its dark marquee advertised Clifton Webb and Dorothy McGuire in *Three Coins in the Fountain*.

Ephraim chuckled. Everett had said there were no coincidences in a quantum system, but perhaps there was still room for irony.

He leaned back in the seat and reached again for a nonexistent seat belt. It was the first time he'd ever ridden without one—just another reminder of all the things that were missing from 1954 and how unfamiliar it all was.

Of course his apartment wouldn't be there yet. His father wouldn't even be born for five more years, and his mother for seven.

Ephraim had heard the story many times; when his mom got drunk, she always reminisced. His parents had met in Puerto Rico, just after she graduated from high school. David García Scott was—would be?—taking time off from college, living with his grandmother and working as a lifeguard at Condado Beach in San Juan. Madeline Watt's best friend, Suzie, swam into a bloom of moon jellyfish on their third day of vacation. David rescued her and drove both women to the hospital. While Suzie was passed out from her stings in the backseat, Madeline and David brazenly flirted in the front.

The odds of the two of them meeting like that seemed so astronomical, it was a miracle Ephraim had ever been born, except it had happened in countless universes. If he ended up living out his life in the past, could Ephraim actually witness their first meeting? It wasn't like he'd have to worry about preventing his own birth. He had no idea how different this world might turn out to be without Hugh Everett in it.

Young Madeline refused to return to the mainland with Suzie after she got out of the hospital. She spent the rest of her vacation in Puerto Rico with David before returning to Summerside for college, and they visited each other every chance they could.

After David's grandmother died, he followed Madeline to Summerside and got a job as a taxi driver. They married, and they had Ephraim, and they moved into the apartment he'd grown up in. Nine years after that, Madeline had kicked David Scott out of their life, and Ephraim hadn't seen or heard from him again. Not even a birthday card at the holidays, as if he had simply ceased to exist.

Ephraim didn't believe in Fate, but would his parents have met if Suzie hadn't blundered into those jellyfish and happened to be intensely allergic to their stings? It seemed to Ephraim that people got together *despite* Fate, when the odds of anyone meeting the right person were so remote—if there were just one perfect match for someone in the entire multiverse.

The funny thing about it was, his mother wasn't even friends with Suzie anymore.

Ephraim leaned forward as they approached the Summerside Public Library.

"Slow down," he said.

Cliff glanced at him. "Is this it?"

"No, but I want to see something."

"We don't have time to sightsee," Nathaniel said. But even he craned his head to get a better look at the library.

It looked bright and new, luminous in the lamplight. It was strange to see it without the stone lions that had flanked the stairway for all Ephraim's life; they'd been a gift from a wealthy family to the library in the 1980s. Jena would have loved to see this.

Then he turned to get a glimpse at Greystone Park, but it wasn't there. It was just an overgrown field surrounded by a peeling white picket fence with missing planks. He could see the dark shape of the Manor House against the night sky in the distance.

"Charming," Cliff said.

"It's going to be a beautiful park one day," Ephraim said.

"The city won't have the money to develop the land until after the Vietnam War," Nathaniel said.

There was a dilapidated gazebo where the Memorial Fountain should be.

"Is that what the fountain is?" Ephraim asked. "A war memorial?"

"You'd think there'd be a plaque. A list of names."

"We looked it up once," Ephraim said. "Even Jena couldn't find anything. It's strange that someone built a fountain to remember something or someone, and it's still there, but no one remembers why."

"That's the way of things, Eph. Even if you forget something, that doesn't make it less real."

"According to Claude Shannon's communication theory, information is everything," Cliff said. "If you extend that to quantum theory, existence *is* information."

Ephraim and Nathaniel stared at him blankly.

"Thanks," Nathaniel said.

"Cheers," Cliff said. "So, what was this war you were blathering about?"

From Cliff's expression, he had just realized that he'd been driving time travelers around for the last two hours and hadn't asked them anything about the future.

"Oh, uh . . ." Ephraim looked away.

"If you're lucky, you won't find out in this universe," Nathaniel said.

Ephraim pointed down the street at the next corner. "That's our turn! Go right. It's at the end of the street, last house on the right. Number two."

Cliff pulled up in front of a two-level house that looked a lot like Jena's in 2012, only smaller. They must have added onto the house over the years.

"This is it," Ephraim said. "Good. Someone's awake." A light was on in the living room.

"It's only ten thirty," Nathaniel said.

"Didn't people go to bed earlier in the 1950s?"

"I'll wait," Cliff said.

"That's okay," Nathaniel said. "You've done plenty for us."

Cliff looked at Ephraim and Nathaniel solemnly.

"All right," he finally said. "But if this doesn't work out, you know where to find me. Here." He fished in his pocket for a scrap of paper and the nub of a pencil and scribbled something on it. "You can call me."

Cliff handed the torn paper to Ephraim. He studied Cliff's phone number: "PRinceton 1-3818." He didn't even know how to dial that. Ephraim stuffed the slip of paper in his pocket.

"Thanks," Ephraim said. He shook hands with Cliff. "Watch where you're walking, all right? And take it easy on the cigarettes."

Cliff laughed. "I will. You watch yourself, too."

Nathaniel reached between the seats to shake Cliff's hand. "Thanks for all your help. It's been good knowing you."

Ephraim and Nathaniel climbed out of the Buick. Cliff waved and drove off.

Ephraim stretched his legs. The old car had more leg room than he was used to, but the seat had been less comfortable than in modern vehicles. He stretched his back out, looking up at the sky.

"Wow," he said. He tilted his head up to stare at the night sky, almost dizzy with the number of stars that were visible. For a moment he felt disconnected from his body, this world, this universe.

Nathaniel looked up. "Wow," he echoed. "I haven't seen stars like that in . . . ever."

"You could get lost in stars like that," Ephraim murmured.

It was strange to think that those lights were always up there, even when he couldn't see them. And it made him feel smaller. There was an infinite number of stars out there. They'd been there long before Ephraim was born and would be around long after he was gone.

Nathaniel nudged him with an elbow. "You ready for this?"

They climbed three steps to the front porch of Jena's house—what would one day be Jena's house, if events played out the same way here.

Ephraim reached above the door and felt for the key that Jena's family hid in a crack between the frame and the wall for emergencies. There was no key, nor was there a crack.

"How do you want to handle this?" Ephraim asked.

Nathaniel picked up a flower pot from the floor beside the door.

"You aren't going to hit Zoe's grandfather with that," Ephraim said.

Nathaniel weighed it carefully in his hand. "No, maybe not." He put it back.

"How about we try asking him for help first?" Ephraim said.

"You really expect that to work?" Nathaniel asked. "'Hi, can we borrow your ham radio to contact your unborn granddaughter in another universe eighty-three years in the future?'"

"People were friendlier and more trusting in the fifties."

"You should have paid more attention in history class." Nathaniel shrugged. "Fine, let's try it your way. But be ready to improvise."

Ephraim pressed the doorbell. Chimes sounded deep inside the house. At some point in the next fifty years or so, the doorbell would be replaced with a buzzer.

After a minute, Ephraim reached for the doorbell again, just as the porch light blinked on.

The curtain covering the window next to the door rustled, and an eye peeked out. Ephraim jumped.

"Yes?" A man said from the other side of the glass.

"We're, uh, stuck and we need to make a call," Ephraim said.

"It's very late," the man said. Ephraim recognized the voice from the radio a couple of days before.

"I know," Ephraim said. "We're sorry to bother you. We're only trying to get home."

The eye looked Ephraim up and down, then slid over to scrutinize Nathaniel. The curtain fell back over the glass.

Ephraim and Nathaniel exchanged a glance. Another thirty seconds passed. Nathaniel put his hand on the doorknob.

The door opened halfway. Jena's grandfather wasn't an old man at all, though that's how Ephraim had pictured him. In fact, he looked just like Jena's father, maybe ten years younger than Nathaniel.

He had short-cropped black hair and wore a pair of round gold spectacles that Ephraim had seen Jena in before. Even in the evening, he wore a shirt and skinny tie, but his sleeves were rolled up to the elbows. He wore gauze bandages on both index fingers.

"Dug Kim?" Ephraim asked.

"Sung Dug Kim." The man tensed. "How do you know my name? Do you live near here?" Dug asked. His English was excellent, but he had a strong Korean accent.

"Yes, sir. My name is Ephraim Scott. I live over on Runyon Street." Not technically a lie, but he hoped Dug didn't know there was only a movie theater and shops on the street now. "This is Nathaniel."

Nathaniel nodded.

"I don't know the Scotts," Dug said. He glanced behind him. "I'm about to go to bed, but if this won't take long." He opened the door wider and gestured them in.

"Thank you," Ephraim said.

Dug nodded. "Please, ah, remove your shoes?" He pointed at the guest slippers lined up inside the door.

Ephraim pulled off his rented dress shoes, glad to get out of them, and slid his feet into cloth slippers that looked about the right size. They were really comfy. Nathaniel grunted and followed suit while Ephraim looked around the foyer.

"You have a beautiful home," Ephraim said.

The house smelled different—sweet, like pipe smoke—but it didn't look much different from the one Ephraim had visited before. It dated back to the turn of the century, and Jena's grandparents had spent every dime they'd brought from South Korea after the Korean War to buy and renovate it. That would have been only a year ago now.

"The telephone is in the kitchen. Would you like something to drink?" Dug started walking toward the kitchen.

"Actually, we don't need your phone," Nathaniel said.

Dug took a step back. "You said you had to call someone." He narrowed his eyes at Ephraim suspiciously and groped behind him as if feeling for a weapon. There was a coat rack with a fedora and a raincoat on it within his reach.

Ephraim put his hands up. "It's long-distance," he said. "Really long-distance. Can we use your ham shack?"

"Who are you?" Dug asked. "How do you know I have a radio?"

"We, uh, saw the antenna?" Nathaniel said.

"Please leave," Dug said. He clenched his fists at his side.

"We can't," Nathaniel said. "We need your help."

"Look, this is all going to sound strange, but I know that your radio has your call sign scratched into the top left corner: WB2IXW," Ephraim said.

"Get out," Dug said.

Nathaniel lunged for Dug. Dug flinched and raised his arms defensively, too late. Nathaniel grabbed his shirt collar in his left hand and pulled him toward him, while punching with the right. Dug cried out. His glasses flew off his face and clattered to the wood floor.

"Nathaniel!" Ephraim said. "Stop!"

Dug flailed and started yammering in rapid Korean. Ephraim recognized one of the words: *Michosso.* Crazy.

Nathaniel hit Dug again, and he folded to the floor. He stopped moving.

"Shit," Ephraim said. "What did you do, Nathaniel?"

"We need his radio," Nathaniel said. "It's the only way."

"No," Ephraim said.

"Well, it was the fastest." Nathaniel glared at him, his eyes nearly feral. "You could have stopped me. You just didn't want this on your hands. Well, it isn't. But you can help me tie him up and make him comfortable," Nathaniel said.

Ephraim bent to pick up Dug's glasses. The frame was slightly bent, but they were otherwise intact. He wiped a dot of blood from one of the lenses with the bottom of his T-shirt, folded the glasses, and hooked one of the legs over his belt.

"We'll talk about this later," Ephraim said.

He helped Nathaniel carry Dug to the couch in the living room. The ham radio shack was set up on a table in a corner of the room.

Ephraim and Nathaniel inspected it. "This looks brand-new," Ephraim said.

"It *is* new." Nathaniel picked up an open user's manual. "He's just starting his hobby."

Nathaniel grabbed a roll of wire and a knife and returned to the couch. He set to tying up Dug's wrists and ankles with the wire. The man's lip was split and bleeding, and the left side of his face was swollen and red.

"Is that necessary?" Ephraim asked.

Nathaniel ignored him. Ephraim turned his attention back to the radio, unable to look at Dug anymore.

"This radio doesn't have the same modifications Zoe made to expand it to the DX range," Ephraim said. He slapped the desk's surface, and a pencil jumped on the blotter. "We can't contact other universes with this."

"Scoot," Nathaniel said. He took the chair from Ephraim and pulled his controller out. "I'm going to hook this up to the radio, just like Zoe did. And hope our luck improves."

Nathaniel opened the controller and switched it on. The glow on his face made him look ten years older.

Ephraim leaned over to look at the device. It was identical to the one Jena had carried, but it was still in its original silver casing, all polished and shining like chrome. It also had a groove for a coin.

Ephraim touched the shallow hollow.

"Is there a coin that goes with this?" Ephraim asked.

"Not that I've ever seen." Nathaniel handed it over.

Ephraim was surprised when the screen stayed lit.

"Nathaniel?" Ephraim tilted the controller to show him the glowing screen.

"Hmm. It was never keyed to a specific user," Nathaniel said. "I guess anyone can operate it."

"Isn't that dangerous?"

"Yeah. I shouldn't have been carrying that thing around with me," Nathaniel said.

Ephraim returned it to Nathaniel. The man smiled.

"What?" Ephraim asked.

"I didn't have to ask you for it, you didn't hesitate."

"It's yours," Ephraim said. "I don't want it. It's safer with you."

"But if you programmed this for your coin, you could travel the multiverse on your own," Nathaniel said. "If we ever get back."

"You must be confusing me with someone who cares about that sort of thing. I just want to go home," Ephraim said. "But speaking of the coin, how will we know we've tuned the right frequency without it?" Ephraim asked.

"We'll hear Zoe's voice," Nathaniel said. "Since this controller is set to detect the LCD, it's essentially a direct line to my home universe. We still might be able to DX on the magic band."

Nathaniel examined the tools on the desk. "Looks like our friend Dug has everything I need to make some adjustments to improve our odds."

He leaned over the radio and rummaged around in the back until he found a place to crimp wire into the radio. Static sizzled from the headphones. He unplugged them, and the sound came through a single speaker on the desk.

"What are you . . . doing?" Dug Kim called from the couch in a raspy voice.

Ephraim jumped and turned around guiltily. Jena's grandfather was trussed up like a turkey with lengths of cable, lying on his side on the couch with his legs torqued to touch the floor. Ephraim winced.

"Anything I can do to help?" Ephraim asked Nathaniel.

"Keep him quiet while I set this up." He glanced at Dug, and his face showed concern. "Get him something for his eye."

Ephraim found a bag of frozen peas in the freezer and brought it to Dug. The man struggled and twisted away from him as he helped him up to a seated position. Bright-red saliva dribbled from a corner of his bloody mouth and stretched in a long line from his chin to his white shirt, which was now speckled with crimson.

"I'm sorry," Ephraim said. He held the frozen peas gingerly against Dug's face. The man moaned. He didn't look forward to telling Zoe and Jena that they'd beat up their grandfather. "This never should have happened."

"Just don't hurt my—" Dug closed his good eye and sighed. "Just go."

"We're working on that," Ephraim said. "We didn't mean any harm."

Dug barked a laugh, and it turned into a cough. More red sprayed from his lips. Ephraim wondered if he should call him an ambulance. They could do that just before they left, if Nathaniel only hurried.

"I'm beginning to think I made a mistake coming to this country," Dug said.

"Why did you?" Ephraim asked.

"To get a good job. To make a better future for my family. I thought Americans were our friends, but . . ." He shook his head and drew in a sharp, painful breath.

Nathaniel fiddled with the radio's dial, speaking softly into the microphone. "CQ DX. CQ DX. Is there anyone on this frequency? Over."

"What do you do?" Ephraim asked.

"Electrical engineer." Dug looked at him. "Who are you? What are you doing with my radio? Are you Russian spies?"

Ephraim glanced at Nathaniel.

"I'm a friend of your granddaughter's," Ephraim said.

"Ephraim," Nathaniel said.

Ephraim saw the moment that Dug started thinking that Ephraim was insane. He'd seen that look before.

"Screw this," Ephraim said. He reached into his pocket. Dug shrank away.

"Easy. I'm just getting my wallet." Ephraim pulled it out and flipped through it until he pulled out the senior picture Jena had given him last week. He held it up close to her grandfather's face.

"See?" Ephraim asked.

The Korean man examined it silently. It showed Jena in a modest blue dress, without her glasses.

"She's pretty, but I don't have a granddaughter," Dug said.

"You will." Ephraim pointed out the gold stamp in the corner that said 2012.

Dug chuckled. "You think you're from the future?"

"You've spoken to her already, actually," Ephraim said. "The other day. You were having a political conversation or something and we found your signal."

"Two days ago, I did hear a girl's voice. What's her name?" Dug asked.

"Zoe or Jena, depending."

"Depending on what?"

That would take too long to explain.

"It's Zoe," Ephraim said. "And if Nathaniel can get that radio working again, you'll be able to talk to her again."

Dug squinted at the picture again. "She does look familiar. Why are you carrying her picture around?"

"We're dating," Ephraim said. "Going steady."

Dug looked at him skeptically.

"It's not like it is now," Ephraim said. "Interracial couples—"

"Do you love this girl? Zoe?" Dug asked.

"I do," Ephraim said. He stared at the picture and tried to figure out which girl he meant.

"CQ DX. This is CHARON1 to CHARON2. Do you read? Over," Nathaniel said.

"That's not a proper call sign," Dug said. "Are you licensed to operate? What is that thing you're holding?"

"Amplifier," Ephraim said. "So we can reach a higher frequency range."

Dug's eyebrows shot up. "That's an interesting notion."

"CHARON2 to CHARON1." Zoe's voice rustled through the speakers. Ephraim froze. Dug looked at him.

Nathaniel whooped. "Boy, am I glad to hear your voice, Z," he said.

"I've been listening all night, hoping you'd be able to get through," she said. "I don't know how you're doing it, but we can save that for later. Is Eph with you?"

"I'm here," Ephraim said. He went over to the desk and leaned into the microphone. "I'm here. And we, uh, have a special guest who would like to say hi."

Nathaniel released the microphone. "Seriously, Ephraim?"

"We owe him," Ephraim said.

Nathaniel sighed. He went over to the couch and sawed through the wires tying Dug's feet. He helped him up and guided him over to the chair gently. Dug lifted his bound hands up and over the microphone. The man suddenly looked unsure of himself.

"Go on," Ephraim said.

Dug squeezed the microphone to transmit.

"This is WB2IXW. Sung Dug Kim," he said.

"Grumps!" Zoe squealed. Dug raised an eyebrow, and Ephraim suddenly knew where Jena and Zoe had gotten that little mannerism.

Ephraim shrugged. "Childhood term of endearment."

"Grandpa Dug, I'm Zoe Kim. John Kim's daughter."

"John . . ." Dug said. His eyes flicked upward. "This is unnatural," he said.

Ephraim drew Nathaniel across the room to give them some privacy. Nathaniel checked his watch impatiently.

A red light flashed against the curtains. Ephraim went to the window and peered out.

"What is it?" Nathaniel asked.

There was a black-and-white vehicle outside with a revolving red light on top. A man in a dark-blue police uniform walked up the path to the door.

"It's the cops!" Ephraim said.

"Damn. Who called them?" Nathaniel asked.

"The neighbors?"

There was loud banging on the door. A baby started crying upstairs.

Nathaniel and Ephraim looked at Dug Kim.

"You have a baby?" Ephraim asked. "How old?"

"My son, John," Dug said. "Eight months. The first Kim born in this country."

"Your wife's upstairs. Did she phone the cops?" Nathaniel asked.

"Don't you dare hurt Eun Hee," Dug said.

"Guys? What's going on?" Zoe asked in a staticky, panicky voice from the radio's speakers. "Grumps?"

The cops pounded on the door again. A deep male voice boomed from the other side. "Open up!"

"We have to get out of here," Nathaniel said. He grabbed the microphone away from Dug. "Zoe?"

"Yes." She sniffled, or maybe that was just more static on the line. "My grandfather—"

"No time. If you're talking to us, then that means the LCD is on?"

"You bet," she said. "Dr. Kim—"

"*Dr.* Kim?" Dug asked.

"I need you to switch it to receive mode in . . ." Nathaniel glanced at his watch. "Twenty seconds? Do you know how to do that?" Nathaniel asked.

"There's a lever with two settings marked in masking tape: 'Receive' and 'Block.' Does that have anything to do with it?"

"Smartass."

"Dr. Kim won't like this," Zoe said.

"I don't like being left behind," Nathaniel said.

The pounding continued at the door, and the baby wailed upstairs. A scared female voice called down in Korean. Dug shouted something back to her.

"This is your last warning. Let us in!" the cop barked.

"But no one can pick you up in that universe," Zoe said. "Everett's in really bad shape."

"I thought he might be. Just set the LCD to receive mode and I'll take care of the rest. Ten seconds later, switch the LCD back to block mode. Over."

"I'm on it. Bye, Grumps. Love you! Over." Zoe signed off, and static crackled on the dead channel.

"Can't I say good-bye to her?" Dug asked.

"You'll be able to say hello in forty years," Ephraim said.

Nathaniel plucked a copper cable from the back of the machine. The other end was coiled tightly around the controller. Nathaniel unraveled it quickly and dropped it to the floor. Ephraim picked it up and collapsed the loose spring into a loop. He slipped it into his back pocket.

Ephraim bowed to Doug Kim. "*Kamsahamnida*," he said. "Thank you. Sorry about all this."

"You know Korean." Dug was astonished.

"Just a few words. Mostly the names of foods I like. I'm learning."

"So what happens now?" Dug asked.

Nathaniel cut the cables around Dug's wrists.

"We now return you to your regularly scheduled programming, already in progress," Ephraim said. He handed the man his glasses.

Nathaniel yanked Ephraim away from Dug. Outside, the cop began shouting a countdown.

"One!" the man shouted.

"I hope this works," Nathaniel said, punching at the buttons of the controller.

"A little late for that," Ephraim said.

"Two!"

"Better hold on, Eph," Nathaniel said. Ephraim took Nathaniel's hand.

"Three!"

The door splintered and swung off its hinges. Two cops rushed in.

Nathaniel pressed a button on the controller. Ephraim locked eyes with Dug Kim. The man nodded.

"*Annyonghi gyeseyo*," Ephraim said. *Good-bye.*

He and Nathaniel shifted away. Zoe's grandfather, the cops, and the house vanished.

CHAPTER 17

They arrived in an empty parking lot in front of a closed shopping mall. Nathaniel's giddy laughter echoed around them.

Ephraim was disoriented, but Nathaniel knew where they were and guided them back to the Everett Institute as quickly as he could. Even at night, the streets were practically as bright as noon, lit up like Times Square.

As soon as Nathaniel palmed the door open and they walked into the atrium housing the LCD, Zoe ran out of the control room to the side.

"Ephraim! Nathaniel!" Zoe said. She hugged Ephraim first, knocking him back half a foot and nearly unbalancing them both.

"Zoe," he said. "Easy there."

She loosened her grip and looked him in the eyes. They were practically nose to nose. Their warm breath mingled. Then she pulled away, glanced downward, and giggled.

Ephraim was still wearing the slippers from the Kims' house. He wiggled his toes in the cotton footies and sighed. He was going to lose his deposit for his shoe rental at the store.

"What is it with you and shoes?" she asked.

He'd been barefoot when he first met Zoe, after he'd had to make a hasty exit from a universe while wading in the park fountain.

"No hug for me?" Nathaniel asked.

Zoe turned and tackled Nathaniel.

"Thanks for the last-minute save, Z," Nathaniel said.

"I was so worried! How did you get back here?" she asked.

Nathaniel showed her his controller.

"You built that with 1950s technology?"

He stashed it in his jacket. "I'm flattered you think I could. I'll explain later. How are things here?"

"Weird," Zoe said.

He glanced at the LCD. The disc was horizontal, the rings around it spinning in opposite directions. He clapped a hand on Zoe's shoulder and went into the control room.

While they waited for Nathaniel to return, Ephraim explained what had happened since Jena and Hugh Everett had left them in 1954.

Nathaniel stalked out of the control room. "Where's Doc?"

"She's been in her office since Jena and Hugh got back. I was worried she'd try to stop me, but I don't think she even noticed what I was up to."

"Then excuse me. I need to have a word with her." Nathaniel strode toward the doors and slapped the panel with his hand. He didn't even wait for the door to lift all the way; he ducked under it as it slowly rose. A second later he crouched in the doorway to peer out at them. "You two did great today."

Ephraim and Zoe waved him off.

"I'm glad you were looking out for us," Ephraim said, as they followed Nathaniel into the building at a more leisurely pace.

"Always," Zoe said. "You're okay?"

Ephraim pressed his hand to the panel on the inside, and the door lowered. Dr. Kim had given him the access she'd promised after all. The sound of the machinery outside was muffled enough that they could talk in a normal voice.

"I am now. Do you think we'll get in trouble?" he said.

Zoe scowled. "I did what I had to do. I couldn't leave you there, Eph. Both of you."

"Was she happy that we found Hugh?" Ephraim asked.

"Honestly? She looked disappointed. Almost . . ."

He gave her a questioning look.

"Heartbroken." Zoe shrugged.

"And Hugh?" Ephraim asked.

"He was unconscious last I saw him, when some of the staff

wheeled him off to his room. Jena's with him now." Zoe watched him closely.

"She is?"

"In his suite."

"Really." Ephraim tried very hard not to look worried. "What do you think will happen now that we have Everett?" he asked.

"He's going to get to the bottom of this and we'll have the multiverse sorted by lunch tomorrow." She met his eyes. "We'll get back to our normal lives and everyone will live happily ever after."

"And a thousand years of peace will reign over the multiverse." He cocked his head. "You suppose he can actually fix everything?"

"I don't know. If I were taking bets, my money'd still be on you." She pressed the button to call the elevator back down to ground level. Ephraim watched the numbers count down from 10 to 1.

"I couldn't even hold onto the coin," Ephraim said. He clenched his hand into a fist. "Without it, I'm just . . . a kid."

"A kid with courage and a good heart. Now, if you only had a brain . . ."

"Ha ha. But I didn't do much. I'd still be in 1954 if not for you, and Nathaniel really came through with that backup controller."

"You think maybe you've been unfair to Nathan?" Zoe asked.

Ephraim pictured Nathaniel beating up Dug Kim. He closed his eyes.

"What's wrong?" Zoe asked.

He couldn't tell her that he'd seen their older friend brutally work over a defenseless man, her grandfather no less.

"I'm surprised that you suggested that, considering how much you despise Nate," Ephraim said.

"The way I see it, Nathan has the potential to become Nate or Nathaniel, and we can help him choose the right path," Zoe said.

Neither of those options looked all that appealing right now.

The elevator arrived and they stepped in. Zoe's finger hovered over the buttons.

"Food or sleep?" she asked.

"I'm not sure if I'm more tired than I am hungry." He yawned widely and covered his mouth.

"That answers that," Zoe said. She pressed buttons 1 and 3 together. "I'm taking you to bed."

He leaned against the wall and crossed his arms. "You wish," he said.

"Wishing doesn't help anything," she said softly.

The elevator deposited them in the secret basement, and they walked down the corridor to the mansion.

"I wasn't sure you'd make it back," Zoe said.

"Me neither."

"It got me thinking."

"Uh-oh."

She stuck her tongue out at him.

"I'm not kidding. Ephraim, I have a confession." She certainly sounded serious.

They walked a while before she said anything else.

"I reassembled the controller a long time ago," she said. "Before I said I did."

"Zoe! Why?"

"My Ephraim was dead. Mary Shelley left. My dad's never around either, off with one of his strumpets practically every night, and when he was around, if I wanted to spend any time with him it had to be with the television on."

"You were lonely?" he asked.

"More than that. I missed *you*, dumbass," she said. "So I decided to go after you."

"We talked about that."

"I didn't care anymore that I don't belong in your universe. I wanted to be in your life."

"Was Jena right? You used the controller at prom?" he asked.

His pulse quickened with sudden panic. What if it hadn't been the multiverse hiccuping? What if Zoe had set this whole catastrophe in motion?

"Give me some credit. I was truthful about that much. For whatever reason, the controller didn't work—like all the other times."

"Other times?" he asked.

"Ephraim, I tried it *every day*. And it never worked."

"Zoe."

"It couldn't find your coin—it was like you didn't even exist. And then I started worrying that something had happened to you, and it was torture not knowing." She balled her hands. "I know it's pathetic. I hate to admit it, but I thought you should know."

They reached the stairs leading up to the house, and he gestured for her to sit down. He sat next to her.

He pulled at a loose thread from a tear in the knee of his jeans. His analog's jeans.

"When the coin went blank, I thought it was all over," he said. "And I wasn't sure if I was relieved or disappointed. But I carried it with me every day, too, and I kept checking it, like I was waiting for it to start working again." He wiped his sweaty hand on his knee and let it rest there. "Hoping."

She put a hand over his. "If the coin had started working, where would you have gone?"

He knew what she wanted to hear, but he couldn't say it.

"Nowhere." He took a deep breath. "I meant it when I said we shouldn't use the device anymore. I'm sorry. I wish—" He shook his head. "I'm sorry things were so awful for you back home, but things were going well for me. My mom was getting help, she started dating Jim. I had my Nathan back, and I had . . ."

"Jena," she said.

He nodded.

"Why'd you give her the coin?"

"I knew if I didn't get rid of it, a part of me would always be waiting for something else." *Someone else.* "I had to put everything behind me and commit to my life, in my universe."

Zoe stood and walked backward up one step.

"So how is she different from me, really?" she asked.

"That's irrelevant. It's . . . a feeling," he said.

"You're happy? With her?"

Ephraim licked his lips. "I've always wanted to be with her."

"That's not what I asked."

"Zoe, if I hadn't met you—"

"Don't say that," she said. She walked up another step. He wasn't sure if he should follow.

"Do you believe in Fate, Ephraim?"

"I've been thinking about that a lot lately. It's kind of hard to believe in Fate, when the multiverse proves that *everything* happens."

"But you and I met. That's not supposed to happen. Maybe there's a reason for it."

Ephraim stood and turned to face her. "You still aren't over him," he said.

He wanted to take the words back right away, but it was too late.

"Good night, Ephraim." She spun and ran up the rest of the stairs. A few moments later he heard a door slam.

"Good night, Zoe."

Ephraim, you are a world-class idiot.

CHAPTER 18

While the first floor of Greystone Manor resembled a hotel, the second floor felt more like someone's home. Ephraim wandered through furnished rooms with worn-out Persian carpets, dusty mahogany tables, and plastic-covered couches.

He found Jena in a drawing room at the back of the west wing—a library—curled up on a red velvet sofa. The plastic tarp had been crumpled up and kicked under its clawed feet. She almost blended into the fabric because she'd changed into a matching red dress.

"Hey," he said softly.

She bolted up. When she saw him, she started crying.

"Easy," he said. He sat down next to her, and a cloud of dust rose in the air around them. She hugged him tight.

"You made it," she said in a low voice. "I was so shocked when I realized what had happened. I would have gone back for you, but Hugh was sick," Jena said.

"It's okay," Ephraim lied. "How is he?"

She nodded at the closed door across the room. Loud snoring emanated from the other side.

"Sleeping," she said.

Jena drew her feet under her legs, draping the short dress over them carefully. She was barefoot.

"What's wrong with him?" Ephraim asked.

"He blacked out after the shift," she said. "He nearly choked on his own vomit. *So much vomit.*"

Ephraim made a face.

"You didn't have to drive in a car with that smell," she said. "I called Dr. Kim and she told me to bring him back to Crossroads right away. Thank goodness Nathaniel has a convertible."

"Using the coin makes Everett that sick?" Ephraim asked.

"Apparently, it gets worse the more he travels. Ironic, huh? He invented a technology he can never use."

"That's why they needed Ephraim to operate it," Ephraim said. He bet it ate Hugh up that he couldn't travel through the multiverse on his own. It had driven Nate mad with jealousy.

"Who lives up here?" Ephraim asked, looking around.

"Dr. Kim," Jena said.

She pulled off her glasses and polished them with the hem of her dress. Ephraim tried not to stare as she lifted it.

"How did you get back?" she asked.

"Nathaniel basically whipped out an ACME portable hole," Ephraim said.

"Never leave home without one," Jena said.

For the second time that night, he highlighted how they'd used the second controller to communicate with Zoe by ham radio, leaving out the part where Nathaniel beat the crap out of Dug Kim.

"Damn," Jena said. "So she got to save you *and* talk to Grumps."

"He's a really nice guy," Ephraim said.

"I wish I could have seen him," Jena said. "I barely got to spend any time in my favorite decade."

"I thought you hated it," Ephraim said.

"There are drawbacks to any era in history. We just trade one set of problems for another. Things are as imperfect in 2012 as they are in 1954."

"I thought I was going to have to live there," Ephraim said.

"Dr. Kim would have come back for you."

"Even Nathaniel wasn't so sure, and he's practically in love with her," Ephraim said. "If it hadn't been for Zoe, we'd still be there. She really came through."

Jena pursed her lips. "What is that supposed to mean? Leaving you was an accident."

"I know. You did the right thing, taking care of Hugh."

"Damn straight. Not everything's about you," she said.

"This isn't—" He sighed. "What are we even fighting about?"

She leaned forward. "It's always 'Zoe this,' and 'Zoe that.'"

"I only mentioned her once."

"Well, I feel like I've been living in her shadow since you came back from her universe."

"You shouldn't feel insecure about our relationship."

"I'm not insecure," Jena said. "I know I'm awesome." She got up and walked toward the large windows on the other side of the room.

He followed her. "So what's the problem?"

The windows faced the Summerside Library. He bet Dr. Kim had chosen these rooms for her own for that exact reason.

"I'm worried *you'll* forget how awesome I am. I'm not used to feeling . . . jealous."

"Jealous?" He frowned.

"I'm jealous of the two of you and your history together and the fact that she kissed you and that she's some kind of hero who swooped in and is going to save the multiverse."

"*We're* going to save the multiverse. All of us. Together."

Ephraim knew what it was like to be jealous of his analog. He'd felt the same way about the other Ephraim and Zoe being together. No, he didn't want to think about that, especially right now.

"It's hard when someone else has something you want, and you ask, 'Why him? Why not me?' Especially when that other person *is* you," he said.

Ephraim had always been envious of other kids' families, friends who grew up with two parents who got along with each other. But in the last year, he'd had the chance to see how other people lived, to actually live some of those other lives, and he'd found he preferred his own.

As imperfect as she might be, his mother was *his* alone and if anything had been different in his life, he'd be different too. His experiences, in the universe he'd been born in, were what made him unique.

"Zoe's just a friend, okay? There's nothing between us," Ephraim said. "You and I have been together a lot longer than I've even known her. And we have twelve years of history on top of that."

She leaned against the window and stared over at the Library.

"Since we're being honest with each other, I was feeling a bit jealous of Hugh earlier tonight," Ephraim said.

Jena feigned shock. "No kidding."

"Come on," he said.

Jena tucked her hair behind one ear. "He's incredibly hot," she said.

Ephraim laughed, but he stopped when Jena's face got pink. "Wait, you're serious?"

"I like a man in glasses," she said. "And a suit."

"You never told me that," Ephraim said.

"You don't wear glasses."

"Poor vision is a sign of inferior genes, which makes for a less desirable mate."

"Really." Jena glared at him over the top of her glasses.

Oops.

"Don't worry, you're plenty cute even without glasses. Especially in a tux." She sighed wistfully. "I was looking forward to taking that off you."

Ephraim cleared his throat. "You know, Everett's going to lose his hair. You saw the pictures in those biographies. And he's going to gain a lot of weight."

"Sexy isn't only about appearances," Jena said. "He's also a *super genius.*"

"Which makes you 'Tastyus supersonicus'?" Ephraim asked. Since he and Jena could never agree on whether to watch Daffy Duck or Bugs Bunny cartoons, they settled on a happy medium: Road Runner cartoons.

"Poor Wile E. tries so hard," Jena said sadly. "But he never catches the Road Runner."

"You really do like the underdog," Ephraim said.

"Coyote," she said. She turned toward him and leaned closer.

"Don't worry, there's a first time for everything. Somewhere in the multiverse, the coyote always gets his bird," he said.

Ephraim kissed her.

"Meep, meep," she said dreamily.

"You look great, by the way. Why are you all dressed up again?" he asked.

She looked down at her dress.

"I needed a change of clothes, after Hugh was sick. This was the first clean thing I grabbed." She didn't pull the neckline up this time. "Prom part two?"

"I'll be right back," Ephraim said.

"Don't go," she said, holding onto his hand.

"It'll just take a second," he said.

He ran back to his room and changed quickly into his tuxedo. On a hunch, he opened the drawer of the night table in his room and found a strip of Trojans stashed inside a worn copy of the *The Mystery of Edwin Drood* by Charles Dickens. He tore one of the condoms off and tucked it into his jacket.

But when he got back to the drawing room, Jena had fallen asleep on the couch. Her fingers were curled around something in her palm.

He pulled at her slender fingers gently, and the coin tumbled into his hand. He found an afghan in the linen cabinet beside the bedroom and covered her with it, then went back to his room, turning the coin over and over in his hands. Heads. Tails.

Does she love me, does she love me not?

Heads. Tails.

Do I love her? Do I love her not?

CHAPTER 19

The next morning, Ephraim found Hugh Everett studying the LCD in the atrium, making notes on a yellow legal pad and occasionally glancing none too subtly at Jena and Zoe over by the door to Everett's lab.

"Feeling better?" Ephraim asked Hugh.

"One hundred percent," Hugh said.

Jena and Zoe had changed back into their matching tank and shorts combos. They were even harder to tell apart because Zoe was now wearing an old pair of Dr. Kim's glasses; her blue contacts were only supposed to be temporary. In fact, Ephraim recognized the gold-rimmed spectacles as her grandfather's.

Still, Zoe stood a little straighter than Jena did, and there was always her nose piercing to give her away, which completely fascinated Hugh.

Hugh reached into his jacket pocket and pulled out a small point-and-shoot camera. He snapped a quick picture of the girls and thumbed a plastic wheel to advance the film. He dropped it back into his pocket and pulled out a pack of cigarettes.

He tilted his head back to watch the rings of the LCD slowly oscillate. Ephraim could practically see him running the equations through his head.

"Ingenious," Hugh said. "It seems incredible that I could have designed this."

"Well, it's the product of modern technology and years of research focused on interdimensional travel," Jena said, wandering over with Zoe.

"And Nathaniel helped," Zoe said.

"In other universes, the US has visited the moon, sent probes into deep space, brought back photographs of the surface of Mars and from beyond Pluto," Jena said. "Which isn't a planet anymore, by the way."

"Don't get me started on that," Zoe said.

"I know, right?"

"Space travel is a waste of time and resources." Hugh lit a cigarette. As he walked around the LCD, smoke drifted up and swirled around the turning rings of the machine. "We already know those planets are out there. We can see them with our eyes. But other universes . . ." He pressed his hand against the base of the gyroscope. "It feels alive."

He continued walking around the base, and Ephraim followed.

"I have no idea why this contraption works," Hugh said softly.

"You and me both," Ephraim said.

"But I'm supposed to have invented it. I'm supposed to explain what's going on in the multiple universes, yet I can barely grasp the basic principles of this machine's design."

"You'll figure it out," Ephraim said. "We'll help."

Hugh shook his head. "I've been reviewing Everett's theories all morning." He stopped. "That still sounds strange."

"You get used to it." Ephraim smiled.

"I feel like my understanding of his probability state theories only scratches the surface. I've read the debates about whether parallel universes exist, and I find myself agreeing with Niels Bohr's theories of the collapsing wave function. Imagine that! My other self would roll in his grave."

Ephraim didn't mention that in all likelihood, Everett was standing on one of his counterparts' graves.

"Maybe I was never meant to share his particular insights. Especially considering what I've learned about what's happening in the multiverse right now," Hugh said.

"What does that mean?"

Hugh threw his hand up and pointed at the LCD. "That this is impossible!" His voice echoed in the atrium. Jena and Zoe looked over at them.

"But multiple universes *do* exist," Ephraim said.

"Obviously. But I think you've recruited the wrong Hugh Everett to tell you how they exist."

"There's no right or wrong. You are Hugh Everett, with the same intelligence, the same potential." The same flaws. Ephraim shrugged. "And you're all we've got."

"Sorry to say, that may not be enough." Hugh sucked on his cigarette thoughtfully.

"Maybe you'll change your mind once we see whatever's in that lab," Ephraim said.

"Well, then, for God's sake, man, let's get on with it."

"We're waiting for Nathaniel and Dr. Kim."

Hugh scowled.

The main entrance opened, and Dr. Kim stepped out, with Nathaniel following a few steps behind. The group assembled in front of Everett's lab.

Dr. Kim's attention focused on Ephraim and Hugh. She brushed her neat bangs away from her forehead, then looked annoyed and shoved her hands into the pockets of her white lab coat. Something was different about her.

She was wearing makeup.

"What's up, Doc?" Ephraim asked.

Dr. Kim stared at him. "I suppose that was inevitable. Good morning, Ephraim. I'm glad you made it back." She nodded at Jena and Zoe before turning to Hugh.

"Welcome to the Ever—uh. Crossroads," Dr. Kim said.

"Thanks," Hugh said.

"You are not what I was expecting," Dr. Kim said.

"I know. But I promise to do my best."

"No one will ever accept you as this universe's Everett," she said.

"I think we're beyond that," Nathaniel said.

"He could be Everett's son," Zoe said.

"And who would his mother be?" Jena asked.

"Never mind," Dr. Kim said. "We do have bigger concerns."

"What . . ." Hugh swallowed. "What happened to the other version of me?"

"This universe's Everett recruited his analog—his double from another universe—to continue his work after his death. And now you're *his* replacement," Nathaniel said.

"How delightfully morbid," Hugh said.

"Hugh, your first task is simple. I need you to open that door." Dr. Kim pointed to the entrance to Everett's laboratory.

"You didn't ask me here to be a glorified key," Hugh said. "Nathaniel explained what you've been observing about the multiverse."

"We need the expertise of someone more experienced with quantum wave states," she said. "Right now you're no more qualified than Ephraim here."

"Hey," Ephraim said.

"Hugh can do this," Jena said. "I've seen the way he thinks. He's brilliant. Give him a chance."

"Thank you, Jena," Hugh said. "And with all due respect, Dr. Kim, you won't need to find another replacement for me."

"Doc, I don't think that's even an option. There aren't any worlds with a version of him in 1977," Nathaniel said. "Not anymore. And, uh, the number of universes recorded in our databases has diminished by half. I was up all night trying to figure out what happened, but I can't explain it. It's as if someone deleted them all. Until we know what's responsible, I've restricted access from the rest of the team."

"Who asked you to run that scan?" Dr. Kim asked.

Nathaniel blinked in surprise. "I just thought—"

"Just keep the machine running. That's all you're in charge of right now," Dr. Kim said.

"Mom, Dad, don't fight," Zoe said.

"*Zoe*," Ephraim hissed. He shook his head.

"I can learn very quickly," Hugh said. "And a fresh perspective might provide the solution we need. I can assure you, Dr. Kim, I'm far more experienced than I appear." He winked.

Dr. Kim's face flushed. "Well," she said. "Why don't we see what you make of your predecessors' notes, shall we?"

"So we can keep him?" Jena asked.

"I'm not a puppy," Hugh said.

Dr. Kim gestured to the door. Hugh approached it slowly. It didn't look like the others in the Institute. It was old-fashioned, with a simple brass doorknob and no hand scanner.

"The biometric sensors are embedded in the knob. Just turn it to the right," Nathaniel said.

Hugh gripped the knob firmly and twisted. A latch clicked, and Hugh swung the door open. Lights flickered on, revealing a vast lab space. Papers littered the floors and tables, drawers were pulled out, file folders and storage boxes were piled haphazardly, lids off. Various computers switched themselves on, and green lines of numbers scrolled vertically down their glowing screens.

"I'm not usually this disorganized." Hugh stepped inside. Zoe wrinkled her nose and fanned his cigarette smoke away with her hands as she followed behind Hugh, but it didn't help because the room already smelled like stale smoke.

"Hugh Two was very private. No one's been in here since he took over," Nathaniel said as he entered.

"Hugh Two," Hugh said dryly. "That's charming."

"I guess that makes you Hugh Everett III the Third," Zoe said.

"Two insisted on the security feature that would incinerate everything inside if we attempted to force entry," Nathaniel said. He tapped at a panel behind the door. "Which I'm disabling right now."

"It looks like someone was looking for something," Ephraim said, drifting into the room.

"Or didn't like what they found," Zoe said.

"It's like a tomb," Hugh said.

"Independent air supply," Nathaniel said. "The walls are reinforced and it's stocked with a decade's worth of food and supplies under the floor panels. Mostly liquor and frozen prime rib. Dr.

Everett was worried about nuclear attacks and designed this room to function as a fallout shelter." He pointed to the yellow and black radiation sign posted above the door. "He hardly ever left this room while I knew him."

"What a terrible way to live," Hugh said. "In constant fear. Didn't he take any comfort in knowing that there are other versions of him in parallel universes?"

"He was more tickled by the idea of all the dead ones," Nathaniel said.

"So what are we looking for?" Jena said.

Dr. Kim stood silently by the door, observing them.

"Anything. Everything. I think we should start with notes on the LCD, the coin, and the controller. There have to be design specs, schematics, doodles. A user manual would be nice. The previous Doctors Everett kept that information close to their vests."

Nathaniel picked up a stack of looseleaf pages from the floor. "Any notes on the coherence of parallel universes, any signs he might have known that things were going wrong. Data sets, research, whatever."

"I've read all of his published papers," Hugh said.

"The first Doctor published at the beginning. But the more attention his work got, the more he withdrew. He had plenty of unpublished theories. Some weren't fully developed, some were plain wacky." Nathaniel sat at a computer station and balanced the stack of papers on his knees. "Once he recruited Two, he only spoke to him, and eventually his colleagues all left to work at other institutes.

"After Ephraim and I disappeared, apparently Two became even more of a recluse. Eventually, he only spoke to Jena—Dr. Kim, I mean. He shut himself up in this room and we never found out what he was even working on before he died."

"Maybe he was just playing computer solitaire," Zoe said.

Ephraim sat at another computer and jiggled the mouse. The numbers scrolling across the screen vanished. He laughed. He'd thought they were related to the parallel universes, running complicated calculations. But it was just a screensaver.

Jena guided Hugh toward another computer station and sat him down in front of the keyboard. He looked at it doubtfully.

"We didn't have machines like this in 1954," Hugh said.

"It's called a computer," Ephraim said.

"I know," Hugh snapped. "But the ones I've seen are bigger than this room."

"These are PCs," Jena said. "Personal computers. Everyone has at least one computer of their own these days. We carry them in our pockets."

"On our *wrists*," Nathaniel corrected her.

Hugh paled.

"Why is all the technology in this lab so outdated?" Zoe asked. "It's not even up to 2012 standards."

"Everett liked what he was used to," Nathaniel said. "He insisted on running his own computers on a Unix operating system."

"Never heard of it," Hugh said.

Jena slid a keyboard in front of him. "It's just like a typewriter," she said.

"My mother types all my papers for me," Hugh said.

"I bet that impresses the ladies," Jena said. "You're going to become a computer wizard one day, Hugh. Your software will save lives. You can do this."

"How do you know so much about me?" Hugh asked.

"I read a lot," she said.

Hugh cracked his knuckles and tapped hesitantly at the keyboard. Jena bent over and quietly explained how to use the wireless optical mouse to navigate on the computer, causing Hugh to stare at her instead of the screen. Ephraim felt his shoulders stiffen. He took a step toward them.

Zoe pulled Ephraim aside. "She can handle him," she said. "Why don't we clean this place up? We can sort the papers into piles that look promising."

Ephraim glanced over at Nathaniel. He was already poking into file folders on the network; he was familiar with this operating system and had an idea of what to look for, so he wouldn't need their help on that.

Ephraim grabbed a messy mound of pages with notes scribbled on them in pencil. "And here I thought we were moving toward a paperless society."

"Well, the man who worked in here was the product of a different time," Zoe said.

Hugh didn't seem to have any trouble embracing the future. In fact, he had one arm around it—Jena. She and Ephraim exchanged a look. She seemed embarrassed, but her eyes warned him not to interfere. She was still taking care of Hugh, in her own way. Ephraim didn't like it, but they needed the man's help.

"I knew one day I would change our understanding of the universe forever," Hugh was saying to Jena. "But I never thought my work would shape the world this much."

Where was the guy who'd confessed his doubts to Ephraim a short while ago?

Zoe blew dust off a stack of books and reshelved them neatly on a bookcase beside the desk. "He sure is arrogant," she said.

"Arrogance has led to many great discoveries," Nathaniel said.

"It isn't arrogance if he's right," Ephraim said. "He made all of this possible. He isn't wrong to feel important. I just don't know why she's encouraging him so much."

"She's starstruck," Zoe said.

He wondered what had captured her attention so much. Most of the things attributed to Everett in his biographies hadn't happened yet for this younger version of him. They were just possibilities, made into probabilities now that he knew where his theories could lead. Maybe they had changed the course of his own reality, and all of this would happen again there when they sent him back.

But that didn't equate Hugh with the man who had developed quantum shifting. There were countless universes where his theories had been ignored, or his research led nowhere. Far more than where it was embraced so wholeheartedly, let alone accepted as real science. This Hugh was no more the man he could become than Jena or Zoe were Dr. Kim.

"Jealous?" Zoe asked.

"No. I trust her," Ephraim said. "But maybe some things should remain in the past."

Zoe lowered her eyes and chewed on her upper lip thoughtfully.

CHAPTER 20

Three days later, Everett's office was clean and organized. Ephraim and Zoe had sorted all the loose papers into three stacks for Hugh to study: "junk," "could be useful," and "we have no idea what any of this means." The last category was actually three towering stacks of its own.

Thanks to Jena and Nathaniel's training, and his own natural ability, Hugh had become good enough with the computer to locate most of his predecessors' work. He claimed he'd already found enough to call a meeting to share his discoveries.

"I'm all ears," Dr. Kim said.

Ephraim almost didn't recognize the doctor. She had ditched her trademark lab coat and changed into a flattering gray wraparound sweater with a deep neck and black slacks that were just the right amount of tight. Her usually unkempt hair was pinned up with a playful fringe of bangs that made her look ten years younger. When she walked past him, she left a strong perfume in her wake.

Dr. Kim sat on a stool facing Hugh and crossed her legs at the ankles.

Jena edged away from Hugh's seat and leaned against a table, eyes narrowed, staring at Dr. Kim.

Hugh swiveled around in his chair and interlaced his fingers in his lap. "Here are the basics as I understand them, building on the work of my predecessors, who, incidentally, were complete geniuses.

"At each moment of decision, there's the potential for more than one outcome. From an individual's perspective, when we make a choice, we experience just one of those possible outcomes. But on a quantum level, *every* outcome actually occurs, and each is observed by an analog in an alternate universe."

Dr. Kim nodded impatiently.

Hugh reached into his pocket and pulled out a quarter. Ephraim's hand immediately went to his own pocket. He relaxed when he felt the coin there.

Hugh held the ordinary quarter between thumb and index finger and showed it to all of them, like a stage magician about to demonstrate a trick.

"Would you all agree that when I flip a fair coin, with an evenly distributed weight, there's a fifty-fifty chance of it landing on heads and the same odds of tails?" Hugh asked.

"That's right," Ephraim said. One of Jena's analogs had used this very thought experiment to explain multiple universes to him last year.

"Not exactly," Jena said. "The outcome is prejudiced by the person flipping the quarter. No human can flip it exactly the same way over and over again."

Hugh bobbed his hand in Jena's direction. "Very good. For simplicity's sake, let's say that from the perspective of a single observer, it has an equal probability of coming up heads or tails. Now consider: In a multiverse, this quantum coin has a *one hundred percent* chance of landing on heads. And a one hundred percent chance of landing on tails."

"Excellent," Dr. Kim said.

"I'm just getting warmed up, my dear," he said.

Dr. Kim actually blushed.

Hugh flipped the coin and caught it. He held out his closed hand. "Call it. Is this coin heads or tails?" he asked. His eyes slid from Dr. Kim to Jena.

"Yes," Jena said slowly. "Right now, it's both. Until you open your hand and we observe which universe we're in. If we're in the one where it displays heads, our analogs in a parallel universe will see tails."

"A-plus," Hugh said.

"She's *essentially* correct," Dr. Kim said. "But under our unique circumstances, this universe can't split to create any other outcome except the one we observe. That's true for any universe that contains a coheron drive, portable or otherwise."

Ephraim understood that this was one of the side effects of the technology; if a universe with a coheron drive could branch off like any other, then the technology would be duplicated as well. There would be countless other Ephraims and Nathans using it to visit other parallel universes. He didn't know if that was a limitation built into the device itself, or if the multiverse couldn't support the kind of exponential growth that would result from such a chaotic force in play.

"Doesn't that create an imbalance?" Jena asked.

"It's countering the natural way of things, that's for sure," Zoe said. "And when does that ever work out well?"

Hugh stood and paced in front of the room.

"Again, for simplicity, let's say that restriction doesn't apply here. This is just any other universe. In point of fact, upon flipping the coin, there are many possibilities beyond heads and tails. I might fail to catch the coin, causing it to roll away or even land on its edge. Perhaps it even falls into a crevice and can never be observed. Naturally, those outcomes have a much lower probability than the chance of it landing on either heads or tails. An almost negligible probability."

"Then why even bother considering them? Except as an academic exercise?" Zoe asked.

"Because it's more than academic—if it's possible, it *does* happen. My esteemed predecessors hypothesized that the multiverse is deterministic: it self-selects the most likely quantum universes from all available possibilities, on what is called a preferred basis."

Dr. Kim leaned forward with sudden interest. "Go on."

Hugh pulled his glasses off and looked at her. "Let's imagine that the multiverse allows for only three outcomes in this case. Three universes. Heads, tails, and edge. It rules out the universe where the coin lands on its edge because it has such an infinitesimally low probability: once in perhaps a hundred million times it will land on its edge. That leaves us with essentially two viable branches: heads and tails."

Hugh reached into the breast pocket of his jacket and pulled out an empty pack of cigarettes. He crumpled it and tossed it onto the table in disgust.

Dr. Kim took a silver cigarette case from a pants pocket and opened it to him.

"My brand," he said in surprise.

"We keep a full inventory of the things you like," Dr. Kim said.

"Indeed," Hugh said.

"These cigarettes haven't been manufactured in this universe in nearly fifteen years, but that's no consequence when you can stock up in another universe."

Hugh took a cigarette. "Thank you," he said.

She flicked a silver Zippo and lit his cigarette, then lit one of her own.

"Why does everyone smoke?" Zoe muttered as the lab filled with cigarette smoke.

"It may not be what you're used to. There's one hundred percent less asbestos in the filter from the brand sold in 1954," Dr. Kim said.

"It's just fine," Hugh said. He suddenly seemed distracted. "*Filter . . . *"

"Hugh?" Jena asked.

"Shhh!" Dr. Kim said. "He's working something out."

Jena pressed her lips together.

Hugh's eyes had glazed and he'd frozen with his cigarette halfway to his mouth. He abruptly snapped out of it and focused on the filter on the cigarette curiously.

"As I was saying." He went on, as if nothing had happened. "Though there may be a universe where the coin landed on its edge, that lone universe is eventually erased as if it had never been created."

"Sounds like quantum Darwinism," Jena said. "Universes with a higher probability of occurring survive, and the others just die off."

Ephraim waved smoke away from his face and cleared his throat loudly. "Nathaniel, you told me once that some universes don't fully exist unless the coheron drive registers some record of them."

Nathaniel nodded. "Ephraim and the first Everett believed that even half-formed—or I suppose half-erased—universes could still be accessed with the Charon device. And once visited, they and their branches would stick around indefinitely and continue branching."

"But that makes it sound like the multiverse is . . . conscious?" Ephraim said. "Intelligent?"

"Let's not anthropomorphize," Hugh said. "I admit that's difficult to accept, but at the heart of the matter, either the multiverse is somehow choosing these realities, or another conscious entity is manipulating them—which is an even more extreme assumption and not worth getting into. I believe, and any sane man would agree: it's all determined by pure statistics. *Science*."

"It may as well be magic," Ephraim said. "You're saying that some of those universes I visited wouldn't have existed if I hadn't chosen them?"

In one of the universes Ephraim had been to, his friend Nathan was a football jock and was dating Shelley Morales. That reality was so improbable it might have been impossible. At the time, Ephraim had thought it had happened because of a magical wish. Now Hugh was saying that, in a way, it had.

Hugh's mouth quirked. "The coheron drive grants them stability. The user becomes a 'super observer,' lending those realities substance. Permanence." He shrugged. "Coherence."

"Fairy dust," Zoe muttered. "If you believe in something enough . . ."

He and Zoe had returned to all of the universes he'd visited when he switched his analogs back to where they belonged. He wondered if there was an expiration date. Were those universes still around now, all because of him and the coin? Their coordinates were stored in the controller—chance had been removed as a factor. With the coheron drive, they were as easy to find as looking up a town on a map and driving there.

What about all the universes that had branched off from them?

"Obviously we can't confirm that a universe doesn't exist if we don't go there," Dr. Kim said. "Just as it's hard to prove a universe exists that shouldn't have, because the coheron drive observed it. That's what the Everetts have been trying to do here: Collect data on the possibility and probability of different kinds of universes and determine how the multiverse handles them. And whether and how we affect the results."

"Kind of sounds like *we* were the experiment," Zoe said.

"It's impossible to remove the scientist from the experiment," Hugh said.

"I think this brings us to the disturbing phenomenon you witnessed at your prom," Dr. Kim said.

"What phenomenon?" Hugh asked. He looked around the room.

"We have footage of the other realities merging with ours," Jena said.

Hugh brought his fist down on the lab table. "Why didn't you mention this sooner?"

"You had enough to absorb here," Jena said. "It seemed better to get you up to speed on the theory before we showed you how it was going wrong."

"I need to know everything you do about what's going on, no matter how insignificant it might seem, if you expect me to be of any help." He stabbed out his cigarette right there on the table.

"It just slipped my mind," Jena said.

Hugh shook his head. "This is incredibly important," he said.

"I agree," Dr. Kim said. She stood and smoothed the back of her skirt. "I have the video in my office, if you'd like to screen it now."

Hugh nodded vigorously. "Absolutely."

Jena moved to join them. Dr. Kim held up a hand. "Carry on with your work here. Nathaniel, I don't want us to be disturbed."

"Sure thing, Doc," Nathaniel said glumly.

"I haven't found any information on the coheron drives yet, so I'd like you to concentrate your search there," Hugh said. "We need to know how the mechanism works in as much detail as possible. And

I'd like to review all the data collected on parallel universes so far." He pointed to his monitor. "On my screen by the time I get back."

"I'm on it," Nathaniel said. He spun around to face his own screen and started typing. "You're starting to sound like Hugh Everett."

"He is, isn't he?" Dr. Kim said.

"I'll take that as a compliment," Hugh said. He followed Dr. Kim out of the lab.

"He sure *acts* like a puppy," Zoe said.

Ephraim looked around the room. "Did anyone else find that a little creepy?"

Zoe whistled. "Hello, Mrs. Robinson."

"What are you two trying to say?" Jena asked.

"Dr. Kim seems interested in taking a more hands-on approach to the situation," Zoe said.

"Hugh can't stand her," Jena said.

"Of course, *you* wouldn't see it," Zoe said.

"What is that supposed to mean?" Jena said.

"This whole conversation was some kind of . . . foreplay," Zoe said. "Nerdy foreplay."

"Dr. Kim wants Hugh. Hugh's a sex-crazed pervert. And you're . . . jealous, Jena," Ephraim said.

"Nonsense," Jena said. "She wants *you*, Ephraim. Or maybe not you, but the one she used to know. Is it really only obvious to me?" She looked at Nathaniel. He put his hands up in surrender.

"Maybe she doesn't know who she wants," Ephraim murmured.

"Or she wants it all," Zoe said.

Nathaniel glanced furtively at the closed door and lowered his voice. "Actually, the Doc and Everett do have a history together."

"What?" Ephraim, Zoe, and Jena said at once.

"She's, like, twice his age," Jena said.

"Last time, their situations were reversed. Hugh Two was sixty-seven," Nathaniel said.

"Ew. That's why she was so insistent on getting one her age this time," Zoe said. "Though I guess she's decided to take the new model for a spin after all."

Jena shuddered in disgust.

"It's just sex," Nathaniel said. "Trust me, it doesn't mean much to him. You read his biographies." He stared at his keyboard for a moment, head down. "I just don't want the Doc to get hurt. Again."

"Regardless of Dr. Kim's motives, we needed a Hugh Everett," Jena said. "So far, he's getting the job done. We should get back to work, too."

They didn't see Hugh or Dr. Kim again for the rest of the night.

CHAPTER 21

The next morning, Dr. Kim called for all hands on deck in the atrium. Ephraim, Zoe, and Jena gathered in front of the Large Coheron Drive, wondering what was going on.

"Maybe we're going on a mission," Ephraim said. He threaded the coin through his fingers in his pocket hopefully.

"Without any warning?" Jena said. "I bet they're sending us home." She twisted her fingers together and stared at the door to the LCD control room.

"You sound disappointed. I thought you wanted to go home," Zoe said.

"I do. But . . . I felt like I had something to contribute, you know?"

"Oh, I *know*," Zoe said.

"Are you implying something?" Jena asked.

"You've, uh, been spending a lot of time with Hugh," Ephraim said.

"So?" she asked.

"Forget it," Ephraim said.

He squinted at the LCD. The golden disc in the center was still horizontal, what he now associated with lockdown mode. It was ablaze with light, reflecting the morning sun from the skylight. Bands and speckles of sunlight danced on the drab walls of the courtyard as its second and third rings circled it steadily.

The middle ring wobbled, and there was an audible grinding sound each time the outer ring completed a circuit. Ephraim smelled the distinct odor of hot metal. How long could it labor like this?

The door at the main entrance opened, and Nathaniel came out, carrying a folded tripod over one shoulder with the camcorder slung over the other.

"Nathaniel!" Zoe called. "Do you know what's going on?"

"Your guess is as good as mine," he said.

"They didn't tell you what this is about?" Ephraim asked.

Nathaniel pushed out his lower lip. "I'm only an engineer, and today, a cameraman. Hugh's putting together some sort of demonstration. I'm sure it will be very impressive."

Nathaniel assembled the tripod directly in front of Atlas, about twenty feet away from the base of the LCD. He started screwing the camcorder into the tripod mount.

"Why do we need that?" Zoe asked. "There are cameras all over this courtyard."

"Dr. Kim ordered it." Nathaniel shrugged.

He opened the flip screen of the camcorder and checked the framing of his shot, just as the door to the control room opened. Hugh stepped out. Jena headed to meet him but stopped short when Dr. Kim appeared just behind him.

Hugh sauntered toward them. Something glinted in his right hand.

"Is that your controller?" Zoe asked Nathaniel.

Nathaniel pressed his lips tight together and nodded once.

"Good morning!" Hugh said. His voice bounced around the atrium. Dr. Kim didn't acknowledge them at all, as though they weren't even there.

"All set here, Mr. Everett," Nathaniel said. "You want me to start recording now?"

Hugh positioned himself between the camera and the LCD and flashed Nathaniel the thumbs-up.

Nathaniel tapped the camcorder's screen, and the red light on the front of the camera blinked on. Hugh was framed in the center of the tiny display. Atlas crouched over him, as if shielding him from an unseen danger above them. Dr. Kim stood just behind Hugh and to his right.

"Now then." Hugh swept his right hand back dramatically behind him and smacked Dr. Kim in the chest. She yelped.

Jena and Zoe snickered.

"Sorry, dear," Hugh said. Dr. Kim backed up a couple of feet.

Hugh cleared his throat. He gestured more carefully at the LCD behind him.

"The Large Coheron Drive is currently generating quantum interference patterns, dynamically adjusting to the superimposed wave functions of other universes. As long as the machine operates in this configuration, this universe will behave as a 'node,' a place of zero wave propagation. Essentially, we're preventing other universes from merging with this one by sending out equal and opposite quantum waves that cancel them out."

He glanced back at Dr. Kim. "My compliments to Jena for conceiving this ingenious stopgap, and to Nathaniel for his superior engineering skills. I couldn't have done it better myself."

Dr. Kim beamed.

"That's the first time any of the Everetts has shown any appreciation for me," Nathaniel murmured. Jena shushed him.

Hugh turned to face the machine, raising his voice. "However, inspired as it may be, this cannot be a long-term solution to what is happening to the multiverse. The problem is still out there, affecting all the other universes, but for the moment we're being spared its influence. Eventually, the drive will cease to function, as man and machine must, or we will encounter a universe that we can't cancel out, and something will make it through. The odds say this will likely happen soon."

He paced in front of the LCD with his arms clasped behind his back. Nathaniel hastily zoomed the camera out to keep him in frame.

"Since we're safe for the moment, right now our most pressing problem is ignorance. Simply put, we need more information. Fortunately, this is also the easiest problem to solve.

"I reviewed the reports that Nathaniel and Ephraim made on their experience in my universe when realities converged and altered the world of 1954 around us. What I found fascinating was the fact that I was completely unaware of any of these changes—I have to take their word for it that the Graduate College shifted location to the main campus at Princeton. I don't remember it any differently."

He paused to draw a cigarette from his breast pocket. Dr. Kim lit it with her silver Zippo. Hugh took a thoughtful pull on his cigarette.

"Think about that: An entire universe reshaped itself around me, and me with it," he said. "That realization is sobering. It also doesn't rule out the possibility that this sort of event has happened before without anyone noticing. Perhaps it is even a frequent occurrence.

"In fact, my theory is that very similar realities must merge once some sort of consensus has been reached—as a way to prune the branches of the growing multiverse, as it were. To test this supposition, I intend to initiate this process artificially."

Zoe sucked in a sharp breath.

"Is that a good idea?" Jena asked.

"Dr. Kim has convinced me that it is," Hugh said. "We need to observe this decoherence effect for ourselves in order to understand it, but our monitoring equipment—the coherence technology—prevents it. The presence of even the portable so-called Charon device makes it impossible for the universe to branch, which accounts for the relative lack of other universes where one of my analogs has developed the technology to visit other universes. And although the smaller units can't generate the same cancellation field that the LCD does, they do disrupt incoming waves enough to limit decoherence."

"Which means what?" Jena asked.

"You want to turn them all off," Zoe said. "Hugh, you *can't*."

Hugh pulled off his glasses and blinked at the camera.

"Of course not. That would be suicide." He chuckled. "Quantum suicide. That's an interesting thought."

"Then what are you proposing?" Zoe asked.

"Last night, Jena and I devised a startling experiment," Hugh said.

Ephraim looked sharply at Jena. She nodded in Dr. Kim's direction and shrugged.

"I barely had anything to do with it," Dr. Kim said humbly. "I just offered a few suggestions."

"I think best when voicing my ideas aloud," Hugh said. "An open ear can't be valued too much. Especially ears as lovely as yours," he said.

He glanced at Jena and smiled. "Yours as well." He turned to Zoe next. He turned away quickly when he saw her dour expression.

He returned to his starting point in front of the LCD. Nathaniel readjusted the camera.

"In fact, the idea had come to me earlier, but my subconscious needed some time, and the right words of inspiration, to work it out. What if we can filter selected universes out of the noise of the multiverse?" He let that question hang in the air for a moment. The LCD screeched behind him, and he flinched.

"What, indeed?" Ephraim murmured.

"Exactly," Hugh said.

"What?" Zoe said.

"Like tuning a radio to a certain frequency?" Jena asked.

"Yes! That's it exactly," Hugh said.

He whirled around and spread his hands wide in front of the LCD.

"Do you think he practiced this?" Zoe asked.

"Several times. Naked, in front of the mirror," Nathaniel said.

"I didn't need that image," Zoe said.

Jena blushed.

"Isn't the camera recording everything we say?" Ephraim asked.

"I hope so," Zoe said. She leaned close to the microphone and whispered, "Hugh Everett is a wanker."

"The idea is to isolate a single universe," Hugh said. "To allow it to interact with this one so we can observe what happens."

"*No*," Nathaniel said. He strode past the camera toward Hugh. Dr. Kim intercepted him and placed a hand on his chest.

"You said you weren't going to turn off the LCD," Ephraim said.

"There's no need for such a drastic measure. I've modified the LCD's software so we can select one universe in our database and allow its wave function to interact with this universe, while continuing to block out the rest."

"How did you reprogram software you were introduced to only a few days ago?" Zoe asked.

"His analog designed it in the first place," Nathaniel said.

"He was very organized. He left remarks throughout the code explaining every function. It was easy to pick up," Hugh said.

"This sounds dangerous," Jena said.

"If we can determine how the universes combine, learn how to control the process, we'll be one step closer to discovering a way to prevent it from happening. Permanently," Dr. Kim said.

"Trust me," Hugh said.

"You think this will work, Doc?" Nathaniel asked.

"I have complete faith in Hugh's expertise," Dr. Kim said.

"No offense, Hugh," Ephraim said. "But I think you're bluffing. When you first got here, you stood right where you are now and confessed that you have no idea how the LCD works or why any of this is happening. If you aren't absolutely sure of what you're doing, then we're taking an unnecessary risk."

"I'm prepared to give Hugh the benefit of the doubt," Jena said. "We have to try *something*. What could possibly go wrong?"

Ephraim, Zoe, and Nathaniel stared at Jena in shock.

"Why would you say something like that?" Ephraim asked.

"Amateur," Zoe said.

"In any event, it's too late." Hugh tugged the bottom of his suit vest to straighten it. "The experiment is already in progress."

He pressed a button on the controller, and the LCD shuddered to a halt. First the inner ring slowed to a stop, then the outer ring, with a horrible rending of metal against metal.

"I'd better take a look at that," Nathaniel said.

The sudden silence in the atrium was startling. When his ears adjusted, Ephraim heard only the tiny whirring of the camcorder.

They all looked around, waiting for something to happen.

Hugh walked toward the camera. "No, look at it through the camera. And keep rolling."

The six of them crowded around the camera as best they could, with Hugh, Nathaniel, and Dr. Kim in front. Jena leaned up on her toes with one hand on Hugh's shoulder. Ephraim and Zoe were able to snatch glimpses of the small screen by craning their necks to peer between the heads of the others.

Hugh extended the controller to Dr. Kim, and she pressed another button with a smile.

The shrieking sound of the LCD began again. Ephraim heard something crack and ping, and a gear dropped from somewhere and settled between Atlas's feet. Nathaniel looked at it worriedly.

"It'll hold," he said under his breath.

The disc in the center of the LCD laboriously turned itself over until the Everett Institute logo was facing down instead of up, and the rings began to rotate again, in opposite directions to each other. Soon they were moving quickly enough that Ephraim couldn't tell which way they were going. A breeze picked up, but it didn't seem related to the spinning bands of metal.

Ephraim smelled water and honeysuckle. It helped to calm the growing queasiness beginning in his stomach, which the others were also experiencing to varying degrees. Hugh was extremely pale, his face beaded with sweat and his shoulders slumping miserably.

The screen of the camera no longer showed the LCD but a smaller version of Atlas, supporting a basin that spilled water into a fountain. Ephraim looked around the atrium, but he couldn't see any quantum phantoms or images from the other universe with the naked eye.

"The Memorial Fountain," Jena said. "It's Greystone Park."

A figure wandered into frame.

"Ephraim . . ." Jena said.

Nathaniel and Jena moved aside to give Ephraim a better view of the screen. He leaned forward and saw a man approaching the fountain. At first he thought it was his father, but then the man turned his face, and Ephraim recognized it as an older version of himself.

Dr. Kim zoomed in the camera. The analog looked about twenty years older, hair thinning, a bit heavier, and with a scraggly beard.

"It's Ephraim," Dr. Kim said. She touched his face on the screen, and the display was momentarily obscured by a warped circular rainbow as she pressed her fingernail against it. She drew her hand back quickly as though she had been shocked.

The older Ephraim turned to look at them. Nathaniel zoomed the picture out again, and they saw that the analog was looking at someone else offscreen. The picture went black for a moment as the lens was obscured by a figure moving through it. Kim shivered as Ephraim was joined by another Jena Kim—the same age as the doctor. She was slimmer, in a pretty yellow sundress, and her long hair was pulled up in a high ponytail. She was laughing.

"Sound," Dr. Kim said.

Nathaniel pressed some buttons, but all they heard was a murky, garbled noise from the camera's small speaker.

"It's working," Hugh rasped. Ephraim heard surprise in the man's voice, and he gritted his teeth. Hugh hadn't been certain this was going to happen.

Hugh took quick, shallow breaths, his right hand clutching his stomach in pain.

"What are we looking at?" Zoe asked.

"This is a single universe overlapping with ours. We wait to see if anything changes," Dr. Kim said. "Here or there."

She fiddled with the controller, and the pitch of the spinning LCD changed subtly. Ephraim's stomach untwisted itself, and Hugh straightened, groaning with relief.

The older Ephraim put an arm around his Jena. Zoe drew a little closer to Ephraim, and he resisted the urge to mimic the motion. His analog reached into his pocket and pulled out a coin. He flipped it into the fountain.

"Make a wish," Zoe said. Her words matched the movement of the older Jena's lips.

A little boy with a bright-blue balloon appeared onscreen, walking along the edge of the fountain, his arms extended like airplane wings for balance.

"Oh," Jena said.

Ephraim's analog picked up the child, lifted him over his head, and lowered him between him and the other Jena.

"Shut it off," Dr. Kim said hastily.

"What, dear?" Hugh asked.

She brushed past him and walked toward the LCD. She stood in front of it, exactly where her other self stood. She reached out a hand toward where the other Ephraim's face would be if she could see him.

"Shut it off," Dr. Kim said again.

"Which? The camera or the LCD?" Nathaniel asked.

"Don't switch off the drive!" Zoe said with alarm.

Hugh pressed a button, and the rings on the LCD slowed. As the central disc turned over slowly to its original position, the outer ring screeched to a stop, then reversed direction to match the inner ring. Atlas shuddered from the sudden shift in balance and speed. It looked like the golden giant was shaking himself awake.

"That was interesting," Hugh said.

They watched the screen as the image from the other universe faded and the LCD and Dr. Kim took its place. And someone else.

"Um," Ephraim said. "I think—"

He was drowned out by a high-pitched scream. A child's shriek reverberated through the atrium. Ephraim clapped his hands over his ears and looked at the LCD.

The boy stared at Dr. Kim in terror. His blue balloon drifted up and toward the LCD. Somehow it navigated between the slowly turning rings without getting battered, crushed, or tangled. Its string caught for a moment, but the balloon tugged free again and continued its long, meandering journey up, up, up.

As the boy continued to scream, Ephraim tilted his head back and followed the balloon's course. It hit the skylight above them and bobbed around lazily until it settled in its exact center. The glass was pointed like a pyramid, Ephraim realized, not a flat square pane like he'd thought it was.

The boy bawled, backing away from Dr. Kim. "Mommy!" he cried.

Dr. Kim stood there stiffly, looking at the spot where Ephraim's older analog had been only a universe away. She didn't seem aware of what was going on.

Jena rushed over to the little boy, and his screams got even louder.

"Shh," Jena said. She crouched and opened her arms, making calming sounds. After a moment he allowed himself to be enfolded.

The boy quieted down, alternately gasping and sobbing. He buried his face in Jena's chest.

She rocked him gently from side to side, eyes closed. "It's okay. It'll all be okay," she said.

"That's a lie," Nathaniel said.

"Well, I'd call this a success," Hugh said.

"I do not think that word means what you think it means," Zoe said.

She joined Jena, and the boy looked between the two of them in wide-eyed wonder, still sniffling.

"What is this?" Dr. Kim asked, suddenly aware of the little boy standing at her feet.

The boy looked at her and screamed again.

"I am not your mother," she said. She looked up and repeated it more loudly. "I am not his mother."

"I think you'd better go," Zoe said. She crouched on the other side of the boy.

Dr. Kim nodded and walked toward the entrance to the Institute.

"What's your name, sweetie?" Jena asked.

"Doug," he said. He grabbed for her glasses. "Doug Kim Scott."

"Holy shit," Nathaniel said. His voice echoed loudly in the court-yard, even over the labored helicopter sound of the LCD.

"Language," Zoe said.

Ephraim approached them slowly. Up close, he noticed the boy had dark-brown hair like his and his mother's eyes. He looked about three or four years old. Doug looked up at him and screwed up his face.

"Daddy?" Doug said.

"Oh, boy," Ephraim said. He prepared for the boy to let loose another flood of tears, but Jena and Zoe kept him calm, while looking at Ephraim accusingly.

"Mazel tov," Nathaniel said.

"You know he isn't really my son," Ephraim said.

Zoe smiled. "Right, because you're a vir—"

"Daddy!" Doug said more confidently.

"Sort of, kid." Ephraim smiled.

"He's your spitting image, Ephraim," Nathaniel said. "Only smaller, cuter, and a quarter more Korean. He's probably smarter too."

"I know you want to see your parents," Jena said. "But we're going to take care of you for a little while, okay, Doug? We're your . . . babysitters."

Doug broke free of Jena and Zoe and ran toward Nathaniel. He tugged on his jacket.

"Yes?" Nathaniel asked.

"Up!" Doug extended his hands upward.

Nathaniel bent and lifted the boy up on his shoulders. Doug reached his arms higher. "I lost my balloon," he said.

"We'll get you another one," Nathaniel said. "We'll get you a whole bunch of balloons. Just don't cry again. Deal?"

"I want that one," Doug said, pointing at the one stuck at the top of the atrium.

"This is the strangest thing I've ever seen," Ephraim said.

"He's adorable," Jena said.

"I guess." Zoe stuffed her fingers into the pockets of her shorts and avoided looking at Ephraim.

"Can we get him back?" Dr. Kim said to no one in particular. She stood in the open door of the control room, staring up at the balloon bobbing gently at the top of the atrium.

"I don't know if we can send him back," Hugh said. "I'll have to study this data extensively."

"Not the boy," Dr. Kim said. "Ephraim. He was right there. Can you bring him back here?"

Hugh frowned. "We already have an Ephraim," he said.

Dr. Kim looked at Ephraim. "Yes, we do. Work on it, Mr. Everett," she said.

Hugh was taken aback at her businesslike tone.

"Let me know if the situation—or anything else—changes. I need to lie down," she said.

She shuffled into the building with her head down.

"So. What do we do with Doug?" Ephraim asked.

"Well, I have a lot of work to do," Hugh said, edging toward his lab. "Jena, when you have a moment, I could use your help."

"I'll be right there," she said.

"What do you think, Eph?" Zoe said.

"We should take him home. We know which universe he came from." Ephraim pulled the coin out of the pocket of his jeans and looked at it doubtfully.

"Keep it in your pants," Nathaniel said.

"Too late for that!" Zoe said, pointing to Doug and grinning.

"No way you're using that coin. After what we just saw, we are not taking any more stupid chances with this universe or any other," Nathaniel said.

"He's got your DNA, Eph. You take care of him," Zoe said.

"He has your DNA too!" Ephraim said.

Jena crossed her arms and arched an eyebrow at him.

Nathaniel swung Doug down and dropped him between Ephraim and Zoe. He ruffled the boy's hair, and Doug ducked away, laughing.

"I have a job for you two," Nathaniel said.

Ephraim and Zoe exchanged apprehensive looks over Doug's head.

CHAPTER 22

"How did *we* become the most useless people on this team?" Ephraim asked.

He was pushing a half-full shopping cart around the Stop n' Shop. Doug, seated in the rear basket, was reaching out to grab every brightly colored package they passed. Zoe followed behind with a small tablet displaying Nathaniel's grocery list, grabbing boxes from Doug and placing them back on the shelves.

It felt like they were playing an all-too-realistic game of house; Doug was an analog of the son Ephraim and Zoe *could* have together. Ephraim was surprised that he didn't mind the idea that much.

"We're serving a very important purpose," Zoe said. "Distraction for the boy."

"Keeping him out of everyone's hair, you mean?" Ephraim dropped five boxes of dry pasta in the cart.

"No. Doug just went through something horrific. I'd be traumatized if I were him. He needs to be doing something normal. And what's more normal than shopping for groceries?"

"With younger versions of your parents," Ephraim said. "In another universe. That's *so* normal."

Zoe shrugged. "I used to love shopping with my dad."

A happy memory suddenly surfaced: young Ephraim sitting in a shopping basket, his mom and dad laughing together.

"At least seeing us doesn't make him scream. I think he likes us," Zoe said. She lowered her face to Doug's, so their noses were almost touching. "You like us, Doug?"

He grabbed her glasses from her face and hurled them over her head. His peals of laughter made other shoppers look their way.

She sighed. "Those are antiques, Doug," she said.

She went to retrieve her glasses from a bin of GenMod apples.

When she came back to the cart, she held two bags of gummy bears, one in each hand.

"If you want to be useful, you can make a big decision," she said.

"What?" Ephraim asked.

Zoe held up the bags. "Haribo Gold or store brand?" She lifted her left hand and lowered her right, then lifted the right and lowered the left, like she was weighing them on a scale.

Ephraim studied his choices with his hand on his chin. "Stop n' Shop gummy bears are two dollars cheaper."

"Yes, they are. They're *very* cheap," she said.

"Uh-huh. Well, just get them both."

"You can't have both, Ephraim! You have to pick one."

"Okay, okay. But I don't even want gummy bears."

"Pretend that you do."

"Fine. It isn't our money, so get the more expensive ones."

"Price isn't the point."

Doug reached out to grab the Haribo bag, but Zoe held it over his head, just out of reach.

"Don't taunt him," Ephraim said. "Put them both in the cart and we'll figure it out later. Sheesh."

Zoe tossed the bags into the cart, pouting.

"Okay," Ephraim said. "Good. I don't even remember seeing those on the list."

"Oh. I'm sure someone wanted them." Zoe put the tablet in her back pocket.

"'Someone,' huh?"

She smiled. "I love gummy bears. They make everything better."

"In that case . . ." Ephraim added another bag of them to the cart. "How many gummy bears do we have to throw at the multiverse to fix it?"

Zoe stared at the extra bag. "You do prefer store brand," she said in a wounded voice.

He sighed and pushed the cart down the aisle. Doug twisted around and grabbed for more candy.

"Doug, stop wiggling," Ephraim said. One of the wheels of the cart got jammed, and he yanked it loose. "You'd think they'd have hover carts or something in the future."

"This place hasn't changed much," Zoe said.

It was almost indistinguishable from the store his mother worked in—a tiny piece of Summerside frozen in time while skyscrapers, condos, subways, and strip malls had sprouted around it. This was the only time he hadn't felt completely out of place in this universe, but he couldn't tell if it was because he was shopping, or because he was shopping with Zoe.

Maybe he'd needed to do something completely normal too; he often picked up groceries for him and his mother. She'd said she didn't want to bring her work home with her.

Was Madeline Scott still in this future? His analog's mother would be in her seventies by now. What did she think her son was doing? Did she know he was dead? Maybe she'd like to meet her grandson-who-might-have-been, and a strangely young version of her own son.

Zoe picked up a jar of peanut butter and tilted her head. "Does Jena have any food allergies?"

"You'd know better than I would," Ephraim said. "I think she doesn't like some fruits. Wait, why?"

"No reason," she said quickly. "Hey, do you realize how much power we have right now? Whatever we buy, they have to eat. We could chuck the list and just bring back fifty boxes of Twinkies." Zoe tossed three boxes of Twinkies into the cart.

"You're going to be an awesome mom one day," Ephraim said.

She opened one of the boxes and gave a Twinkie to Doug. He bit into it happily, smearing white cream all over his nose and chin. Ephraim grimaced.

As they moved down the frozen food section, a middle-aged woman with a red shopping basket followed Ephraim with her eyes.

Zoe rummaged in one of the freezers and dumped five boxes of fish sticks into the cart.

"Who are these for?" Ephraim said.

"Who do you think?" Zoe asked.

"Doug?" Ephraim asked.

Doug stuck his tongue out and blew a raspberry. Bits of Twinkie sprayed everywhere.

"Nice." Ephraim brushed the crumbs off his T-shirt.

"Nathaniel likes them," Zoe said. She tapped the screen of the tablet to cross fish sticks off the list. "Now we just need a box of wine."

"Aisle Seven," he said. He guided the cart around a corner, narrowly missing a cart with a little girl sitting in the back. Doug and the girl smiled at each other as Ephraim headed for the beer and wine section.

"Did you see that?" Zoe asked. "They start young."

"Speaking of young: Will they sell alcohol to us?" he asked.

"I saw a sign. The drinking age in this universe is eighteen," Zoe said. "And marijuana's legal. Somehow it's less appealing when you aren't breaking any laws."

"That reminds me: belated happy birthday." Jena had turned eighteen two weeks before prom.

Zoe picked up a six-pack of Summerside Special beer and raised it to him. "Cheers."

"Put it back, Zoe," Ephraim said.

"My ID, my beer," she said.

"Didn't your license expire like seventeen years ago?"

Zoe fixed her eyes on him for a long, terrible moment. She put the beer back on the refrigerator shelf.

"I should have borrowed Dr. Kim's," she said. "No wine, then." She deleted it from the list.

A camera flash went off. Ephraim saw an elderly man aiming his wristcom at them, about to take another picture. The man quickly lowered his arm and pushed his cart in the opposite direction.

"What is going on?" Ephraim murmured. "People keep staring at me."

"Maybe they think you're someone else," Zoe said.

"My analog hasn't been around for over a decade." Ephraim ran a hand through his hair. "Whatever. Did we get everything?" he asked.

Everything on Zoe's list was crossed off. "Yup," she said.

Ephraim aimed the cart for the bank of checkout machines. They were all self-serve. There wasn't a single human employee in sight. A seven-foot-tall blue robot that looked like a refrigerator on tank treads was restocking a display with cans it pulled from inside itself. Some things had changed here, after all.

"Let's go," he said.

"Ephraim, wait." Zoe grabbed his arm. Cold air from the cooler washed over them. Goose pimples dotted her bare forearm. Did Jena have that mole there, just above her right wrist?

"I have to ask you something important," she said.

Ephraim looked pointedly at the shoppers around them.

"Here?" he asked.

"Before we get back to Crossroads. Before I lose my nerve." He'd never known Zoe to be nervous about anything. She took a deep breath and let it out. It misted in the refrigerated air.

"Ephraim . . ." She put her hands on her hips. "Seriously? You're staring at my boobs?"

"What?" he asked. "I'm not—" He was. She'd forgotten her hoodie, and her tank top was eminently more fascinating at the moment, thanks to the cold temperature. "Sorry. Was that your question?"

"No. Hold on," she said.

She put her hands over Doug's ears. He giggled and closed his eyes.

"So why haven't you slept with Jena yet?" Zoe asked.

"Huh?"

"Simple question," she said.

"Yeah, but it's also blunt. And unexpected." Which described Zoe perfectly. "You know what? I'm not having this conversation."

He yanked the cart toward the checkout machine and started running items through the barcode scanner and dropping them on the scale.

"Jena and I have talked about you," Zoe said. "At length."

"I am shocked by this startling revelation," Ephraim said. He dropped a can of peas. It rolled under the machine. He decided to leave it there.

"I assumed Jena was holding out on you. She seemed like the type. But she says *you* wanted to wait. That sounded so improbable, I was certain she was making it up."

Ephraim's eyes flicked to Doug.

Doug put his own hands over his ears and grinned, his eyes flitting between Ephraim and Zoe. The kid was going to need therapy one day.

"He doesn't know what we're talking about," Zoe said.

"I'm not sure I do either," Ephraim said. He put down a box of generic corn flakes and looked at Zoe. "Fine. You know we were planning to do it the night of prom."

"Jena said she was ready to have sex months ago and she gave you plenty of hints. Even you can't be that clueless. I'm curious why you didn't jump her bones at your earliest opportunity."

"She was telling the truth. I wanted to wait," Ephraim said.

"You wanted it to be special?" Zoe asked.

"Yeah, of course. Duh. But that wasn't it." He met Zoe's eyes. A serious question deserved a serious answer.

"Giving Jena the coin meant admitting I would never travel to another universe again," he said. "Sleeping with her . . . was admitting I would never see you again." He gripped the handle of the cart. His slick palms slipped on the glossy plastic. "I wasn't ready for that."

"Oh," Zoe said.

She numbly picked up a box of macaroni and cheese and pulled it against her chest instead of running it through the scanner.

"Happy now?" he asked. He grabbed the box from her and scanned it. He fed a couple more boxes through the machine without noticing what they were.

"Yes," she said.

Ephraim looked up. She had a goofy grin on her face.

"Are you okay?" he asked.

"I love you," Zoe said. "For what that's worth." She pushed her hair back from her face and suddenly found something intensely interesting about the rear wheels of the shopping cart.

When he was with Zoe, he only wanted to be with Zoe. But when he was with Jena, sometimes—it was less often, now, but it still happened sometimes—he thought about Zoe. If he really thought about it honestly, if he had to make a decision right now . . .

"I love you, too," he said.

Her head snapped up. "That was fast. You're not saying it because I said it, right? Like an automatic response that you didn't think about before you opened your mouth? I know you have that problem, saying whatever comes into your head, but it isn't supposed to work that way. Don't just say it because it's what I want to hear. Only if you mean it—"

"Zoe!" Ephraim said. "I mean it. I didn't have to think about it because it's what I feel. What I've felt since I first saw you at the fountain last year."

"When you thought I was Jena," she said.

"I only thought that until you kissed me, thinking I was your Ephraim. You're a very good kisser."

They looked at each other.

"I might have waited too long to tell you that," Zoe said.

"To tell me what?" Ephraim smiled.

"I love you," she repeated.

"Yes," Ephraim said. "You waited too long, but it isn't too late."

"So what do we do now?" Zoe asked. She leaned over the cart between them. He did not look down her shirt, except once, very quickly.

"Kiss!" Doug said.

"Don't encourage us," Zoe said. "Wait a minute. Kid, can you hear what we're saying?"

Doug shook his head, hands still over his ears.

"Hmmm," Zoe said. She flipped a panel up on the front of the child seat to reveal a video screen. A 3-D cartoon came up. Doug's eyes glazed over instantly. She pulled out the attached earbuds and poked them into his ears.

"Should he be watching that?" Ephraim asked.

"Sure. That's what it's for. Where were we? Oh, yeah. 'Kiss.'" She leaned toward Ephraim.

"Uh. There's just one thing," he said.

Zoe sighed and stood straight. "Jena."

"It's awkward," he said. "I sort of love her, too."

"You can't love both of us."

"I do."

"No, I mean you aren't allowed to if you want to be in a relationship with me. Maybe that's selfish or narrow-minded, but it's the way I am."

"I'm just being honest, Zoe. I love her, but I don't want to be with her. I want to be with you."

Her stupid smile was back.

"Jena and I are good together," Ephraim said. "I know I could be happy with her. I *am* happy with her. Or I was."

Zoe's smile faded.

Doug handed Ephraim the bag of apples from the cart, and he put it on the scale. He pressed a button on the touchscreen to accept the price.

"It takes effort though, for me at least," Ephraim said. "It's not as easy as it is with you."

"You think I'm easy." Zoe frowned her disapproval.

"No, I'm more comfortable with you."

"You find me *comfortable?*" She was only teasing him.

"Come on! I mean you and I fit better." He rolled his eyes. "We belong together."

"Does Jena know?" Zoe asked.

"She suspects," Ephraim said.

Zoe started bagging their groceries while Ephraim emptied the cart.

"She knew it before we did," Zoe said. "That isn't your fault. But you have to talk to her before we . . ."

"I know. Notice how I'm not kissing you right now?"

"Sadly, yes." She pouted. "You would have banged her eventually?"

"Oh, yeah," Ephraim said. "Definitely. I'm not that virtuous."

"Then you might like to know that my Ephraim and I had sexual relations. *Constantly*," Zoe said.

"Good for you," Ephraim said. He clenched his hands.

"Um, you're not supposed to squeeze bread," Zoe said.

Ephraim dropped the squashed loaf to the side of the checkout counter. The soft white bread slowly regained some of its shape.

"In my universe, you can't afford to wait for the good stuff. You might not live long enough," Zoe said.

"It's fine," he said.

"No regrets?" Zoe asked.

He shook his head. "Despite the strong motivation, talking to Jena's going to be difficult. All this time I've been insisting she's wrong about us, but she was right all along. Having that conversation might be the hardest thing I've ever had to do."

"Including that time you stopped Nate from terrorizing the multiverse?"

"We did that. Together," Ephraim said. "And it was much easier, in retrospect."

The last items in the cart were the three bags of gummy bears. He stared at them.

"I get it now," he said. "You're the Haribo brand!"

"You're cute, but you're kind of slow sometimes, Ephraim," Zoe said. He felt an eerie sense of déjà vu; another of her analogs had said that to him once before.

Ephraim handed the bag of Haribo gummies to Zoe and left the other two bags on the side for the robot to re-shelve.

Zoe tapped Nathaniel's credit card against the screen and paid the bill. Ephraim loaded the cart with their bagged groceries. He looped his fingers through the wire mesh of the cart and looked at Zoe solemnly.

"There's still one significant problem," Ephraim said.

"The end of the multiverse." Zoe shrugged. "One issue at a time."

"And even if we fix that, we still come from different universes."

"Here's a wild thought: We could just enjoy being together for now." She walked backward, pulling the cart with her. Ephraim's fingers were still threaded into the metal, so he went with them. Doug laughed. He liked going backward.

They pushed the cart out of the store. Ephraim blinked in the bright sunlight, and sweat formed as soon as he left the refrigerated comfort of the Stop n' Shop. He pulled his fingers free from the cart and massaged them.

She took his hands. "We can at least have lots of sex. After you dump your girlfriend."

Ephraim widened his eyes. "But that would make you a felon. I'm still a minor."

"Not in this universe." She flashed him a wicked grin.

"Kiss!" Doug said.

CHAPTER 23

As soon as Ephraim, Zoe, and Doug returned to Crossroads, Ephraim went looking for Jena at Everett's lab. He wanted to get this over with.

She was leaning against Hugh's desk with a hand draped over his shoulder while he typed at his keyboard. He murmured something in a low voice. She laughed.

"Jena?" Ephraim said.

Jena jumped. She looked at Ephraim guiltily. She pulled away from Hugh and clasped her arms around herself.

"Ephraim!" Jena said. "You're back."

"Sorry to interrupt," Ephraim said.

"Nonsense. Come in," Hugh said. "I've been waiting for you."

"You have?" Ephraim and Jena asked.

"You didn't get my message?" Hugh asked. "I told Nathaniel to send you here as soon as you got back."

"I haven't seen him. I came straight here," Ephraim said.

"Doesn't matter. I need a helping hand and only yours will do." Hugh turned to Jena. "Dear, could you give us some privacy?"

"Sure," Jena said. She looked at Ephraim questioningly.

"Um, Zoe could probably use some help with the groceries," Ephraim said. "She has her hands full with Doug."

"I thought he'd get tired out from shopping," Jena said.

"He might have if he hadn't eaten three Twinkies."

"Ephraim!"

Jena walked toward the door. Hugh patted her on the rear and she slapped his hand away.

"What did I say about that?" she said.

"Force of habit." He smiled.

"I thought you learned quickly," she said. "Some genius."

"I am who I am, darling."

"Work on that," she said. She hid a small smile from him, but Ephraim saw it.

She stopped to give Ephraim a kiss, but he turned his head slightly so her lips only brushed his cheek.

"Eph?" Jena said.

"We have to talk," he said softly. "Later. When I'm done here, I'll find you."

She steadied her eyes on him. Then she brushed past Ephraim, and after a long pause, he heard the door close behind him.

"Ephraim, pull up a stool," Hugh said.

"I'd rather stand," Ephraim said.

"You've got a bee in your bonnet."

"I don't even know what that means." He stared at the closed door. He wanted to go after Jena. "What can I help you with?"

"She's a bright and beautiful woman. I've never met anyone like her before," Hugh said.

Ephraim laughed. "That's funny, considering how many Kim analogs we have in one place."

Hugh lit a cigarette and regarded Ephraim carefully. "And yet Jena isn't anything like Dr. Kim or Zoe. You see that, don't you?"

Ephraim nodded. "I thought you and Dr. Kim were . . ."

"I like women," Hugh said. "I simply used her in the same way she wanted to use me. It was consensual, no strings attached, cosmic or otherwise. And it was lovely. It's just sex, Ephraim." Hugh tapped the ash from his cigarette into an ashtray.

"It's more than sex to her," Ephraim said.

"Dr. Kim was only trying to recapture what she had with my predecessor." Hugh blew smoke from the side of his mouth. "Or were you referring to Jena?"

Ephraim remained silent.

"You're lucky, Ephraim. Jena's in love with you. She's made that quite clear." Hugh examined the glowing tip of his cigarette. "How serious would you say you are about her?"

"That's none of your business," Ephraim said.

"It could be."

"If you're trying to justify flirting with her—" Ephraim said.

"I don't need justification or your permission," Hugh said. "Only hers. I make no apologies for my behavior. Except to her."

"Good luck with that, *Pudge.*"

Hugh scowled. "Where did you hear that?"

Ephraim waved a hand carelessly. "I read it somewhere. Biographers know everything about you here, including your nickname."

"I've always despised that name." Hugh stood up from his chair. "I deserved that, though." He pulled off his glasses and rubbed his eyes wearily. "I've been at this for too long. I'm sorry. I'm under quite a bit of stress, and if I can be truthful, I may have overestimated my ability to understand all this. Jena has been the one bright spot about this whole situation."

"I know what you mean," Ephraim said.

"I'd like to be friends with you," Hugh said.

"'Friend' might be too optimistic, but I'll try. For the sake of the multiverse," Ephraim said.

"Good man. You'll see in a moment that we have no choice but to work together. Follow me."

Hugh led Ephraim to a workbench at the back of the laboratory. There was a dusty file box labeled "Top Secret" in black marker.

"That's a great way to prevent prying." Ephraim looked inside the carton and found an old tape recorder and a locked metal box with an index card taped to the top of it, bearing a handwritten note in tiny letters.

Ephraim picked up the metal box. It beeped softly at his touch, and a light on top turned green.

"Ah," Hugh said. "Excellent."

"Biometric scanner?" Ephraim asked. The box was about the size of a doorstopper novel. He turned it over. Something rattled inside.

He read aloud from the yellowing card taped to it: "'Do not open until Doomsday.'" He tried to lift the lid, but it was still locked. He jiggled it in case it was only stuck, but it stayed closed.

He put the box down on the bench. It beeped again, and the green light faded away.

"I guess they're serious," Ephraim said. He tapped the note thoughtfully. Something about it bugged him.

"Someone may have had an odd sense of humor," Hugh said. "Though the end of the multiverse would qualify."

Ephraim picked up a pencil and a scrap of paper from the lab table. He scribbled on the page for a moment, stared at what he'd written, and then passed it to Hugh.

Hugh held Ephraim's note next to the one on the box to compare the handwriting.

"A perfect match," Hugh said. "You're either a master forger, or that's—"

"My analog's handwriting," Ephraim said. He dropped the pencil on the floor and stepped away from the table. "What's the deal?"

"The deal is that this universe's Ephraim and one of my predecessors wanted to be very certain that only they could access whatever's inside this box. It's coded to open only at their touch."

"Or two of their analogs," Ephraim said.

"We're both keys," Hugh said.

Ephraim grinned. He was needed after all. Even if it was just to open a box.

"What do you suppose is in there?" Ephraim asked.

"Hope, perhaps," Hugh said. "There's a simple way to find out."

Hugh placed his left hand on the left corner of the lid. The box beeped, and a light on his side turned green.

Ephraim put his right hand on the right edge. The box beeped, and another green light flashed.

The lid unlatched. They lifted it together.

The box contained a black foam rectangle that was flush with its sides. A smaller one-inch-deep rectangle had been cut into the middle of the foam, with an audiocassette nestled in the cushioned hollow. "Play Me" was written on its label in fading pencil in handwriting Ephraim didn't recognize.

"What is that?" Hugh asked.

Ephraim glanced at him in surprise. "It's a cassette. A way of storing audio on a strip of magnetic tape."

"Like reel-to-reel tape," Hugh said, his voice filled with wonder. He picked up the cassette delicately between his index finger and thumb and examined it. "I heard someone was working on this. But I never dreamed it could become so compact."

"The Summerside Library has a ton of audiotapes like this in storage. But the format's way old-school, even in 2012. I mean, *vintage*. In my universe, anyway."

"My other self resisted change as he got older," Hugh said. He rubbed his thumb across the label. "This is our handwriting."

"At least he left us a way to follow his instruction." Ephraim pulled the tape recorder out of the cardboard box, its purpose now clear.

He plugged the device into an outlet on the lab table. He pressed the black button marked "Eject," and the tape deck popped open. He took the cassette from Hugh and inserted it in the machine open end first, with the "Play Me" side facing up. It didn't fit.

Ephraim rotated the cassette so the tape end faced out and tried again. It slid in easily. He pushed the deck down until it clicked closed.

"Should we get the others?" Ephraim asked.

"This was meant for the two of us," Hugh said. "Let's listen to it before we decide whether to share it with a broader audience."

"I don't know," Ephraim said.

"We don't have much control in this situation, Ephraim. But knowledge is power, and I won't give up that advantage easily."

Ephraim hesitated, then nodded his assent.

They pulled two stools over to the table and settled in front of the tape recorder. Hugh lit another cigarette and puffed on it, staring at the tape recorder intensely.

Ephraim pressed "Play."

CHAPTER 24

The tape played the soft hiss of air and a series of clicks and pops. A man cleared his throat. Then Ephraim heard Hugh's voice.

"This is Hugh Everett III. I am eighty-eight years old as of the date of this recording, August 12, 2019."

The recorded voice sounded rougher and more tired than that of the younger man sitting next to Ephraim. "The first thing you should know is: I'm a fraud."

Ephraim and Hugh exchanged curious looks.

"People credit me with the theory of many worlds, but the proof that they exist found *me*," Everett's voice said.

Hugh gripped the seat of his stool with both hands and leaned closer to the tiny speaker, tipping his head with his eyes closed as though praying.

"It took seventeen years for me to unravel the secrets of wave harmonics and develop a machine that could generate the quantum vibrations necessary to reach other worlds. But the coheron drive, my life's work, was nearly useless.

"Rather than creating a two-way door between universes, as I had intended, it simply made things . . . disappear. Like half of a magic trick. We didn't know where the objects went, or *if* they went anywhere at all. And if they were not destroyed, as my critics claimed, we had no way to bring them back.

"Even if someone were foolish enough to step inside the machine, we would never be able to learn what he found on the other side, if he survived the trip. My crowning achievement was a failure.

"We sent recorded messages into the machine, in every media format and language known on our world, in the hopes that another Earth with the same technology would be able to respond. What you don't know is that one day, we got an answer."

The voice paused. Ephraim heard the clink of ice in a glass and a match being struck.

"You won't read anything about this in any history books, or even in my autobiography. Only a handful of people, sworn to secrecy, know about the small metal capsule that appeared at the base of our gyroscope, in the exact spot from which we'd sent our own probe. The cylindrical container was of an alloy that included elements not found on this planet, at least not in this reality. Inside was a metal disc the size of a quarter, made of the same material. It was suspended in a Meissner-Ochsenfeld field, releasing a steady amount of heat and harmless EM radiation."

"Uh-oh," Ephraim said.

"Shh," Hugh said.

Everett wheezed and started coughing. Ephraim heard fumbling at the microphone then a loud click and a second of silence before the sound resumed.

"Ephraim Scott," Everett intoned.

The back of Ephraim's neck crawled.

"Everyone knows the name of the first man from our world to visit another Earth," the recording continued.

"I'm famous?" Ephraim asked. That was why everyone in the supermarket had been staring at him. He must have looked similar enough to his analog to make people notice, even after all this time.

He heard liquid splash into a glass and the clink of ice and crystal. Everett sipped at his drink and his voice rasped.

"But his first trip didn't happen the way you heard. In fact, it happened a year before the public demonstration we staged, and it was entirely an accident." Everett laughed. "Just like many great scientific discoveries.

"You see, Mr. Scott was studying the capsule in my laboratory late one night when instruments detected that his scans were disrupting the magnetic field. When the disc began to fall, he instinctively reached out and caught it. And disappeared.

"Footage from surveillance cameras revealed that at the moment the disc landed in his hand, he was transported elsewhere. A spike registered by the coheron drive left no doubt that he had gone to another universe.

"Three days later, he phoned me from Seattle.

"He refused to say where he had been or how he'd gotten to the Pacific Northwest—he would only tell me in person. I picked him up myself in our private jet. On the way home, Mr. Scott told me he had been to a universe on the brink of death. An advanced human civilization had been trying to contact their ancestors in a parallel timeline, so that our universe might avoid their fate.

"I might have thought Mr. Scott was attempting an elaborate hoax, but he brought back more than a wild story. He delivered the key to interdimensional travel: a *portable* coheron drive, which negated the need for a machine in the destination universe to enable a return trip. I had considered that as a solution, of course, but it's impossible to build one with the technology available today. It would be like trying to manufacture a wrist-computer in 1910. Even if you had detailed schematics or a working device, you need the intervening one hundred and nine years of industrial, scientific, and technological advancement just to fashion the parts you need and understand how to put them together.

"Mr. Scott explained that the 'transhumans' who summoned him had been waiting for a younger world to discover interdimensional travel so they could help us move forward.

"Though anything that *can* happen in the multiverse necessarily *does* happen, the probability of that event can be infinitely close to impossible. Our universe was the only one in all the multiverse that discovered coherence at a critical turning point in history. According to the transhumans, man's ultimate role in the cosmos is being determined *right now*, in every choice we make as a race.

"If our technology grows *too* quickly, beyond our ability to use it intelligently and morally, then probability dictates that we will destroy the planet or kill ourselves off. If our technological and sociological development lags too far behind, our universe will begin to burn out before we can transcend to the next level—just as it did for the transhumans. As Goldilocks would say, this universe, this particular moment in time, is 'just right.' And with the transhumans' gift, we remain on track for our great destiny."

"No pressure," Ephraim said.

Hugh looked at him sternly over his glasses. He'd picked up that mannerism from one of the Jenas, Ephraim was sure of it.

"Mr. Scott and I agreed not to reveal the true origin of the device, to give mankind the best chance at achieving its best possible future. But he had two conditions: He wanted to use the device to visit as many other universes as we could find that were like ours. According to the transhumans, recording the coordinates of other universes with the controller affords them permanence in the ever-changing multiverse and links them to our own. When our descendants millennia from now reach what some call the Omega point—the transition from corporeal life to noncorporeal existence—all the universes we've visited will make that final journey with us."

Hugh widened his eyes.

"This seems a frivolous use of the technology to me, but since the coin was configured to respond only to Mr. Scott's touch, and currently only he is able to assign new users, I had little choice. In return for my endorsement and his continued employment here, he has graciously authorized me to use the coin as well," Everett said.

Ephraim frowned. Hugh shot him a disconcerting look.

"He similarly programmed the controller to work only for his friend Nathaniel Mackenzie—his second condition," Everett said. "This seemed like a sensible security measure, and in return I gained the benefits of Mr. Mackenzie's loyalty and expertise. He has already modified what he's now calling the Large Coheron Drive to match the functionality of the portable unit."

The older Everett drank, then coughed violently. He slammed his glass down with a thud and a clatter of ice.

"We are still unable to replicate the coin, and I'm running out of time to continue this phase of my work. I've decided to recruit someone to replace me. And I can think of no one better than myself." He chuckled. "One day you will hear this tape and you will know the truth. It's up to a younger mind than mine to figure out what to do with it. Don't make the same mistakes I did."

The recording stopped, and a couple of seconds later the machine clicked and the "Play" button sprang up.

Hugh jumped. "Don't stop there!"

"The tape ended," Ephraim said.

Hugh let out a long breath and ran his hand through his hair.

"He was so hard on himself," Ephraim said.

His mind spun, trying to figure out his analog's part in all of this. He'd set all these events into motion. He'd been complicit in Hugh's decision to keep the origin of the coheron drive a secret and use it with no consideration about the consequences, on the word of strangers who had essentially abducted him. What had he seen in that other universe?

"The first Everett was a failure," Hugh said. "And he had to live with that every day. No wonder I couldn't find any notes on the Charon device—he was taking credit for technology from the future. On one level, I understand why my analog did that. I hate the thought of only achieving mediocrity. But lying about it . . . I'm disturbed that I'm capable of that."

"Join the club. I've had analogs like that," Ephraim said. Nothing bared the soul more than seeing the choices your other selves made— and the consequences. "Just keep in mind that you aren't him. You shared the same potential, but your actions, your beliefs, your choices make you different. You can follow the same path and lead someone else's life, or make your own course."

Hugh nodded. "Your analog went along with this when he could have taken the device and claimed it as his own discovery."

"He didn't want the responsibility," Ephraim said. "Or the attention. I think he just wanted to help people, help them to transcend to this other plane of existence."

"Assuming that those transhumans were honest with him. Or that he was honest with Everett," Hugh said.

"You're a very suspicious man," Ephraim said.

"It's no worse than being *too* trusting," Hugh said.

"Was there anything else in the box?" Ephraim asked.

Hugh pulled up the foam from the lockbox, but there was nothing under it. Ephraim turned over the cardboard box and shook it out, but it was empty.

"You still want to share this tape?" Hugh asked.

"I don't know," Ephraim said. "I think there are too many secrets around here already."

"I'm very close to figuring this out. I just need more time. Maybe we don't need to spoil Dr. Everett's legacy," Hugh said.

"There's a lot more than his reputation at stake," Ephraim said. "Dr. Kim told us that the second Everett insisted on trying to build a portable device of his own—out of pride. But if he heard this tape, he knew that it was an impossible task."

"And he was trying to buy himself time to figure it out. Like I wanted to."

"When he failed, it killed him," Ephraim said.

Hugh shook his head. "'Don't make the same mistakes I did.'"

Ephraim ejected the tape from the deck. "I can't figure out why he and Ephraim left this for both of us," he said. "I should at least tell Nathaniel. He'd want to know about his best friend."

"His 'best friend' decided not to share any of this with him. Just be careful. Nathaniel is loyal to Dr. Kim, and who knows how she would react to all of this."

"If you don't trust her, why are you helping her?"

"I'm placing my bet on the winning side. She is determined to keep this universe alive, and I plan to be in it when she succeeds. You're a survivor, too, Ephraim. Just don't do anything foolish."

"Excellent advice," Dr. Kim said.

Ephraim and Hugh turned. Dr. Kim and Nathaniel were standing at the front of the lab, watching them.

Ephraim stood. "Uh. How long have you been standing there?" He casually slipped the cassette into his back pocket.

"We heard everything," Nathaniel said in a grim voice. He glanced up at the ceiling.

Ephraim saw a camera above the workbench. And another one in the corner. Everett had mentioned that the lab had surveillance cameras in his recording, but he didn't know Dr. Kim had been monitoring them.

"Smile. You're on *Candid Camera*," Dr. Kim said.

"We're as surprised by this tape as you are, Jena," Hugh said.

"It's Dr. Kim from now on, Mr. Everett," she said. "I'm disappointed that you were going to keep this to yourselves."

"I just need a little more information," Hugh said. "I'm almost there. I can almost taste the solution to all of this. The first Hugh said that the universes are linked to this one, that we all share the same fate—"

"It's already too late," Dr. Kim said. "I realized something after our experiment earlier."

"What's that?" Ephraim asked.

She lit a cigarette and approached Ephraim.

"I think the other Ephraim we saw, your older analog, might have merged into this universe if you didn't have that coin. Instead we got that little brat."

"His name is Doug," Ephraim said.

"Doug, Cousin Oliver, whatever." She waved her cigarette carelessly. "At least his unexpected appearance told me that my backup plan is going to work."

"No." Hugh stood. "You can't."

"What?" Ephraim asked.

"You wanted that other reality to merge with this one," Hugh said to her. "You used me."

"You said it yourself, *darling*. We used each other," Dr. Kim said. "He belongs here."

"Who?" Ephraim asked.

"Ephraim," she said. Frustration was creeping into her voice.

"*I'm* Ephraim," he said.

"You're the wrong one," Dr. Kim said.

"So is that other guy!" Ephraim said. "You can't replace the one you lost, Dr. Kim. You saw them in the camera. The other Ephraim and Jena are happy together. At least they were until their kid was pulled out of their universe." He paused. "Face it: You missed your chance."

"*This* is my chance. The one I've been waiting for. None of us have to be alone anymore."

"Oh," Ephraim said. He looked at Nathaniel for help. "You see it, don't you? She's completely lost her mind. You can't go along with this."

"The Doc thinks that if we can't stop the collapse of the multiverse, perhaps we can control it. Save as much of it as possible," Nathaniel said. "That sounds pretty good to me. I thought you'd be all for helping others."

"It sounds like giving up to me," Ephraim said.

"That's why you wanted me to modify the LCD software to filter universes," Hugh said. "To try to manage the process of decoherence. There are hundreds of thousands of universes in the database. By using that data, we can choose those that are compatible with this reality and combine with them safely."

"She wants to allow other universes to merge with this one?" Ephraim asked.

"Just elements from them," Hugh said. "You filtered it even further, didn't you?"

"That's enough, Mr. Everett," she said.

"You used the biometric records we have for Ephraim Scott to target his analog, but because there was already one of him here, protected by the coin, the closest match was his offspring," Hugh said.

"Oh, shit," Ephraim said. "You did that on purpose? Why? To create some kind of perfect universe?"

"Smart boy. I knew you'd understand," Dr. Kim said.

"But all those universes," Ephraim said. "Those people . . . you'll just let them disappear?"

She took a drag on her cigarette and blew out a cloud of smoke. She studied it thoughtfully.

"They would have disappeared anyway. But this way, we can save some of them," she said.

"Like another Ephraim. Do you think any of my analogs could love *you*?"

"One did, once. And I let him get away."

"You were clearly a different person then," Ephraim said.

Dr. Kim looked at Nathaniel.

"I need you to give me the coin, Eph," Nathaniel said.

Ephraim put his hand in his left pocket. "Why? It won't do you any good," he said. He glanced at Hugh. He met Ephraim's eyes and nodded slightly.

"We can't have you interfering," Dr. Kim said. "We can make this the best of all possible worlds. You can still help be a part of that."

Hugh quietly opened a drawer in the workbench and withdrew one of the controllers. He flipped it open and pressed a button, then lowered it back into the drawer and closed it.

"Hell, no," Ephraim said. "I already know you plan to replace me, so you'll understand if I'm not that enthusiastic about cooperating," he said. "What about Jena and Zoe?"

Dr. Kim didn't respond.

The sound of the LCD outside the lab had stopped. He glanced nervously at Dr. Kim. She hadn't noticed. But Nathaniel tilted his head, listening intently.

"The universe will never stabilize if there's more than one analog in any universe," Hugh said. "I think that's why your friends merged with each other. The multiverse couldn't distinguish between identical twins and analogs."

"How did this happen to you, Jena?" Ephraim asked. "Your plan is the most self-serving thing I've ever heard. You're going to pick and choose who lives and who dies."

"And who do you really want to save? Worlds full of strangers you've never met, never will meet? Or do you want to preserve the people you love? Your mother. Your best friend. Your girlfriend?" she said.

"There has to be another way," Ephraim said.

"'E pluribus unum,'" Dr. Kim said.

"Excuse me?" Ephraim asked.

"That's written on the coin. It's Latin," she said.

"'From out of many, one,'" Hugh translated.

"I know what it means," Ephraim lied. "It's on all our currency. It doesn't mean anything special."

"It's the answer to everything," Dr. Kim said.

Ephraim squeezed the coin in his left pocket tightly.

Dr. Kim narrowed her eyes. "You're free to leave, Ephraim. But not with the coin. It was never yours. Nathaniel, reclaim our property."

"I'm sorry, kid." Nathaniel approached and held his palm out, like he was reaching out to take Ephraim's hand in friendship.

"Nathaniel . . ." Ephraim tensed.

"You might have been able to beat me in a fight back in junior high, but not anymore, Ephraim."

"Right. I've seen what you're capable of," Ephraim said.

"Please don't let it come to that."

"Don't do this," Ephraim said. "'The needs of the many outweigh the needs of the few. Or the one.'"

"You're actually quoting *Star Trek* to talk me out of this?" Nathaniel asked.

"It would have worked on Nathan," Ephraim said.

"I'm not Nathan. Here's another movie quote for you: 'There can be only one.' And this universe has to be the one. Now stop playing around and give me the coin, Eph."

"You know, Judas got more than a quarter for his betrayal." Ephraim pulled the quarter from his pocket and dropped it lightly into Nathaniel's open hand.

"And he hung himself for it," Nathaniel said sadly.

"Hanged," Dr. Kim corrected.

"It'll work out," Nathaniel said. He patted Ephraim's arm and returned to Dr. Kim's side. He studied the coin curiously as he passed it to her. He snapped his head around to look at Ephraim and opened his mouth.

But it was too late. Ephraim had one hand in his right pocket, grabbing the real coin while already forming the wish in his mind.

"You should have known better, old man. You've fallen for that trick before." Ephraim flipped the coin and snatched it from above his head a moment later.

Just before the room disappeared, Nathaniel winked at him.

CHAPTER 25

Ephraim appeared in his bedroom, seated at his desk. He was disoriented for a moment; he'd forgotten that using the coin without the controller swapped him with his analog in the destination universe. Since he, Jena, and Zoe had used the controller to shift, there shouldn't have been an Ephraim in his universe to swap with, but it was possible one had merged into his reality in his absence.

In fact, without the controller to confirm quantum coordinates, he couldn't even be sure this was his home universe.

After his experiences with the coin last year, Ephraim had frequent nightmares that he had slipped into a parallel life without even knowing it—or that someone else was leading the life he was supposed to have. So he'd developed the habit of checking that things were the same as he remembered whenever he came home.

He pocketed the coin and looked around his room. The photo on the bookcase of him and his mother had been taken at a dinner celebrating six months of her being alcohol-free. A photo next to it showed her with her boyfriend, Jim. That was a very good sign that Ephraim was where he belonged.

Had he left that book open on his desk? He picked it up. It was a collection of science fiction stories by Philip K. Dick. Not something you wanted to read when you were already feeling paranoid—or when people really were after you.

He noticed it was a library book, and it was a day overdue. He owed the Summerside Library twenty-five cents.

"Ha," Ephraim said.

The bed was unmade. Ephraim always fixed it before he left. He considered it an active crusade against entropy. There were a lot of things he couldn't control in life, but he could make his own bed in the morning.

"Someone's been sleeping in my bed." He chuckled and quickly silenced himself.

Was Dr. Kim's madness contagious? If cell phones were supposed to be bad for you, hanging around a coheron drive—or carrying part of one in your pocket—had to be much worse. That might explain Nate's megalomania and his Ephraim's psychotic tendencies.

It would be so easy to attribute their behavior to external causes, but it was far more likely that their darkness had come from within, that everyone was capable of making selfish choices, regardless of who had to suffer.

Ephraim wondered who would come for him: Dr. Kim or Nathaniel. Either one of them could use the controller to track the coin and follow him whenever they wanted, but they wouldn't be able to transport themselves directly to his apartment. That gave him an hour on the outside if they walked from Greystone Park, but as little as twenty minutes if they took a cab.

Nathaniel had winked before Ephraim shifted. He'd realized Ephraim had switched the coins, but had he let him get away with it anyway? Or was he just showing Ephraim that he was unconcerned about catching up to him? He'd seemed pretty firmly on Dr. Kim's side.

Maybe Nathaniel had gotten dust in his eye and it didn't mean anything.

An instant message dinged on Ephraim's computer. He recognized Jena's screen name, uhny-uftz. It seemed another Jena analog had merged into this universe along with another Ephraim.

uhny-uftz: u still there?

Jena would never have substituted "u" for "you" or abandoned proper capitalization, not even in a text message. Ephraim scrolled back through some of the history of the conversation she'd been having with his analog just before Ephraim had shifted in. He'd interrupted them in the middle of some hot and heavy sexting.

Ephraim checked the list of users. The screen name Jimmy01sen blinked green as he stared at it. Nathan. But was it his Nathan?

Ephraim typed.

intrst11r-pig: Nathan? I'm back. From the future.

He waited impatiently for Nathan's response.

Jimmy01sen: welcome home!!!!

Ephraim let out a breath.

intrst11r-pig: Good. You're still you. Right?

Jimmy01sen: how's my camera?

Ephraim grinned. That was Nathan, all right. He'd forgotten Nathan's camera, but considering his sudden exit, he had a perfectly good excuse.

intrst11r-pig: Thank you for your concern. Had a rough time over there.

Jimmy01sen: I was having a rough time over here.

intrst11r-pig: Of course you did. I'm sorry.

Jimmy01sen: I thought you might be back though. My webcam went nuts a few seconds ago. Some of the local news stations picked up faint quantum ghosting, and social media feeds are exploding with people talking about what they saw on their TVs and cameras.

intrst11r-pig: Is it still happening?

Jimmy01sen: No. Everything's back to normal now.

Ephraim switched on his webcam. When he looked at his room through the tiny video screen he saw something moving directly in front of him—over him. He slid his chair back and saw a ghostly image of one of his analogs typing at his computer. No, there were two phantoms, and one of them was apparently looking at porn.

Ephraim hastily tilted the camera to take in more of the room. It was full of other versions of himself, watching TV, playing video games with Nathan, jerking off, making out with analogs of Jena, making out with analogs of Mary—or Shelley.

He could barely pick out individual versions of himself, the screen was so full of them, many more than he'd seen on Nathan's camera at prom. The multiverse was getting worse, and he worried that just having the coin in his pocket was doing more than letting him see it. Maybe its presence in this universe was making it less stable.

How did the multiverse ever sort all of this out? It was just arbitrarily mashing universes together. Maybe Dr. Kim was right—if it was that senseless, if one Ephraim was as good as another on that macrocosmic scale, then why shouldn't someone enforce some order?

The coin would protect him for a little while, but what about his mother? And Nathan? They couldn't hold hands forever to stay in contact with the coin. Eventually the coin would run out of power, and even he would be vulnerable.

Ephraim put his head down on his desk, wrestling with the idea that there was nothing he could do.

He lifted his head and stared at the computer screen. He'd left the camera facing his bedroom door. He saw another Jena standing there, looking at him as though she could see him.

He'd left her and Zoe behind in Nathaniel's universe. He would never get to see either of them again.

"I'm sorry, Jena," he said.

"For what?"

Ephraim jumped out of his seat and spun around. The Jena standing in the doorway was real, not a phantom.

"Jena!" he said.

She smiled.

If this was Jena, and not her analog who'd been sexting with a different Ephraim a few minutes ago, she had to have come here with a controller.

"How'd you get here?" he asked.

"Zoe sent me. She slipped me her controller as soon as Nathaniel told her you'd left."

"So he did let me get away. Why didn't they come with you?"

Jena's smile faltered. "Zoe stayed to reason with Dr. Kim."

"How's that going?"

"Not well. Dr. Kim doesn't know I've left."

Ephraim sat on his bed, suddenly overwhelmed with fatigue and relief. "I'm glad you're here. I didn't mean to leave you. I just didn't know what to do."

"I know," she said. "You didn't have time to think about it. I'm glad you got away."

Ephraim had needed to hear that.

Jena sat close to him on the bed and wrapped an arm around his waist.

"You got here fast," he said. He'd arrived here only ten minutes ago, tops.

"I took Nathaniel's car before I used the controller to follow you," she said. "Since a pantsless analog of yours swapped places with you, we figured we'd probably find you at home."

He laughed.

"I don't know how anything can be funny when everything is so screwed up," he said.

"Not everything. We're together." She leaned her head against his shoulder and wrapped her arm around him, sliding her fingers into the right pocket of his jeans.

"How'd you get in my apartment?" he asked.

"Your mom let me in," Jena murmured.

"Mom's home?" he asked.

He disentangled himself from Jena's arms.

"She's supposed to be at work now, but maybe that's different too," he said. "She could walk in on us at any minute."

"She reminded me that it's a little late to be coming over to see you, but that she trusts us." Jena placed her hand on Ephraim's thigh, and he closed his eyes. "She also said that if we're quiet for too long in your bedroom, she's coming in here with a Super Soaker filled with cold water. I thought she was kidding, but I saw her put it in the freezer."

His mom's sense of humor hadn't changed, at least.

Jena kissed Ephraim on the back of his neck. "Tell me what happened," she whispered against his ear. He felt a shiver run down his skin.

"Mmmm," he said. "Jena?"

"Don't mind me. Go on."

"This is really not the time." He pulled away and stared at her.

He hadn't had a chance to tell her that he wanted to be with Zoe, but this wasn't the time for that conversation either.

He stood up and paced between his bed and desk.

"Dr. Kim's exploiting the collapsing multiverse to create a perfect universe for herself, with handpicked analogs of all of us to keep her company."

"When you put it that way, it sounds pretty bad," Jena said.

"It sounds bad no matter how you put it. She's going to throw all those other universes away to save herself."

"And to save the people she loves," Jena said. "Is that so wrong?"

He stared at her. "Are you serious?"

Jena stood up and smoothed her hands against the back of her shorts.

"I'm just saying, maybe we should hear her out," Jena said.

"No, Jena. She's *evil*. How can you even consider her plan?"

"Dr. Kim's had more time than any of us to figure out what's happening. If there were a way to stop it, she would know. Maybe she's right, we should just get the people we care about into her universe. Sort it all out once everyone is safe."

"Jena, she only wants one of each of us there. You and Zoe . . . she was going to get rid of you, somehow."

"She wouldn't do that to herself."

"She certainly doesn't want me in her ideal world," Ephraim said.

"But I do," Jena said. "Come back with me. She won't be angry. I promise. She just wants your help. Or if you won't help, she wants you to agree not to interfere."

"She wants the coin," he said. "Did Dr. Kim send you here?"

"No," Jena said.

"You're lying," he said.

"She didn't send me." Jena looked Ephraim in the eyes. "I volunteered. This was my idea."

Ephraim groaned. "Why?"

"She told us what she's planning and I know she's right, Eph," Jena said. "I could just feel it. I just have to bring the coin back to her and everything will be okay. She has the coordinates for this universe. She can save my parents, and Mary and Shelley."

"It's too late for Mary and Shelley, remember?" he said.

Jena's eyes teared up. "I don't want to lose anyone else," she said. "And I don't want to die."

"Hugh says what happened to Mary and Shelley suggests that multiple analogs can't stay in one universe for long, not while the multiverse is this unstable. You'll just merge or disappear. Dr. Kim knows this. She was there when he told me. She doesn't care about anyone but herself anymore—*her*, not her analogs. I've seen the way she acts around you. She's jealous of me and Zoe and you and Hugh."

"What are you talking about?" Jena said.

"I know you like Hugh. He certainly likes you."

Jena shook her head. "What did you mean, you and *Zoe*?"

Ephraim licked his lips. "I tried to talk to you before, when I came to the lab."

"After you got back from your shopping trip. With her." Jena pursed her lips. "Did something happen, Ephraim?"

"Not like you think. We only talked. Jena, I'm so sorry. I've always wanted to be with you, you know that. But . . . it turns out that I love Zoe."

Jena stared at him blankly, which unnerved him more than if she'd reacted with anger or sadness. Then she laughed.

"I'm not joking," he said.

"I know, but . . ." She wiped a tear from her eyes and tried to stop laughing. "I told you so!" she gasped out. "And I can't believe you're telling me this now!"

"Uh. This wasn't what I was expecting. Not that I want you to be devastated or anything, but are you all right?"

She held a hand up and sat on the bed, still laughing.

"Not to flatter myself, but I thought you'd be more upset. After the way you acted at prom," Ephraim said.

"That was ages ago, wasn't it?" Jena looked up at him. "Eph, I'm not surprised. I knew you still had feelings for her. The kiss I saw only confirmed it. Of course I was upset, but we didn't expect this to be for forever."

"I wanted it to be," he said. "I thought I did."

"Oh," Jena said. "I just assumed, with college next year . . ."

"Yeah," he said. "Now there might not even be a next year for any of us."

"It doesn't have to be that way," she said. "I love you, and I still want you in my life. Come back with me. Help us. You'd be helping Zoe, too."

He looked at her sharply. "Is she onboard with Dr. Kim's plan?"

Jena hesitated.

"I wasn't lying about that. Zoe really is trying to get them to change their minds," she said. "Looks like you chose the right girl."

"We're just back where we started," Ephraim said. "She's in another universe, and you and I are in this one."

"Oh, I'm not staying," Jena said.

"You don't have a choice. I'm not bringing the coin to Dr. Kim's universe," he said. "And the controller can't take you back there without me."

"I'll manage."

Ephraim's bedroom door opened. Jena's eyes flicked behind him. "See? My ride's here." She stood up.

Dammit. Ephraim should have realized Jena wasn't alone. She had said "We figured *we'd* probably find you at home." He turned around to see her companion, with a sick sense that he already knew who it was.

Ephraim's analog sauntered into the room like he owned the place, which he had only half an hour ago, before Ephraim had bumped him out. He had a backpack slung over one shoulder.

Even after meeting multiple analogs of his friends, Ephraim had yet to talk to one of his own. It had always been a possibility, but it had seemed like a remote one; the nature of the coin's design had prevented him from ever running into himself unless he was also using the controller.

The analog looked between Jena and Ephraim. "You were right," he said to Jena.

"I told you it was a stupid idea. I don't know how to seduce someone. Even my boyfriend." She glanced at Ephraim. "Ex-boyfriend."

The analog's eyes lit up. "I can teach you a few things," he said.

"I doubt that. Feeling better?" she asked.

"You could have warned me the trip would make me throw up," the analog said.

Jena smirked.

It was incredibly surreal to see himself standing on the other side of the room, not so much like looking in a mirror, but more like an out-of-body experience—like he was somehow standing outside of himself, looking at his own body.

His other self seemed just as fascinated, but a moment later his stunned expression changed to contempt.

"This is yours," the analog said. He threw the backpack to the floor at Ephraim's feet. Then he put an arm around Jena's waist. "And *this* is mine."

Jena stepped on his foot. The analog yelped and let her go.

Ephraim checked inside the bag. His tuxedo was crammed in there. Nathan's video camera was on top, along with the paperback Dickens novel he'd found in his room at Greystone Manor.

"Nice of the Doc to return my stuff," Ephraim said. "She didn't expect me to come back either."

"Hugh packed those," Jena said. "He says good-bye."

"Tell him I said thanks. For everything." Ephraim couldn't have used the coin to get away if Hugh hadn't switched off the LCD.

"Hold on." The analog strode to the bag and snatched the strip of condoms peeking out from the Dickens book. "You won't be needing these," he said. He winked at Jena.

"Ugh," Jena said. "You won't need them either. Not with me."

The analog shrugged. "There are plenty of options in the multiverse. Where does he keep the coin?" he asked.

Jena glanced at Ephraim. "Right pants pocket," she said. "I checked. It's there."

"Jena," Ephraim said.

The analog walked up to Ephraim, smiling thinly, and punched him in the face. Ephraim saw stars and ended up face-down on the carpet. His eye was already throbbing.

Through the dull buzzing in Ephraim's ears he heard Jena shout his name, but he didn't know which of them she was talking to. She sounded freaked.

The analog reached into his right pocket. Ephraim tried to twist away. He kicked out at him, but the analog danced away.

He held the coin up between his finger and thumb to show Ephraim. It flashed once in the light before he flipped it over to Jena.

"Last summer I went through hell because of you," the analog said. "I didn't know what had happened, but I learned pretty quickly that I had to stop telling people that the world had changed around me. No one remembered anything was ever any different.

"Eventually I figured out I was in a parallel universe, but I kept that to myself. You turned my mother into an alcoholic, you douche. You made me live like a poor person."

"I tried to swap everyone back where they came from," Ephraim said.

"Only so you could feel good about yourself."

"No," Ephraim said. "I'm sorry. I don't know why it didn't work." He sat up, massaging his temple. He winced with the pain.

"I think I do," Jena said. "Eph, it wasn't your fault. While you're in a universe with the coin and someone has a controller, that universe can't split off. But as soon as you and Nate left, it was able to branch just like any other universe. Every decision spawned another, similar universe—with whichever Ephraim analog was in it at the time."

"Even though Zoe and I backtracked through the universes I'd visited with the Charon device, we only returned the analogs from the parent universes." He closed his eyes, but he opened them again when he saw bright spots against his eyelids. He was having trouble focusing his left eye.

"You're from one of the universes that branched off." Ephraim climbed to his feet slowly. "I had no idea. I wanted to put everything right."

His analog scowled. "You ruined my life, so I'm taking yours."

"It's time to leave," Jena said to the analog. She slotted the coin in the controller. "If you wanted revenge, you got it. If I know Eph, this is going to eat him up with guilt."

She looked at Ephraim. "You did your best, like you always do. But you should know by now that you can't fix everything."

She pressed a button, and the coin hovered and spun to the coordinates she'd set.

"No, Jena!" Ephraim headed for her, but the analog shoved him back. Ephraim swung at him. The analog ducked and tackled him to the floor.

"I'm ashamed to share the same DNA as you." The analog pinned Ephraim under him.

"I'm more than my DNA," Ephraim said through gritted teeth.

"I'm sorry you've wasted your potential."

"Boys, please," Jena said. "Don't be an idiot, Eph. The coin is programmed for the lab. If you grab it now, you'll just end up exactly where you don't want to be. They're waiting for you. This is over."

She pulled the analog off Ephraim. She took the analog's hand, and he grinned.

"Jena," Ephraim said. "You're way too smart for this. You have another plan, right? Your mother, your father . . . Dr. Kim can't protect them." She was just pretending to go along with Dr. Kim. She had to be. But he couldn't figure out why.

"Neither can you," Jena said. "Good-bye, Ephraim."

The analog closed his hand over the coin, and they disappeared.

CHAPTER 26

Ephraim sat on his bed, staring at the spot where his analog and Jena had been a second ago.

The only advantage he'd had was gone with them. Without the coin, Ephraim was at the mercy of the decohering universes. He could become a different person at any moment or disappear entirely and he'd never even know it; worse still, no one else would notice either.

Someone knocked on his open bedroom door. His mom poked her head in.

"Honey? Is everything—" She took one look at his face and flew into the room. "Oh, my God! What happened? Are you all right?"

"No," he said.

"How did you hurt your eye?" she asked.

"I sort of did it to myself." He laughed.

She sat next to him on the bed. "Where's Jena? Did she hit you?"

He shook his head.

She wrapped her arms around him and he closed his eyes. He pressed his face against her shoulder like he had when he'd been a little kid, running to his mother with a skinned knee.

"You're, um, crying, sweetie," she said.

Ephraim swiped the back of his hand against his cheeks and brushed away the hot tears.

"Something got in my eyes," he said.

"I believe it's called sadness. What's going on? I didn't see Jena leave."

"She left in a hurry," Ephraim said. "With the other me."

"*Other* you?" Her eyes widened. "That boy Jena was with—"

"Mom. I'm the real one. It's me. Ephraim."

She stared into his eyes, and he saw the moment she understood him. "Eph?"

"Yes," he said. "I'm home."

"Oh, thank goodness." She hugged him even tighter than before.

"I saw the video Nathaniel recorded of how you left the prom, disappearing with that device," she said.

Ephraim tensed at her mention of Nathaniel before he remembered that she always called Nathan by his full first name.

"So. Two Jenas, huh?" she said.

Ephraim ducked his head.

"What's her name? The other one? Zoe. Is she . . . are you two . . . ?" she asked.

"We are. But I don't think it's going to work out," Ephraim said.

"The morning after prom, I found you lying in bed. With a hangover and a hickey." She frowned disapprovingly. "If I hadn't known you'd left, I wouldn't have realized someone else had replaced you. Even though your double kept calling me Mad, and he was unbelievably rude to Jim. Isn't that awful?"

"He's okay? Jim?"

"He doesn't understand any of this. Not that I get it all either. He bought all these DVDs about quantum physics and we've been watching them together."

"They wouldn't really cover this sort of thing," Ephraim said. "The Ephraim who's been here the past few days was another version of me from another universe. Like that body you saw from last year."

She nodded thoughtfully. "I wanted to kill this one myself. He's a punk. Whenever I started to forget that he wasn't you, I watched Nathaniel's video again. To see you. To remind myself that you were still out there, somewhere." Her eyes brimmed with tears again. "I knew you'd come home."

She looked exhausted, like she usually did after work. She was even more tired lately with the paralegal classes she'd started taking in the spring.

"Are you here to stay?" she asked. "Is everything . . . done?"

"Depends on your definition of 'done.' It's out of my control now. It's a long story, Mom, and I'm tired."

She was distracted by something on his computer screen. "It's still happening," she said softly.

Ghosts flickered on the screen, brighter and more opaque than they'd been in the video. A parallel version of Madeline Scott walked past them and picked up some socks from the floor. A phantom Ephraim and Jena were fooling around on the bed, where they'd been a short time ago. A man leaned over the computer screen. She sucked in a short breath.

"*David*? Ephraim, is that your father?"

The man walked into the bedroom, looked around for a moment, and peered at the screen. Ephraim got a good look at his face. It sure looked like his father, the way Ephraim remembered him.

"Is that possible?" his mother asked.

She turned, but the space where his father should have been was empty. She reached a hand out, but there was nothing to touch. When she looked back at the screen, David Scott was gone. Ephraim had watched him walk out of the room, fading with each step.

"That wasn't Dad," Ephraim said. "He just looked like him. Parallel universes are overlapping with ours. And once in a while, something or someone gets through."

A phantom Ephraim on the bed slipped his hand under a phantom Jena's shirt, and she arched her back. He leaned forward and kissed her neck. Ephraim's mother squinted at the screen.

"Well, that's enough of that," she said. She switched off the monitor.

"Mom, we've never done that here before. I swear," he said.

"'Here'?" she asked.

"I mean *ever*. I don't even know what they're doing."

"It's too late for that talk, I imagine." She tousled his hair. "But you'll always be my little boy. My little, virginal boy."

"*Mom*," he said.

"Even when you and Jena—sorry, *Zoe*, give me cute little grandchildren, I'm going to assume they were made without sex."

"Too bad you can't meet Doug," Ephraim said.

"It's weird that cameras can pick up those . . . what do you call them?"

"Quantum phantoms. You're right. It is weird." Ephraim got up and headed for the desk. He switched the screen on.

"I really don't need to see any more of that, Eph," his mom said.

He studied the phantoms moving across the screen. "Why is my camera still picking up other universes?" Ephraim asked. "I don't have the coin anymore."

"You mean a coin makes that happen?"

"It's half of a really powerful device, the thing we used to travel between universes," Ephraim said.

"Where's the other half?"

"Jena has it. Hugh Everett has one too." Her eyes widened when she heard the name.

Ephraim looked at the bag his analog had dropped in his room.

He dumped it out onto his bed, and he and his mother studied the contents. The rumpled tuxedo, Nathan's camera, the book. Good thing his analog had taken the condoms with him.

He checked all the compartments of the backpack, but there was nothing else inside it.

His mother picked up the tuxedo jacket and shook it out. She reached into the inner pocket and pulled out something small and silver.

"Whose phone is this?" she asked.

"Phone?" he asked. "That's it!"

"It was in your jacket." She handed it to him.

"This is the controller," he said. "The other half of the device." Hugh must have slipped the device in there, knowing that Ephraim's analog would bring it right to Ephraim.

"Does that do you any good?"

"I don't know, but it's the best I've got. Now I might be able to do something. What, I'm not sure, but something," he said.

He flipped the controller open. It still responded to his touch.

This was a total game changer. The game still sucked, but it was like he'd just been handed a secret code that had gotten him an extra continue.

"You'll figure it out, honey. How about some tea? Tea solves everything. And maybe you can try to explain this to me a little better."

He smiled. "Do we have any gummy bears?"

"I'm sure we do. Jim is always buying candy. But he's probably eaten all the green ones. I'll put the water on."

She smiled and left the room.

Ephraim took a quick shower and got dressed. It felt good to be wearing his clothes again. He pocketed the controller and threw Nathan's camera, Everett's audiocassette, and the loop of copper wire from 1954 into Hugh's backpack. Then he arranged the rental tuxedo on its hanger, minus the shoes, and brought them both out to the kitchen.

A man was slumped over the table.

"Jim?" Ephraim said. He rushed over to the man's side.

It wasn't Jim. The man had black hair with a scattering of silver and only the first signs of thinning. His skin was a rich brown, like he'd spent a lot of time in the sun. He was breathing shallowly.

"Dad?" Ephraim asked. "Mom! You'd better get in here!"

He didn't know how she'd missed her ex-husband passed out in her kitchen when she was making the tea. Ephraim glanced at the stove. There was no kettle on the burner.

"Mom?" Ephraim called.

He left his father at the table and ran through the apartment, checking all the rooms for his mother. She was gone, and so was any sign that she lived there. Ephraim broke into a nervous sweat.

He hurried back to the kitchen and grabbed the cordless phone from the wall. He nudged his father's shoulder. He couldn't believe this was happening to him again, with his other parent.

The man lifted his head and groaned. "Ephraim?" he said in a thick voice.

Only his dad pronounced his name that way: "Eff-ra-heem." He knew that voice too, though he hadn't heard it in person in nearly eight years; the rumbling baritone with its shadow of a Latino accent had read books to Ephraim when he was a boy. He still heard some books that way in his head when he reread them.

"Dad?" Ephraim asked. "David Scott?"

Ephraim leaned on the table for support. The last time he'd seen his father, Ephraim had been ten years old. He went to bed one night, and the next morning, when he came out of his room for breakfast, the bookshelves in the living room were bare and his mother was crying on the floor with a split lip and a black-and-blue cheek.

He'd thought his father had abandoned them, but later he found out that Madeline Scott had kicked her husband out of the apartment, and out of their lives. After that, he stopped wanting his father to call him.

"Did I fall asleep?" David Scott asked in a slurred voice.

Ephraim made a fist.

His mother standing up for herself, protecting Ephraim, divorcing his dad—that was the bravest thing Ephraim had ever known anyone to do. Even if she fell apart after David Scott was gone.

Ephraim hadn't seen the man's face since then, except in old pictures his mother had hidden from him. She'd sent everything that belonged to his father to an address in San Juan. Ephraim had only gotten two birthday cards, on the wrong day, and a single phone call from the man since.

"Dad," Ephraim said.

"I heard the voices again," his father said.

"The voices?" Ephraim said cautiously.

There was a Sudoku book, a pencil, a box of Entenmann's donuts, and a mug in front of his father on the table. Ephraim lifted the empty cup and sniffed it. Vodka. There hadn't been any of it in the house for a year, or alcohol of any kind. The smell of it made Ephraim feel sick.

"Dad, look at me," Ephraim said.

David Scott looked up blearily. His eyes were bloodshot and he was unshaven. He seemed fifteen years older, not eight. His hair needed a good trim. It was late at night, but it didn't look like he'd been out of his threadbare pink terrycloth robe all day, if all week.

"What?" his dad said.

"Where's Mom?" Ephraim asked. His voice choked up, and he blinked back tears.

His father slapped the table. The pencil bounced and rolled off the table.

"Don't start that." He glared at Ephraim. Just like that, his anger disappeared and he looked sad, tired, and old. "I don't want to talk about her anymore. I . . . can't. The doctor said . . . it upsets me." He looked down at the Sudoku book. The top row of nine squares were filled in. Ephraim shivered when he saw the numbers: 9, 0, 9, 8, 7, 7, 11, 1, and 9. The coordinates for Nathaniel's universe

"She was just here," Ephraim said. "Mom. I spoke to her."

Something flickered across the man's face. Hope? But it was quickly replaced by the deepest sadness Ephraim had ever seen on another person's face.

"You don't really believe she was here." His father looked at him with fear and concern. "Ephraim. You don't, do you?" He grabbed his wrist in a surprisingly strong grip.

"No! Of course not. Let go of me."

His father shoved his hand away. "I don't want you to get like this. Like me."

"What's wrong with you?" Ephraim asked. He sat next to his father.

"What isn't?" David Scott said.

His father's shoulders sagged, and he squeezed his Sudoku book between his hands.

"I heard her voice. I don't know where she's gone, but she's never coming back," his father said.

He rubbed at the Sudoku page with an eraser, scrubbing away the numbers from the squares at the top. Ephraim looked more closely and saw that the entire page had been filled in with numbers and erased.

"Things haven't been the same since . . ." His father tapped a staccato rhythm on the table with the eraser.

"Since Mom left?"

His father shoved the Sudoku book away from him. "Since you were born."

Ephraim froze.

"My life would be so different," his father said.

"You'd still be a loser," Ephraim said.

The blow came so suddenly Ephraim didn't even see it. His head whipped to the left. His cheek burned and blood filled his mouth. At least it wasn't the same side that his analog had punched. He laughed. Turn the other cheek.

Ephraim got up and stumbled away from the table, holding his hand to his face. The skin was tender and stung.

"Or maybe you'd be dead," Ephraim said. He spat blood onto the worn linoleum of the kitchen floor. The memory of another, identical kitchen covered in blood flashed in his mind.

"You'd like that, would you? You should have gone with her." His father stood up. He grabbed Ephraim by the shirt and shoved him against the refrigerator.

"I'm leaving as soon as I can," Ephraim said. He felt the controller in his pocket.

His father leaned close to his face. His breath stank and tears mingled with the sweat on his face.

"Why don't you fight back?" he asked.

"Because I'm not like you," Ephraim said.

"I raised a coward." He mumbled something in rapid Spanish.

"No, a coward is someone who hits a woman when he's drunk," Ephraim said.

His father dropped him and went back to the table. He pressed his forehead against the table and covered his ears with both hands.

"Shut up, dammit!" he cried.

Ephraim straightened his shirt. He stretched his jaw and heard something click into place. He wiped bloody saliva from his lips and staggered back over to the table, watching his dad guardedly.

"What do you hear?" Ephraim asked.

His father tilted his head, listening. "Maddy," he said. "And you. Whispering. Voices just whispering, like ghosts. I even hear myself."

"Maybe you're hearing other worlds," Ephraim said softly.

"Can you make it stop?"

"I don't know how."

His father looked up and met his eyes.

"I know it was my fault," his father said. "I drove your mother away. All of this is my fault."

"You can't blame yourself for all of it. Trust me, I know."

His father picked up his mug, saw it was empty, and put it back down again. What was wrong with him? Did his mental illness really let him hear analogs from other universes, or had the voices made him sick in the first place?

"Let me make you tea," Ephraim said.

"I hate tea. Don't you have a date tonight? Or was that last night?" his father asked. "What time is it? I need my meds."

He pointed to an amber bottle on the kitchen counter. Ephraim grabbed it for him.

"What are these for, Dad?" Ephraim asked.

"The voices," he said. "But they don't seem to help."

Ephraim opened the bottle and handed over one of the small pink tablets. His father popped it into his mouth, dry swallowed it, and winced.

Ephraim really didn't have anything left. Zoe, Jena, his mother . . . they were all gone. At least his mother wasn't dead. She was out there, maybe even somewhere in this universe, but as removed from his life as if she was dead after all. She wasn't the same person who had raised him.

He missed his mother.

He took a deep breath. He wasn't changing realities this time. The world was changing around him. The controller allowed him to remain aware of the altered universe, but he couldn't do anything about it.

"I have to go," Ephraim said.

His father went back to his Sudoku puzzle, filling in squares with random numbers and erasing them again.

"Take the car," his father said.

"We have a car?" Ephraim asked.

"You get this weird sense of humor from your mother," his father said. He pulled keys from a pocket of the robe and tossed them to Ephraim.

The keychain was made from a US quarter enclosed in a metal bezel that was attached to a ring.

Ephraim turned it over and saw that it commemorated Puerto Rico, his father's birthplace, as an American territory. Ephraim rubbed his thumb over it. It was perfectly ordinary, but the coincidence disturbed him.

"Um." Ephraim clutched the keychain tightly. "Where's our car parked? And what does it look like?"

"You're so forgetful." His father swiped his hand over his eyes. "It's the old Volkswagen across from the basketball court."

"Thanks. Don't wait up, okay?"

Ephraim wondered what would happen to this man if Ephraim never came back. This wasn't his father, this was just one possible version of him, but he still felt protective of him—and sorry for him.

Ephraim had hated David Scott for what he'd done to his mother, and for not being there. There was obviously more to the story than he knew. He looked at the bottle of pills on the counter. He wasn't sure of anything anymore.

One thing was certain: Ephraim wasn't going to stay here. He was going to his date with Jena, but he had to make one stop first.

CHAPTER 27

Nathan was strangely quiet as he buckled into the passenger seat of David Scott's car.

"You okay?" Ephraim asked.

"I'm just thinking about your mother," Nathan said.

"*Nathan*," Ephraim said.

"Not like that." His friend ran a hand through his hair. "It was bad enough when Mary and Shelley merged, but now Maddy's gone too. I'm sorry, Ephraim."

"Thanks," Ephraim said.

"At least you got a car out of the deal." Nathan reached over and opened the glove compartment. "Too bad it's like twenty years old and belongs to your crazy, abusive father."

He looked at Ephraim's face and winced. Ephraim had cleaned himself up and changed shirts, but his left eye and cheek were swollen and red.

"Yeah," Ephraim said. "But I'm glad you remember my mom and the way things are supposed to be."

"Why is that, anyway?" Nathan asked. "I saw my dad on the way out and I asked him if he recognized your car. He knew it was your father's. Everyone else remembers things differently from us."

"Before my mom disappeared, she said something about forgetting that my replacement wasn't me."

"But he was a dick," Nathan said.

"Even so. She said she remembered what had happened whenever she re-watched that video you sent her. I think that might have something to do with it. Speaking of which." He handed Nathan his camera from the backpack on the seat between them.

Ephraim started the car and caught his friend up on events since the prom while he drove them to Jena's house. He ignored the camera in Nathan's lap, pointing at Ephraim and recording everything he said.

"I can't believe Jena stole the coin," Nathan said. "Does she like that Everett guy that much?"

"She thinks she's doing the right thing," Ephraim said.

"That's even worse."

"But Hugh sent me the backup controller, so I think he might be on my side."

"Which side is that?"

"The one in favor of not destroying the multiverse for personal gain."

"Right. I'm on that side, too. But what can we do?" he asked. "Maybe this Dr. Kim has a point. I mean, she's a doctor."

"She's a psychologist." Ephraim clenched the steering wheel. "I really need you to be with me on this, Nathan," he said.

"I'm just musing aloud. I'm with you, Eph. No matter what wildly improbable scheme you come up with." He drummed his fingers nervously on the armrest. "But you have to stop looking at me like that."

"Like what?" Ephraim said.

"Like I have spinach stuck in my teeth and you're trying to find a polite way to tell me," Nathan said.

"Sorry."

"I'm not going to disappear or change on you," Nathan said in an exasperated voice.

"You don't know that. What if the coin and the controller make it happen to the people close to me? Like, physically near me, but not in contact with me?"

"Or realities are cohering completely at random, like everything else in the multiverse."

"Decohering," Ephraim corrected.

"Huh?"

"The universes are *de*cohering," Ephraim said. "'Cohering' is when the Charon device stores their coordinates and prevents them from disappearing. Decohering is when they fade away or merge."

"Okay, well, that sounds backward. Whatever. The bad thing that's happening isn't going to affect me," Nathan said.

"Why's that?"

"For one thing, I know too much." Nathan patted the side of his camera.

"And why else?" Ephraim asked.

"I'm obviously the best Nathan Mackenzie in all the multiverse," Nathan said.

Ephraim laughed. "The very best. No room for improvement."

Nathan opened Ephraim's backpack and pulled out the audio-cassette from Everett's lab.

"Is this that old recording?" Nathan asked.

"Yeah."

Nathan slid the cassette into the tape deck in the car. "I want to get the sound on the video, too," he said.

Ephraim shrugged.

The hiss of the tape filled the car. Ephraim jumped when he heard his own voice. The car swerved.

"This is Ephraim Scott. If you're listening to this, then that means I never came home."

Ephraim pulled over quickly. He cut off a car, which honked as it sped by them.

"Is that your older self?" Nathan asked.

"It must be," Ephraim said. He turned up the volume on the radio. He was listening to the Ephraim Scott who had started all of this.

"I've made a terrible mistake. I've thought about it every day since I got the Charon devices. And I've finally realized that we aren't supposed to have this technology. I never should have let Dr. Everett convince me otherwise."

Nathan strained against his seat belt to get a better shot of Ephraim's face with the camera.

"That isn't fair. It wasn't just him—it was my decision to keep all of this a secret. The transhumans lied to me. I think they did something to my mind," the older Ephraim went on. "The more I use the coin, the more universes I visit, the more I remember. I have two sets of memories, like I lived another life in those three days. They must have brainwashed me so I would do what they told me. So I would bring the machine back and start recording the existence of other universes. I don't know what they're planning, but I'm afraid they aren't trying to help us. They're using us. They're using *me*.

"Some of those universes we visited shouldn't exist. Maybe most of them." The older Ephraim took a deep breath. "I haven't told Jena or Nathan what I'm planning to do. If you two are listening to this, then I'm sorry. I have to do this on my own. You would try to stop me or come with me, and it's too dangerous. This is likely a one-way trip.

"I'm returning to the transhumans' universe to find out what's really going on. Whether I'm right or wrong, I don't know if I'll be able to get back to you, but I'm going to do whatever I can to fix this.

"Jena, I love you. I know I tell you that every day, but I want it on the official record." The older Ephraim laughed. "Nathan . . . Hell, I love you too, man. I wish I hadn't made you part of all this. Take care of things while I'm gone.

"I told Hugh Two the truth and played Dr. Everett's confession for him. He agrees that I should go, while he tries to figure out more about what the coheron drive's real purpose is. He'll share this recording when the time is right. I hope you can forgive me.

"I hope I can forgive myself."

The recording ended. The tape popped and crackled until Ephraim ejected the tape. It had been playing the unlabeled side.

"You didn't hear that before?" Nathan asked.

"No. I didn't think to check both sides of the tape. And I'm guessing Hugh Two never played it for Dr. Kim, either. He probably decided it worked in his favor if Ephraim was out of the picture, and better to keep his predecessor's secret and preserve his own reputation. My analog trusted him because he'd trusted the first Everett."

Ephraim stowed the tape in his backpack. "It doesn't matter anyway, because my analog never went through with his plan. He died in Zoe's universe and stranded Nathaniel there with his coin."

"It was still a nice message," Nathan said. "He sounded just like you."

Ephraim started the car silently. They were pretty close to Jena's house.

He drove past Greystone Park. He glimpsed the lights of the Memorial Fountain through the trees.

"What's this Jena like?" Ephraim asked.

"Piña coladas and walking in the rain," Nathan said.

"That's not what I meant."

"I don't want to ruin the surprise." Nathan grinned.

"I've had enough surprises."

"You'll like her."

"Now I'm really nervous." Ephraim leaned forward and peered through the windshield. He saw his own reflection looking back at him in the glass, but when he refocused, he could see Jena's house ahead of them. He pulled over in front of it. Her parents' car wasn't in the driveway. That should make this easier.

Nathan turned his camera around to record through the windshield.

"So do you have a plan?" Nathan asked.

"Of course," Ephraim said. "Come on."

"Are you planning to come up with a plan?" Nathan asked.

"Busted. But we have to start somewhere."

"Maybe we should consult a physicist like Michio Kaku or Reed Richards."

"Reed Richards isn't a real person," Ephraim said.

"In every universe?" Nathan asked.

"Yes."

"Sue too? She's invisible—you can't be sure she doesn't exist."

"I'm pretty sure."

"Do you think Jena will help us? She doesn't know anything about this."

"I just need something from her," Ephraim said. "I shouldn't be long."

"You came here for a booty call?" Nathan swung the camera around and zoomed in on Ephraim's face. "That should help relieve some of the stress of saving the multiverse."

"You really haven't changed at all." Ephraim smiled. Though he'd often encouraged his friend to act more mature, at the moment he appreciated something being constant in his life. "Wait in the car until I come out."

"I'll try not to cohere *or* decohere while you're gone," Nathan said.

"Just keep rolling tape," Ephraim said.

"As if you have to tell me." Nathan pointed his camera toward Jena's house. "If she starts undressing, try to get her over to the window."

Ephraim shook his head and got out of the car.

CHAPTER 28

The analog of Jena who greeted him at the door had red and blonde streaks in her hair, which was longer in the front than the back. A small silver bar pierced her right eyebrow, and she had a silver loop through one nostril. She was wearing a cut-off white T-shirt over a black lace bra and black denim shorts. And she had green eyes.

"Uh," Ephraim said. "Hi."

"You're late," she said. "OMG, what happened to your face?"

"I'm getting tired of that question," he said.

"You've been fighting?" she asked.

"Sort of."

"That's so hot." She grabbed Ephraim by his belt buckle and pulled him into the house. She closed the door behind him and pushed him against it.

She leaned close and touched his raw cheek gently with a cool hand. "Does this hurt?"

He winced. "A little."

She kissed it gently. Then she rose on her toes and kissed his eye.

"Wait," he said. "I can't—"

"Shhh," she said. She kissed him on the lips. A moment later, he discovered she had a third piercing.

He jerked away and bumped the back of his head against the door.

She laughed. She stuck her tongue out and wiggled it at him. Silver glinted on the end of it. "I just got it today. I wanted to surprise you."

"I'm surprised," he said. He squeezed past her. "*So* surprised."

"You're freaked!" She clapped her hands with delight. "Can you imagine how my dad will react?"

"You should find a different way to tell him," Ephraim said.

"Ew," she said. She tilted her head. "Although I *am* his type."

"Ew," he echoed. He moved toward the stairs and put one hand on the banister.

"Guess what? I have a surprise, too, Jena," he said.

"Is it that you hurt your head and have selective amnesia?" she asked, hands on her hips. "Because I remember telling you never to call me that again."

He paused. "Zoe?" he asked.

"Good. Your memory's coming back," she said. "Now I don't have to kill you." She smiled.

"Zoe, I'm not who you think I am. I don't have time to explain. But I'm not the Ephraim Scott you know."

"So who are you, then? A clone? Doppelganger? Time traveler?"

"You forgot shapeshifter," he said.

"Right. You could also be an android."

"Long-lost twin," he said.

"Recipient of scientifically implausible facial reconstruction surgery."

"A wizard did it," he said.

"Or one of us is hallucinating."

Ephraim frowned, thinking about his father's analog, who was clearly mentally disturbed. A moment later she realized her mistake.

Zoe put her hand on his arm. "Sorry. I guess I'm the one with selective amnesia. It's all fun and games until someone puts her foot in her mouth."

"Don't worry. He isn't really my father."

"I know exactly how you feel," she said. "We both got a raw deal in the daddy department."

He folded her hands in his. "Zoe, I'm from an alternate universe. I'm a parallel Ephraim from another dimension that is starting to merge with yours. And time is of the essence." He flinched. "Did I really just say that?"

"Very convincing," she said.

"I just came over here for one thing," he said.

"Oh, good," she said.

"Keep your pants on," he said. "Please. I need to borrow your grandfather's old ham radio."

She blinked. "Huh? What do you want with that old thing? How do you even know about it?"

"Like I said, I'm from a parallel universe." He retrieved his wallet and pulled out Jena's senior picture, the same one he'd shown her grandfather in 1954. He handed it to Zoe.

"Did you have Nathan Photoshop this?" she asked.

"This is real. Your double in my universe, *Jena* Kim, gave it to me last week."

"Uh-huh. And she's your girlfriend?"

"She was, but we just broke up."

"If you're trying to dump me, this is a shitty way to do it, Ephraim." Zoe turned away.

"No, no! I'm not dumping you." He sighed. "We were never together. Not you and me. That's what I'm trying to say. I've never seen you before today. I'm a different Ephraim."

"That's impossible," she said.

"'When you have eliminated the impossible, whatever remains, however improbable, must be the truth,'" Ephraim said.

"Where'd you hear something ridiculous like that?"

"From Jena. Quoting Sherlock Holmes."

"She sounds like a geek."

He smiled. "Completely." He turned and headed up the stairs.

"Where are you going?" she asked.

"Attic," he called over his shoulder.

"Ooh, we've never done it in the attic," she said.

"*We've* never done it anywhere," Ephraim said. "And we aren't going to."

"You're in a very strange mood today," she said.

"It's been a very strange day."

Zoe followed him up to the attic door. "I haven't seen the radio in years. Dad probably sold it. We had a big garage sale a couple of years ago."

Ephraim groaned.

"I'll get one on eBay for your birthday," Zoe said.

"I need that specific machine."

Nathaniel had said he needed to use the same ham radio, because they were all connected with each other on some quantum level.

They went into the attic. Zoe turned on the light, a dim bulb in the middle of the ceiling. The ceiling sloped at an angle the deeper you went, and the cramped space was warm and musty. Dust coated everything like a fine gray snow.

"It would probably be in the back," Zoe said. "The older stuff is farther in."

She shoved a box of Christmas ornaments aside. Ephraim picked up another box to move it out of the way. It was too light to hold the radio, but he lifted the flap to check the contents anyway. It was filled with shiny, colorful clothes. He touched the bright-blue shirt on top. It felt smooth like silk but stiff like a heavily starched collar.

"Those are Grumps' old Korean clothes," Zoe said.

They worked side by side to excavate disintegrating boxes of books, videocassettes, and a broken air conditioner, making a narrow path toward the back of the attic. He had to crouch on the far end because the ceiling was so low.

"This isn't my idea of a fun date, Eph." Zoe wiped her hands on her shirt, leaving grimy handprints over her breasts.

"Too dirty, or not dirty enough?" Ephraim grinned.

She made a face. She turned and knocked a small box from the top of a stack of cartons, and he heard glass break. She leaned over to pick it up.

"Uh-oh," Zoe said.

"What?" he asked.

"I think I found the radio. Most of it."

He helped her clear the pile of boxes out of the way so he could get to the ham radio. It was in an open carton, caked with dirt. The lid was loose and wires spilled out of it. Zoe blew on it, and a cloud of dust rose around them.

"It looks like Dad cannibalized some parts," she said.

Ephraim found another box of radio components near it, with bits of wires and vacuum tubes. He grabbed everything that he recognized from Zoe's room and piled them into the carton with the radio.

"You think it still works?" she asked.

"I'll make it work," he said. He tried to lift the box. It was heavier than it looked. "Can I borrow this?" he grunted.

"You can have it," she said.

"I thought it was like a family heirloom."

She gave him a funny look. "It's only junk."

He dragged the cardboard box toward the door. Zoe pushed from the other side, and it went more quickly. The two of them managed to carry it downstairs. They rested by the front door.

"Ugh. I need a shower," she said. He watched her chest rise and fall as she caught her breath.

She caught him staring. "Care to join me?"

He shook his head.

"You're really going to leave?" she asked.

"I have what I came for," he said. "Thanks, Zoe."

"Sure," she said. "But you owe me."

She put her hands on his shoulders. She was quick, just her lips brushing against his lightly. At the same time, she pushed the right sleeve of his T-shirt up to expose his bicep.

"You aren't my Ephraim," she said.

"What made you believe me? The kiss?"

"The kiss. The fact that you usually can't keep your hands off me. You couldn't carry that radio by yourself. And you don't have a tattoo."

Ephraim rubbed his bare arm. "What was the tattoo of?"

"My name." She pulled the neck of her T-shirt lower. He saw a word written in calligraphy just above her left breast. *Ephraim.* "We both got ambigrams. The word looks the same in a mirror."

"If that's all it took to prove it . . ." He sighed. "Why did you kiss me first?"

"I didn't think you'd let me later." Zoe opened the door for him.

"I'll get Nathan to help me carry this out to the car," he said.

Nathan was exactly where he'd left him, in the car playing recorded footage on his camera's tiny screen.

"You were in there a long time. Get what you came for?" Nathan waggled his eyebrows.

"Yes. I need you to help me carry it to the trunk."

Nathan was disappointed when he saw the radio. "This is really what you wanted? An old radio?"

"It's vintage," Ephraim muttered. "Where did Zoe go?" He'd wanted to say good-bye, but she wasn't in the foyer.

He heard a TV in the living room though. He poked his head in and saw an old man thumbing through the Tivo listings. The man jumped when he saw Ephraim.

"Who are you?" he shouted. He reached for his walker.

Ephraim put up his hands. "Calm down, Grumps. Dug. Mr. Kim." It was shocking to see the man with wispy white hair and so shrunken, wrinkled, and hunched over after meeting him in his twenties.

"How do you know my name?" Dug Kim asked.

"We've met before. Almost sixty years ago."

"Nonsense." The man scrambled up from his seat.

"I'm a friend of your granddaughter, Zoe," Ephraim said.

"I don't have a granddaughter," Dug said.

"You live here alone?" Ephraim asked. "What about your son? John?"

"Get out of my house!"

"Ephraim?" Nathan came into the living room. "What's going on?"

"Don't hit him!" Ephraim said.

"I'm not going to hit an old man." Nathan looked scandalized. "But we should get out of here before he calls the cops."

Dug was already dialing on an old cell phone that looked a lot like the controller in Ephraim's pocket.

"Okay. Er, sorry to trouble you," Ephraim said.

He and Nathan grabbed the box from the foyer and hurried out to the car. Ephraim's arm muscles burned with fatigue, and a tiny splinter of broken glass had worked its way into the palm of his right hand. He picked it out carefully and wiped his bloody hand on his jeans. Nathan popped the trunk, and they heaved the box inside.

Ephraim started the car. "We have to fix the radio and set it up. Not at my place. My dad might be there."

"My house," Nathan said. "Mom's making her famous kugel. And Dad has every tool we could need in his workshop."

Ephraim examined the ham radio in the Mackenzies' garage. The glass facing was cracked and one of the knobs was loose. He shook it. Something rattled inside, but he hoped it wasn't anything important. This radio was over half a century old. They built stuff to last back then, didn't they? He really needed it to still work.

He cleaned all the dust from the machine with a cloth and a small vacuum. He sneezed three times in quick succession. Then he plugged in the radio at Mr. Mackenzie's workbench and concentrated on sorting the jumbled cables and wires, inserting them where he thought they belonged. Nathan found a scanned copy of the radio's manual online and plenty of schematics.

Ephraim flipped the power switch and held his breath. Nothing happened.

He tapped the dial lightly. He rapped his knuckles against the side of the old metal cabinet.

Tears blurred his vision. It hadn't been much to hope for, but he didn't even have that anymore. He was never going to see Zoe again, or his real mom.

He wiped his eyes and cleared his throat. He made some hero. He had to pull himself together.

"If you're done feeling sorry for yourself, the radio's working," Nathan said.

Static burst from the radio, and the dial began to glow a soft orange. He put a hand on the box and felt it humming, like the coin always did.

"It takes time to warm up." Ephraim laughed.

He quickly wrapped the controller in the copper wire from Dug Kim's house the way Nathaniel had in 1954. He plugged it into the back of the radio. He fiddled with the controller, but he didn't really know how it worked.

"Let me see," Nathan said. "I'll figure out the new tech while you mess with the old."

Ephraim nodded and handed it to his friend. If Ephraim was uncannily attuned to the coin, Nathan and his analogs were natural mechanics.

There were no speakers, but he optimistically pulled on the headphones he'd found in the box, with the rusted metal earpieces and fraying cloth covers over the cords.

He leaned closer to the console and held onto the microphone while Nathan worked the controller. He tried to find the spot on the dial that Zoe had tuned to, but all he got in that range was dead air. He didn't know if anyone would be monitoring his transmission; they had no reason to expect him to try to make contact.

"This seems promising," Nathan said. "There's an option here for something called 'tracking mode'?"

"That should do it. Nathaniel configured it to link up with the Large Coheron Drive."

Ephraim coughed and squeezed the handle on the microphone a few times and started transmitting. "Hello? This is Ephraim Scott. I'm looking for Zoe Kim." He remembered her call sign. "CHARON2. This is Ephraim Scott to CHARON2."

Nothing.

He whirled the dial as far to the left as it would go and tried again, making his way through the bands incrementally. He got a few irate ham operators telling him to get off the radio, and some who were more helpful, warning him that he needed to get some training and a license before he started operating on public channels. He ignored them, pressing the headphones against his ears, listening intently for a familiar voice. Listening for Zoe.

"Anything?" Nathan asked.

Ephraim pulled the headphones off and left them dangling around his neck. He slumped back in the chair.

"It was easier when I had the coin," Ephraim said.

Nathan rummaged in his pocket. "Have you ever tried putting a regular coin in the controller?" he asked.

"I never had a reason to," Ephraim said. "What do you think would happen?"

"One way to find out. Only I don't have any quarters. I'll run and grab one from the change jar."

"I have a quarter," Ephraim said. He fished out his dad's car keys and popped the quarter out of its bezel on the key ring. He held it up and squinted at it doubtfully. He passed it to Nathan.

Nathan slotted it into the disc-shaped indentation in the controller.

Ephraim pushed his chair back, and Nathan backed away a step, but after thirty seconds, there'd been no reaction. Nathan leaned over it to check the readout on the screen.

"Careful," Ephraim said.

"It isn't doing anything," Nathan said.

Ephraim tapped the coin lightly with his index finger. Then he pressed his fingertip against it more firmly. "No change in temperature."

Nathan snapped his fingers. "I forgot to engage the gyro mechanism." He pressed a button on the controller, and the coin jumped.

They scrambled backward and watched the quarter skitter on the controller like the Mexican jumping bean Ephraim had made his father buy him when he was six. It hadn't been a bean at all. He'd been amazed, disillusioned, and disgusted when a tiny moth eventually hatched from it.

"Isn't it supposed to float?" Nathan asked. He aimed his camera at the controller and zoomed in so they could observe it from a safer distance.

"It's doing something," Ephraim said.

The coin was glowing now, a dull red, growing brighter.

"Dude," Nathan said.

Now the quarter was bright white, blotting out everything else on the video screen. Nathan tilted the camera to look at the controller's display. It was cycling through a series of numbers and broken characters.

"Looks like an error message," Ephraim said.

"Uh, how do we stop this?" Nathan asked.

"Usually it stops when it finds the right frequency and then I grab the coin to shift."

"Yeah, I wouldn't touch that if I were you."

Nathan put down the camera and hurried over to the wall where various tools were mounted on corkboard. He found a pair of long pliers with a rubber handle and brought them over to the controller.

"What's that horrible sound?" Nathan asked.

Ephraim lifted the headphones and listened with one ear. A high-pitched whine came out of the earpiece. He winced and pulled it away from his head. The frequency became more piercing. He spun the dial, but it was the same on every channel, with the addition of a cacophony of voices complaining about interference.

"Some kind of feedback loop," Ephraim said. "Get the coin out of there!"

Nathan held the shaking pliers closer to the controller. He winced as he clamped the ends around the coin. As he lifted the coin, the controller went with it.

"It's stuck," Nathan said.

"Great. Is it melting?" Ephraim asked.

Nathan pulled on a dark visor from the bench and peered closely at the coin and controller. "They're separated by about a half-inch of air, but there's some kind of force holding it to the controller."

"Can we slide something between them to break the connection?" Ephraim asked. "A sheet of metal?"

"On it," Nathan said. He dumped a box of odds and ends open on the concrete floor and pawed through it while the dark garage got brighter and brighter with light from the coin, now glowing like a tiny star. Their shadows elongated across the room in harsh relief.

Ephraim felt the heat of the coin against his bruised cheek, even from a couple of feet away.

He kept cycling through the stations on the radio until he heard something under the crackling static and whining frequency. It might have been his imagination, but the lights on the dial were getting brighter too and the radio was generating heat of its own.

A vacuum tube popped and a wisp of smoke rose from the vents on the radio. The lights on the dial darkened, and the headphones went quiet. Ephraim smelt burnt ozone.

"Shit," he said.

The controller itself was rattling now too.

"Nathan, do something!" Ephraim said.

"Got it!" Nathan jumped up and hurried over with a steel ruler. He pulled on a thick gardening glove and clutched one end of the ruler, while he slowly slid the other end under the coin like he was trying to flip a pancake on the stove with a spatula. Sparks flew and the ruler vibrated.

"It's resisting." Nathan gritted his teeth. He wrapped his bare left hand around his gloved right and pushed harder. Blue electricity crackled over the steel ruler, and Nathan's hair drifted up from his head. "Not good," Nathan said.

Suddenly the coin disappeared with a cartoonish *zing*, and they heard a crash on the other side of the room. The controller settled down on the table, and Nathan threw the steel ruler to the floor.

Nathan leaned against the table and pulled off his face mask. "That was a terrible idea," he said. He held up the tinted visor. A thin crack ran down the left side. Nathan touched his cheek.

"Are you okay?" Ephraim asked.

"I'd swear the coin hit me," Nathan said. "I think it went *through* me. I felt it plink against the mask and there was a hot pinprick on my face."

"How's the controller?" Ephraim asked.

"It's still on," Nathan said. "It looks like some of the coin melted off on it and the edges are a little scorched." He poked at the controller with his gloved finger. "I can scrape it off, I think."

Nathan rubbed his cheek again and shook his head in disbelief. "What about the radio?"

"It kinda blew up," Ephraim said.

"I'll take a look under the hood. You find the coin before it starts a fire or something." Nathan lifted the top off the radio and held up a wiring schematic for comparison.

Ephraim found his father's quarter on the other side of the room, embedded halfway into the plaster wall like a thrown shuriken. The area on its edges were burned, but it had been even more of a close call—the coin was lodged just to the right of a small propane tank for the barbeque grill. He decided not to mention that to Nathan. He held his hand above the coin and waited for it to cool off enough for him to touch before trying to retrieve it. It still took him a couple of minutes of wiggling to pry it from the wall.

He brushed off the loose plaster and examined the damage. The edge that had hit the wall was actually bent flat. Washington's face was distorted, melted half off. He turned the coin over. The other side was blank; all he could make out was the faint lettering at the top: "E PLURIBUS UNUM." His hand tingled.

Ephraim went back to the bench. Nathan was poking around in the radio's guts.

"One of the tubes blew," he said. "I replaced it. Who knew my dad had a collection of old vacuum tubes?"

"You're a genius," Ephraim said. He flipped the coin to Nathan. It wobbled awkwardly through the air, and Nathan caught it.

Nathan took one look at it and whistled. "Any idea what happened?"

"Yes. We did something incredibly stupid." He sat down. "But hopefully there's no permanent damage."

Nathan came around to the front of the radio. "Give her another try," he said.

"Her?" Ephraim asked.

"I feel like I've bonded with 'Arciay' now that I've had my hands inside her." He swung the rusted RCA logo around on one loose screw on the face of the radio.

"And you gave it a name. You're rather bizarre, Nathan Mackenzie."

"Thanks."

Ephraim flipped the radio back on and crossed his fingers. Two of the dials remained dark, but the one in the center glowed faintly amber. The buzzing noise was gone, replaced with the hissing background noise of an active frequency. He didn't touch the knob—this was the station that had seemed strongest during their little experiment. He turned up the audio volume and set the headphones on top of the radio so Nathan could listen with him.

"This is Ephraim Scott," he said. "Reaching out to *anyone*. Zoe Kim. Nathaniel Mackenzie. Anyone read?"

The radio crackled, and he repeated his message. Then he heard an eerily familiar voice reply through the headphones:

"Are you there, Ephraim? It's me, Ephraim."

CHAPTER 29

Ephraim stared at the ham radio in shock. He'd made contact . . . with himself?

Nathan jostled his shoulder. "What's going on?"

"It's one of my analogs," Ephraim said. He twisted the right earpiece of the headphones so it faced out. Nathan leaned close to listen in.

Ephraim fumbled with the microphone and squeezed the transmit bar. "Am I really talking to myself?"

"Yes, but for the first time, you're getting an intelligent response."

Nathan laughed. "I like him."

"He's me," Ephraim said. But which him was it? Was he talking to the analog he'd just swapped with? If so, he doubted he would be much help. "Where are you?" Ephraim asked.

"Seattle Below."

"Just below Seattle?"

"More like *under* it. My turn. How old are you?"

"Seventeen," Ephraim said.

A sigh. "Are they recruiting kids now?"

"I'll be eighteen next month," Ephraim said.

"Ah, youthful optimism. Good attitude to have, squirt."

"Don't call me squirt," Ephraim said.

"Sorry, Junior."

Ephraim clenched his jaw. "And what should I call you?" he asked evenly. "It seems weird to call you Ephraim."

"I've been Ephraim for much longer than you have," his analog said. "But call me Scott, if that's easier for you."

"Scott." Ephraim tried it out. "How old are *you*?"

"Forty-two," Scott said.

"So you're twenty-five years older than me. You were Nathaniel's partner?"

"You're brighter than you sound."

"Aren't you supposed to be dead?"

"Give it time," Scott said. "It won't be long now."

"You abandoned your best friend in a universe with no way home," Ephraim said.

"That was his own damned fault. I warned that idiot not to follow me," Scott said.

"Asshole," Nathan said.

Ephraim released the transmit button. "Quiet. We need him."

"Hello? Are you still there?" Scott asked.

"He sounds panicked," Nathan said. "Maybe he needs *us.*"

Ephraim started transmitting again. "I'm here."

"I got your signal just in time," Scott said.

"My signal?"

"That transmission you just sent pinged every universe simultaneously. I would have noticed it even if I hadn't been listening. How'd you do it?"

"Oh, yeah. That," Ephraim said. Nathan handed him the misshapen quarter. He turned it over in his hand. "It was, um, child's play. Who were you listening for?"

"Everyone. Anyone. I've been trying to get in touch with Nathan or Jena, but I guess they aren't taking my calls," Scott said.

"Probably not. You aren't expected. In fact, they think you're dead," Ephraim said.

Scott sighed. "That's what I wanted them to think. I suck at good-byes."

"I know. I heard the message you left for them," Ephraim said. "I guess you made it to the transhumans' universe after all. Did you find what you were looking for? Are we causing the multiverse to collapse?"

"Yes and no. It started the moment the first universe was formed.

It's an ongoing process that we've been interfering with. Now the multiverse is just overcompensating and speeding it along, a bit recklessly if you ask me."

Ephraim leaned forward. "What do you mean?"

"It's what we're good at. We're an unnatural element that disrupts the natural order of things. But it's more serious than forcing a few thousand species to extinction. Now we're all endangered, us along with everything in the multiverse. Go, humans. We're not supposed to communicate with other universes, let alone visit them and bring back souvenirs and tourists. Just talking to you right now is like pulling at a loose thread."

"Are you sure?" Ephraim asked.

"As sure as I can be about anything, Junior. And you know it too, or you would still be with Jena and the others instead of in a universe twenty-five years in its past, talking to me with an amateur radio. I'm betting you ran just like I did."

"You think you know a lot," Ephraim said.

"Information is my business." Static crackled on the speaker. "Which means I'm working myself to death." Scott laughed harshly.

"I don't get it," Nathan said.

Ephraim transmitted. "Why is that funny?"

"Information is everything, Little Eph. That's all we are. That's all the universe is. And right now the universe is suffering from a bad case of TMI."

"Too much information?" Nathan shook his head. "I think he's nuts."

"It does make sense though," Ephraim said. He squeezed the microphone. "Dr. Kim, your Jena, she's trying to sort through all that information and force the multiverse to collapse into just one universe: hers."

"So that's what she's doing," Scott said. "That's like trying to cram ten pounds of shit into a five-pound bag. But she *might* be onto something."

"Can we reverse it?" Ephraim asked.

There was a long silence. "Hello? Scott, are you still there?" Ephraim asked.

"I'm here," Scott said.

"Can you repair the multiverse?" Ephraim asked.

"No. There's no reversing this. There's no separating universes or people that have already merged. We can't stop it, either. But we can let it run its course and mitigate the damage." Ephraim heard dead air, then the radio clicked on again. "But it's all up to you, little buddy."

Ephraim slumped in his seat. "That's what I was afraid of," he muttered.

CHAPTER 30

Nathan handed Ephraim the controller. "That should do it. As far as I can tell, it's in 'receive mode.' Like he instructed."

"Great work," Ephraim said.

"I didn't do much. That other you knew all the codes to get into the debugging subroutines for the controller. You could have done it without me."

Ephraim considered the controller in his hand. He held it out to Nathan.

"I don't think so," he said.

"You want me to come with you?" Nathan asked.

"It might be your last chance to see another universe," Ephraim said.

Nathan grinned. "I thought you'd never ask." He took the controller and tucked it into his pocket. He picked up his camera and checked through its settings. "Man, if I come back here with footage from a parallel universe on the brink of destruction, I might be able to win a Pulitzer."

"You'd at least be able to get on *Good Morning America*. If you can get up that early."

Nathan pointed the camera at Ephraim, and the red light flashed on.

"So, after we save the multiverse, who are you going to do?" Nathan asked.

"You mean 'what.' Then I say, 'I'm going to Disney World.'" Ephraim sat in front of the silent radio and idly spun the dial. He watched Nathan's reflection in the glass window over the dial as he panned his camera over his dad's workroom.

"I stand by my original question," Nathan said. "You can't celebrate heroism with a mere theme park. You deserve an entirely different kind of ride." He swung the camera toward Ephraim. "I'm referring to sex."

"I got that." Ephraim grinned.

A muffled ringing sound filled the room.

"Your pants are ringing," Ephraim said.

"That isn't my phone," Nathan said. "Oh, that's the signal!" Nathan slid the controller out of his pocket. It rang again.

"I thought it only *looked* like a phone," Nathaniel said. "Are you telling me we could have just called for help?"

"Answer it," Ephraim said. Scott had simply told him to be ready for the dimensional shift, but he hadn't given any useful details like how or when to expect it. Ephraim grabbed onto the camera strap around Nathan's neck and wrapped it once around his wrist, to make sure neither of them would be left behind.

Nathan opened the controller and held it up to his ear.

"Hello?" he said. "This is ridiculous. There's no speaker on this—"

A moment later the Mackenzie garage disappeared from around them and they reappeared in a vast room. Ephraim's ears popped painfully and he winced. When he opened his eyes, the lights went out, plunging them into darkness, except for blue lightning crackling above their heads.

That had been unlike any other dimensional shift he'd ever experienced. He realized he was now holding the camera from the strap.

"Nathan?"

Ephraim turned to see if Nathan was next to him, but the sudden motion in the darkness made him lose his balance. He tipped forward, caught himself, then doubled over and threw up.

He heard an echoing splash a few feet away that told him Nathan had shifted with him and was similarly incapacitated.

"Ugh," Nathan said. "Something I ate didn't agree with me." He coughed and spat. "Actually, I think that was everything I ate, ever. My whole life flushed before my eyes."

Ephraim was glad he couldn't see anything. "It's the shift to another universe. You'll feel better in a second," he said.

"You knew this would happen? That's why you gave Jena that bucket at the prom," Nathan said. "You could have helped a bro out."

"I've been to so many universes with your analogs, I forgot you've never shifted before. I'm more worried about the fact that *I* just got sick."

He was okay, though. Ephraim straightened slowly. His balance was back to normal, and his hearing wasn't muffled like he was underwater. The space they were in was stifling, with the volcanic smell of hot machine oil. He heard clanking, the slow grind of metal against metal, a gentle humming sound that made him think of the coin, and something else. Footsteps on a metal catwalk?

"You all right?" Ephraim croaked. He spat in the darkness and hoped he didn't hit anything or anyone.

"Yeah. Aside from the bad taste in my mouth. And the blindness," Nathan said. "Life isn't worth living if I can never see a woman again."

"At least you'll have an excuse to touch one."

Ephraim opened his mouth. That had been his voice, and he'd been having that very thought—but someone else said it first. The voice came from Nathan's other side.

"True. Where are you?" Nathan asked.

"I didn't say that," Ephraim said. "The other me did. Scott."

Lights strobed on overhead, and Ephraim could see the large room they were in. The lit area was easily the size of Greystone Park, but the edges receded into blackness, so he couldn't tell how big the space was. It was painted a gun-metal gray, and the light sources were several stories above him, like little suns floating in a dark sky.

A giant silver disc hovered directly above his head. It was illuminated by spotlights and encased in a shimmering transparent sphere, like a coin in a floating bubble. Blue electricity jumped from the metal disc and struck the sides of the globe as the disc slowly rotated horizontally inside it, reminding him of one of those novelty electric balls that he'd seen at science fairs.

The air itself vibrated with energy, and the floor trembled beneath Ephraim's feet. He looked down and saw that he and Nathan stood on a raised platform with a silver mesh floor that sparked with electricity.

"Wow," Ephraim said.

Nathan took the camera from him. Ephraim had forgotten he was holding it.

"Get a shot of that thing," Ephraim said, pointing up.

But Nathan was already interested in recording something behind Ephraim. "Shazam," he muttered.

Ephraim turned . . .

And saw himself.

It was like looking in a mirror—if the mirror also dropped a hundred pounds, gave you long greasy hair, a bushy beard, and premature balding.

It was inarguably another, older Ephraim.

His skin was pasty with sallow patches, blemishes, and blisters. He had long, cracked, dirty fingernails. He smelled like a gym locker.

What was the protocol for meeting yourself? Should they hug or shake hands? The older Ephraim just seemed content to glare at his younger self and Nathan.

"You brought a plus one," said Scott. He stomped across the floor toward them, his face red with anger. "No wonder we blew a fuse. I wasn't expecting to transport two people."

"Chill, old dude," Nathan said. "We made it safely."

"I've never done that procedure before. You're lucky the two of you weren't fused together. Or that Nathan wasn't dead on arrival," Scott said. "I used my DNA to lock onto yours, Ephraim, and followed the signal from the controller to pull you here. Just you and whatever was immediately in contact with your skin. When you both came through, it took me an extra moment to reassemble his molecules."

Ephraim and Nathan had been connected only by the thin nylon strap of the camera, but it had been enough to bring his friend along when Scott triggered the shift. The strap must have passed through Nathan's body while he was still materializing, leaving Ephraim holding the camera.

"If I'd told you he was coming, would you have let him?" Ephraim asked.

"Definitely not," Scott said.

"There you go," Ephraim said. "I figured."

"The shift put too much load on the Coherence Engine. If it had blown a circuit or been drained too much, it would all be over. *Everything*. As it is, I'm not even sure I can send you away again." He turned and squinted up at the slowly rotating disc. "It's going to take a while to recharge, if we even have enough power to complete a cycle."

"I wouldn't have brought him if I didn't think he would be helpful," Ephraim said.

"I remember having better judgment at your age," Scott said. "No offense, Nathan."

"Plenty taken," Nathan said. "What's your problem, man? We're on your side."

"What are you recording with that camera?" Scott demanded.

"Right now? A loud dumbass."

Scott's eyes bulged and he sputtered. Then he laughed.

"Don't mind him. You forget the camera's there after a while," Ephraim said. "He's filming everything, like for a documentary."

"Are you, now?" The older analog scratched at his beard thoughtfully. "Everything?"

Nathan lowered the camera uncertainly.

"No, no. Keep doing what you're doing. Been at it for a while?"

"Since the prom," Nathan said.

"And you still have all that footage? With you?"

"You bet." Nathan patted his camera bag. "I haven't had a chance to edit any of it yet."

"Edit . . ." Scott faced Ephraim. "You might be right about him, Junior. You have good instincts after all."

"Not sure if that's a compliment, coming from you."

"We're our own harshest critics. I'm doing you a favor. If I can't be honest with you, no one will be."

"I will," Nathan chimed in.

Ephraim saluted him. "I can always count on you giving me your own skewed perspective on things. Whether I want to hear it or not."

"Well, come on," Scott said.

Ephraim hopped down from the platform. "Uh, sorry about the mess," he said. "I don't know why I got so sick this time. Hasn't happened in a year."

"For some strange reason, the human body doesn't take it well when its molecules are ripped apart, tunneled into another universe, and slammed back together again on the other side. It's even more stressful when you get pulled across space as well as across dimensions. You're in the Pacific Northwest now, about a thousand feet below the surface. That's a bit outside the range of the controller."

"Are there any side effects?" Nathan wiped his mouth with the back of his hand. "Any *other* side effects?"

"I wouldn't eat anything for a couple of hours, which is good because the food here's terrible, unless you like Meals, Ready-to-Eat. Oh, and you're probably sterile now," Scott said.

"What?" Ephraim asked.

"You don't even want to have kids," Scott said.

"I've changed my mind recently," Ephraim said.

He'd never wanted to be responsible for disappointing a kid the way his parents had so often disappointed him. But meeting Doug had given him a different perspective.

Scott shook his head and walked away.

"No, seriously. Are we sterile?" Ephraim asked. He jogged to catch up with his older self.

"Hey. Is anyone going to clean this up?" Nathan almost slipped on the wet platform as he climbed down from it. He was pale and still a little shaky.

Scott glanced over his shoulder and considered the vomit dripping through the grating. He shrugged.

"No point," he said.

Nathan walked backward, recording the giant gyroscope turning slowly over the platform. Ephraim realized the bubble was slowly descending, like the crystal ball in Times Square at New Year's. Rainbow patterns swirled over the surface of the globe, and sometimes he caught flickers of cities and faces.

"If we're underground, what's topside? Zombies? Dinosaurs?"

"Toxic levels of radiation and an atmosphere you wouldn't want to breathe for more than ten minutes. And billions of rotting corpses. For humanity's last trick: mass suicide."

Nathan blanched.

"So people went underground to survive," Ephraim said. "Where are they now?"

"They escaped to other universes," Nathan said. "Right?"

"Some people did," Scott said. "They went to younger universes like ours. Or they migrated to worlds where they could start all over again on unspoiled land. But plenty of people refused to give up their technology. They'd made it this far, and they wanted to keep moving forward, not go backward.

"As the universe ages, there are fewer choices for how things can go," Scott continued. "The multiverse is like a balloon—it expands, and then it contracts. New universes replace old ones." He spread his hands wide. "And all roads lead here."

"You're saying there are no other universes in this timeline?" Nathan said.

"Quick study," Scott said. "You're close. All the universes in this timeline are just like this one. So the minds of this universe decided to share their technology with younger worlds, in the hopes that this would lead to a better future for humanity. That's what they told me, anyway."

"I'm guessing they had an ulterior motive," Ephraim said.

They walked in silence for a short while, Ephraim impatient for Scott to continue with his story, Nathan busy recording their surroundings. The cavernous room they'd been in had narrowed to a corridor barely wide enough to accommodate the three of them walking side by side. Lights came on just ahead of them as they walked and switched off behind them, giving the impression that they were moving through an endless dark void.

"So if they didn't leave, where is everybody?" Nathan asked. His voice echoed ahead, then seemed to creep up on them from behind, reverberating against the walls.

Scott stopped abruptly. Ephraim and Nathan walked past him a few steps, then turned to look at him.

"All around you," Scott said, wild eyed.

Nathan coughed, covering his mouth with one arm. "We're breathing them?"

Scott laughed, the echo effect adding a maniacal quality to it. "The walls are a multiplexing storage matrix for a quantum computer the size of this entire arcology."

"We're inside a computer?" Ephraim said.

"We're surrounded by it. *They're* inside the computer. They uploaded themselves as bits and bytes. Boots and bots." Scott giggled. "Bats and butts."

Ephraim looked at his other self, wondering if he needed to smack him. "Okay." It sounded like Scott had been alone here for too long.

"So everyone transferred themselves into what, a simulation?" Nathan asked.

"You got me. They were gone when I arrived and there's no way to communicate with them once they've crossed over. I've tried. They thought they were saving themselves, but personally, I think they're dead."

Scott walked on, brushing past Ephraim and Nathan.

"What about the rest of the world?" Ephraim asked.

"Maybe they have their own computers," Scott said. "Some of them went to space stations before things got really bad."

"What's the point of living without their bodies?" Nathan asked.

"So their minds would still be around when humanity reaches the next, and final, level of evolution: pure mental energy. Incorporeal consciousness. They won't need bodies then."

Ephraim stuffed his hands in pockets. "He's kidding us," he said.

Scott laughed. "Am I? It took me a while to piece it all together. Maybe I've gotten it wrong, but I don't think so. I've thought of almost nothing else for the past ten years. It was their master plan."

Scott's face was drenched in sweat, and he was panting. The last thing they needed was for the guy to keel over from a heart attack before they found out what they were supposed to do here.

Scott grunted and moved ahead of them, walking more quickly now.

They finally emerged into a smaller space than the one they'd just left, which consisted of a video screen embedded into the wall and a large flat console.

"This is like the Batcave. You even had a giant penny back there, sort of," Nathan said.

"More like the Fortress of Solitude," Ephraim and Scott said at the same time. They stared at each other.

For a moment, Ephraim saw himself in that older man, but then the moment was lost and he was looking at a man with unsightly wet patches under the arms of his baggy gray jumpsuit. He had to stop himself from becoming . . . that. Scott had given up on everything.

No—he hadn't given up. He was still fighting to protect the people he loved. That realization allowed Ephraim to sympathize with his older self.

"What?" Scott asked.

Ephraim blinked. "When did you start going bald?" he asked.

Scott ran a hand through his thinning hair.

"Junior, we have bigger problems right now."

"Right. Sorry."

Scott tapped the onyx console with three fingers, and it lit up. It was a touchscreen with multicolored icons and a virtual keyboard. Scott pressed one of the panels, and two egg-shaped chairs rose out of the floor on either side of his cushy recliner.

"Have a seat," Scott said.

"The future is just like I imagined it." Nathan put a hand on the back of his chair reverently.

"Me too," Scott said. "Everyone's dead or dying."

CHAPTER 31

Ephraim sat in his chair. It was as uncomfortable as it looked, and when he leaned back, he could only see Scott leaning against the console in front of him.

"How did you get here?" Ephraim asked. "Nathaniel had your coin."

Scott smiled. "You should know by now that there are two sides to every story, just as there are two sides to every coin." He held out a hand, and something flashed. He rolled a silver coin down his knuckles, then brought it back around and did it again. Light glinted off the shiny metal. Scott expertly flipped it to Ephraim.

Ephraim caught the coin and studied it. It was a blank silver disc, which should mean that it was drained of power, but it was warm and tingling. It felt alive.

"You had two coins?" Ephraim asked. "That's why there were two controllers!"

"Do you remember eighth-grade science class? When we used a magnet to turn an ordinary paper clip into a weaker magnet?"

Ephraim nodded.

"This works on a similar principle. That's a master token. If you place it in a controller along with a second disc of similar properties, you can make a functional duplicate of the original."

"So this is kind of a template, and that state quarter was a copy of it?" Ephraim asked.

"That was my Dad's quarter. He gave it to me on the first day of high school. For luck. If you use an object from your own universe, it makes shifting easier since you both have the same quantum wavelength."

"Naturally," Nathan said. "Everyone knows that."

Ephraim weighed the silver token in his hand. It was heavier than his coin, but it still felt very familiar and comfortable in his hand. Like it wanted to be there.

He shook his head. It wasn't a living thing.

"Why didn't you tell Everett that you could make more coins? Or Nathaniel?" Ephraim asked. Then the answer came to him.

He squeezed the disc, staring at his older self. "If they'd known they could make copies of the coin, for any other user, they wouldn't have needed you," Ephraim said. "Is that right?"

Scott didn't respond.

"I'll take that as a yes."

"Does it matter?" Scott's voice was pained.

"Tell me you didn't want to burden Nathaniel with your secret," Ephraim said.

"That's true!" Scott said. "If I'd told him, he might have told the others."

"That's not the same thing," Nathan said. "That sounds more like you didn't trust him."

Ephraim glanced at his friend uncomfortably. He'd shut Nathan out in the same way—he hadn't trusted him enough after seeing what his analogs were capable of. That was another thing he had in common with Scott, and it wasn't an encouraging resemblance.

Scott shook his head. He was retreating more and more into the mental world that had been his reality for ten years. All that time, alone here, surrounded by ghosts in the machine. Buried deep underground. It was a perverse coincidence that Dr. Kim had nicknamed the portable coheron drive the Charon device—for this other Ephraim Scott, the coin had paid his passage to a very real underworld.

"I didn't trust Everett," Scott said. "He was out of control. He ignored everything I told him about this universe. He was only interested in taking credit for the invention and collecting more data. He made me program the coin so he and Jena could find another version of himself." Scott laughed. "But I configured it so the trip would make him sick, every time. He couldn't go on using it."

"Jeez," Nathan breathed. "We're depending on this guy to save the multiverse? We're doomed."

Ephraim held up a hand and waved it. "Scott," he said. His other self didn't look at him. "Eph," he tried. This time he responded.

"You stranded Nathaniel in another universe," Ephraim said. "Why?"

"I tried to ditch him to come here, but he tracked me with the controller. I realized the only way to escape was to use the token he didn't know I had. I left him the coin where he would find it, in the park fountain in another universe, and disappeared."

Ephraim flipped the token. Scott's eyes followed it.

"Why didn't you just use the token to leave from your own universe?" Ephraim asked. "Then you wouldn't have jeopardized your best friend."

"The LCD would have detected that I'd shifted. If I ever went back, they would want to know how I did it," Scott said. "I checked first—my analog and his family were living in Summerside, so I knew he would be able to find another version of me to get him home."

"The only problem was that our analog was five at the time. Then when he was finally old enough to help, he ended up using the coin selfishly instead."

"What?" Scott asked.

"Then my analog tried to pull the same disappearing act you did, only he was accidentally killed in a hit-and-run in my universe. That's kind of where I came in."

"How long was Nathaniel trapped there?" Scott asked.

"Ten years," Ephraim said. "He waited for ten years."

Scott groaned. "I never meant for that to happen."

"Scott, why did you really leave?" Ephraim asked. "I heard the tape. You nobly wanted to find out the truth from the transhumans. You got what you came for, yet you're still here. So what happened?"

"Jena got . . . close to the second Everett."

"Please tell me you didn't leave because you were *jealous*," Ephraim said.

"I loved her. We'd been dating off and on since high school. I thought she was the one." He laughed. "The *one*. I know how ridiculous the idea of that is, now."

"Unbelievable," Nathan said. "Eph, I'm sorry, but your analog is a total loser."

"I asked her to come with me," Scott said. "I told her my suspicions about the transhumans and Everett's intentions, but she refused to leave. She believed in Everett—both of them—too much. She was more in love with the idea of working at the Institute than she ever could be with me."

"But she was with you," Ephraim said. "You threw it away."

"I wanted her to come after me," Scott said. "The controller worked for her. Every time I tried to get away, I thought she would find me. But it was always Nathaniel."

"You drove her and Everett together. You left, then Nathaniel left and couldn't get back. Dr. Kim tried to hold up the Institute with Everett, but he didn't know what he was doing and he couldn't build his own coheron drive."

"I wish it could have turned out differently. But as it happens, it's a good thing I left."

They were silent for a moment that stretched on too long. The only sound was a steady, distant beep from one of the consoles.

"How do you figure that any good came of this at all?" Ephraim asked. "The three of you have been miserable and alone for more than a decade."

"I'd been wondering for a while if the transhumans were as benevolent as they seemed. I wanted Jena to come with me so I could show her this place. She could have helped me work out what was going on. Instead, I ended up here on my own, learned how to use all this abandoned technology myself. I've been taking care of the machine. And I discovered my hunch was right. They gave us the portable coheron drives to sacrifice the multiverse for their own gain."

"Isn't that what Dr. Kim is doing?" Ephraim said.

"They have something worse in mind." Scott waved his hand over the console. A screen behind him displayed a white circle.

"This is the universe," Scott said.

Nathan yawned. "It looks like a donut," he said.

Ephraim struggled out of his chair and stood next to Scott.

"Go on," Ephraim said. "I'm listening."

Scott input a sequence into the console. More circles started appearing in different colors, beside the original circle.

"Each of those circles represents another adjacent reality," Scott said. "The multiverse."

More circles began appearing around it, many of them close enough to touch the circle in the center and each other. Some of the first circles began disappearing the farther the circles spread out.

"Most parallel universes are meant to be fleeting. They come into existence when individual actions diverge at a quantum decision point, but they often disappear or merge back into each other, according to the decisions with the greater probability. Have you ever misremembered something that happened to you?" Scott asked.

Ephraim nodded.

"Sometimes our memories are faulty, but other times it's the universes merging, without us consciously noticing. Déjà vu is another one of those side effects, when you merge with a universe a split-second ahead of yours," Scott said.

"Consider it, Ephraim," he went on. "Every single person in the world, billions and billions of people, each causing a new universe to appear with each decision . . . choosing pancakes over French toast, turning left instead of right. Every electron in the universe causes a new universe to appear to account for its erratic motion. The multiverse can't sustain that for long. Think of it as a kind of buffer, a backup system. As the queue fills, it purges itself of old data, at more or less the same rate. It remains in balance."

"How long does a universe stay in the buffer?" Ephraim asked.

"Until a certain probability establishes itself as more likely than the others," Scott said.

Those were those phantom universes Nathaniel had told Ephraim about, the ones that exist in their own quantum state, half-real, half-imagined.

"When the controller stores a coordinate for one of these universes, the act of observing and recording its existence strengthens its reality. It becomes a permanent fixture in the multiverse. Instead of disappearing when it's supposed to, it becomes a new anchor point that in turn spawns other universes. Now look at what happens."

The screen showed circles appearing much more quickly, and now they were overlapping with each other like Venn diagrams. They were also appearing stacked over each other, barely separated in space but clearly overlapping precisely when Ephraim tilted his head one way to see them in three dimensions in the holographic display.

"Getting pretty crowded, isn't it?" Scott asked. "Multiverses are being created at an exponential state, and they're sticking around."

The universes were represented as multicolored cylinders now, piling over each other. Ephraim closed his eyes and squeezed the bridge of his nose.

"Stop," he said. "I get it."

"You can't stop it, Ephraim. That's the point," Scott said.

Nathan joined them at the console, camera aimed at the screen.

"But it turns out, it *has* to stop. The transhumans discovered that the multiverse is finite. It's the ultimate data storage mechanism, but it's running out of space. The system's overloading and now it's writing over parts of itself just to keep going. It's merging universes at an accelerated rate, randomly and arbitrarily, forcing disparate realities together in ways they don't belong—probability be damned. When everything happens in the multiverse all at once, there's no way to decide which event is more likely than any other."

Scott took the coin from Ephraim and laid it on the console. "*We* did this," he said.

"Did the transhumans know what they were doing?" Ephraim asked.

"Oh, they knew," Scott said. "They set us up. And we went for it."

"I thought they wanted to save humanity."

"Yes, but what does that mean? To them, humanity's manifest destiny is to become pure consciousness. Some scientists call this the Omega Point, and there are two ways to reach it. One way is to advance your technology so far that you transcend into a new kind of noncorporeal life. Sometimes that's referred to as the Singularity."

Scott spread his hands to take in the room.

"The transhumans came close, but they didn't quite make it in time. Heat death of the universe, and all that. They've preserved themselves as quantum minds in the computer. Noncorporeal life, but not all that satisfying," Scott said. "They want to be *energy*, right?"

"So what's the second way?" Ephraim asked.

"The universe fills up with too much information. At that point, *everything* becomes information—same result, but it's the brute force method."

"They wanted to give us a head start, they said," Ephraim said. "But they were really giving themselves a second chance."

"If a *multiverse* reaches its Omega Point, every universe in it reaches it, too. Not so great for most of them. Our universes still had millenia of living to go. But it's a great deal for the transhumans whose clock was running down," Scott said. He looked up. "Tick, tock. Tick, tock."

"Bastards," Nathan said.

"They were willing to wipe out most of the multiverse to save themselves?" Ephraim asked.

"They used us," Scott said. "It wasn't enough for them to commit suicide, they had to take everyone else with them."

"I assume there's a way to change the plan, if you brought us here," Ephraim said.

"A massive dump," Scott said.

Nathan giggled. Scott and Ephraim glared at him.

"Of *data*," Scott said. "If we're approaching the kill screen of the multiverse—game over—then the only thing we can do is hit reset early. Before it runs out of space."

Scott waved his hand over the console again, and the circles started disappearing from the screen until there was only one left, right in the center. He put his coin on the console, and the circle became a silver disc, which slowly rotated.

"We have to start over," Scott said.

Ephraim gazed at the screen.

"This is what Dr. Kim's trying to do," Ephraim said. "You agree with her?"

"She's a very smart woman," Scott said. "She's picking up the multiverse's slack, adding order to a chaotic system. She's bought us some time, but she's being too selective. It's like bailing water in a paper cup—you'll never work fast enough and the cup won't hold together for long. More realities are spawning every nanosecond, taking the place of the ones that are gone.

"Entropy has to take its course. Nature abhors a vacuum, but it abhors artificiality even more," Scott said. "And too much order is just as unnatural."

"You want to get rid of everything all at once," Ephraim said.

"This is the last thing I *want* to do, Ephraim. But this isn't about what I want. It can't be personal. That's where Jena is getting this wrong."

"But all those people in the multiverse . . ."

"We can't save everyone."

Zoe had told him the same thing. He knew it made sense, but . . .

"How do we choose one universe out of all those possibilities?" he asked.

"Pick one randomly," Scott said. "That seems fair. It doesn't really matter, so long as some life goes on somewhere and has the chance to split into new realities when the multiverse settles down again."

"Why haven't you done this already?" Ephraim asked. "What do you need us for?"

"To make this work right, we have to delete all the data we have on those other universes and disable all the coheron drives— simultaneously. And funny as it seems at the moment, I can't be in two places at once," Scott said.

"So call them and tell them what to do," Ephraim said.

"If I contact Jena and ask her really nicely to please destroy her drive, she probably won't listen. I need someone I trust implicitly to pull this off." Scott looked at Ephraim and Nathan. "You two will have to do."

"Thanks," Nathan said dryly.

"You have to delete all the recorded coordinates for every universe you've visited, except for the one universe you're going to preserve as the template. Every file, every backup. If it's even written on a piece of paper, that might be enough to keep it real. Information is that powerful."

"What if someone's memorized the coordinates to a universe?" Ephraim asked.

"Kill them." Scott stared at him impassively then burst out laughing. "Just kidding. I think we only have to worry about physical records, but then again, I've never done this before." He smiled. "Or maybe I have. Maybe we're all part of the multiverse's grand design."

"Does a video recording count?" Nathan asked, looking at his camera.

"You asked which universe to save," Scott said. "I think the one we have the most information about makes a good choice. That'll stabilize it and give it preferred basis. You have a lot of footage of your universe."

"But every universe has tons of footage. All those security cameras. All the videos uploaded to the Internet. That's probably even more true in the future, right?" Ephraim asked.

Scott nodded. "But this is the only footage of a universe that exists outside of the universe it was recorded in." He snapped his fingers at Nathan. "Keep recording."

Nathan gave him a thumbs-up.

"This feels awfully selfish," Ephraim said. "I don't feel much better about this than Dr. Kim's plan. Why is my universe any better than hers?"

"I'm not saying it is."

"Are you sure there's no way to prevent more than one universe from disappearing?"

"It's risky to try to save too many. Some universes will probably stick around anyway, once there's enough room in the buffer. When we erase the information we've been saving and remove the coheron drives from the multiverse, it'll all be up to chance—as it should be. The universes may simply disappear, or they could merge in unpredictable ways. But that's better than wiping the slate completely clean and pushing all of us to the Omega Point, yeah?

E pluribus unum. One from many.

"Okay." Ephraim took a deep breath. "Tell us how to pull this off."

CHAPTER 32

Ephraim and Nathan appeared in the atrium of the Everett Institute. Ephraim grunted as his ears popped from the change in pressure and elevation while Nathan knelt and retched.

Ephraim stretched his jaw to clear his ears and helped his friend to his feet. Nathan had tears in his eyes.

The gyroscope of the Large Coheron Drive was still. Ephraim reached into his pocket and touched the token Scott had given him. The smooth metal disc vibrated gently against his fingers, as if reacting to its proximity to its sister machine.

"Is that it?" Nathan cocked his head back to study the LCD. "It's smaller than Scott's."

"Uh-huh," Ephraim said. He checked the cameras positioned all around the atrium, wondering if Dr. Kim was watching them. He'd expected alarms to go off when they arrived, but it just showed that she no longer counted Ephraim as a threat, and she didn't know about Nathan at all.

"Put your hand on that panel." Ephraim pointed at the flat black plate mounted beside the door to the control room.

Nathan glanced at him skeptically, then pressed his palm against the biometric scanner. A moment later it pulsed green, but it didn't open. A numeric pad appeared on the screen.

"Crap. Your analog is more paranoid than I thought," Ephraim said. "What would you use?"

Nathan thought for a moment, then typed in 1-2-3-4-5.

"That's a stupid password," Ephraim said.

"That's why no one would try it," Nathan said.

"Well, it didn't work." Ephraim squinted at the skylight. He'd lost all track of time in Seattle Below, but it looked like early morning here.

Doug's blue balloon bobbed lazily against the glass. "We'll have to find Nathaniel or Zoe for access, then." Preferably Zoe. "Let's head up."

Nathan's handprint opened the doors to the main portion of the building without any difficulties.

They walked quickly down the corridor to the elevator.

"Should we take the stairs?" Nathan asked. "To preserve the element of surprise?"

"If anyone's paying attention, they already know we're here," Ephraim said. He pushed the call button, and the elevator started down from the top floor.

He tensed as the doors opened, but it was empty.

"What floor?" Nathan asked as they entered.

"Ten."

Nathan jabbed the button and hummed his own elevator music as they rode up. Just as Ephraim was going to throttle him, the elevator dinged.

"Tenth floor. Mad scientists, evil doubles, and ex-girlfriends," Nathan said.

The doors opened. Ephraim peered out, but there was no one waiting for them.

"It looks clear," he said.

Nathan nodded. "I'll cover you."

"With what?"

Nathan smiled and pointed the camera at him.

"Great."

Ephraim stepped out of the elevator and looked around. It was empty. Where was everyone?

"It's quiet," Nathan said.

"Don't you dare say what you're about to say," Ephraim said.

He held up a hand. There were voices coming from the conference room on the left. He turned back to Nathan.

"You hear that?" Ephraim whispered.

Nathan nodded.

"I'll check it out," Ephraim said.

"What if it's Dr. Kim?"

"Maybe I can reason with her. I have to face her sometime."

"That's your brilliant idea? You're going to talk to them?"

Ephraim eyed Nathan's camera. "It works in movies. Er. It sometimes works in movies. For a little while."

"It never does," Nathan said. "Well, hardly ever. She isn't going to listen to you."

"Probably not." Ephraim eyed Nathan's camera. "I have a cooler mission for you, in case talking doesn't work out."

Nathan grudgingly gave him the camera, and Ephraim told him what he wanted him to do. Then they split up. Ephraim took the left side of the lab, and Nathan went to the right.

Dr. Kim's office was dark, but the conference room was lit up and occupied.

Ephraim approached the door. The last thing he expected to see inside was Nathaniel, Zoe, Jena, and Hugh playing poker.

The door was locked, but his handprint released the latch. He opened the door.

"Surprise," Ephraim said. He grinned.

"Get him!" Zoe said. Nathaniel and Hugh jumped from their seats on either side of the door and closed in on Ephraim.

Ephraim held up his hands. "Guys! It's me!"

Hugh pinned Ephraim in a bear hug from the right. Nathaniel glowered at Ephraim.

Ephraim flinched, waiting for the blow.

"No!" Jena said. "That's Ephraim!"

"Duh," Zoe said.

"Not Ephraim," Jena said. "*Ephraim*. Look at his face."

"Nice. Who did that?" Zoe asked. "I'd like to congratulate him."

"*Et tu*, Zoe?" Ephraim said.

This was hardly the welcome he'd hoped for from his friends.

Zoe stared at him hard, and her mouth parted slightly. She approached Ephraim slowly.

"It *is* you, isn't it?" she asked.

"Good to see you, too," he said.

Zoe kissed him. For a moment, it was just the two of them.

"Guys, get a universe," Nathaniel said.

Zoe broke off their kiss. She looked at Hugh. "You can let him go," she said. "He's the real deal."

Hugh released Ephraim and brushed off his T-shirt. "Sorry about that," he said. "Glad you made it back. Can't wait to hear how."

Ephraim met Zoe's eyes. "Not so easy to tell analogs apart, is it? I'm waiting for an apology."

"I didn't expect to see you again," she said.

"Now why does that sound so familiar?" he said.

"So. Maybe this isn't the best time for a romantic interlude," Nathaniel said.

Zoe showed him her middle finger.

"I have a new philosophy. You should always take time to let people know how you feel," Ephraim said. "Or what are we trying to save?"

"Eph, I'm so sorry," Jena said. "I didn't know what else to do. I believed Dr. Kim."

"What changed your mind?" Ephraim asked.

"She's bonkers," Jena said. "She took the other Ephraim to scout other universes. She's looking for analogs to bring back here. You were right. She isn't leaving anything to chance anymore."

"I'm glad you found the controller," Nathaniel said. "Hugh and I hoped you would use it to sneak back here."

"You two worked together?" Ephraim asked. "Thanks, it was brilliant. I'm sorry I doubted you, Nathaniel. I thought you were with Dr. Kim."

"I was on the fence. I figured I was better off playing along until I knew for sure. But as soon as she sent your analog and Jena after the coin, it was evident she wasn't thinking clearly," Nathaniel said. "And I told her so."

"Is that why you were all locked up?" Ephraim asked.

"Dr. Kim is convinced that we're conspiring against her," Hugh said.

"She was right about that much," Nathaniel said. He and Hugh pulled two laptops out from under the table. They opened them and started typing while Zoe gathered the cards together.

Ephraim looked around the room. "Where's Doug?"

Nathaniel rapped on the table. "Come on out, champ."

Doug slowly emerged from under the table. He beamed at Ephraim.

"Eph!" Doug said. "You came back."

"Hey, kid." Ephraim ruffled his hair. Doug's face was sticky. He clutched a nearly empty bag of gummy bears. Ephraim smiled.

"Seeing that other Ephraim totally flipped the boy out," Jena said. "That's why he was hiding under the table. He's better at telling analogs apart than anyone."

Ephraim sat down, and Doug crawled into his lap. "Show me what you guys are working on," Ephraim said.

"Nathaniel got us into the mainframe," Hugh said.

"Tricky, because Dr. Kim set up so many password blocks," Nathaniel said.

"Fortunately, I designed this software. Or rather, my analog did," Hugh said. "So I know all the backdoors." His fingers flew rapidly over the keyboard.

"And we're exploiting them to copy the database of all the coordinates," Nathaniel said.

"That's wrong," Ephraim said. "We have to—"

Hugh held up a hand. "I finally figured it out. The multiverse is all about observation. And observation is about acquiring information," he said. "As long as information about these universes is stored somewhere, in some universe, they can't decohere. Once Dr. Kim has everything she wants in this reality, she's planning to purge all the rest. But she won't be able to if we take backups to other universes."

"We may not have the portable coheron drive, but the LCD can still send each of us on a one-way trip," Zoe said. "We can get back home!"

"I'm impressed, Hugh. You're right. This plan will definitely work," Ephraim said. "If we were going to follow it. But we can't."

"We have to," Jena said. "We have to save as many universes as we can."

Ephraim shook his head. "We have to delete all but *one* of the coordinates we've recorded, disable the LCD and Charon devices, and let nature run its course. Only one universe will survive, but it should be enough to start off a new multiverse."

They all stared at him in disbelief.

Nathaniel stood. "Kid, you were against Dr. Kim's plan from the start. You wanted to save every universe. This is how we do that."

"I was wrong. But that doesn't mean she's right. I have it on good authority that we need to wipe everything in the database." Ephraim checked his watch. "In exactly forty-seven minutes."

"On whose authority?" Nathaniel barked.

Ephraim locked eyes with Nathaniel. "I met one of my analogs. An old friend of yours."

"Ephraim's still alive?" Nathaniel said. "How? Where?"

Ephraim flashed the coin Scott had given him.

"He had another coin?" Nathaniel said. "That bastard."

"He did what he thought he had to," Ephraim said. "And so are we."

A wave of nausea passed over Ephraim. Jena and Zoe lowered their foreheads to the table, and Nathaniel slumped in his seat, face pale and sweat glistening on his forehead. Hugh moaned pitifully. Doug started bawling.

Then the feeling passed.

"Shh," Ephraim said. He hugged Doug and rocked him gently. "You're still here." He scanned the room with his eyes. Everyone was accounted for. "We're all still here."

Doug pressed his face into Ephraim's T-shirt. The boy's tears and snot soon wet a spot on Ephraim's shoulder.

"What was that?" Ephraim asked.

"Dr. Kim and your analog are back," Nathaniel said. "The same thing happened when they left with the Charon device. They'll be upstairs any minute."

The group gathered in front of the elevator. The elevator was already descending, the numbers above the doors counting down from ten.

Nathan wandered over, hands in his pockets.

"Did you guys feel that?" Nathan asked. He belched and held a hand to his stomach. "Pardon."

Nathaniel gaped at his younger analog. "I'll be damned."

"Probably." Nathan sized up his older self. "Not bad, old Nathan."

"Where did *you* come from?" Nathaniel asked.

"I had to keep Ephraim out of trouble." Nathan grinned.

"Good to see you, Nathan!" Jena said. Zoe nodded.

Hugh shook Nathan's hand and introduced himself.

"You've been holding out on me, kid," Nathaniel said to Ephraim. "What are you up to?"

"You'll see." Ephraim raised his eyebrows questioningly at Nathan. "Did you . . . ?"

"Mischief managed," Nathan said. "Pretty sweet setup, like you said. And my best work ever, if I do say so myself."

"How about the other thing?" Ephraim asked.

"Couldn't find it," Nathan said.

"Okay. Well, you have perfect timing." He checked his watch. They had forty-two minutes left. The elevator numbers were counting up from the ground floor.

They lined up in a row facing the elevator: Ephraim, Nathan, Nathaniel, Zoe, Jena, and Hugh. Ephraim held Doug's hand, but the boy hid behind him, peeking out around Ephraim's legs.

"Cute kid," Nathan said. "He takes after his mother."

"Thanks," Ephraim said.

When the elevator doors opened, Dr. Kim's face briefly registered shock before she composed herself and stepped out. Ephraim's analog trailed behind her. He flipped the coin over and over like a movie gangster, one hand in his pants pocket.

"Looks like we're just in time for the party," Dr. Kim said. Her eyes fell on Nathan. "Terrific. Just what we needed. Another Nathaniel."

"Hi, Dr. Kim," Ephraim said.

"If you're here to beg for a place in my universe, it's too late," Dr. Kim said. She tucked her hands into her lab coat pockets.

Ephraim looked at his analog standing beside her. "This isn't the Ephraim you want. I know you were out looking for his replacement."

The analog fumbled the coin. He recovered it and turned to her. "That's not what you—"

"Shut up," she said. "Both of you. *All* of you. I won't listen to any more of this."

"I figured as much," Ephraim said. "But I know someone you *will* listen to."

"Oh?" Dr. Kim's eyebrows shot up.

"Your Ephraim's still alive, Dr. Kim."

Her expression was unreadable. "That isn't possible."

"Nothing's impossible in a multiverse." Ephraim nudged Nathan with his elbow.

Nathan pulled a small remote control from his pocket and pointed it behind him.

Scott's face appeared on every monitor in the lab. His voice came from hidden speakers all around the room, like the voice of God: "*Jena, I love you. I know I tell you that every day, but I want it on the official record.*"

This time, the expression of shock remained on Dr. Kim's face. But they had her attention.

"Who wants popcorn?" Nathan asked.

CHAPTER 33

"I've made a terrible mistake. I haven't told Jena or Nathan what I'm plan-ning to do. If you two are listening to this, then I'm sorry. I don't know if I'll be able to get back to you, but I'm going to do whatever I can to fix this. I hope you can forgive me."

Ephraim frowned. Nathan had taken some creative liberties with Scott's recording. But Ephraim had to give his friend credit: He'd edited hours of footage into a "Best of Seattle Below" highlights reel in record time on the terminal in Nathaniel's office. It was a bit too heavy on what Nathan called "money shots" of the transhumans' Coherence Engine and Scott's console, but the narration got the point across.

"Most parallel universes are meant to be fleeting. They come into existence when individual actions diverge at a quantum decision point, but they often disappear or merge back into each other, according to the decisions with the greater probability," Scott said onscreen.

"We aren't supposed to have this technology. It's risky to try to save too many. Some universes will probably stick around anyway, once there's enough room in the buffer. When we erase the information we've been saving and remove the coheron drives from the multiverse, it'll all be up to chance—as it should be. The universes may simply disappear, or they could merge in unpre-dictable ways. But that's better than wiping the slate completely clean and pushing all of us to the Omega Point."

Scott had carefully outlined the plan for Ephraim and Nathan back in the transhumans' universe, and now for everyone else in the video recording. Nathaniel had a hard expression on his face as he watched, but Dr. Kim looked pale and a little lost.

"As soon as you get back to Crossroads, here's what you have to do. Choose the universe you're going to keep and queue the rest for deletion in the LCD mainframe. Wipe all the backups. Destroy the other Charon device."

"Use the remaining controller to set the coordinates to the universe you already selected, then erase the controller's memory; the coin will hold the coordinates until you touch it." Scott handed Ephraim the token onscreen.

"He had another coin?" Dr. Kim said. Her eyes were riveted on Scott's face. She slowly walked toward the screen on the wall opposite the elevator.

"Exactly an hour after you get back there, wipe the LCD and disable it." Ephraim checked his watch. "Thirty-nine minutes."

"Destroy it if you can. Take the coin and whoever's coming with you and get the hell out of there. When you get to your destination universe, destroy the controller and the coin. That's very important, Ephraim, if you want that universe to branch and rebuild a multiverse from that template."

"Wouldn't it be easier to stay in the same universe as Crossroads?" Ephraim asked.

"No. You should go to a universe where parallel universes are only a theory," Scott said. *"Or someone else will come up with their own coherence drive one day and this will just start all over again."*

"How do we choose who gets saved?" Nathaniel asked, a beat before Nathan asked the same question onscreen. They glanced at each other.

"That'll be the hard part, especially for you, Ephraim. The universe you go to can't have more than one analog of each of you in it. That universe could never make a stable multiverse. I can't predict what might happen if it branches with multiple versions of you or anyone else, but it won't be good. We might end up with other problems down the road."

"That's what I was afraid of," Jena said, looking at Zoe. They both looked at Ephraim.

"But if this works, and I think it will, it will put the last universe and its offshoots back on track, buying the human race millennia to become whatever it wants. That's all we're buying ourselves: a chance."

Scott's face faded to a shot of Ephraim's face. Nathan zoomed out and aimed the camera from low to show Ephraim standing on the Coherence Engine platform with electricity crackling dramatically above his head. It was the only flattering image of him that Nathan had ever captured.

The camera moved as Nathan climbed the steps to the platform and took his position beside Ephraim, just before they were zapped back to Crossroads. The shaky camera frame focused on Scott at the control panel in the distance, a tiny, lonely figure.

"*Energize, Mr. Scott,*" Nathan said on-camera, in his best Shatner impression.

The sound fizzed and popped. The image exploded into colorful static and broken pixels as Seattle Below disappeared with Scott. The screen faded to black.

Ephraim saw the thoughtful look on Dr. Kim's face reflected in the dark screen.

She reached into her pocket for her silver cigarette case and lighter. She put a cigarette into her mouth but didn't light it.

"He left me," Dr. Kim said.

Nathan pressed the power button on his camera's remote. The 3-D video feed of the atrium reappeared on the screen. Dr. Kim leaned closer to it, but she wasn't looking down at the LCD. She was looking up, at the blue balloon floating by the skylight just above her head.

Doug slipped his hand out of Ephraim's and toddled toward her. Ephraim grabbed for him, but the little boy was too fast.

"Doug!" he whispered loudly. "No!"

Doug stopped next to Dr. Kim and stared at the balloon with her. He reached up and tugged on her white coat. She looked down at him.

"Why are you so sad?" he asked. "You lose a balloon, too?"

She knelt next to Doug and took his hands in hers.

"Sort of," she said. She hugged Doug.

"I know you're not my mommy," he said. "You're mean."

Ephraim winced.

"I was upset because I don't have a little boy like you," she said. "I was too jealous of what other people have."

"Mommy gave me that balloon. You can have it," Doug said.

"Thanks, sweetie." Dr. Kim looked at the screen. "But I can't get to it either. It's too far away."

She straightened and put her hand on Doug's head. "Eph can be such an idiot sometimes," she said.

The boy ducked away from her and stared at the screen on his own.

"Jena, we have to let it all go," Nathaniel said. "It's time."

Her shoulders slumped in defeat. "I won't try to control the outcome. Realities can merge or disappear as they will. The way they were always meant to."

Ephraim cleared his throat. "We need your access codes, Dr. Kim," he said.

"No." She turned around and looked Ephraim in the eyes. "I'll take care of the Large Coheron Drive myself."

"All right," Ephraim said.

"Eph?" Zoe said.

"We have to trust each other if we're going to get through this," he said. "You heard Scott's plan. There's still a lot to do. We have to work together to meet his deadline."

Dr. Kim handed Nathaniel the controller from her pocket. "I'm going down to the control room now," she said. "How much time do we have?"

Ephraim checked his watch. "Half an hour."

"I'll disable the LCD. You do whatever you have to. Whatever you want." She waved a hand dismissively and headed toward the elevator.

"What about me?" Ephraim's analog asked.

"What about you?" Dr. Kim brushed past him into the open elevator. The doors closed and whisked her down to ground level. The analog grimaced.

Nathaniel looked at the controller in his hands. "Okay, I'll dismantle this. Jena, Zoe, can you two work on deleting the backup files? Hugh and Ephraim will queue up the universes for deletion."

"*Ahem*," Ephraim's analog said.

"What is it, Two?" Ephraim asked.

The analog shot Ephraim an annoyed look. "I'm not a number," he said. "I have a name."

"No, but you do need a nickname," Nathan said. "Ephraim and Scott are both taken. How about . . . Dick?"

"No," Dick said.

"I think it suits you," Ephraim said.

"You don't mind, do you, Dick?" Jena asked.

"I do mind. Stop calling me that."

"Oh, this makes it so much easier to talk. Dick is a lovely nickname," Jena said.

"It isn't even remotely related to Ephraim," Dick said.

Hugh clapped a hand on Dick's shoulder. "My condolences. I know what it's like to get stuck with a poor nickname. You'll get used to it."

"I hate all of you right now," Dick said. "I just wanted to help."

Nathaniel nodded toward Doug. "Take care of the kid."

Dick rolled his eyes, but he wandered over to stand next to Doug at the monitor.

"Ow!" Dick said. "The brat pinched me."

Hugh typed in some commands on the terminal. A list of coordinates scrolled down the screen, organized by date. There were thousands of entries. Hugh highlighted them all.

"We're supposed to leave one universe," Ephraim said.

"Which?" Hugh asked.

"That's the question," Ephraim said.

"Shall I pick one at random?"

"Scott said it should be one that doesn't know about parallel universes. The only ones we know for sure where the multiverse is only a theory is my universe and Zoe's," Ephraim said.

"And mine," Hugh said. "It isn't even a theory there. If I never publish my paper, maybe it won't even be that much."

"Good point. Pull it up."

Hugh scrolled through the list, looking for the coordinates to his universe.

Jena and Zoe arrived. Zoe joined Ephraim, and Jena leaned over Hugh, looking at his screen.

"We erased the backups," Zoe said. "And reformatted the servers, just to be sure."

"Time?" Jena asked.

"Fifteen minutes," Ephraim said.

"Guys!" Dick called from one of the monitors displaying the atrium. "Ephraim!"

"Does it ever not feel weird to hear yourself?" Ephraim asked.

"No," Jena and Zoe said. They sighed.

They went over to see what was going on. Nathaniel was already at the monitor, looking down at the LCD alongside Dick. Doug was jumping up and down excitedly.

"Dr. Kim's up to something," Dick said.

Ephraim pressed his forehead to the glass and watched as the LCD began rotating and electricity crackled along its frame. A faint, transparent image shimmered into view in the center of the ring, with the disc spinning so quickly it looked like a solid ball. He saw Scott standing on the other side of the portal. Dr. Kim walked under the statue of Atlas. She vanished.

"Where'd she go?" Jena asked.

"To Scott," Nathan said.

"Wow, that's romantic," Zoe said.

"What a waste," Dick said. "Isn't the transhumans' universe done for? She's too hot to die."

"See? Your nickname's perfect for you," Jena said. "Dick."

"That was sweet and all, but Dr. Kim said she would destroy the LCD," Ephraim said. "Now one of us has to get down there to—"

"It isn't over." Dick pointed down at the atrium.

The group watched as the rotating disc of the LCD picked up speed. It was sparking now, the disc glowing white-hot at its center.

"Uh. We're safe in here, right?" Nathan asked.

"This place is practically an impenetrable fortress," Nathaniel said. "I designed the shielding myself."

Nathan glanced at his analog skeptically, then took a few steps away from the wall separating them from the runaway machine below.

They heard a horrendous tearing sound, an agony of rent metal, and the frame of the LCD started to buckle.

"It's melting," Jena said.

One of the metal rings broke away from the machine. It careened at high velocity and ricocheted off the walls, rising five stories before clattering back down to the ground and wobbling to a stop. They felt dull thuds in the floor from each impact, and the wall-mounted monitor shook from the force.

The second ring shot out horizontally and slammed into the steel-plated wall on the opposite wall, which crumpled inward. It stuck there for a moment, quivering, before it tumbled down to the cobblestones, bent into a rough crescent.

"Huh," Nathaniel said.

Doug clapped his hands and laughed.

The disc suddenly catapulted straight up into the air, turning over and over itself, still glowing white-hot. It flipped past them before hitting the skylight and breaking out of the atrium. Glass rained down, glinting in the noon sun like a shower of diamonds. Bricks and chunks of metal crumbled down from the shattered edges of the skylight. Something hit the camera, and the image cut off.

Nathaniel glanced up nervously. "I didn't reinforce the roof. I didn't expect the LCD to drop on us."

Ephraim ran to the monitor around the right corner and saw Zoe head for the one around the left.

The monitor facing Dr. Kim's office blinked the gray message "Signal Lost" over and over. He kept going around the next corner just as Zoe arrived from the opposite direction. The monitor facing the elevator still worked. The camera was tilted at a forty-five-degree angle, and snow dotted the picture, but he could see what was happening on the other side of the shielded wall.

"Over here!" they said.

The disc shot back down through the hole above the atrium, still turning over and over.

It hit the ground on its edge, a few feet in front of Atlas, and embedded itself three feet into the ground with a deafening crack that reverberated through the atrium and made the building tremble around them.

"What are the odds of that?" Nathaniel asked.

Hugh pulled a pad from his breast pocket and started scribbling calculations.

Jena poked him in the side with her elbow. "Rhetorical question," she said.

The frame of the LCD was twisted and warped, like the ribs of a mighty beast. But Atlas himself amazingly still stood, his burden gone at last. His arms were raised not to carry a heavy weight but in triumph. Blue electricity arced between his outstretched hands and flickered along his bronze biceps before fading in the bright sunlight.

"She really did it," Zoe said. "I didn't think she would."

"Too bad she destroyed it ten minutes too early," Ephraim said. "With the LCD gone, we'd better get a move on and hope that other universes don't merge with this one before we can purge them. One working Charon device isn't going to protect all of us."

CHAPTER 34

The group studied the list of universes Hugh had called up on his screen.

"These two are ours," Zoe said, pointing out two coordinates that differed only by a couple of digits. "There's Hugh's. This is the one we're in, and this is where Dr. Kim went to be with Scott." She glanced at Dick. "We don't know where Dick came from, though."

"That can't be helped now," Ephraim said.

"Nice," Dick said.

"Which one do we keep?" Zoe said.

"I have a better question," Dick said. "Which of us are going there?"

"Oh, yeah. Only one of each of us can go," Jena said.

"What if one of our analogs is already in that universe?" Zoe asked.

They all looked at each other awkwardly.

Nathaniel broke the silence. "Hugh and Doug are a given, because there's only one of them. But there's a pair of each of us. Two Scotts, two Kims, and two Mackenzies."

"Nathan and Nathaniel are different enough that they might be okay in the same universe," Zoe said.

"I wouldn't risk it. He's younger, so he gets to go," Nathaniel said.

"This sucks," Ephraim said.

"Rock, Paper, Scissors?" Dick asked.

"That won't work," Ephraim said.

"Why not?" Dick asked.

Ephraim held up his fist. Dick copied his motion, and together they counted it out. "One, two, three!" On three, Ephraim flattened his hand—and so did Dick.

"Paper," Dick said.

"Again."

This time, on three they both shaped scissors with their fingers. Then paper again. Rock. Rock. Scissors.

"I see how it is," Dick said. "I know! Why don't we try 'Rock, Paper, Scissors, Gun'?"

"Rock, Paper, Scissors, *Gun?*" Nathan asked. "I guess gun would—"

Dick drew a small gun from his pocket.

"Oh . . ." Nathan looked at Ephraim. "That's why I couldn't find the gun you said was in Nathaniel's office."

Nathaniel glared at Zoe. "*This* is why you don't bring firearms to Crossroads. When has a gun solved anything?"

"There's a first time for everything," Dick said. "If I kill Ephraim, there'll only be one of us. Problem solved."

Ephraim grabbed Doug and pulled him behind him.

"You don't have to kill me," Ephraim said. "You can take my place."

Dick stared at him. "Dammit! You're really that fucking noble?"

"He is," Zoe said.

Dick put the gun down on the desk. "Screw it. I don't even know how to use a gun," he said.

Nathaniel snatched it up. "I do." He pointed it at Dick and pulled the trigger.

Dick flinched. Jena screamed. But there was no gunshot.

"You think I'm stupid enough to keep a loaded gun around *kids?*" Nathaniel asked. "And I'm not referring to Doug. Sheesh." He tucked the gun into his pocket. "Now where were we?"

"Dick was demonstrating why he doesn't deserve to live," Zoe said.

"Should we draw straws?" Jena asked.

"Forget it." Zoe lowered her eyes. "Eph, you and Jena go," she said.

"Zoe," Ephraim said.

"It's okay." She took his hand. "You picked me. That's good enough."

Ephraim glanced at Jena. That wasn't going to happen.

"I'm staying with you, Zoe. Whatever we decide," he said.

Dick rolled his eyes.

Ephraim stood up. He had been so sure of their plan, but the longer he waited, the more uncertain he became.

"Hugh, Jena, Doug, Dick, and Nathan will go to whichever universe we pick." He looked at Zoe and Nathaniel. "The three of us have taken this kind of risk before. We already decided what it was worth to us to keep the rest of the multiverse, and our friends and family, safe."

Nathaniel clapped him on the back. Zoe chewed on her upper lip, nodding.

"Great." Dick clapped his hands once. "So let's go home."

"No," Jena said.

"Jena?" Ephraim asked.

"We can't ask you to sacrifice yourselves for us," she said.

"You don't have to ask. That's what makes it a sacrifice," Zoe said.

"Be selfish for once, Eph," Jena said.

"Excuse me?" he said.

"There's no happy ending, Jena," Nathaniel said. "Let us do this."

Jena whirled to face Ephraim. "Eph, you don't have to do this."

"I don't see anyone else volunteering."

"You didn't give us the chance," Nathan said. "If I thought it would do any good, I'd let you take my place. But I can't. So I'm not going. Nathaniel, you can have my spot."

"I've spent enough time in the past," Nathaniel said. "I'm not doing that again. That's your time. You have to lead the life you were meant to."

Zoe slapped the table. They all looked at her.

"Am I hearing this right? *No one* wants to go?" she asked.

"I didn't say that," Dick said.

"Neither did I. I'm going," Hugh said.

Jena glared at Hugh. "How can I live my life knowing what it cost?" Jena said. "I have enough pressure without that on my conscience."

"That's your problem," Zoe said. "You'll get over it."

"Hold on," Jena said. "Hold *on*." She stared at the screen, biting her lip.

"What?" Ephraim asked.

Jena waved him off. "Shhh. I'm thinking."

She furrowed her brow and looked at the numbers again.

"We only need to maintain *two* universes to accommodate all of us," she said.

"Which is still one too many," Ephraim reminded her.

"Says Scott. But he also said some universes might remain anyway. When we were planning to copy coordinates to those laptops, we were going to take them to as many universes as possible. Why, Hugh?"

"I thought that would improve our odds of at least one universe surviving," he said.

"At *least* one. So there's a benefit to trying to preserve more than one?"

"As a mathematician, I agree with that. But with a couple of stipulations. Each of those universes would have to be radically different from the other, or it wouldn't work. Similar universes are too prone to decoherence and convergence." He pulled his glasses off and polished them on his lapel. "In other words, they're more likely to merge."

"Right," Jena said. "You used the words 'likely,' and 'odds.'"

"It's all about probability. It's a game of statistics," he said.

"What are you getting at, Dr. Everett?" Nathaniel asked.

Hugh smiled. "Not a doctor yet."

"Sorry. For a minute you sounded just like him."

"I think I get it," Ephraim said. "If we send ourselves to more than one universe, distributed so each has only one analog of each of us, maybe they *all* have a chance of surviving?"

Ephraim felt the first real hope that they actually could make it through this.

"Just a chance," Hugh said. "From a statistical standpoint, it makes sense to provide an initial pool of universes for the multiverse to choose among. If we pick only one to start with, that runs counter to its tendency to self-select on a preferred basis."

"Scott would have considered this," Nathaniel said.

"No, he wouldn't have," Ephraim said. "Because he had no one he wanted to save badly enough. Maybe the answer lies somewhere between Scott and Dr. Kim's plans. A compromise."

"You're just looking for justification to save the people in this room," Nathaniel said.

"Hell, yes," Jena said. "You say that like there's something wrong with it."

"But that doesn't invalidate the point," Hugh said.

"It's no better than the Doc's plan," Nathaniel said.

"It's no *worse* than Dr. Kim's plan," Ephraim said.

"Tell me the truth. Can this actually work, Hugh?" Nathaniel asked.

"Scott doesn't have access to the data we have, and for all his talents and intuition, he's no scientist. Everything remaining equal, so to speak—no coheron drives, no duplicate analogs, and the universes being as dissimilar as possible—the multiverse could sustain a handful of realities. It thrives on diversity as much as individuality—one of its many paradoxes."

"So let's give it something to work with." Ephraim cracked his knuckles and sat down at the computer. "It just so happens that we have a diverse selection of universes available today. Here are our options." Ephraim pointed to one set of coordinates. "The past, circa 1954." He looked at Everett. "That's your universe."

Ephraim slid his index finger to the next one down.

"This is the universe in the far future, where Scott and Dr. Kim are. I don't think any of us want to cramp their style in the time they have left together.

"This is the universe we're all in, the present, relatively speaking. And finally . . ." There were two coordinates left.

"Our universes," Zoe said. "The present for me, Jena, Ephraim, and Dick."

"Crap," Ephraim said. The numbers were almost identical. Despite the big differences in each universe, as far as the multiverse was concerned, they were interchangeable. "We can only keep one of those, or risk them merging with each other."

"Damn," Dick said.

Hugh cleared his throat. "Jena, I don't suppose you would consider coming back with me?"

"To 1954?" Jena asked. "Are you asking me out?"

"It was just an idea," Hugh said.

"I don't know," she said. "I'd have a lot to get used to. Women didn't have equal rights. Asians didn't have it easy back then either. There's no Internet."

"Perhaps you would change that," he said. "I'm quite convinced you can accomplish anything you want to."

"You're not seriously considering this, Jena?" Ephraim asked. "I know you have some romantic ideal of the fifties—"

"It's more than that. I mean, I do want to go to a real sockhop, and see one of those drive-in restaurants with the waitresses on roller-skates. And ooh, drive-in movies! But when we were back there, I felt free and excited and . . . useful," Jena said. "More than I've felt in a long time. There was this amazing sense of change. Like anything was possible. I already know things will get better, and maybe I can play a part in creating a new future."

"You're most remarkable, Jena," Hugh said.

She smiled. "I'd like to go with you," she said. She turned to Ephraim and Zoe. "The present is for you two. Don't waste it." She looked pointedly at Doug. Ephraim blushed.

Zoe abruptly grabbed Jena in a hug. Jena was startled, but she returned the gesture. After a moment, she started to squirm.

"This feels kind of weird," Jena said. "Could we maybe stop?"

They broke off the awkward embrace and grinned at each other.

"We should vote on this," Nathaniel said.

"Don't we all prefer living?" Hugh said. "I'm prepared to take the selfish road and hope for the best."

"I don't have a better idea," Zoe said.

"It's worth a shot," Nathan said.

"We have to hear from one more person. The one who has the biggest stake in our decision." Nathaniel crouched to look Doug in the eyes. "What do you want, Doug? One universe or four?"

The boy blinked at him.

Ephraim leaned over and whispered in Doug's ear. "How old are you?"

The boy held up four fingers. "Four!" he said.

"You heard him," Ephraim said. "Four universes."

"You cheated," Nathaniel said. "He didn't answer the question."

"He didn't understand the question. Dr. Kim changed her mind and took a huge risk because she wanted Doug to have a future. This is the closest thing to the only home he's ever had. He doesn't even have proper parents anymore. Do you want to take even more from him?"

Nathaniel eyed Doug. Ephraim tickled the boy's belly, and Doug laughed, squirming away.

"He's so freaking cute," Nathaniel said.

"Shall we make it unanimous, old man?" Ephraim asked.

"Fine," Nathaniel said. "We'll try it your way. But if you're wrong and the multiverse fizzles out, I'm going to say I told you so."

Ephraim took Zoe's hand. "One more thing to settle. Your place or mine?"

"No contest. Yours," she said. "It has no war, no draft, and a better library."

"Are you sure?" Ephraim asked. "Zoe, once we erase the coordinates to your universe, that's it."

She covered her mouth. "We may not have a choice anyway. I just remembered something. Does *any* record of a universe count?"

"Digital or physical," Hugh said.

"Don't tell us there's a napkin at your house with your universe's coordinates scribbled on it," Ephraim said.

Zoe turned her right wrist out to display her barcode tattoo. He hadn't gotten this close a look at it before, but now he realized that it had ten digits. The numbers were familiar . . .

He checked the screen between them. It was one of their five choices.

"So much for that," Ephraim said. "I guess we're going to Zoe's universe."

Zoe shook her head.

"We could cut her arm off," Nathan said.

"Nathan!" Jena said.

"Or burn the tattoo off," Nathan said.

"Ephraim—" Zoe said.

"Don't worry. You aren't losing your arm," Ephraim said.

"I know," Zoe said. She put a hand over his on the mouse and gently guided the cursor to the second set of coordinates. 101.899.3441. "These are the coordinates for my universe."

He compared them to the numbers on her arm again. 1018993212.

"*My* universe?" he asked.

"I wanted to be sure I could always find you," Zoe said.

Jena sniffled. "Jeez," she said. "I must be allergic to something."

"Romance?" Nathan asked.

Dick crossed his arms. "I hate to break up this lovefest, but aren't we almost out of time?"

"We have three minutes," Ephraim said.

"So who gets me?" Dick asked.

"You could go with Jena and Hugh." Ephraim grimaced.

Behind Dick, Jena waved her hands and shook her head vigorously.

"Nah. What would I do in the fifties?" Dick asked.

Nathaniel leaned forward. "You could stay here."

"Hmmm. Let me think. No," Dick said.

"I could use help raising Doug. And maybe it'd be good for you, too," Nathaniel said.

"I assumed Doug was coming with us," Ephraim said. The boy looked close to tears.

"You aren't ready for a son," Nathaniel said.

"Thank God," Zoe said.

Ephraim raised an eyebrow.

"I mean, maybe one day," she said. "Sure. But I can't be a mom now."

"He should be with his father," Ephraim said. "Or a reasonable facsimile."

"Dick's close enough," Nathaniel said.

"Fine. I'll stay. At least you can stop calling me Dick when I'm the only Ephraim around," Dick said.

"Don't bet on it. I have a hard time adjusting to change," Nathaniel said.

Ephraim knelt and drew Doug to him. "Bye, kid. I'll miss you."

"You're leaving?" Doug asked. His lower lip quivered.

"I have to go. But you'll be in good hands here." Ephraim kissed Doug on the forehead. "Just listen to Uncle Nathaniel."

He pried Doug's arms from him and pushed him gently to Nathaniel.

Jena embraced Ephraim next. "I'll miss you, Eph."

"Is this what you really want?" he murmured.

"Yes. He may not be the cutest guy I've ever known, but he's definitely the smartest. Besides, we've all got to go somewhere." She kissed Ephraim on the cheek, then stepped aside to let Hugh come up.

Hugh and Ephraim shook hands.

"Good luck," Ephraim said. "Don't let this happen again, okay? Maybe you can go into a safer line of work, like video games."

"What are video games?" Hugh asked.

"You'll like them. Jena will explain. Just don't build any more coherence devices."

"Consider us duly warned."

Jena picked up the controller and flipped it open. Ephraim

dropped Scott's token into it, and she punched in the numbers for Hugh's reality from the computer screen.

"We only have one controller, but we can use it to program both coins. This one's set for 1954." Jena pulled the token out of the controller. "Ow! Hot!"

She dropped it quickly into her pocket. "I'll hand it to Hugh downstairs. We don't want to shift from up here. It's a ten-story drop."

Hugh called the elevator.

"Don't forget to destroy that coin when you get there," Nathaniel said.

Jena nodded. "We'll take it straight to Mount Doom."

The elevator arrived. "Okay. I guess this is good-bye." She looked at Zoe. "Take care of Eph. He's too dumb to live, a lot of the time."

"I will," Zoe said.

Jena and Hugh linked hands and stepped into the elevator. The doors closed.

Dick handed his coin to Ephraim. "This belongs to you," he said.

Ephraim pocketed it and checked his watch. "Three minutes." He nodded to Nathaniel. "As soon as we're clear, delete the coordinates of all but the four universes we decided on."

Nathaniel crushed him in a hug. "You're a good kid, Ephraim." He grinned. "A good man."

"You aren't bad yourself, old-timer."

Zoe stepped up and kissed Nathaniel on the lips. "'Good-bye, Scarecrow. I'll miss you most of all.'"

Nathaniel touched his lips. His face flushed.

"Do I get one of those too?" Nathan asked.

"Loser," Zoe said.

Nathan shook Nathaniel's hand. "See you, man."

"In about twenty-five years. Enjoy our youth."

"I'm sorry we didn't get to talk more. There's a lot I wanted to ask you."

"On your nineteenth birthday," Nathaniel said. "And it's amazing."

Nathan smiled broadly. "I look forward to it."

"Good luck, Ephraim," Dick said.

"You too, Ephraim." Ephraim smiled.

Dick leaned closer. "If your girlfriend's anything like my universe's Jena, she'll like it if you nibble—"

"We have to go," Zoe said. She grabbed Ephraim's hand and pulled him into the elevator. Nathan scooted in after them.

They gathered in the shadow of the vertical disc embedded in front of the statue of Atlas.

"That'll be fun to clean up," she said. She ran a hand against it. "Cold," she said.

The three of them stood in front of it, studying their reflections in the sheer surface.

"This is it," Ephraim said. He flipped his coin and caught it.

Zoe held out the controller, and Ephraim slid the coin in. She typed in the coordinates of Ephraim's universe, and double-checked them against her tattoo. The metal disc lifted and rotated.

"Okay, it's programmed for your universe," she said. "I'm erasing the controller's memory now."

"When we left, we didn't have any analogs back home. Let's hope that's still true," Ephraim said.

They linked their arms together, and Ephraim grabbed the coin for the last time.

"Bamf!" Nathan said as they shifted.

As soon as they arrived in front of the fountain at Greystone Park, Zoe threw the controller to the ground as hard as she could. It bounced and broke into two halves still connected by wires and cables. She stomped on it with her foot, and the case cracked and splintered further.

He and Zoe stomped the pieces over and over again until the case's metal guts were strewn all over the courtyard.

The people sitting on the benches or in the middle of an afternoon stroll gaped at them.

"Good afternoon," Ephraim said. He, Nathan, and Zoe scooped up the broken fragments of the controller and dumped them in the fountain for good measure.

Ephraim trailed his hand in the cool water. The sunlight glinted on the coins on the bottom of the fountain. He was tempted to toss his own coin in there, but he had other plans for it.

Nathan stared glumly into the burbling fountain with his hands in his pockets. This smaller-scale Atlas still carried a weight on his shoulders, but to Ephraim, his expression no longer looked pained but joyful.

"You about to hurl in there?" Ephraim asked.

"No." Nathan pouted. "I just realized I left my camera in the future, with my video in it. Good-bye, Pulitzer."

CHAPTER 35

Zoe smiled from behind the circulation desk when Ephraim entered the Summerside Public Library at closing time. The last patron shuffled out past him. Ephraim flipped the sign to "Closed" and locked the sliding glass doors.

Zoe stood and stretched her arms, arching her back.

"Need any help?" he asked.

"What kind of help are you offering exactly, mister?"

"Well, we are all alone." He leaned over the counter, and they kissed.

"You know how much books turn me on," she said. "But we aren't quite alone."

"Nathan and M.S.?" he asked.

"They're in the stacks," she said.

"He's always wanted to do that," Ephraim said.

Zoe grabbed his hand. "Eph, I have to show you something in the back."

"Subtle." But then he saw her troubled expression. "What's up, Zoe?"

She led him to the small room where they repaired damaged books. She opened a creaky wooden drawer and pulled out an old book. The blue cloth cover had black spots, and the binding was coming apart at the seams.

"I debated whether to show this to you, but we decided we wouldn't have any secrets, right?" she said.

He nodded.

"Okay. I was restoring this and I found something interesting. I'm not sure what it means," she said.

She positioned the book on the counter in front of him. He ran his fingers over the title engraved in gold on the spine. *Alice's Adventures in Wonderland and Through the Looking Glass.*

"This is one of Jena's favorite books," he said. "She gave me a copy for Christmas." He still felt self-conscious talking about her around Zoe.

Her mouth twitched. "It's one of my faves, too. That's why I was taking particular care with it. Anyway . . ."

She carefully lifted the front cover to reveal a fading bookplate fixed on the inside of it. Ephraim read it aloud.

"Generously donated to the Summerside Public Library on March 3, 1992, by Mrs. Jena Kim Everett," he read. The hair on his neck rose. "What?"

"March third. Her birthday," Zoe said. "*Our* birthday."

He fingered the silver ring on his right hand nervously, twisting it counterclockwise. He'd had the coin melted down and molded into two thin bands; Zoe wore the other ring as a necklace.

Every now and then, Ephraim felt a phantom tingling sensation from the metal, or thought it was warmer than it should be.

"How?" Ephraim asked.

"I'm only guessing, but if universes can branch and merge, maybe they can also be grafted onto each other. At some point, our different timelines connected and merged. It might have been because of Jena. Ultimately, she belonged to this universe, and that was one way of putting things right."

He turned the first page of the book. "This is a first edition . . . printed in 1954."

"It shouldn't have been in circulation. Rare books belong in the case upstairs. After I freaked out about my discovery, I was curious. So I did some research."

"Of course," Ephraim said. He was counting on Zoe's investigative skills to locate his mother's analog in this patchwork universe. If the other Madeline Scott didn't want to be a part of his life, at least he could see her one last time and say a proper good-bye.

"I searched through ledgers going back to when the library was built. Jena donated thousands of books to the library. And I finally found out who funded the Memorial Fountain in Greystone Park: The Kim Foundation."

Ephraim perched on a stool beside the desk. He paged carefully through the fragile book. Jena had handled this same volume, two decades ago.

"I already checked for other messages," Zoe said.

"The book *is* the message," he said. "What else did you find?"

She wrung her hands. "An obituary." Tears filled her eyes. She pulled off her glasses and swiped at them, smearing mascara in dark slashes under her eyes.

The page he was turning fluttered as his hand trembled. "She's dead?"

Zoe slid a grainy and blotchy photocopy of a small clipping from *The Herald Statesman*.

"It's dated March second, 1994," he said numbly. "The day before you were born."

"There was a short news article with it. She left a suicide note."

"No," Ephraim said.

"But they never found a body," Zoe said. "It's like she just . . ."

"Disappeared?" he asked.

"This is Jena's universe. Maybe she couldn't exist here after she was born. She would have been, like, her *own* analog?"

"The multiverse correcting itself? Even if she realized that could happen, why make it look like a suicide?"

"She had plenty of time to plan for that day. She would have wanted to make sure no one was blamed, or blamed himself."

Ephraim pushed the obituary away.

"She lived a good life," Zoe said.

"She was only fifty-eight," he said.

"Well, you should read that obituary. She wrote it herself. It's beautiful. She led the life she wanted. She was rich, because of a few smart, almost prescient investments over the years. And she gave all of it back to Summerside."

"Did she have any kids?"

"There are Everetts, but they aren't Jena's." She looked at Ephraim. "I did do a little more digging."

He smiled. "You had a busy day."

She stuck her tongue out at him. "Hugh Everett and Jena Kim were married for a year before she broke it off. He continued his work on parallel universes," she said.

"He promised he wouldn't," Ephraim said.

"Thank goodness no one believed him," Zoe said. "It must have been frustrating knowing he was right, but not being able to prove it. In the end, he got married and had two kids, a daughter and a son. He started a video game company in the eighties: Crossroad Games."

Zoe stashed the obituary and book in the desk drawer.

"She always wanted to leave Summerside, but she just ended up coming right back here," Ephraim said.

"She could have gone anywhere, Eph. She came back because she wanted to. Sometimes no matter how much you want to get away, there's no place like home."

He pressed the palms of his hands against his eyes. "Thanks for telling me."

"Sometimes it's better not knowing, isn't it? Imagining that all our other selves are still out there, living their own lives, going on when we stop?"

"And maybe they are. Jena's universe might have spawned another reality before it crossed ours."

"Anything's possible." Zoe smiled. "I'm more interested in the future right now."

"Dinner?" he asked.

"You know me so well." She pulled him to his feet and gave him a quick kiss. "Let's order something at my place. My parents are visiting Grumps tonight."

The shifting multiverse hadn't only taken people away; mercifully, it had also given back Zoe's mother and grandfather.

"I'm in the mood for Mexican," he said, as Zoe said, "Let's have Chinese."

"Hmm," Zoe said.

Ephraim reached into his back pocket and pulled out the quarter he'd gotten from his dad's key ring. Half-melted, with one edge dinged, it was no longer a fair coin.

"Let's flip on it," he said.

"Ephraim, let's not." Her hand covered the coin in his hand.

He grinned. "Heads, I pick dinner."

He flipped the coin and caught it easily. He turned away and peeked at it.

"Mexican it is!" he said.

Zoe grabbed his right hand and forced his fingers open. She laughed when she saw his hand was empty.

He made the quarter appear in his left hand. He rolled the coin down his knuckles, then passed it back to his right hand.

"Show-off," she said.

"How about best out of three?" he asked. He flipped the quarter again,d but she grabbed it out of the air before he did. She clutched it to her stomach with both hands.

"Afraid to see if it's your lucky night?" he teased.

"I just want to stay in *this* universe a little longer. I can do magic too," she said. She waved her right hand in front of his face. "Now you see it, now you don't!" Ephraim noticed her slipping it into her bra with her left hand, but pretended he didn't.

"If you get it back later, it'll be *your* lucky night," she said.

They compromised on dinner: They ordered Mexican *and* Chinese and stayed in for a movie that neither of them saw much of.

As Zoe and Ephraim kissed, he was distantly aware of the sound of a coin clattering to the bare wood floor and rolling under the living room couch. It spun for a few moments and stopped. *Heads or tails?* he wondered.

Zoe sighed and pushed him away. "Fine. Check if you want to," she said.

He checked under the couch, but he couldn't see it there or anywhere else in the vicinity. He slid his hand along the dusty floorboards.

The quarter was gone.

"So? Heads or tails?" Zoe asked.

He smiled. "Both."

ABOUT THE AUTHOR

E. C. Myers was assembled in the United States from Korean and German parts and raised by his mother and a public library in his hometown of Yonkers, New York, on which Summerside is loosely based. He has worked as a doorman, food server, security guard, web designer, software consultant, technical writer, video editor, tape librarian, digital media manager, and blogger, and he now writes copy for a pediatric hospital. E. C. attended the Clarion West Writers Workshop in 2005 and is a member of Altered Fluid, a prolific writing group in New York City. His website is www.ecmyers.net.